Levi's Labyrinth

An Origin Story

By: Ralph M. Edgerson Jr.

ISBN 978-1-943159-27-7

The publisher would appreciate notification where errors occur so that they may be corrected in subsequent printing and/or editions. Please send comments to the publisher by emailing to deeprivers67@yahoo.com Printed in the United States of America

Thank You and Dedication…

First off, I want to thank The Almighty for blessing me with the gift of storytelling. I couldn't do this without Him. This book is dedicated to my supportive and loving wife Darlene D Edgerson, I love you baby. Her support truly means everything to me, no matter how boring it gets (inside joke) …lol. Thank you to my children Ralph III and Bryanna for the inspiration to be a better man and father for them. My R&B, the best music I ever help create. Thank you to my partner in crime Dawn "Deep Rivers" Blanchard for believing in me when I doubted my talents. Special thanks to my cousin Ayanna and the entire Bourbon Street Bookers aka BSB book group for all the support and encouraging words. I love you all so much.

#keeppushing #keepwriting #MrWrite

INTRO

Levi's lies or Levi's truths…Levi could have been me; Levi could have been you. The life of a man is measured by his deeds, good or bad. But what if Levi's bad was the lesser of two evils, does that make him a bad man? Born at the turn of the century in 1999, Ronald Levi Sweed was a complexed enigma that had more battles going on under the surface than anyone could imagine. To walk in his world, one must be careful because the shadows aren't the only things that can kill you. Every year was a game of chess on a battlefield in a dense forest peppered with emotional, physical and psychological land mines. Levi became a master at the game and took control of the hand he was dealt. Was it right or was it wrong? Read his life and you come up with your conclusion to the Labyrinth that is Levi…

Year 2005

"Yo daddy wasn't shit, you ain't shit and ya damn kids probably gone grow up not to mount up to shit!", was the words little Ronald Levi Sweed and his siblings heard their grandmother shout to their father.

Ronald's grandmother wasn't the typical gray-haired sweet old lady anyone would imagine, in fact she didn't have a gray hair insight and his father Roger was only 13 years younger than she was. She was upset with Ronald's father because she had been babysitting his three kids all day. He promised to bring her 100 dollars when he returned but he showed up empty handed. Roger shuffled his kids in the backseat of his old '96 Chevy Impala SS as he could hear his mother fuss at him from the front porch of her project apartment. Roger's oldest son Brock, who was 11 at the time, gave zero fucks and had a bad attitude just like his grandmother, smiled out the back window as he poked out his tongue at his grandma.

"Fuck you boy!", blurted out Roger's mother as she slammed her door shut.

Roger quickly drove down St. Bernard Ave and asked his kids did their grandmother feed them while he was gone, his baby girl Darlene just smiled as she answered yes. The little hellion Brock told him they ate earlier around lunch time, which was a bologna sandwich and that he was hungry now because it was almost 6. Roger let them all know that they had to go pick up their mother first and then they would all go get some Popeye's for dinner. Roger and his wife Olivia were what you would call common law married, they been together for over ten years. Olivia Stranton was 16 when Roger met her at a block party and she was infatuated with him from the first time she seen him, the only thing was Roger was 26 at the time. As bad of an idea as it was for them both, Roger pursued Olivia and they had been going strong for almost 12 years now. Ronald was the middle child at 6-years-old, with little Darlene being the baby at 4 and big brother Brock was 11, all of them was the light to their father's eyes. The kids never really knew where their mother worked, only that she was always picked up at the same spot every day on Chef Menteur Hwy and most of the time she had a purse full of money with her. The honest truth was Roger was a street dealer, a transporter of pretty much anything illegal and Olivia's pimp, along with three other girls but Olivia was

Roger's number one. They kept their activities away from their kids as best as they could because they wanted to avoid the questions, but Roger wasn't one to hold back any punches if one of his kids was to ask him anything. The shiny black Impala pulled up to the usual corner store on Chef Menteur and Olivia walked out right on schedule like always as she got in the car and greeted her beautiful babies,

"Hey y'all. Y'all had fun by granma?"

"No. All grandma did was look at the stories on TV."

"Mama, we had fun. Brock wanted to go in and out all day and grandma wasn't havin it."

Olivia laughed at her rambunctious little man as she listened to Brock tell her that his grandmother fussed when they kept going outside to play in the courtyard and come back inside for a drink. Roger let Olivia know they're going to have to find someone else to watch the kids when they head out for work because his mother was pissed about not getting her money that was promised. The Sweed family made their way home after stopping to pick up some chicken for dinner that night.

It was early Saturday morning when Ronald woke to his little sister crying, when he went to see what was wrong, he found Brock teasing Darlene by swinging her favorite doll in the air by the hair. Frustrated with his big brother's antics of being the sibling bully, Ronald calmly asked him,

"Give her, her doll back."

"If I don't, what you gone do about it? Nothing. So, no."

"Just give her da doll, damn."

"Nope."

Ronald knew his brother was almost twice his age and pretty much way bigger than he was but that didn't stop him from charging towards him. He buried his shoulder into Brock's stomach, tackling him to the floor and Darlene's doll went flying in the air. The loud commotion of the boys struggling in the front of the house woke their mother and she walked in with nothing but whipping little asses as she entered the living room. Before Olivia could lunge at the boys fighting on the floor, Darlene shouted for them to stop and told her mother that Brock started it. Ronald walked off outside, proud of his accomplishment and Brock went to his room as Olivia had Darlene help her with breakfast. Once he was outside, Ronald found his dad working on his car like he always does and asked if he could help his pops with it. Roger was tickled that his little man wanted to help and handed him a wrench to make him feel like he was doing something as he scooted under the car to change the oil. Ronald peeked up under the car while his dad was loosening a nut and Roger noticed his son had a swollen lip,

"Boy what happened?"

"Nothing."

Ronald looked down to the ground, afraid to tell his father that he had a fight with his brother because he always pressed that they stick together no matter what. When he stopped working on his car and asked Ronald again what happened, the youngster had to give him an answer. Little Ronald told his dad that their horse playing got a little out of control and he got hurt. Roger knew his kids and just let that be the answer he was going to accept. Deep down he was proud that his son stood strong to protect his siblings, even if it meant taking the blame for lying. He continued to show his youngin' how to change the oil on his car but then the laughter of kids caught Ronald's attention. When he looked up from under his dad's car, Ronald seen his friends across the street playing in the yard and asked his pop if he could go over to play with them. Roger had no problem with it but made his son realize one thing as he laughed,

"Son, you do know you outside in yo Backyardigans pajamas, right?"

"Dang! I need to go change."

Across the way from where Roger was working on his car was the Daniels family, Cedric Sr and Delores had three beautiful kids with one on the way real soon. Delores was sitting outside on the porch watching her 6-year-old twin girls, Alonna and Shalay play with their little brother Cedric Jr. Her husband, Cedric Sr had been a deputy for Orleans Parish Sheriff's Office for over 15 years and Roger made sure that all his extracurricular activities stayed far away from home because of that fact. The Daniels thought Roger was a mechanic with Olivia being a secretary somewhere and that's how little Ronald's parents wanted it to stay. The anxious lad darted across the street to play with his friends when his father shouted for him to stop,

"Hey! What I tell you bout that?! Coulda been a car comin and you woulda ran right into it!"

"I'm sorry. I'm sorry."

"I got him Roger, they little behinds don't see anything around them except what they want to get to", responded Delores as she stood up gesturing that it was safe for Ronald to come over.

Roger admired the motherly/wifely way Delores was and all of her inner beauty matched or fell short to her outer beauty, which was sometimes captivating to him. Even at nine months pregnant, Delores was absolutely beautiful, to the point of being classified as a model. Not one of those thin malnourished runway models but a thick thoroughbred of a specimen. She loved to have the neighborhood kids play in her yard, with her children and most of the time if anything was going on in that city block it was at the Daniels' household. Delores really liked to entertain or have some sort of get together at her house on occasion. The Sweeds been to a few but Olivia didn't really care for, what she called "doing too much" or "showing out" and her pettiness usually kept the family from attending too many functions. Most of Olivia's insecurity came from an underlining jealousy because she seen how her man would look at Delores in a wanting way and Roger got caught staring again,

"Keep gawkin' over there and ya fuckin' eyes gone fall the fuck out."

"Fuck you talking bout? I was just makin sho Ronald got cross da street."

"Yea, okay. Nigga I ain't stupid."

Olivia rolled her eyes at him after telling Roger that she fixed breakfast for everyone and that one of his potnas called about a pickup of "dust bunnies" that had to be dropped off. Roger and his associates had their own language for the different assortment of drugs he transported. Just by the name he knew what, where or even who was talking without being on the phone with them. Marijuana was called pretty much any vegetable that was green like broccoli, collards, spinach and so forth. Cocaine had an arrange of different names like snowflake, horse, whiteboy and angel. Heroin carried names like dust bunnies, superman, foil or charcoal. Roger ignored his woman's attitude about him staring across the street at Delores, grabbed a quick bite to eat and headed to go pick up a package to be delivered to his corner boys in the east. His older boy Brock always wanted to run the streets with his dad and when the little badass seen his pops getting ready to go, he rushed to put some clothes on to go with him. Roger was getting ready to walk out the door when Brock asked to come with him and figuring it was a simple transaction Roger had no problem with his big boy tagging along. Brock darted outside when he seen his little brother playing with the Daniels' kids across the street and he walked over to tell Ronald he was going with their dad. Little Ronald was cool with staying home playing tag with his friends when one of the twins, Shalay, walked up asking Brock if he wanted to join them and the annoyed adolescent responded,

"Getaway from me before I pluck you in the forehead."

"Pluck me in the forehead and I'm a kick you in ya nuts."

"Oh I can't stand you."

"I don't like you either!"

Brock was about to answer her but then he heard his father's engine start-up and knew it was time for him to go.

Ronald had gone back home to get his baby sister Darlene to bring her with him across the street to play with his friends, while their mother chilled in the house. All the kids were playing in the front yard when Cedric Sr showed up in his squad car for lunch and the twins dismissed everything they were doing as they ran toward their father. Ronald looked at his dad as his "superhero", strongest man ever but Mr. Cedric looked like a real-life superman in his sheriff's uniform to him. The girls stood outside of his cruiser, cheering for their dad to get out of the car while little Cedric Jr stood in the front of the vehicle waiting for his pops to do the one thing, he always does for him. Delores was standing on the porch and shouted,

"Now you know he ain't moving until you do it Ced."

Ronald was curious as to what she was talking about because this was his first-time seeing Cedric Sr in his squad car. Then the car lit up like a Christmas tree, strobe lights blinking across the top, with the siren blaring and little Cedric took off running like the cops was chasing him as his dad ran behind him. Darlene and the twins laughed as Cedric Sr pretended to arrest a giggling Cedric Jr on the porch but for some reason the sight was something uneasy for Ronald as the police dad shouted to him,

"You want some?!"

The little lad's soul felt like it jumped out of him as he froze in place looking at the handcuffs on the petite boy in front of him because it just wasn't funny to him and Delores noticed the fear in his eyes. The heavily pregnant mother walked up to Ronald to pull him out of the trance he was in, as she laid her hand on his back, softly talking and told him it was just her boys playing around. Ronald knew it was them playing but it was his first time seeing somebody get real handcuffs put on them. He explained it to Delores that he doesn't ever want to be handcuffed and Cedric Sr told him that he's a good kid, so it would never be anything he would have to worry about. The Daniels clan headed inside for lunch and Delores invited the two Sweed kids to join them. Ronald knew his mother would have a conniption fit if they went inside without her permission, so he declined as he went back home with his baby sister. Darlene wasn't ready to go back but Ronald promised to fix her favorite toasted PB&J sandwich and the little angel complied with the biggest smile on her face because she loved how her brother made them. Ronald always looked out for his little sister because their big brother was too busy trying to be grown, wanting to be a big man like his father. When their mother wasn't working, most of the time all she did was watch TV, so all they had was each other. The two walked in the house to their mother doing her usual and Darlene made a straight shot for the kitchen but was stopped by her mother,

"Don't you go in my kitchen making a mess without washin' ya damn hands, smelling like outside."

"I don't smell like outside."

"Yes you do. Smell like a musty puppy."

Ronald walked his little sister to the bathroom, placed the wooden step stool in front over the large porcelain sink, turned on the water and handed her the soap. He really took pride in taking care of his sister as best as he could and after they cleaned up, they both went to the kitchen to make their lunch. Darlene loved peanut butter and jelly sandwiches, but her bread had to be toasted first with butter. She watched her brother like a hawk to make sure he did it just the way she likes, and she was truly pleased with the finished product when Ronald slid the plate in front of her. The little toddler was tickled with her sandwich as her little feet just kicked as she ate her lunch.

Roger pulled up on side of a warehouse off of Tchoupitoulas Street, right by the Mississippi River. They were so close to the water that Brock could smell it in the air. The pre-teen was just stoked that his dad allowed him to tag along, sitting in the front seat like his partner and it made him feel like a boss on the ride but then his pops shocked his system. Roger leaned over to open the glove compartment in front of his son, pulled out a large chrome .45 as he told Brock to stay put,

"Look, I'm a be right back, don't touch nothing, don't play with my radio and don't get out of the car. I'm serious."

"Okay."

Brock's eyes were wide as two silver dollars, focused on his dad walking into the warehouse, tucking the big tool in his waistband and his body was froze to the front seat, scared to move a muscle. His 11-year-old mind ran with all types of imaginary scenarios of his father. One was him being a killer vigilante like his favorite comic book character or maybe he was a secret spy like the guy in the movie he saw once. Brock didn't know what to think because until just then, he didn't even know his dad owned a gun. Roger walked through a low-lit warehouse to the back office where he met up with one of his associates that had two large duffle bags waiting for him. He didn't think it was going to be that much product he was transporting through the city, but Roger picked up the two bags and headed towards the exit door. A Haitian drug runner walked up to Roger. Papa Sha really didn't care for the transporter because he felt Roger was an unneeded middleman and just held an evil grin while looking in his eyes. The Haitian's gang leader liked Roger because it eliminated them from being implicated in any distribution, but Papa Sha had his issues with Roger because he wasn't Haitian. The two had words before but Roger was protected by the leader's bond with him and Papa Sha knew it would have been bad for him if anything happened to the carrier. With his chrome insurance tucked under his shirt, Roger bumped pass Papa Sha wishing the gang's lieutenant would give him a reason to draw down on him, but all the gang member did was laugh,

"Chen plezi!"

"Ya mama the dog bitch."

Walking back to his car, Roger could hear footsteps behind him, and he went straight to his trunk to load the duffle bags, but the first thing he did as he dropped the bags on the ground was pull out an AK47 from the trunk. The statement was made that Roger was ready for anything as the assault rifle hung on his shoulder by the strap and he secured his cargo in the trunk, occasionally glancing over to Papa Sha's goons staring him down. He tossed his rifle in the backseat, sat down in the driver seat and drove off to his next destination. Brock sat there completely quiet because he didn't know what to say after seeing his father brandish another weapon in front of him. Roger's eldest boy sat there just looking out the window not knowing what to say to his dad and his uncomfortableness could be seen as he fidgeted in his seat, tugging at his seatbelt. Roger knew it all was new to Brock seeing that his father owned several firearms and asked,

"You good?"

"I'm good."

Roger explained to his son that some parts of the city was a little more dangerous than the others and he has to walk around with protection on him sometimes. Brock listened as his father told him he needed them for protection, protection for himself and the family. Roger drove through the east of New Orleans on Downman Road to a rundown house that had a few undesirables hanging out in front. He got out, opened up his trunk and two guys took the duffle bags out as they went straight inside while another guy came out to hand Brock's dad a dark green backpack. The two talked for a second when the guy looked over Roger's shoulder to see Brock sitting in the front seat and went over to talk to him,

"Whaz up lil man? Runnin' with ya pops? Lil pup looking like a big dawg, ya heard me."

After his dad drove off, Brock didn't know if the idea of the risk was pure excitement or his nervousness was just taking over, but one thing he did know was he wanted more. Then his pops made him keep a secret which made Brock's ego even bigger,

"Don't let ya mama, ya brother or ya sister know about this, alright."

"I ain't saying shit."

"Watch yo mouth lil nigga."

Olivia was prepping to cook dinner when she got a call from a potential client that wanted to have her and one of her girls accompany him for some "fun time" at his hotel. She usually didn't work on weekends because Roger had other girls for that, but the guy was one of her regulars and asked for her personally. After going over cost, time and location Olivia told the guy she would see him later that night with nothing but freaking him on her mind. Her baby girl Darlene walked in the kitchen to see what her mama was doing and like turning off a light switch Olivia went into "mommy mode" asking her little one if she wanted to help her cook. The baby of the bunch was excited to do whatever her mother wanted her to do as she waited at the counter for instructions when Ronald walked in telling them that his dad just pulled up. Brock walked in the house still embellishing the time he spent with his pops on the road and Roger followed right behind him looking for his woman. The two parents made eye contact and just by the look on Roger's face Olivia knew he wanted to meet her in the bedroom to talk some business. Roger closed the bedroom door as Olivia listened to him tell her that he had to make another run to drop off the backpack he got from his delivery. He told her how he thought he was about to have words with Papa Sha again and having her with him this time might help. Olivia knew the beef the two had with each other was an ongoing thing. Roger's gorgeous bottom bitch was always the catalyst that eliminated a lot of that with her smiles, soft caresses and compliments though. Papa Sha had a weakness for her, especially when she wore a tight low-cut top showing off some cleavage and smelling good to match her sexiness. She started looking through her closet for the right outfit to wear in front of the second in command Haitian gang member. She then told Roger that she had an escort service appointment that just came up. Anything that brought money into the house, Roger was comfortable with as he looked for something to put on when he takes Olivia to her appointment. The two had a lucrative set-up of high paying clients from different walks of life. One of Olivia's regulars, Benjamin, was part owner of the cable company that supplied all of the New Orleans area, he just enjoyed paying for sex. When Roger met Olivia, he had two girls under his management, working the streets and truck stops to supply Roger with the money he demanded them to bring in. As a teen, Olivia was captivated with the idea of the risqué acts, and she was wrapped around Roger's pinkie. She wanted nothing more than to please him in any way possible, so she joined in making him money. Her safety became his utmost priority when she was working and the two became a power couple as they worked the escort scene. They built a clientele, made it exclusive to the well off and had a few hotel personnel in their pockets for information that would arise, such as events or police stings. After finding the right fit to wear that night, Olivia went back to cooking dinner for everyone with her little girl.

The Sweeds had just finished the dinner Darlene helped fix with her mom, which was now her favorite jambalaya, baked fish and buttered corn on the cob. The kids were sitting in the living room looking at TV while their parents were in their bedroom getting dressed. Roger walked in, giving the kids the rules for the night when he told them that he and their mother was about to step out for a minute. Darlene didn't like when her mom would leave in the middle of the night, but Olivia did it regularly, so she got use to her brothers putting her to bed at night sometimes. Ronald always made sure to read her a book to ease her little mind. Brock jumped up as his pops was heading to the door,

"Daddy, who in charge tonight?"

"Ronald in charge. Make sure everybody take they bath and in bed by 10, ya heard me."

"Yes sir."

Roger headed to the car after kissing his baby girl good night and Olivia kissed every one of her kids repeatedly, even though her boys couldn't stand when she did that as Brock wiped her kisses off when she closed the front door. Roger was focused as he drove uptown towards where the Haitian gang was waiting for him to arrive as Olivia sat next to him holding onto his hand. She always was nervous when Roger would meet up with them because the gang members were ruthless and only dealt with Roger because of the leader's grace on him. The gang leader use to date Roger's mother before he was born and took him under his wing at an early age, but the full-blooded Haitians didn't care for the outsider. He made his bones running errands and completing task that called for someone that wasn't sporting dreds as a common headdress like his gang member counterparts. Roger made them a lot of money transporting weed, coke and heroin through the city but still had to prove himself every time he showed up in their territory but mostly because of one individual. The couple pulled up in front of a double shotgun house where two dreadlocked goons were sitting out front like guards. As soon as Roger stepped out of his car, Papa Sha walked out on the porch,

"Estipid, you bless us again with yo presence."

"Ya mama."

"Why you always bring up my mother?"

"Stay in yo lane and I won't."

Roger had been around the Haitian community long enough to catch on to a few words and he knew "estipid" meant "asshole" in Haitian creole. The passenger door of Roger's Impala opened, and Olivia stepped out, looking as delicious as she wanna be. The trick worked as Papa Sha was completely focused on her and her only. Her red six-inch heels, the black spandex tights, the bright red low-cut blouse that accentuated Olivia's ripe C cup breast and her smile simply melted him where he stood,

"Mademoiselle, your beauty is everything."

"Sha stop flirtin with me. Lookin handsome as always. Is that silk?"

"Che, you know nothing but silk touches dis skin."

Roger knew he wouldn't have any more problems with his rival as one of the goons walked him in the house to the gang's general who was waiting for him to arrive. While Roger was inside getting his cut for the delivery, he took care of for the Haitians, Papa Sha was doing his best at shooting his shot with Olivia. She pampered his ego like she did with any of her other clients but nothing the Haitian gang member could tell her would sway her away from Roger. Papa Sha pretty much offered her the world if she would leave Roger and be with him, but all Olivia would do is laugh off his attempts as she gently caressed him. Besides being completely captivated by Roger, Olivia was attracted to grimy niggas, which Papa Sha was definitely not grimy by the least. He had gold rings on almost every finger, at least five gold chains on his neck, a shiny silk Versace shirt, tight jeans and pointed gator shoes, he was entirely too flashy for her. Olivia looked at guys like him as "marks" but the only saving grace for Papa Sha was that he and his gang was well-known throughout the city, so no one would touch him because they knew the repercussions. Roger walked out the house with his money tucked away in his jacket, took Olivia by the hand as he escorted her to the car and looked at Papa Sha with an evil grin. When he got in the car, he made sure his nemesis was looking as he rolled down Olivia's window, put his hand on her throat and put his tongue deep in her mouth in a passionate kiss. The couple laughed as Papa Sha flashed both of his middle fingers to the car as it drove down the street. Olivia teased with her make-up, so that she would look perfect for her client as she asked Roger what the old man had to say about his work. Roger chuckled,

"He liked my shit as always, ya heard me. But dem old folks know they superstitious fareal, say he can smell a storm coming. Like nigga, it's clear outside."

"Bae, you know how they are."

Olivia was on her way to the hotel where her date was patiently waiting on her and one of Roger's girls. She called to make sure her tag team partner was at the hotel and the young woman told her that she was waiting in the lobby for her when Roger pulled up in front. The sexy Olivia stepped out of the car as the valet held the door open for her and Roger escorted her in where they met up with Cynthia, one of Roger's hardworking street strollers. Cynthia was a 19-year-old country girl from a small town outside of Opelousas, Louisiana that came to New Orleans for the exciting city life. The thing is she ended up entangled in Roger's web and became one of his top girls. She was a thick pretty yella-bone with green eyes, smooth silky skin, perky plump B cups and an ass that clapped when she walked in her floral sundress. Olivia wasn't a rusty trinket standing on the other side of Roger. The creamed coffee toned beauty queen matched her partner's insatiable sexuality as they walked to the elevator. Eyes in the lobby followed their every move. Roger walked his girls down the hallway to their client's door, tongue kissed them both as he told them he'll be downstairs waiting. Olivia knocked on the door as she watched her man get back on the elevator and was all smiles when a middle aged old white businessman opened the door dressed in nothing but a snow-white terrycloth robe. Her along with the eager Cynthia made their way in the room to a wide-open living room, Benjamin had ordered some room service ahead of time for them. Benjamin was a big businessman that was more concerned with making money than having a relationship with a woman, so when he got the urge to be with something soft, he would call for an escort to satisfy that yearning. Olivia was used to the pampering when she was with Benjamin, but Cynthia was loving the catered exotic fruit, gourmet cheeses, shrimp cocktail and champagne. The veteran knew Benjamin really only did it just to show off how much money he had, and it wasn't to actually have food for them during their stay. Olivia pushed

Benjamin on the plush sofa in the living room and pulled the strap loose on his terrycloth,

"Fuck all this food, white boy. Where my dick at?"

"Right here, waiting on you."

Cynthia watched as Olivia stroked him to a blood red hardness while Benjamin laid his head back, enjoying the feeling and the young escort took her sundress off as it fell to the floor. Olivia coasted her partner to stand behind the couch and put her nipple in Benjamin's mouth while she inserted his man meat into her mouth. Benjamin's tongue twirled around Cynthia's perky nipple, while she rubbed his chest reaching down to hold the base of his dick while Olivia went up and down on it. The bottom bitch went deep on Benjamin, and he moaned in pleasure as she came up,

"You like that shit, huh? You better not stop sucking her titty. You stop, I stop, ya heard me."

He reached up, holding both of her breast in his hands, while he gave both of her nipples equal attention as Olivia rigorously stroked his meat. Cynthia came around the sofa to help with the oral pleasure with Olivia as they both fought over who was going to suck on his dick the most. Their lips and tongues provoked him to pull his rod from them in an attempt to take a break, but the temptress wasn't having it. Olivia had dealings with Benjamin on several occasions, so she knew what would make him bust quick and laid on the floor as she took her tights off revealing her plump shaven pussy while she rubbed her clit. Cynthia went down on Olivia, sucking on her juicy clit with her fat round ass up in the air for Benjamin and he went in for the bait but not before spreading Cynthia's ass cheeks taking a taste of her tight hole. The youngster wasn't ready as his tongue slid deep in tickling her inside while he fingered her wet pleasure pocket and continued to push his tongue in as far as it could go. Olivia held onto Cynthia's head, enjoying her oral skills as she commanded Benjamin,

"You better eat that sweet ass, you nasty muthafucka."

"Oh my goodness! He eating my ass. He so deep in my ass."

"Eat dat ass, she lovin dat shit."

"Wait, wait."

"Bitch, who told you stop eatin dis pussy?"

Olivia pushed her head back down as she commanded her suitor to fill up Cynthia's insides with his steak and Benjamin did as he was instructed, sliding all of his hardened meat in the young woman's warm juice box. Olivia's partner moaned deeply, vibrating on her clit while Benjamin pounded away, and Cynthia's ass jiggled to the motion. Benjamin was enjoying the sight of watching the young woman orally please Olivia while he fondled the young apprentice's insides with his dick. The job was almost complete as the visual sent him over the top. The businessman sped up his motions until he pulled out stroking his meat in his hand and Cynthia held open her ass while he exploded all on her back. Olivia got up from the floor while Benjamin sat there trying to catch his breath and Cynthia followed her in the bathroom to clean up after their erotic escapade. The women were taking a shower together in the double wide glass shower when Benjamin walked in, and he couldn't help but join them as he started rubbing on Olivia's ass. She grinned as she whispered,

"Now you do know this gone be extra right white boy."

"You already know I got it."

"Shower sex is my favorite. Wha cha wanna do?"

Benjamin pushed both of them against the shower wall as he took turns eating them both out until they came in his mouth. Cynthia returned the favor as she sucked him rock hard again and had him bend her over in the shower. Olivia watched as the business mogul stroked his meat in and out of her to another spastic orgasm. He had his fill of the ladies and went to bed as Olivia left out with her partner in crime, grabbing an overstuffed envelope waiting on the nightstand for them.

It had almost been a week since Roger dropped off the payment for the packages he delivered for the Haitians and the statement the elder said to him about smelling a storm coming came true. A category 5 hurricane by the name of Katrina was about to touchdown in New Orleans in a few hours and city officials called for their residents to evacuate. The Sweeds usually stayed home most of the time during hurricane season and this one was no different. Olivia watched the news broadcast stating how devastating this storm may be and got a little nervous. Roger really wasn't worried about the storm that was coming their way more than the thought of looters that he knew would take advantage of empty houses in his neighborhood. He sat outside watching neighbors pack their cars to leave for higher ground when he seen the Daniels group load up in their suburban. Delores had just given birth to their fourth child, Kareem, earlier that week and Cedric Sr wasn't taking any chances with his family as he got them ready to leave. The law enforcement officer seen Roger relaxing in front of his house,

"Say big dawg, they say this gone be a serious storm. Y'all not leaving?"

"Nah chief, the one right before this one they told us evacuate and that wasn't shit. I'm a stay put and watch over everybody houses, ya heard me."

"You sure?"

"Man we good. Probably gone be some rain and dem water pumps gone push dat shit right out."

Cedric pleaded with his neighbor to leave and even offered that the family join his at the hotel the sheriff department supplied for all of their employees. Roger turned down the gesture as he stated he's going to be the "neighborhood watch" while they're gone and went inside when the clouds started getting real thick in the sky. Olivia was sitting with her little girl trying to catch up on one of their favorite sitcoms, but it kept getting interrupted with broadcast of the upcoming hurricane. The mother of three started feeling uneasy about staying home. She asked her man if he thinks they should leave like they seen a lot of their neighbors do because the weatherman made the storm sound so dangerous,

"Baby they showed it on TV and dat storm is huge."

"Katrina right? Girl I ain't ever run from a bitch and I be damn I run from this one. We good."

"Alright big man. I'm a hold you to it."

"I got something you could hold."

Olivia shook her head at her man's jokes while she looked at all the broadcast that told her different from what Roger was spilling out, she fell asleep in front of the television. Roger later woke to a loud thunderous crack from the storm system overhead but when he got out of bed, he was surprised by a soaking wet carpet floor, and he immediately went looking for Olivia. Another thunderous crash woke everyone else in the house and Roger could hear sounds of his kids calling for him as they realized there was water in their rooms. It sounded like a freight train was right outside the door as the wind blew pass the house. The rain imitated the sound of iron pellets slamming against the windows as lightning strikes seemed to light up the entire home. Little Darlene clung to her mother's side as she walked through the house, the agitated look on Olivia's face when she looked at Roger said a thousand words and his arrogance came back to bite him. Roger told his boys to go to their room to grab only important things as he told Olivia to do the same and he went to their bedroom to get essentials as he flipped over their mattress. Under the mattress was Roger's emergency kit which was a few stacks he saved for times like this, a couple of guns and Olivia found it strange that was the first thing he went to,

"Really Roger, that's the first you grab?"

"The way this water coming up, we won't be coming back here no time soon and we gone need this shit."

"Grab some stuff and lets go, c'mon."

Olivia went along with what he said as she gathered other things for them like clothes. Ronald was grabbing a few clothes as he watched with bafflement all over his face because he noticed Brock unhooking their game console from the TV. The middle child tried to tell his older brother that the game wasn't important, but Brock ignored his little brother as he packed the console in his backpack. Roger walked through the house calling for all his family members to meet him in the front of the house and everyone filed in one at a time. He had looked outside to see their car wasn't going to make it as the street was completely flooded and watched as everybody's eyes bucked wide open when he told them they would have to walk through the water to higher ground. The Sweeds made their way out the house as the storm let up for a while and light began to peek between the dark clouds that blanketed over the city. The water was chest high to 6-year-old Ronald, but he pushed through as he watched his brother struggle with the heavy game console weighing him down in his backpack. Just like he told Brock earlier, their father had noticed the unimportant item poking out the backpack and the sight pissed him off. The head of the household snatched the game from his son and tossed it in the murky water,

"Fuck is you carrying dat stupid shit for. Hurry yo ass up."

Ronald held his mother's hand as he escorted her down the street making sure she kept her footing. His father held Darlene on his shoulders as he led the way and Brock walked aggravated upset over his game. The city looked like an overgrown swamp as houses sat partially submerged in water, the streets they sat on were non-existent as the family tracked on to their destination. The sounds of people crying out for help, splashing water and flybys of helicopters were occasionally interrupted with distant gun shots. Roger's head stayed on a swivel as he walked his family forward as Olivia shouted,

"Where are we going? Everything under water! We shoulda been left yesterday."

"Livia I know! Just keep walking."

"Where are we going?"

Before her man could answer her, a small boat came floating through towards the family and the guy on it told them that the water only gets deeper down the street. The boater offered to bring the Sweeds closer downtown because he heard that the city opened the Superdome for the residents to shelter there. Roger was a little skeptical of taking the ride from the stranger, but he seen that the water they were standing in was already up to Ronald's chin and knew it would only get higher. He thanked the guy as he loaded his family on the boat, and they made their way downtown as the dark clouds started to rumble again in preparation to open up another downpour on the city.

It was completely chaotic at the Superdome, people fighting for space, food and any other resource they could fight over as Roger watched over his family. Ronald held tightly to his little sister's hand as crowds of people pushed pass while his father attempted to find a spot for the family to rest their tired wet feet. Olivia had a feeling they would be tracking through high water so she packed a lot of their clothes in plastic garbage bags and told the boys to get out of the damp clothes they had on. Brock looked for a place to change when his mother told him to just get out of the clothes where he stood but the youngster was completely uncomfortable getting undressed in front of a bunch of strangers. Ronald immediately started peeling off the wet garments to freshen up, but his big brother wasn't having it and complained to their dad about it. Olivia nor Roger was trying to hear any of the grumbling Brock was doing while they attempted to figure out their next move and the aggravation was starting to come to a head with Roger. The constant whining worked Roger's last nerve when he finally snapped on Brock,

"Say man, you supposed to be the oldest and you doing more crying than your baby sister and she four. They got people that done lost everything they own and you over here crying like a little bitch because you gotta change clothes in front of people who ain't even worrying bout yo ass. Change ya damn clothes, stay in them shits, I don't give a fuck but one thing you gone stop doing is all that damn whining."

"But dad…"

"What da fuck I say?"

Ronald watched as his brother backed down, sitting next to a large concrete column, sulking from the chastising he just got from his father and sat there completely in his feelings about the whole situation. The middle child looked around the large lobby area of the Superdome at all the people in there. The smell of sour cloths, sewage and decaying filled the air as his family waited to see where they were going next. A few law officers started to open up other parts of the dome to the general population and people started to rush to claim their spot as Roger pulled his family to a vacant corner spot in a large hallway. The head of the family had a little conversation with a guy who had an extra tent he wasn't using and Roger bought it from him for shelter for his family. Ronald had never seen his father do any outdoor activities before, like put together a tent but he watched as his father maneuvered through the task to have something for his family to lay their heads. Olivia pulled small packs of peanut butter crackers from her backpack, handed them out to her family and they all sat in the tent Roger put together as the parents worried what to do. The cracks of lightening and rumbles from the clouds outside could be heard inside the structure as everybody feared the worse from the storm battering their city. Horrid smells passed through the building, with an occasional scream and rumors of dead bodies being found throughout the building ran rampant, but Roger wasn't going look to see if it was true or not. As night began to fall back on the city, the rains continued to come down, the shadows started to come out from their hidings and Roger went into protective mode, watching for anything out of the ordinary. Ronald watched as the laid-back relaxed man he has always seen at home turn into a lion on a hunt, eyes scanning over everything, searching for anything that needed to be stopped. Roger sat Indian style at the entrance of the tent with a blue steel .357 magnum in his lap while his family laid in the tent and Ronald watched his father with pure intent to secretly learn whatever he could from watching his every move. The young 6-year-old inched closer to his father silently sitting in the entrance of the tarp opening and was shocked when he heard is dad call his name,

"Ronald stop creeping, come sit ya lil behind out here."

Roger usually instilled the manly stuff into Brock because he was the oldest, but his youngest boy was showing interest in what his father was doing. Little Ronald absorbed everything his father told him that night and kept it close to him as his own personal gospel. The lights were dim in the dome because of the lack of power running through the building but Ronald's eyes were glancing over the sea of people that were sprawled out in front of him and his father, looking for anything out of the way. He could see his father's grip to the handle of the gun resting in his lap tighten when sounds of a woman's scream spark in the air. Ronald's pops stared out into the shadows,

"Son, I want you to remember one thing bout humans. Angels and demons are always around us day or night. But at night, no matter what, the demons will always show they face, you just gotta make sure you ready for dem bitches. Ya heard me."

"Yes sir."

YEAR 2006

The Sweeds got bussed from New Orleans to the city of Houston after their hometown was considered unsafe for anyone to stay and the family made the new surroundings home for the time being. Word of family members and friends dying during or after the storm became a normal occurrence for them but the news of Roger's mother passing away was the hardest for him to hear. He got his stubbornness from her because just like Roger wanted to do, she stayed during the storm. Roger's mother found herself at a friend's house in the lower ninth ward when the levees gave way and the house they were in was engulfed with water as it washed away. Her body was found under an overturned shed a mile from where she originally was. He paid for her to be cremated and delivered to his house because they had no other family to take care of her. Olivia still had family in Louisiana but after she hooked up with Roger, they all cut her off, so her man and her kids were all the family she really had. The couple made do with what they had and being in a new environment never slowed down their resourcefulness as Roger recruited a new stable for the ones he lost in New Orleans. Olivia really wasn't with walking the streets of Houston like she used to do in the city, so she became the madame of the young crew of girls they had put together.

Roger also connected with a few of his boys from back home that he used to transport for. H-Town along with other Texas cities became some good connects for the pipeline he created. As for the money flow, everything was running smooth for the Sweeds, but the boys had their issues with the big city and its occupants. Going to school was kind of rough for the Sweed boys because they were the outsiders from another city, got special privileges from teachers and didn't understand the gang affiliations. Ronald tried not to get into too much trouble, but it would always find him and the now 7-year-old had no problem defending himself. As for Brock, who was 12, he went out looking for trouble on a regular. The kids at school would always say that the NOLA boys were like night and day, but they knew that no matter what the issue was, Ronald was going to defend his big brother at all cost. It was Brock's first year in junior high and walking from school was a task for the juvie as he walked through heavy gang territory to get home. He made his way down the streets of the 5th ward when he seen some bigger boys sitting on a stoop of a house in the middle of the block. 5th ward was nicknamed "The Bloody Nickle" by some of the residents there for several reasons, one being the dangerous gang affiliation there. Brock attempted to just buzz pass them because they all were dressed in all red and he knew they were going to say something to him. He was almost past their house when Brock heard them laughing and one shouted out,

"Say blood, you know where you at? Hey! I asked you a question fool."

When the nervous youngster turned around, all he seen was four tall teens standing in front of him and Brock readied himself for a fight but said nothing as he looked them in the eyes. One of the teens grabbed their prey by the shoulder strap of his backpack. He then pulled him close to him as he told Brock that he needs to pay a toll to walk on his street. Brock nervously told him that he didn't have any money on him, but the teens didn't want to hear that as they began to dig in his pockets. Right when Brock thought that he was about to get beaten beyond recognition all he heard was his little brother shout,

"Get off my fucking brother bitch!"

When one of the teen boys turned around to see who the little voice was, Ronald swung his backpack at the boy striking him on the shoulder and the elementary school kid did not stop. He kicked his victim square between the legs, dropping him to the ground, as he rushed him with a closed fist, ready for war. Except for the teen that was getting pummeled by Ronald, all the others found it hilarious how much courage the little guy had, and the laughs continued as they pulled Ronald away. One of the older teens held onto the feisty little guy while trying to see who he was, and Ronald didn't let up as his main goal was protecting his brother from the neighborhood bullies. They had finally let the Sweed brothers know they were just teasing Brock because they were new to the area, but Ronald stayed on the defense while he backed away from the four teens. The crazy thing was, instead of Brock thanking his little brother for coming to his rescue, the older Sweed boy was pissed that he was saved by him as they walked home.

After being showed out by his little brother, Brock had a point to prove to anyone that was willing to watch him act a fool. Where Ronald claimed the nickname "pitbull", from the teens in the hood, because of his small size and heart of a lion. Brock was brandished the name "crash" as for "crash dummy" because whatever scenario the neighborhood hoodlums came up with for Brock to do, he would attempt to accomplish. The challenges started out as simple vandal type acts but then it got more demanding until the test turned criminal and the naïve Brock went headfirst every time. Their dad was a stickler for his kids to always be in school to better themselves no matter what, but Brock would always test Roger's patience. Calls from teachers, days of detention and even one run in with a policeman aggravated Roger so much because his son was bringing too much unwanted attention to his family,

"Nigga, da fuck wrong with you?"

Roger knew if people started looking into his house, they would notice things he and Olivia been keeping under wraps. The kids' parents never really kept them from making friends or associate with a certain class of people, but Roger seen that Brock's new friends were endangering his operation. He called for his son to end the friendship with his bright red flag wearing friends. The only thing Roger didn't know about his son's new acquaintances was that they had jumped Brock into their gang, and he was in deep. Ronald knew of his brother's affiliation but didn't want to have anything to do with it because he didn't understand it. The gang members actually respected him for standing his ground and not joining them. He didn't tell his father about Brock becoming a Blood because like always Ronald was protecting his own but ended up getting in trouble anyways when Roger found out he knew. Little Ronald had gotten used to taking on the responsibility of being the "big brother" of his siblings and the caliber of liability his father held him to. The 7-year-old had gained a lot of respect from the gang members because of the grown man attitude he held, and it carried over to the rest of his family when they would be out in the neighborhood. Darlene never knew how many eyes watched over her as she played in the front yard, Olivia didn't know how protected she was as she would carry her groceries in the house from her car and most of it was just out of respect for Ronald. Just seeing his little brother getting more respect from his own gang would push Brock to do extra stunts to get noticed and the extra notoriety got the wrong attention. Brock had ventured out to the southwest side of Houston one day and assaulted a couple while they were at a park. What the eager attention seeker didn't realize was that the female of the couple was the sister to a very dangerous Mexican gang member, the mistake was made and a greenlight was lit for Brock or any of his members. When Roger found out about his son, his first thought was to kick him out of the house because he didn't want anyone coming to his home looking for Brock. Olivia pleaded with him not to because she couldn't see her oldest boy pushed out on the streets at the age of 12 and Roger really couldn't see putting his own child out either. As always Ronald wanted to be the protection for his siblings, but this wasn't anything a kid could fix. Roger went to one of the "OG's" of the click Brock was connected to with a band of 100-dollar bills and asked him to hold his son in his house until Roger was able to get Brock out of town. The gangster was 10 years younger than Roger and his juvenile ways showed but the father was desperate to have a safe haven for his son. The young gang leader stressed that Brock created a beef between them and the southwest Mexican gang but agreed to hold up the newbie if Roger brings the same amount of money every week. The request was granted but Roger addressed,

"Say lil nigga, don't think you getting over on me. I'm only agreeing to this shit cause that's my seed we talking bout, ya heard me. Please don't think y'all the only ones walking around strapped. My son come outta here with a scratch on him and I'm leveling this fucking shack, we good."

"Fool we good. You just make sure you keep dem stacks comin and we won't have a problem."

The arrogant leader looked at Roger and took his money with a smile.

Olivia didn't know what to do with herself after her eldest baby was no longer under the same roof as she was, but she knew it was for the betterment of the entire family that Brock wasn't there. She tried to keep herself busy with her other kids when she was home but the demand for her escort service kept her away from home a lot. Houston had way more money to splurge on her girls than New Orleans did, she had become the true big mama of their little clan. With Olivia running the prostitution ring, Roger was able to completely focus on transportation of his products between Texas and Louisiana. Ronald had gotten accustomed to his dad not being around for a few days and took on the burden of being the man of the house but the sudden appearance of what his mother called his "aunts" felt a little off to him. The traffic of sexy young women back and forth through the house was a bit strange for Ronald but he trusted his mother's decision to have them around her kids. The women never stayed long, only to have a quick conversation with his mama, drop off an envelope, a quick hello with the kids, maybe a bite to eat and off they went. Darlene loved seeing the visitors at her house and was comfortable calling them her aunties, but Ronald made sure they didn't talk to his little sister alone. Olivia would find it funny how guarded her little man was over his family, but she also understood Ronald had been like that ever since that first night after the hurricane that moved them to Texas. She had wished her oldest boy had inherited the same mentality, but Brock went in a totally different direction, and it was evident that he wasn't going to change after hearing the latest news. During a visit with one of Olivia's girls, she found out that the young woman seen the now highly active gang member known as "Crash" selling on a corner she frequents for drive-thru Johns. The mother of three knew she was losing her boy to the streets and knew she had to do some drastic shit to get him back to her before the streets eat him alive. Olivia had loaded her kids in the car to drive over to where the call girl had told her she seen Brock, but Ronald's gut was telling him it was a bad idea. He had heard from some kids at school that the area where his brother was holding up was extremely dangerous and was known for high gang activity. Ronald borderline begged his mother to allow him and Darlene to stay home but Olivia wasn't hearing it as she headed to the east side of Houston. The streets looked completely strange to Ronald as they made their way towards where Olivia was told her son was hanging out. The element of danger was deep, and Brock's mother was oblivious to it at the moment. Olivia's middle child seen drugged out street walkers, aggressive pimps, groups of red bandanas wearing teens and abandoned houses that held addicts for its residents. Eyes followed their car as it slowly drove down the street and Olivia was blind to them because she was too concerned with finding her son, but Ronald kept a close watch on every sly look. They pulled up to a group of teens Olivia was familiar with and she rolled down her window,

"Hey, any of y'all seen Brock around here?"

"Man, you looking for Crash? Dat fool up da street."

A few of the teens laughed as they pointed to a corner store, telling Olivia that the juvenile was stationed over there. Ronald's mom rushed towards the convenience store, only to find Brock fighting with a crackhead that was trying to beat him for his product. Olivia seen the frail man tugging at Brock's hand, trying to get him to release whatever was in it and Brock repeatedly punching the man in the side of the head. Ronald watched as his mother darted out of the car to help her son and the reaction Olivia received wasn't what she expected as Brock shouted disapproval to her assistance. His mother stood there in disbelief as she watched Brock storm off away from her and a young man walked up to her,

"Say lil mama, I got some work for ya if you need some."

"I don't need no work lil boy, what I need you to do is what my husband paid y'all to do and that's keep him safe."

"Damn, calm down. We good round here."

The young thug realized who Olivia was and backed off from her, telling her that Brock was safer with him than staying in the house, as he revealed a large gun tucked in his waist. The cockiness of the gang member didn't satisfy Olivia's worries at all, but she left them to their vices but not before shouting to Brock to take care of himself. Olivia knew her son was getting himself in deep with his new clique and desperately wanted to get him as far away from them as she could.

Roger had just gotten home when he seen Olivia getting out of the car with the kids,

"Where y'all coming from?"

"We just got back from by Brock, bae you gotta do something. He out there selling, fighting crackheads and who knows what else. My baby not built for that shit."

"I'm a take care of it bae. I promise."

Roger knew he had to get his kid off the streets, especially with a rival gang looking for him and the concerned father already had things in plan to get his whole family out of Texas. After they all got settled inside, he sat Olivia down to tell her how he had been traveling back to New Orleans not only for product but to find them a place. Roger knew he couldn't keep up with the amount of money the "OG" wanted him to pay for protection for his son. After finding out that they had Brock on the corners working, the payments were useless. He had his lady start to pack up because they were going to head out the following week back home, but Olivia's business sense kicked in asking what would they going to do with their collection of girls. Roger looked at her with the coldest stare,

"Man, fuck dem bitches, ya heard me. I'm worried bout mines and mines only. Dem hoes gone be good."

"But bae…"

"Man fuck'em."

Olivia had did the one thing Roger had never done and that was get connected to the workers that supplied them with money from street walking. It wasn't that she caught feelings for the girls but the fact that her man wasn't always around and the girls kept her company sometimes, Olivia concerned herself with them. Roger could care less if the escorts would be okay or not and let it be known when his lady asked to take a few of the girls with them back to New Orleans,

"Girl what you trying to build here, a fucking hoe house? You do understand we can't have dem in our house, we got kids nigga."

"I know dat. I was just thinking we could set something up. I don't know."

Olivia seen she was going to lose the battle with Roger on the subject and left it alone as she got her priorities in order with getting things together for the move next week.

Ronald could hear his parents talking in the other room about moving back to New Orleans and he couldn't be any more excited about it because he didn't like Houston at all. He couldn't stand how the H-Town kids treated him because he was not from Texas, always calling him a refugee. He hated when they would tease him when it would rain or making fun of how he talks different than them. The move back home was something Ronald was truly looking forward to, back home to some familiarity and kids just like him. The young lad tried his best to keep his cool while his family got things together for the upcoming week. But it was like the days dragged and everything the neighborhood kids did began to work his last nerve. The day came when one of the hellions tested Ronald's patience one time too many and the neighborhood badass found out the hard way why the teens gave him the nickname "Pitbull". The kids were on the bus being rambunctious as always, but one kid kept flicking balled up pieces of paper at Ronald, just being annoying as ever. The calm natured Ronald kept repeating himself to the kid,

"Dude, stop it."

"Or what? You ain't gone do shit!"

His little sister Darlene was sitting at the front of the bus with the other smaller kids when the bus stopped at their street and Ronald walked up to escort his baby sister home. The boy that was taunting Ronald got off the bus too. He continued his terrorism of the youth, but he made the ultimate mistake by hitting Darlene in the back of the head with a ball of paper. Ronald turned around with rage in his eyes as he charged towards the boy, but the bully's agility allowed him to avoid the attack and slipping to the ground only enticed the assault that ensued. Ronald quickly got up from the ground, snatching the boy by his shirt, threw him to the concrete and dropped bombs of clinched fist to the boy's face. Darlene's brother landed several strikes to the bully's face before her scream stopped him,

"Ronald!"

Ronald got up off the battered boy, leaving his victim on the ground, dazed from the assault he just got. He didn't want to fight the boy because he knew he would have to see him again at school but protecting his baby sister was top priority to Ronald and he wasn't going to let that boy disrespect her.

Olivia was packing clothes in a large cardboard box with two of her top girls that came over after they finished a service call for some visiting businessmen. The girls brought in a lot of money for Olivia, and she didn't want to lose them because of that, along with the fact that they all connected like close colleagues. She let them know that she was leaving with her family in a few days, moving back to New Orleans and asked them to come with her to start a new business there. The girls were game for the change of scenery, but Olivia knew she would have to convince Roger to take the girls with them. Right when the triplets were laughing about all the money they could make in New Orleans, Ronald walked in the house with Darlene. The bundle of joy rushed to her mother, spilling all the tea about the fight she just witnessed. Olivia looked over to her son standing at the door, still with anger plastered on his face from the recent event and called him over to her,

"Boy, what you do?"

"Mama, he started with me. And he hit Dee in her head."

As he made his way to his mother, Ronald began to explain himself to her and Olivia commended her son for standing up for his sister. The kids pretend "aunties" began to ask them about school and Darlene was ecstatic to tell them about her whole day. Ronald was still a bit leery of the women as he went to his room while Darlene rambled on. It wasn't that he didn't like his mother's friends, he found most of them extremely attractive and they were always sweet to him, but he knew the women weren't family. The long three days stuck in the Dome after the hurricane really changed Ronald to view family as something sacred and it took a lot for him to trust anyone. Ronald went to his room thinking of what he may have to do the next day he seen the boy he had the fight with, but all his contemplating was interrupted when he heard his father come home. Roger was arguing with his lady about her inviting two of their call girls with them to New Orleans and the fact that they didn't have any room for them,

"Livia, you lost yo damn mind! You had to lose yo muthafuckin mind."

"Bae, we could work this out. We just gotta find da right house. We got this bae, c'mon."

Olivia was confident that they could find a place for all of them, but Roger always ran his operation where business was never under the same roof where he laid his head, and his woman just wasn't listening to reason. Keeping the two separate was key for Roger when he had his first child, but Olivia made it clear that overprotecting them wasn't working and used the issues they're having with Brock as evidence. The father of three caved into his woman's request to have the girls join them in New Orleans but made it known that his standard of no business in their home will stand no matter what. Little Ronald stood there silent in the hallway listening to his parents, wondering what his father meant by "the business" and the 7-year-old's mind just wandered with explanations. He was so busy trying to figure out what he had just heard that he didn't realize his mother told his pops about the fight he had earlier after school. Roger walked up to his son asking him what happened, and Ronald stood strong on his convictions for standing up for his sister, accepting whatever punishment his father had in store for him. The middle kid was surprised when his dad was proud of him and sat him down to spill a little knowledge to him,

"Son don't ever be scared of anything on two feet because they feel pain just like you do. Family always comes first, no matter what and the ones you consider family, until they show you different. If a nigga puts you in a predicament that could jeopardize your life, cut that nigga lose and don't look back. Cause if he comfortable enough to put you in danger, he comfortable enough to leave you there too."

The Sweeds had loaded up their moving truck to head back to New Orleans and Ronald couldn't be anymore ready to get out of Houston. After he encountered a fight almost every other day after school with a different kid trying to take the title. Little "Pitbull" was heading back to New Orleans undefeated after his talk with his dad about never fearing anyone. The family had brought Brock back home with them, but the active gang member was reluctant to leave his clique. He voiced it continuously as they packed in the last couple of boxes in the back of the truck. Roger was getting frustrated with his eldest complaining, disrespecting his family connection and checked him,

"Say my nigga! Dem niggas could care less for yo ass. A nigga had to pay dem bitch ass niggas to watch ya while you was there but you claiming dem muthafuckas got love for ya. I had a good thing going on here but I'm leaving to try and save yo ass from dem Mexicans that wanna put fiya to ya ass but if you don't wanna go, fuck it stay here. But I'm protecting da rest of my family, ya heard me."

Roger figured the stern talk would break through Brock's thick skull, but it worked in reverse and the pre-teen walked off down the street in the direction of his "OG's" house. He watched as his son stormed down the sidewalk and shook his head at the decision Brock made. He knew he would go down the street to convince his child to come with them anyways, but he had to let him walk away. Olivia came out with a few bags for Roger to add to the load when she seen that Brock wasn't out by the truck like everyone else was and inquired his whereabouts to Ronald. When her little soldier told his mother of the fuss his dad had with his older brother, Olivia gave Roger the dirtiest look and he knew it was time to go get his son back. Roger started walking down the street to go get Brock while Olivia waited with the kids, and she started texting her girls to let them know they all should meet up soon to head out. Jazzy was one of the girls she texted, and she stated she was right around the corner from them, but Eve called Olivia frantic,

"Tell me Brock with y'all!"

"No, Roger going get him now. Eve, what's wrong?"

"Oh Lawd."

It scared the mother why Eve was looking for Brock but when Eve told Olivia why, she freaked out looking for her son also. Eve overheard that one of Brock's gang buddies took a payout to give one of the Mexican gang members his whereabouts and they were on their way to the house.

Olivia rushed down the street as she called Roger's phone, but he didn't answer and then the sound of a warzone erupted in the distance. The sound of multiple gunfire echoed through the entire neighborhood as tires screeched off, a woman's screams followed and a few pops from smaller gunfire came after. A black old school four door car sped pass her on the street and she could see the Hispanic faces stare back at her as she froze still, until they left. Olivia could hear screams down the street, and she ran as fast as she could towards the screams only to find her husband on his knees with his back to her. Roger's lady didn't want to see what he was holding on his lap but when she seen Brock's tennis shoe in the middle of the street, she knew exactly what it was in front of her man. Olivia's body literally collapsed to the ground in disbelief of what she knew had just taken place. Roger silently held his eldest's lifeless body in his arms as the liquid life source poured out staining the area all around them. Nothing but regret, what if's and pain filled the father's heart as he stared out into nothingness of the life he use to have. Roger began faulting himself for letting his son walk away, blaming himself for not going get him earlier. He condemned himself for not noticing the danger he seen his son walk into when he seen the black car turn the corner in front of Brock. The sounds of police sirens could be heard in the distance, but Roger knew it was far too late for any type of police security at this moment, only a coroner because his child was gone.

After all the dust had cleared, after all the police questionings, after all the souls of the neighborhood exited from in front of the Sweeds house. It was only the family left to their own devices. Eve gave Roger the info she gave Olivia. When he found out that his son was set up by the same guys he was running to for cover, Roger had one thing rushing through his veins and it wasn't anything good. Olivia was nowhere near capable of trying to talk her man out of the revenge filled rage he was going through at the moment because she still couldn't get out of the hole of despair, she was in. He knew it had to be quick whatever he did because his entire family was packed up and ready to go back to New Orleans. Roger was glad the girls were coming back with them because he had someone to drive Olivia along with the kids back home and an alibi just in case questions arise after what he had planned. Jazzy was all game for whatever Roger had in store for the hoodlums up the street, but Eve was the mind of reason trying to talk the bitter father out of his decision,

"Baby, I know you hurtin but this won't bring him back. Let's just go, start all over in New Orleans. C'mon, please daddy."

"Fuck dat daddy! They killed yo son!"

It was as if Roger had an Angel and a Devil on his shoulders trying to sway him in their direction, but his mind was made up once he opened the trunk of his car. He had loaded the kids in Olivia's car with Jazzy behind the wheel, Eve was driving the moving truck with Olivia sitting in the passenger seat. He told all his girls he will see them at the Texas-Louisiana border and told Ronald he's in charge. Roger watched as they drove off to the Interstate and he went back inside to prepare himself for battle. He knew it wasn't going to be easy, but the element of surprise was on his side as he loaded the clips to the arsenal of firearms in front of him. Roger waited until dusk because he wanted to make sure all the kids were inside when he set his rage on the street, plus he wanted to make sure no police were around. He watched through the mini blinds as the neighborhood went quiet and the only ones roaming the block was the ones he really wanted. Dressed in all black with a black bandana around his neck, Roger loaded the large duffle bag in his car. He removed the license plates from his car, to avoid any witnesses pointing him out and made his way to his mark. The time had come, and the angel of death left to meet with his victims, ready for the worse as he drove down the street. Brock's ex-associates all were out front of their "OG's" house doing their usual shenanigans they did every night and truly thought they had gotten over on everyone. They had no idea what was coming for them in the form of a heartbroken father until they heard the screech of tires in front of the house and a black shadow jumped from the car. The silence of the street was awaken with a barrage of warfare focused on one house and everyone dove for cover as the dark shadow walked the sidewalk gunning down anything moving. The gang members attempted to fire back but they were assaulted with a swarm of bullets in their direction every time they would raise their heads. The main culprit Roger was looking for ran up the street but was halted with one shot to the back of the leg and then the father went looking for the leader of the group. He kicked in the door to two youngster hovering in a corner scared of the boogeyman terrorizing the neighborhood and he shouted for them to run. As the teens took off down the street, Roger found the one man that owed him his life and repeated to him what he said the first time,

"I said if my son come back with a scratch I'm leveling this shack. Consider it leveled, bitch."

"Nigga I ain't do shit! Dem fuckin Mexicans shot that nigga, not me."

The images of his son being riddle with bullets right in front of him blasted through his memory, ripping at Roger's heart, cutting the oxygen from his lungs and fueling the rage he was feeling. Roger pulled his .45 from his waist, pointed at the guy's head and pulled the trigger without thinking nothing of it. He left the house looking for the guy that set his son up still trying to crawl away from danger. The death dealer walked right up to him, place the gun to the back of his head, whispered goodnight in his ear and the bark of the large gun could be heard down the street as the flash of light was the last thing seen.

Ronald had been in his new home almost a year now and he is reminded of losing his brother to a drive by shooting every day. His mother has yet to recover only to get out of bed to go to the bathroom. The two women that came with them from Houston has taken on the motherly or wifely duty in the house. Jazzy would recruit for the escort service, take care of the top-notch clients and made sure the kids got off to school on time. Eve worked various strip clubs, made sure Roger stayed on schedule with his deliveries and always took care of all the kids' needs. The ladies had become a replacement for the woman that struggled just to open her eyes when someone would bring her food. It was rough but they all managed to make it work because everyone in the house was determined to make it work, especially Ronald. He had to grow up fast, taking on the responsibility of being Darlene's only big brother and seeing his father treat two women like he would his mother. Ronald was always trained to give adults respect at a very young age no matter what. But watching his father completely disrespect his mother when Jazzy would cater to him was too much for the youngster. Jazzy had taken the wifely duties to another level one day when Roger was home after a long trip from Texas. Ronald had to stay home from school that day because he was carrying a high fever and Eve was watching over him. He had become accustomed to Eve over time because she was truly a caring woman with the softest of hands and her eyes were like two green jade disc. Her smile drew any man in, be it old or young and Eve held a class of elegance like Ronald's mother. Even after working two different clubs the night before, Eve came home to cater to Ronald's every need but fell asleep on him in the process. The now 8-year-old Ronald seen his makeshift mother peacefully sleeping at the foot of his bed and he didn't want to disturb her, but he was extremely thirsty. He went downstairs to the kitchen only to find his father sitting at the table with Jazzy on her knees in front of him. Even at a young age, Ronald snuck and seen enough porno videos to know what was going on at the table. The moans his father was making was drowned out by the sounds Jazzy was creating and the little man ran back upstairs, to avoid being seen. The rumble of feet going up the stairs alerted Roger, who knew exactly who it was and went straight to his son's room. The father didn't feel he had to explain himself for getting service to a little kid poking his nose in grown folk's business, but he went to check on his ill son. Roger walked in his son's room to Eve still asleep on the bed and Ronald sitting there with questions on his face, but his questions weren't answered that day, only lessons for another day. The youngster didn't know what to think, his mother barricaded in her bedroom for who knows how long, his baby sister tuned into the mother figure that took over and his father tangled in the web Jazzy spun. Ronald seen his close-knit family falling to the wayside since his brother's death, but the year was only getting started.

A lot had changed since Roger came back to the city and not for the good in his case because Papa Sha took over as the leader of the Haitians. The old man perished after the hurricane, leaving his second in command in charge and the dreadlocked Dracko taking on the rank of lieutenant. The two collectively couldn't stand Roger because he wasn't a purebred and only tolerated him because of the old man but now the old man wasn't there anymore. Just like he did with Olivia, Roger tried to use the female persuasions in Jazzy, but she was too eager for the island gangster and Eve wasn't having it. Eve was loyal to the Sweeds, especially to the kids because they were like hers, but Jazzy was loyal to whoever had the most money. After meeting with Papa Sha, Jazzy seen potential of being a boss bitch and not just

Roger's "special girl" when he needed to release some stress. The pimp didn't know he had written his own ticket to Hell when he introduced Papa Sha to the call girl. The gang leader played along with Roger, feeding him just enough rope so he could hang himself high with all the info the devilish Jazzy was giving up. She told them about Olivia being ill, his son Brock dying in front of him and even the situation with the Houston gang he lashed out his wrath on. Roger was too busy trying to keep up with young guys that was working for the Haitians in transportation and distribution to notice Jazzy's deceit. He kept up with some of the guys he was cool with before Katrina who ran loads of reefer between Louisiana and Florida, but it still wasn't enough. The market for heroin started dying off after the storm and prescription pills became the new buzz with the Haitians. It was easier to get to, easier to cut out the overseas element and it was ten times easier to transport through the city. Roger's profitable scheme was falling apart right in front of him, and he had to figure out a way to stay in the good graces of his hateful associates. Eve tried to convince Roger to dive deep into the escort service they had going but he didn't see the service growing like he wanted to. Sex was something that fell to the back burner with many men in the city because they were too concerned with how they were going to rebuild and pills from the Haitians helped them to forget. Eve tried to show Roger that the city was building up and that the need he and his girls provided would definitely come to the forefront once things clear. He didn't trust the thought because he was too caught up in the quick cash method,

"You telling me to hold out for these niggas to come around and these dreds are offering me bands right now to bring their product to Texas? Nah, I can't do it."

"Baby, we just have to hold out a little longer. There's no one out here doing what we doing, no one giving out the service we provide and you can come out like a fat rat if we do this right."

"I ain't got time to wait. I gotta take care of deez kids, Livia zoned out and this damn house ain't gone pay for itself."

Olivia was usually the brains behind the operation and with her out, Eve took on the job without a hitch. It was all falling on deaf ears though as Roger looked at all the bills he had in front of him and waiting for someone to call was not an option.

Papa Sha would always have Roger bring Jazzy with him when picking up his shipments, the unaware transporter thought it was because the call girl was his type, but it was only for more info. The gang leader would pay Jazzy off with pills to feed to Olivia which kept her dependent on them and handicapping Roger in the process. Jazzy stepped out of line scorning Roger one time stating,

"You running errands for Sha and only getting his scraps. Dracko said you was soft."

"Bitch, my hand ain't gone feel soft. I'm over here supporting you hoes and you disrespect me like that? Bitch I'll kill ya and drop yo ass in the river, ya heard me."

"Sha said you was jealous of him. Said he would let me…"

"Bitch!"

The call girl had started feeling herself on that day after leaving from by Papa Sha and caught the back end of Roger's hand in the car. That day was the day that sealed Roger's fate and Jazzy was bent on watching him fall apart. It was the first time Roger ever put his hands on her and Jazzy had set in her mind that she was going to destroy Roger no matter what. Giving Papa Sha all the ammo he needed was all that was on her mind at that point and keeping Olivia drunk on pills was her first step. Turning his kids out was next on her agenda but Jazzy knew Eve was going to be a problem as the kids' protector, so she had to pick her time right. The call girl had truly become an evil presence in the home, feeding Olivia prescription pills and pocketing money from escort jobs. The ultimate act was her new attraction to Ronald, walking around him naked, asking him for passionate kisses when he would be alone with her and enticing him with soft caresses,

"Ronald, you getting so strong. I bet those girls at school be chasing you down. You bet not be showing them girls yo big dick, you can't show nobody yo big dick but me."

"Huh?"

"You gone let me see it? C'mon, lemme see it."

The young 8-year-old didn't really know how to handle a grown woman prancing in front of him, but he liked how she made him feel. He figured if his dad could do it, he could do it too and no one needed to know about it, but little Ronald was just a pawn in Jazzy's game.

Eve caught the spiteful Jazzy one night at a strip club she worked at, hanging with Dracko and a few of his goons. At first, she didn't think anything of it, assuming that Jazzy was working a John for the night,

"Bitch, what you doing here, you out here on a date? Roger know where you at? Don't be out here taking all my money."

"Fuck that nigga Roger, he a whole hoe outchere."

"Bitch what you talkin bout?"

The smell of strong green bud filled Eve's nose when she felt a man's large hand lay on her lower back and the strong Haitian creole dialect vibrated her ear as Papa Sha whispered to her. He started to tell her to relax with them for the night, but Eve gracefully declined the offer as she looked over to Jazzy with confusion in her eyes. The girls knew Papa Sha didn't care for Roger at all and any fraternizing with him could be looked at as betrayal. The thing is Jazzy been turned her back on Roger a long time ago and was just building a strong enough net to trap him in, but she needed Eve's help,

"C'mon girl. They got all the top shelf drinks over here, as much weed you wanna smoke and Dracko fine ass already said he willing to pay for all yo time."

"Nah, I'm good. I'm going make this money, y'all have fun."

Eve could feel something wasn't right but kept it to herself because she didn't want to have the Haitian crew looking at her strange. She left the group as she went back to dancing for the men in the club, but she kept one eye on Jazzy and Papa Sha in the VIP section. Images of the Haitian gang leader taunting other girls, pouring champagne on them as they pass, pushing bouncers around and Jazzy laughing at it all was a little too much for her to tolerate. She left for the night after making her quota only to find Roger outside of the club, talking with Dracko. Eve's lover seen her walk out and gestured for her to come over. The dancer unenthusiastically made her way towards the gentlemen and her face showed it because Roger looked at her with concern. He knew something had to be wrong that Eve didn't want to come to him, she was always ready to help him in any way. After his shoot out with the Houston gang, Eve was the one who went in the rest stop bathroom and cleaned him up. She held the entire family down, working any John she could find until Roger got back on his feet, and he respected the green-eyed beauty for it. For her not to want to be around him felt off,

"What's the matter baby? Dem duck ass niggas broke in there? Daddy gotcha, go head and go home."

The relief on Eve's face was evident and she went straight to her car. She had nothing but information for Roger when he got home about Papa Sha, Jazzy and Dracko, who all looked like they were in there plotting. Eve could have just let the events play out and watched from a distance as everything fell apart, but her spirit wouldn't let her. She was truly loyal to the family because she could have been homeless on the streets still if it wasn't for Olivia pulling her in. Eve was born Evelyn Tisdale, as the result of an incestual rape between her mother and a close cousin back home in Oklahoma. When she found out who her actual biological father was Eve couldn't look her family in the eyes because they all knew of the incident. After she reached her womanhood, eyes from perverted first cousins started to feel like wolves on the hunt after smelling blood. She ran away to Texas when she turned 15 to avoid the same fate of her mother but ended up having sex with old pedophilic men just to survive. Olivia found her leaving the county jail one morning after a night in lockup, cleaned her up, gave her a roof over her head and some money in her pocket. She showed her the ropes, gave her the game, taught her how to make money and not just scraps for ramen noodles. From that day forth Eve was loyal to anything that involved the Sweed family and tonight seeing Roger with Dracko bothered her to no end, she had to tell him everything.

Roger crossed the state lines and knew something wasn't right after his talk with Eve the other night, but he went anyways. The money he would make off of this run would put him over the top but the route he had to go put him in direct line of the gang he had issues with. Papa Sha got word to a few HPD officers that an illegal package was going through their city, with the guy that wreaked havoc on their streets a year ago. Jazzy in return got in touch with some gang members in the Sweed's old neighborhood, telling them that Roger was on his way back and slipped in the address he was heading to. The stage was set for Roger's downfall, and he went into the lion's den with sights on stardom but was about to be faced with nothing but darkness in the form of betrayal. Right when he entered the city the sky opened up to a serious downpour and it was like sheets of water falling from the clouds. Eve called him nervous for her man,

"You reach Houston yet baby? I know you said not to worry but I couldn't get you off my mind and Darlene kept asking about you before she went to bed."

"Girl if you don't stop it with the stressing. I'm good, ya heard me. Just touched down in the city, bout to hit these fools up and I'm a head my ass back cause I can't stand being here foreal."

"Ok, I need you to be safe. We need you to be safe."

"C'mon nah, you forgot who you talkin to?"

Eve didn't want to get off the phone with him until he got to his destination, but Roger ended the call because he needed to find the address he was heading to. The poor honorable family member was a nervous wreck as she waited by the phone for Roger's call, but the Judas of the family walked by with her arrogance on high. Jazzy made it known to Eve that she hopes Roger doesn't return from his trip and Eve felt she knew something was going to happen, she just didn't know what. The only thing was Jazzy made one fatal mistake and that was leaving her phone hanging around for Eve to see it alone with all the messages. She looked through numerous messages from Papa Sha, stating that Roger was worthless to him and promises of her being his number one girl. Plans for keeping Olivia strung out on pills were all through the text and suggestions about the kids were disturbing. The killer was the text from an unknown number with a Houston area code stating that they were waiting on Roger at the house. Eve immediately called Roger but only got his message service. Panicking that the worse is about to take place, she went straight to look for Jazzy for answers. She walked in Jazzy's room with rage all over her, ready for war but couldn't find her anywhere in the house. Eve went in Olivia's room to her zoned out on the pills Jazzy been feeding her, she went in Darlene's room to the precious angel still sleep and then she rushed in little Ronald's room. The sight of a topless Jazzy, erotically breastfeeding the 8-year-old boy while she fondled around in his pajama pants sent Eve into a rampage,

"You BITCH!"

She snatched Jazzy by the back of her head before she could react, dragging her down the hallway kicking. Eve pushed her out the front door and Jazzy fell backwards on the front porch, still trying to get away from her. The enraged female pounced on top of her and commenced to beat Jazzy's face in until she got tired of punching her. After destroying the half-naked traitor's face and chasing her up the street, Eve rushed back inside because she remembered she needed to get in touch with Roger. She called him again but there was no answer,

"Roger baby, please pick up, please."

Eve calmly walked back in the house to Ronald standing in the hallway, terrified of the woman he seen moments ago. Eve was always sweet, calm and gentle to Ronald but the woman he seen drag Jazzy out of his room was nothing like that. The young boy apologized repeatedly, in fear that he was about to receive the same treatment his molester got but Eve just sat down with fear on her face. She pulled Ronald close to her, as she wrapped her arms around him and explained that what Jazzy was doing to him was wrong. With fear still stabbing at her heart of what may be happening to Roger in Houston, all Eve could concern herself with is the wellbeing of the rest of the family.

The rain showers came down with no letting up in sight as Roger parked in the driveway of the house he was looking for. He waited for someone to come out as he texted the number he was given but there was no movement. Roger kept sending Eve's repeated calls straight to voicemail as he waited on his connects to answer his text. His patience was running thin, and Roger got out of his car to walk up to the front door, but a sudden lightning strike revealed some shadowy figures hoovering on the side of the house. When Roger turned around to retreat back to his car he could see between the storm a large van that resembled a police vehicle less than a block away from him. He knew he was set up and shooting his way out of it was not an option as he tucked away his chrome cannon in his waistband. As soon as he reached for the handle of the car door, he could hear a man shouting at him, but Roger could tell from the tone it wasn't a cop,

"Don't move bitch."

When he turned around Roger was face to face with the two teens he spared in the house that night last year and their guns were drawn out for battle this time. The barrels of their guns shivered in Roger's face as their tight grip to the handles cringed. Two more guys rushed over and went straight to Roger's car, snatching the medium sized duffle bag from the back seat. It was all a set up and Roger was stuck in the middle but then he thought about the van up the street. He had a feeling his robbers were going to shoot him anyways, but he blurted out,

"Say round, we all need to get outta here. Dem people right up the street."

"Bitch, shut da fuck up."

"Nah fareal, 12 is up da street my nigga."

With a swift swing of the gun, Roger was struck in the mouth to shut him up but then it was too late because the van began speeding towards them. The stormy night air was filled with red, white and blue lights as black tactical suited officers rushed out of the van with their assault rifles pointed at everyone's head. Roger fell to the ground as he was kicked in the back by an overzealous officer, but the two teens found their destiny as they began firing at the lawmen while running back to the house. One was struck right between the eyes while he ducked behind a garbage can shooting at the cops and the other teen was shot in the spine as he ran around to the side of the house. Roger watched as the two teens laid there motionless, one alive but assumed very paralyzed and the other very dead as his skull emptied out on the concrete. The transporter was handcuffed alone with the other guys that were holding the duffle bag and they all were carted off the property in police units. Roger's plan for one last run fell apart in the matter of minutes as he watched from the back of a police squad car.

YEAR 2008

Ronald had officially become the man of the house after his father was given a double life sentence for distribution and first-degree murder of a cold case in Houston. Things hadn't been the same since Roger been in prison and it didn't look like it was going to pick up any. The 9-year-old had to grow up fast because his mother wasn't holding up her end of the agreement of being the guardian of the children in the house. Eve was there to be the adult in the house, but it wasn't the same as the mother figure Ronald relied on. The growing young boy felt comfortable with Eve and voiced himself with her,

"I know she still hurting bout Brock, but she got two other kids to look after and mama slacking for real. She mo concerned bout them pills than what Darlene doing, she don't care no-mo."

"Ronald don't say that, ya mama going through it right now and she just need yo support. She gone come round."

"When? When Darlene in high school?"

"Ronald. Alright nah. Give ya mama a break."

The honorable family member had confidence that Olivia would turn it all around, but it was looking real bleak for the mother of the family. Olivia lost a lot of clientele because of her growing drug problem and rumors from her now rival Jazzy didn't help at all. Eve tried to support the family as much as she could, but it wasn't enough to keep them afloat and the bank wanted the house back after several missed payments. Ronald and his family went from a four-bedroom duplex with one side as rental property to a three-bedroom shotgun house on Section 8 housing. The silver lining for the 9-year-old was that the new house they were moving to was close to the family's old house before the hurricane. Ronald enjoyed bringing his little sister to the playgrounds they use to go to when they were younger and seeing some familiar faces. Similarity was everything for him at this point because everything he was use to was gone, including the compassionate mother he used to have. Olivia's strong attraction to prescription opiates started changing her, the trend Jazzy started in order for her to cope with the death of Brock had become an everyday act. Papa Sha made sure that one of his pushers stayed nearby to keep Ronald's mother supplied with at least a minimum amount because it brought him pleasure watching her fall apart. The image of Olivia as Roger's number one freak in his stable had completely faded away and now Papa Sha was the man with Jazzy as his number one. Dracko tried to pull Eve in with them because he found her green eyes so sexy and she was already popular in the stripper scene. The only thing was Jazzy didn't want to encounter Eve ever again and black balled her with the Haitians. She still remembered the ass whipping she received from Eve, the night she was caught molesting Ronald and it was something she didn't want to face again. Ronald on the other hand was ruined when it came to girls because none of the young girls at school could compare to the woman that took his innocence. He had become the more advanced kid in school when it came to sexual content, but it also created a hunter. Ronald's suave mannerism would convince the naïve girls to follow him behind the bleachers for dry humping and soft kisses, while he caresses them. He didn't realize that he had turned into the person that took advantage of him because the temporary moments brought him some sense of enjoyment. The quiet kid began to wither away and the one that emerged was no longer looked at as prey. Ronald would usually keep to himself because he still had trust issues with anyone new, but he made sure that everyone knew who his baby sister was. The first guy that picked on Darlene felt his wrath and it was clear that Darlene Sweed was off limits.

Without that older male to guide him, Ronald was left to his own devices and most of the time it wasn't always the right choice. He had a mother figure in Eve until his real mother ran her off with allegations that Eve was trying to sleep with him. Eve couldn't believe what was going on,

"Liv are you serious? I treat that boy like he's my own. Everything I do is mainly for you and dem. The one that was touchin' him, you was all in her damn face but because I show him the attention you suppose to I'm trying to feel on him. I bet if I show up with some oxy, I would be yo best damn friend"

"Bitch get out and leave my damn key. Yo ass ain't gone be shit without me."

"Really Liv?"

"Yes!"

The accusations was the last straw for Eve and she cut her ties with Olivia but still kept a watchful eye on the kids from afar. The secondhand mother tried her best to keep Ronald on the right track, but it was hard to accomplish when she wasn't in the house with him anymore. She had been gone from the Sweed home for more than two months and things in the home went downhill. Food was running scarce and the kids were being neglected. The lack of guidance was evident when Eve caught Ronald running out of the corner store one day with the store clerk in hot pursuit of him. Little Ronald darted through the neighborhood leaving the store clerk gasping air, but Eve knew where he was headed as she drove her car two houses down from his front porch. She waited as she watched him walk up the sidewalk,

"Boy what you call yaself doing? You was never one to bring heat to the house."

"Mama, I'm not doing it for fun. Me and Dee gotta eat."

"Y'all don't have food in the house?"

"No. I only snatched a few packs of Ramen and deez cold drinks. Dats it."

The sight of the boy she so considered her own son, resulting to shoplifting to eat, hurt her to her soul. Eve wanted nothing but to take Ronald and Darlene with her, but she knew it would turn into a true fight with Olivia. She reached into her purse, pulled out a rubber band wad of ones and placed it in Ronald's hand, begging him to call her when that money runs low. Eve knew she would have to come check on the Sweed kids periodically because Ronald wasn't one to ask for a handout. The little man of the house made his way up the steps to his front porch and waved Eve off as she drove down the street with eyes full of tears. Ronald went inside to his mother zoned out on the couch as usual, Darlene playing in her room and he went straight to the kitchen to prepare them something to eat. When the smell of the food hit the air, Darlene came out her room,

"I'm tired of eating noodles every night."

"Shid, you can eat this or go hungry cause this all I could get to."

"Maybe tomorrow you can get some Spaghetti O's."

"Yeah, maybe."

He felt the money in his pocket and promised her he will have something different for her the following day. The kids sat in the kitchen eating their food when Olivia woke from her catatonic pill filled state to the aroma of the food in the kitchen. She asked Ronald why he didn't get her anything from the store and the agitate youngster simply replied,

"With what mama? You ain't give me money to get this."

"Boy! Who da fuck you talkin to?!"

The aggressive reply was followed by a slap to the face from Olivia as she stumbled out the kitchen to her bedroom. Darlene had had enough of her mother, even at the tender age of 7, she knew this wasn't what their life was supposed to be. She knew Ronald's feelings were hurt, even though he didn't show one sign of pain, she pulled him to her room and they finished their dinner in there. Even as a toddler, Darlene knew that Ronald was the one that would look out for her no matter what and at these times they needed to stay together. Thoughts of just running away from home ran through both of their minds but they knew that wasn't a feasible option. Ronald was a calculator and knew if two kids under the age of 12 were to disappear from their home it would turn into a massive search. He knew he would have to stick it out a little bit longer to get to where he wanted and that was away from his mother, with Darlene right behind him.

Even in prison Roger tried to keep in touch with his family as much as possible and Olivia attempted to make it always sound as if everything was fine when he called. She figured he had enough on his plate in jail and worrying about something he can't control was one less thing for him. Stories of school truancy showing up at their front door about Ronald was covered with the latest episode of Darlene bringing home all "A's" on her report card. The continuous ring of her phone with bill collectors was masked as potential clients for her pretty much non-existent escort service. It would be the only time Olivia would sober up just to put on a front for Roger so that he wouldn't think something was wrong at home. Ronald found it embarrassing to see her go out the way to make things seem fine and Darlene would always find an excuse to get off the phone because she knew she couldn't lie to her father,

"Daddy, I gotta go finish this science project before I go to bed. I promise I'm a send you a copy of my report card when it come in. I love you daddy."

"I love you more babygirl."

For Darlene, knowing she would never see her father again was enough turmoil on her and lying to him constantly was too much to bear. Olivia knew not to put Ronald on the phone unless Roger asked for him because the little man wasn't going to put on a show like his mother or his sister. Roger always tried to help with the family finances by getting Olivia connected with some of his associates on the outside, but it would always fall apart because they didn't trust Olivia. After Roger was taken out of the equation, Olivia was left to run her business all by herself. She was good at seducing men, but Roger was good at making sure they pay. With her muscle no longer there, being stiffed on money or customers coming up short had become a regular occurrence. Olivia's escort service resulted down to cheesy motel meetings for traveling truck driver quickies and stragglers looking for some head in the middle of the night. Her growing addiction to prescription pills wasn't helping her situation any either. Guys started taking her for a dope fiend when she accepted a bottle of oxycontin for a night of fun from a few Haitian dope boys. Jazzy found it amusing that the once madame fell from grace so quickly as she laughed,

"Bitch talked all that shit, like she was a boss. Now she suckin' dick just to pay section 8 rent."

"Don't get a big head, che. If we cut you off, you one trick from being broke, nah", replied Dracko as he rolled his blunt.

"I am essential to Sha. He needs me and you know it. If it wasn't for me, Olivia and dat bitch ass Roger would still have control of all dem high paying tricks out there."

"Need you? Che, he needs you like he needs a pet monkey. Something to play with for now but sooner or later will end up in a zoo."

Papa Sha's little princess felt disrespected by the lieutenant and went to voice it to her supposed lover. When she went to him with her complaint, Jazzy found out that she was as valuable to Papa Sha as the pitbull puppies he raised. Papa Sha had zero tolerance for anyone that thought they carried any sort of value to him except for making him money. Jazzy was in her feelings about being pushed to the side, but she also knew she had no other choice but to shut up about it. The Haitian drug lord had finally become the head nigga in charge when it came to the sex trade in New Orleans. No street stroller like Jazzy was going to destroy that for him. As much as he couldn't stand him, he envied Roger because he had it all together in Papa Sha's eyes. The only thing keeping Roger in the picture is the fact that he is still alive and Papa Sha was working on that. Even though Roger was in jail for the rest of his life, he still had loyal followers that looked up to him. Corner boys that wanted to enter the lifestyle looked at how Roger came up in the ranks. Street hustlers that tried to make a name for themselves modeled their every action behind how Roger handled himself. Papa Sha couldn't stand the fact that no one looked up to him in that manner but the gang members that were under him. He felt if there was no more Roger to talk about that everyone would look to him for guidance and not the jailbird, he so despised.

Papa Sha used his charm on Jazzy like he always does and had her contact the Houston gang members that was locked up with Roger in Texas. She promised sexy nights, erotic photos and even help with a lawyer to get out of prison early, if they did her a favor. The prison gangsters were all game to gain some stripes as hitters and agreed to do Jazzy that favor, but she had to agree to visit them. The call girl didn't want to have to travel back to Texas but was coasted by Papa Sha to complete the task he had set out for her. The trip back to Houston was quick because Papa Sha wanted the hit done fast and Jazzy set up the visits for that weekend with both of the prisoners. She didn't want to go back to Houston because she didn't want to run into any old ghost of her past. Jazzy's real name was Jasmine Green and she had been a woman of the streets since she was 16 years old. Jasmine was one of those problem teens that had everything handed to them but still wasn't satisfied. She was raised by a single mother who tried to keep Jasmine out of the system because she knew how it ran, but Jazzy did everything possible to get in that same system. School fights turned into brawls at the mall, which lead to gang affiliations in the streets and then more dangerous crimes were added to her list. The wholesome lifestyle her mother wanted for her had been replaced with drug transactions, prostitution and even robbery set-ups on men that wanted to date her. Jasmine was out of control before she was able to drink alcohol legally and most law enforcement officers were lenient on her because of her mother. One of Papa Sha's men dropped her off in front of the county jail, the place that employed her mother for the past 30 years and the one place Jazzy didn't want to visit. As soon as she stepped on the sidewalk, an uncomfortable ease came over her as she heard,

"I know that's not Jasmine Green. Girl where you been hiding?"

"Excuse me."

Jazzy turned around to an older gentleman in a sheriff's uniform, smiling at her and she couldn't recognize him, but he knew her. She glanced over her shoulder looking to see if anyone else was out that knew her, but most people were just buzzing by trying to get to their destination. The older guy just rambled on about how much she had grown since the last time he seen her but most of his words were mumble mumble because Jazzy wasn't paying attention to him. She tried to make up an excuse that she had to go but then the mumbling cleared up when she heard the gentleman state that her mother was in the visitation center. Jazzy froze in place thinking she would have to see the woman she had been avoiding for the past 10 years and how awkward it would be.

While Jazzy was in Houston taking care of his dirty work, Papa Sha took the opportunity to visit Olivia and taunt her with his prominence in the city. The female he desired to be his was just a shell of the woman he lusted after when she was with Roger. Papa Sha had his driver pull up in a brand new all-white BMW SUV, parked right in front of Olivia's house off St. Bernard Avenue in the 7th ward and Ronald stood on the porch eyeing the vehicle. Papa Sha smiled as he rolled down the limo tinted back window,

"Di ti gason, kote yo manman"

"What?"

"I said, where is yo mama, boy."

"For what?"

"Haha, I just wanna talk to here."

Ronald looked over the flashy foreign speaking guy in front of him and told him that his mother was inside but stood his ground not letting Papa Sha step onto the porch. The Haitian gang leader laughed as he admired the little boy's manly mannerism as he protected his house. He complimented the young boy for his protective stance, stating he showed more heart than a lot of guys he knew and then stated he wanted Ronald to work for him when he gets older. Papa Sha informed the kid in front of him that he was a friend of his parents and was just coming over to check on Olivia. Because he never seen Papa Sha before, Ronald was a little indecisive about allowing the man in front of him any closer but then Olivia came outside, moving Ronald to the side. He walked off down the street after giving Papa Sha's driver a dirty look as he passed by and could hear the gangster state that he looks like Roger's twin. Ronald couldn't understand why the island thug was at his home but the smile his mother held while he was there said a lot about his presence. The former Princess of Erotica in the city was adorned in tattered clothes, eyes blood shot red and carried an odor as if she hadn't showered in a few days. Papa Sha could see Olivia was struggling, money wasn't flowing in like it use to before Roger's arrest and he offered to help her get back on her feet. He wanted Olivia to start delivering packages for him through the city,

"You can make a lot of money, che. Me know that boy not comin' home no time soon."

Papa Sha knew if she would take the offer, she would be in debt to him but also knew the dope fiend would eventually be addicted to his product and work for him for free. Olivia knew she had a weakness for Papa Sha's narcotics and turned down the offer,

"Sha, I know I would end up coming up short if I was to deliver your pills. I ain't doing that to myself."

"Nah che, I can't trust you with my pills. I'm talking bout me guns, che. My guns need a driver."

"Just dropping off a few guns, that's all?"

"Yes. Just a few drops, here and there."

The deal was done with a handshake and the thug walked back to his vehicle with a smile on his face. He told her to meet him at their warehouse later that night to pick up her first shipment as he drove off. Little Ronald was coming up the sidewalk, after leaving from the corner store with a bag of chips and a cold drink. Papa Sha had his driver stop, rolled down his window and reached out a wad of ten-dollar bills to the little lad standing on the sidewalk. At first Ronald didn't want to take the money but then thought about his little sister and tucked the money in his pocket. The evil grin on Papa Sha's face was the last thing Ronald seen as the tinted window went back up.

Jazzy waited in the visiting lobby for her name to be called when she heard a woman, with a familiar voice, call out her name. The eerie feeling that she was about to see her mother came to fruition when she turned around and Jazzy's mother stood there with concern on her face. The flare of designer clothing, gold jewelry and top shelf designer handbag was wrapped around an unconcerned demeanor. She stood there silent, where anyone else would have been excited to see a person they haven't seen in over a decade. Jazzy's mother shook her head in disappointment as she turned to walk away,

"I was just making sure it was you and that you're still alive."

"Yeah, I'm still alive and doing damn good, as you can see. Without none of yo help either. I see you still strugglin' as always."

"Damn shame."

"Shame? What's a shame is you still at this tired ass job working for pennies and I'm walking around with yo salary hanging off my shoulder!"

A deputy walked up because Jazzy was getting loud in the lobby, drawing attention to herself and the officer asked her to quiet down or leave. Knowing she no longer had the security blanket that was her mother anymore, Jazzy sat down as she waited for her visit. Whispers at the information desk drew eyes to glance over at her as the gossiping continued. The confident New Orleans escort knew they were talking about her, but she could care less about their opinions. Right when she was about to tell the desk clerk how she really felt, a deputy called out Jasmine Green and she walked pass them with a smirk on her face. The deputy walked Jazzy down a long hallway, to two large puke green double doors,

"Take you a seat in there and your visitor will be with you shortly."

The seats were stainless-steel, and they were connected to a large stainless-steel table that was bolted to the floor. The floors were concrete with peeling puke green paint on it, the walls also were concrete cinderblocks, and the room echoed the deputy's footstep every time his combat boots would contact the floor. Jazzy nervously looked around the room at other people visiting their incarcerated loved ones. She was so ready to leave but she knew she needed to make sure that her two accomplices handled their end of the deal. Jazzy focused her attention on the secured door the inmates were entering through, when one of the deputies gestured for her to come over to him. Assuming something went wrong with the paperwork, Jazzy got up agitated and asked the deputy what was wrong. The jailer informed Jazzy that her visitation was cancelled with both of the guys she was coming to see. Thinking she did something wrong,

"I filled out all the paperwork y'all sent to me and even did a phone interview with some lady. What's wrong now? I just wanna see my people."

"Ma'am it's nothing you did. The two gentlemen you're trying to visit with are unable to have visitation at this time because of a situation that took place last night."

"A situation? What situation, are they okay?"

"I can't get into that with you because it's an ongoing investigation right now."

Jazzy was confused as to what happened and wondered if her two co-conspirators jumped the gun on what she wanted them to do but the deputy wasn't giving any clues. The visitor left the center with all kinds of questions running through her mind until she seen her mother standing out front patrolling the entrance of the visitation center. She reluctantly went to her mother trying to get any information she could on the two gang members. Jazzy's mother was just as uneager to help as her daughter was to talk to her but she went looking for info anyways. One of the jailers that was really cool with Jazzy's mother looked up reports on both of the guys she came asking about and the information she got was wild. In a "gen-pop" area of the prison the two gang members had an altercation with Roger Sweed. One of the gang members was stabbed in the throat by Roger with a sharpened long metal screw, where he died from his injuries. Roger was stabbed repeatedly in the back and stomach with a sharp wooden pencil, in which he bled out on the floor before he could get to the infirmary. The only guy left was placed in solitary confinement until his arraignment on the case. Jazzy didn't even thank her mother for the information and immediately headed back to New Orleans to give Papa Sha the info in person.

When word of Roger meeting the angel of death in prison hit the streets, every debt collector came knocking at Olivia's door claiming that he owed them outrageous amounts of money. Guys knew Roger had stashes of money hid for rainy days and they were raining on Olivia like a monsoon. The respect for him as a hustler left the day he died, and vultures were hovering over her waiting to take whatever scraps were left. Most of the ones that were coming at Roger's widow was already loyal to Papa Sha and were just making running guns for him look very promising. Olivia made two runs for him to Texas and Florida but slacked off after that because she couldn't keep an eye on a very active Ronald anymore. The 10-year-old was getting out of hand because his adult guidance wasn't there anymore to steer him on the right track. It wasn't Ronald rebelling against the world but the young boy trying to take care and support his little sister because no one else was there to. He stayed on Darlene to focus on school just like his dad did with all of them because Ronald needed at least one of them to succeed. The youngster had gotten to the point where he no longer cared about school and only went to school in order to have an alibi for his criminal activities. At the young age of 10, he found himself calculating perfect times to get away with pawn shop runs to sell a backpack full of things he stole from cars the morning before. Once Ronald gained the reputation for being the young booster in the neighborhood, he got the attention of some questionable guys that wanted him to get them some more pricier items. It was easy for a young boy to slip by adults unbothered because of the buzz of the city bringing home its first Championship title in football. No one really looked at a 10-year-old as a crook and Ronald had became too good to get caught by an amateur. He had managed to create a clientele for almost anything he could get his hands on and the pressure to get bigger things started to come into play. Some chop shop guys started asking the juvenile to get them certain cars for their business and that called for Ronald to get himself a team together. He liked to work alone because that eliminated anyone snitching or running their mouth to the wrong person, but Ronald knew he needed back-up for these jobs. It was crazy for older guys to see this youngster handling himself like a grown man when around other adults, but they didn't know Ronald had to grow up fast. His mother was still a struggling addict and most of her money went to rent, or her opiate addiction, food or clothes fell to the side. Ronald's main priority was making sure his little sister never went to bed hungry, the clothes she wore to school was clean or up to date and she wanted for nothing. The pressure was rough on him, but he managed the best he could with what he had. Street dudes that knew Roger always reminded him that he was his father reincarnated and Ronald wore that like a badge of honor.

"I know that's not Ronald and little Darlene Sweed over there. Get y'all behinds ova here and give me a hug", was the words blurted out by a lady standing in line at the neighborhood deli store.

Ronald had walked to Triangle Deli corner store with Darlene because she asked for a fish plate for dinner. When they both turned around, there stood Delores Daniels with her twin girls Alonna and Shalay. The smile on Mrs. Daniels' face was an immediate sunshine to Ronald's heart and he couldn't help but to run to her as he hugged her as tight as he could. Delores simply melted in his arms because she could feel all the love, he had for her. She didn't realize how much she needed his hug as much as he needed hers. Darlene followed with her excitement for the lady that was the beacon of light for her when she was a toddler. The twins smiled as they watched their mother

reunite with their old neighborhood friends and greeted
Ronald with a synchronized hello. He couldn't help but to
laugh hearing them speak at the same time, but he also
noticed the twins grew up to be as beautiful as their mother.
Darlene looked around for the boys because Cedric Daniels
was the same age as her and she hadn't seen the baby boy
Kareem since he was an infant,

"Where's Ced and Kareem at? They with Officer Daniels?"

"No..."

Once the question was asked the reunion instantly became
very somber as the twins' eyes fell to the floor and Delores
informed the Sweed kids that Officer Daniels was killed.
The mother of the Daniels kids' eyes welled up with tears
as she told Ronald and his sister that her husband was
killed while evacuating the hotel they were staying at.
During the chaos of Hurricane Katrina battering the city of
New Orleans, the flood waters began to take over the hotel
the Sheriff Department held all the family members of its
employees. The department decided to move everyone to
higher ground on buses that was ready to pull out and
Cedric Sr was standing guard making sure the families got
on the bus safely. A small crowd of people attempted to
take over one of the buses, forcing the sheriffs to have to

fight them off and Cedric Sr got into a struggle with a large guy. The two fell to the ground in the fight, Cedric Sr's shotgun went off, striking him in the chest and he bled out in front of his wife as she rushed her children onto the bus. The information of the "Superhero" passing away brought back all the bad memories of his own father dying in prison. Ronald shared the news with the Daniels that they were fatherless also. Delores' face told it all as she heard that Roger was killed, and the sorrow continued when Darlene told them that their brother Brock was murdered in a drive-by shooting. The mother figure fell to her knees as she wrapped her arms around the Sweed kids,

"Baby I'm so sorry. Y'all know I am always here for y'all."

"Thank you."

"I'm serious now. If you need anything, please call me."

Noticing that their mother was nowhere around Delores asked about Olivia and Ronald's face of frustration showed through that she wasn't a factor at the moment. The twins' mother wanted to investigate more but didn't want to pry into the kids' problem, if there was any. But the problem was bigger than Delores could imagine when she seen Ronald pull a mass of assorted bills from his pocket and pay for their food at the deli. The kids were making their way out the door and Delores took it upon herself to hand them her cell number so that they could keep in touch with her, Darlene smiled as she walked out. Delores worried about the kids she watched grow up with her own children and wondered what they had been through since the last time she seen them as she watched them cross the street.

The last day of school had passed and summer was here, Ronald was walking home from the bus stop when he seen Darlene standing outside talking to a boy that was obviously older than her. Protection mode kicked in as he stepped to the boy aggressively,

"Say round, who is you?"

"Calm down lil nigga, I was just speaking."

"Man, move around somewhere."

"Or what, lil nigga?"

The older kid didn't know who Ronald was, so the respect level wasn't there when it came to the little pitbull standing in front of him. Darlene tried to tell her big brother that the older boy was just asking her a few questions, but Ronald didn't like how the older kid was looking at his sister. Right when Darlene's big brother was about to cross the line and assault the kid eye balling his 8-year-old sister, a kid he knew from the neighborhood shouted his name. Mook was the same age as Ronald and was known as the hood's little demon, always getting into something. Ronald was cool with Mook, they held a sense of respect for one another, and the little mischief-maker knew what Ronald was capable of while the older kid in front of him had no clue. Mook had to tell Ronald that the boy was his cousin from the Westbank visiting and that he didn't mean any harm. The feisty pitbull told Mook to take his cousin on the other side of the street and for him to never talk to his sister again. Darlene was embarrassed at the way her brother was acting because one boy showed her some attention. Mook's cousin wasn't trying to listen to a kid younger than him or tell him what to do. He walked up to Ronald, trying to intimidate him with his size but the young bull didn't budge one inch and stared his opponent down. Mook knew his cousin was a little throwed off and attempted to deescalate the situation with cracking jokes. But the two warriors were set for battle. When the older kid realized simple scare tactics wasn't working, he reached in his pocket and pulled out an all-black .38 special, pointing straight at the middle of Ronald's forehead. Mook had gotten frustrated with his cousin at this point,

"Dammit cuz, you on that dumb shit. I gotta live here and you gone be on the other side of the water."

"Nah cuz, this lil nigga think he hard."

"Nigga that was suppose to scare me? Pull the fuckin trigger or get that raggedy shit outta my face, ya heard me."

Darlene's only brother stared over the barrel of the shiny black pistol, straight into the kid's eyes without an ounce of fear in his face. Mook stood in front of his cousin, pleading with him to put the gun away, stating that Ronald was his good friend. The cousin evilly smiled as he listened to Ronald's newfound friend and slowly put the tool back in his pocket. The same unbothered face Ronald had when Mook's cousin stepped to him was the exact face he had when Mook walked his cousin across the street. After seeing her brother stare the guy down all the way from across the way, Darlene knew her brother was on another level and being a kid wasn't in the cards for him. As she went to go inside, Ronald's baby sister gave him some advice,

"Daddy always told us don't be scared of nothing on two feet but that don't mean challenge everybody. Somebody gone challenge you back one of these days."

"Well when dat day happen, I'll be sure to let you know."

It had been a few days since Ronald had his little run in with Mook's cousin in front of his house. The neighborhood friend continuously apologized for his family member's actions every chance he got and Ronald appreciated the consideration. Ronald started to see that Mook was genuine with his words and even stated that he got into an altercation with his cousin over what he had did that day. The two started to really mesh together, Ronald teaching Mook how not to draw attention to himself and Mook teaching Ronald about the city hotspots where he could make some quick cash. They really worked good together and the friendship had become a strong bond between the two. Mook introduced Ronald to one of his running mates one day when they were just hanging out at the house. Desmond Price was a true hot head at heart but if he considered you his friend, a person always had someone watching their back. Desmond lived a few streets over from where Ronald and Mook was, but he roamed the neighborhood constantly because the parental guidance he should have had was non-existent. His father was nowhere to be found and his mother was more concerned with where her next 6 pack of beer was coming from than her only child. Desmond overheard the story about Ronald and Mook's cousin,

"That nigga straight pussy dawg, ya heard me. Mook, I know that's yo cousin and all, but we need to go touch that nigga. He pull a gun on ya once, he feel he can do it anytime."

"Shid, I don't like da nigga that damn much anyway. I'm down for whateva."

Ronald chuckled at his two buddies but knew if they were really going to reach out at Mook's cousin they all needed a plan. The fire boiling in Desmond's gut barely had him paying attention to what Ronald was saying. All he wanted to do was swing the aluminum bat he kept wringing his hands around. The three amigos headed to the Business District on the bus, where Ronald found the perfect car to boost and they made their way across the river. Ronald was a fairly tall 10-year-old, with features of a teenager, so seeing him behind the steering wheel of a car didn't raise any eyebrows. He was on a mission and his two goons were ready for whatever he had planned. To say it was three adolescents in a stolen vehicle, Ronald drove around like he was running errands but being careful all the same. Desmond wanted them to stop at a gas station so that he could grab some snacks, but Ronald turned down the suggestion,

"Nigga, we in a stolo. We pull up to a gas station and ten cameras gone be on us. You trying to get caught?"

"Damn dawg, a nigga just wanted some Chee Weez and a pineapple Big Shot."

"Think next time, shit."

Ronald didn't know it, but he had become calculating just like his dad, thinking five steps ahead and he schooled his partners with the same mentality. They had finally made it to their destination and Ronald parked the car a block away from the house. He told Mook to get his cousin to come outside while he and Desmond hid on the side of the home. When the older kid stepped out on the porch he was confused as to how his younger cousin made it to his home. The city of Algiers known as The Cutoff was 35 miles from where Mook lived and there wasn't a single adult in sight. Mook made up a lie stating he had caught the bus to come see him and hash out any beef they were having. With arrogance in his tone, Mook's cousin told him he was right to apologize first because he was out of line for stepping in front of him,

"You shoulda let me pop that lil bitch."

"Pop this bitch!", shouted Desmond as he rushed out with bat in hand.

One swift swing to the back of the knees and Mook's cousin fell to the ground. Desmond stood over him as he repeatedly swung the bat at his legs and the teen's childhood voice screamed in pain. Ronald walked up and stopped Desmond's attacks as he stared into his victim's eyes,

"Don't come on my side of the river again. Or next time I won't stop this nigga, ya heard me."

"Oh, and you tell my mama or Teedy what happened and we comin' back", stated Mook as they walked off.

The crew had made themselves known that they were not to be messed with, you fight one you fight all three.

They had each other's back no matter what, even if one of them were wrong, which was usually Desmond and Ronald always had to correct him later. They got to a point where Grand Theft Auto was a normal occurrence for them, with Mook or Desmond as lookouts. The city's chop shops knew their faces as the young bulls taking over in the field. Older guys put in request for special cars all the time because they knew the musketeers would complete the task. Ronald and his crew studied the art of boosting a car, but Desmond got impatient with the act of waiting for the right time. He would take it on his own to physically carjack someone at gunpoint but only brandishing a replica or pellet gun. Ronald and Mook threatened to cut Desmond off if he continued to jeopardize the operation they had set up,

"Say round, you gone bring too much attention to us. You outchea flee-flickering and we trying to make some money. Ain't nobody looking for three 11-year-olds jacking cars. You keep that shit up dem people gone be on our ass."

"Aight damn! Y'all all in my shit like rough ass tissue paper. A nigga was just trying to bring the crew some extra. Niggas still like extra don't cha."

"Yeah, but my nigga you going bout it all wrong. Shit can get real real quick and you out here fuckin up."

"My bad. My bad."

They understood Desmond's good intent, but Ronald had too much to lose if he were to get caught or arrested. He had become pretty much the sole provider for his little sister and the household with his criminal activities. Ronald tried to shelter Darlene from the things he was doing but it was evident to her that her brother wasn't working at a fast-food spot or grocery store, bringing home the kind of money he had. He would take out time just to spend with her and even made an effort that they both visit the Daniels' home on occasion but trying to live that double life was tiring for Ronald. His trips to the clean-cut family he adored to be around when he was younger became less and less, until it was only Darlene coming to visit. Ronald had bigger fish to fry, trying to keep up with debts or the bills in the house because his mother couldn't and keeping his crew happy. Money was rolling in, with orders for special vehicles and imported cars. The excitement of stealing a car was a rush for Ronald at first but now it had become a chess match to him, and he was the chess master. The crew's latest request was a 2009 Maybach Mercedes and at the time there was only three of them in the city. Ronald knew it would be near impossible to boost the car without its special key to operate it and getting a key from an owner would involve being physical with them. Desmond was completely fine with getting a little physical with someone standing in front of him making money,

"Ole boy done gave you da list. Bruh, we just need to find one of dem bitches. Run up on a nigga with that tool in his face and he gone give up the key."

"I hate to say Dez right but he telling the truth, that's how it's gone have to be with this one Pitbull. It's no way around it."

"And that nigga talking bout paying us boo coo money for this shit."

Ronald was chilling on his porch with Darlene, talking about what movie she wanted to go see this weekend when Papa Sha pulled up in front of their house. The Haitian gangster was in an old school Jeep that was custom painting the New Orleans' team colors and he stepped out the vehicle bearing gifts for the kids. He placed a replica of the Championship ring the players had in Ronald's hand and gave Darlene a team photo with several player's autographs on it. The hoodlum walked pass the kids as he made his way in the house and Ronald's mind went to wandering on how to steal the tricked-out Jeep in front of him. He knew it was an older model, so just popping the steering column would be a breeze for him. Every car Ronald encountered; he went through the same scenario of how to steal the vehicle to make money but this particular automobile he just wanted to steal it to wipe the smile off of Papa Sha's face. The thought of the man he really couldn't stand fell to the side when Darlene seen Ronald's partners walk up the sidewalk,

"Hey Dez."

"Hey Dee, what's going on lovely?"

"Watch it nigga."

"Damn dawg, I was just speaking."

"What's good withcha? Who this fuckin' whip foe?"

"Bitchass Sha. Muthafucka gave me this stupid ass ring. I don't like that dude foe nothing, never have."

"Mane, Papa Sha in yo house right now my nigga, and you out here?"

"Fuck that nigga. It's something bout that muthafucka I just don't like, I should snatch his fuckin' Jeep."

The boys laughed as they walked off, but Ronald was so serious about stealing the Haitian gang leader's car. He went over to the driver side door and tugged on the handle, but the chirping of the alarm stopped him. Mook nor Desmond knew Ronald meant he wanted to steal the Jeep and the shock on their faces showed it when they heard the warning beep from the vehicle's alarm. Ronald rushed off with his friends as they made their way to Broad Street to catch the bus to New Orleans East. Desmond told them about where they could find one of the Maybach Mercedes, they were looking for at a convenience store owned by an old Vietnamese man. He figured the old man wouldn't be an issue and give up the keys to the car with no problem. The plan sounded like it would work in Ronald's head and Mook came completely prepared with all the accessories in a backpack he had on. The boys got on the Broad bus and siked themselves up on the big payout they were going to get with this heist. Images of some brand-new kicks and new clothes ran through Desmond's mind, while thoughts of leaving mystery money in the mailbox for his parents ran through Mook's mind. All Ronald could think of was supporting his baby sister so that she never had to ask any nigga for anything. The idea that his mama was working with Papa Sha was uneasy on him and he had to make this money to get her from under his thumb. The boys got off the bus one stop before their destination on Haynes Blvd, so they could walk and plan out their route. Haynes Blvd was a long street with neighborhoods on one side and a levee on the other, with Lake Pontchartrain behind it. The crew knew they had to be quick because police could be on top of them in a minute and if they get the car, they needed to be out of the area fast.

They walked along the top of the levee, watching as cars darted by on the street and then they came up on the convenience store Desmond was telling them about. The corner store was prime for jacking because it had a vacant wooded lot next to it and very little traffic in or out. The boys sat on the levee, watching as customers came and went but the vehicle they had came to get was nowhere to be found. Disappointment started to set in for them because it started to look like they came all the way from the 7th ward for a blank trip but then a sparkle caught Mook's eye. A shiny cream-colored Maybach with limo tinted windows drove up the street and parked itself right in front of the store. Ronald released an evil grin,

"There go my bitch."

Mook opened his backpack, pulled out gloves, face mask and three pellet guns that resembled the real thing, the boys were all set. They split up going in three different directions towards the store and Ronald's eyes were focused on the front door of the store. He walked up to the car, while Mook walked over to the vacant woods and Desmond stood at the corner pretending to wait on the bus. The closer Ronald got to the car the more he realized that the engine was still running, and the music was playing loud. He figured this was going to be the easiest carjacking he ever had to do as he reached for the driver side door. When Ronald pulled at the door, surprisingly it was open and he jumped in but the big surprise was that a boy was sitting in the passenger seat. Ronald instantly drew down on the teen with his pistol pointed directly at the young Vietnamese boy's face. The boy was frozen with fear and Ronald shouted for him to get out of the car. Mook and Desmond immediately showed up on the side of the vehicle, opening the doors as they attempted to get in. Right when Desmond sat down in the backseat, he noticed someone rushing out the front door of the corner store,

"Ro, we got company!"

"Don't move or I shoot. I shoot you niggas", shouted the old Vietnamese owner.

Mook was standing by the front passenger side door and all he could see was a gray-haired Vietnamese man pointing a loaded AK47 directly at them. Ronald felt he had leverage over the old man because the boy in the car looked just like him and he just knew the old man wouldn't shoot his own family. He grabbed the teen by his collar and pressed the gun against his temple,

"Let us go old man or I'm a paint the inside of this car with him."

"My son ready to die, but are you?"

"My pops serious, he will light this car up before he see you drive off with it", replied the teen sitting next to Ronald.

"I'm not playing old man!"

"If you serious, you would have pulled trigger already. Get out my car, I let you live."

Desmond pleaded to just run away and go after another car, but Ronald was determined to leave with the Mercedes. Mook was in agreement with his partner and put his replica gun away in his pocket as he backed away from the car. The old man seen that Ronald's back-up was fading away and focused the barrel of his firearm directly at the black boy sitting in the driver seat. The teen tried to reason with Ronald, stating that stealing the car wasn't worth his life and that he could get his dad to give him some money if he just let him go. But the frustrated youth was hell bent on a big payout from the chop shop for the Mercedes and didn't budge as he told the old man to go back inside. The tension was extremely thick between the two staring one another down but then the old man's face of anger changed and he focused the barrel of the AK to the ground. He walked up to the driver side door and calmly spoke to Ronald,

"How far do you think you can get? Serious question. How far? Because if I let you leave, you won't make it."

"Go back inside and watch me old man."

"This car come with tracker in computer. Satellite find you like it find cellphone, quick. You no get far friend."

"He's not lying. My dad bought this car for my mom and that was one of the things that got his attention. You might get up the street, but the police gone be waiting for you."

Ronald was defeated and he knew it, but he wasn't giving in just yet. He told the teen that he wants all the money out of the register and then he would get out of the car. The old man hesitantly went back inside and emptied his cash register into a plastic grocery bag. It felt like the old man was in the store forever, but it was only 30 seconds that had passed. Desmond was ready to sprint off, his nerves had him on edge and Mook held the same thoughts as they waited for the old Chinaman to come back out. He exited the store with two bags in his hands and a proposition for Ronald to consider,

"You smart boy. I like your courage, you scared of nothing. Come work for me, we make lot of money or take money bag and broke tomorrow."

"What if I just take both of yo bags old man?"

"My name is not old man; my name is Chou. You take both bags, I find you and I kill you. I find yo friends and I kill them too. I find yo parents and they die. Take my car, take my money. Not worth it my friend. Take this bag, worth it, we make lot of money and you can buy real gun next time."

"What?"

"You know real gun that go pew pew. Not the pop gun in yo hand."

At that moment, Ronald realized that the old man Mr. Chou was a lot smarter than he looked and that he knew their guns were fake the whole time. He couldn't turn down the proposal as he reached for the bag and Chou told him how much to bring back when he's done. Ronald slowly stepped away from the luxury car, he and his partners walked away with the bag the old man gave them as Chou watched them walk up the street.

The thing none of the boys knew about Mr. Chou was that he was a member of a very dangerous Vietnamese gang from New York known by the tag name BTK. He had a hand in pretty much anything illegal in the city of New Orleans along with having a few police in his pocket. The old Chinaman was far from what a person would perceive him to be because he wanted it that way. He owned three different corner stores and he was respected by the residents in the neighborhood. If a kid or woman came up short on their total, Mr. Chou would always tell them,

"You pay me next time you come."

The thing is the old man would never ask for the money they owed him the next time he would see them. Neighborhood block parties would always get catered food sent to the party from Mr. Chou's corner store kitchens. Everybody was called friend and the residents in the neighborhood all liked the old man. Most people just thought he was the owner of a few convenience stores but the ones that knew the real Mr. Chou was far and few and not speaking a word of his other ventures. There was one instance where one of his stores was robbed by two men. His sister-in-law was raped and then pistol whipped for the cash in the safe. Both men were identified but it was too late by the time the police found them. One guy was found beaten to death in the trunk of an abandon car with a broom stick shoved so far up his ass the handle could be seen in his throat. The other guy was found dead in a vacant house, naked, tied to a chair with his penis cut off and hanging out of his mouth. The police had no clue or idea who did the horrific crimes to the men, but the entire neighborhood knew Mr. Chou's family was off limits. His criminal business was so fruitful that laundering money through shell companies had become second nature for him. Making money by any means had become a sport to Chou and he seen that same desire in Ronald's eyes. Taking a chance on three 11-year-olds was just an experiment to see if he was going to make a profit off them but he knew the little gunman was going to be special. Chou's teenage son, Justin was skeptical of his father's decision to take in three hooligans that just tried to steal his car, but the old man had his reasons. With agitation in his voice Justin questioned his father,

"Pops, those fools just tried to steal your fucking car and you in return offer them work."

"First, you watch you mouth. You know I no like cussing. Son, if you feed the wolves, they no come back to steal more food. I make ally and not enemy. City has enough money for all us to eat."

"Really pop?"

"Yes. Now bring yo ass inside."

Justin tried to understand his father's logic but couldn't get pass Ronald pointing a gun at him, even though it was fake.

The bus ride back home was somewhat quiet as all three boys imagined their lives no longer existing if the old man Mr. Chou would have began shooting instead of talking. They've all been in some sketchy situations before but never someone pointing a loaded gun at their face, except for that one incident with Ronald. Ronald knew one false move in that car and Mr. Chou would have unloaded on him. He literally started to admire the old man for how he kept his calm through the whole situation. Ronald thought the old store owner was nuts offering him a job after he and his boys tried to steal his car, but he wasn't going to turn the opportunity down either. Desmond was still a little shaken up about the botched carjacking but made fun of it to ease his mind,

"That old man was about to pop all our asses. I'm telling ya, a lil pee came out when I seen that choppa."

"Yo scary ass."

"Fuck you nigga. You was scared too."

"Shid, scared shitless."

The boys started laughing as they made their way home and Ronald started looking in the bag Mr. Chou gave him. Inside the bag was more than a hundred individually wrapped dime bags of premium cannabis. Just by opening the bag the aroma of weed hit Ronald's nose and his eyes lit up to the sight of the bright green baggies. The crew all went to Mook's house because Ronald nor Desmond trusted their mothers and knew their product would get smoked by them. As soon as they walked through the front door the hard nose thugs they portray in the streets left and three 11-year-old kids walked in the house. Mook's parents were both two hard working, every Sunday Baptist church going, law abiding citizens that had no clue their son was a little criminal. Mook's mother never called him by his nickname,

"Jason, wash yo hands before dinner. Ya friends staying? I made smothered potatoes and fried pork chops."

"Jason, wash ya hands pumpkin", laughed Desmond.

"Nigga, fuck you. Least my mama cook. What yo mama do? DRINK."

"Why you gotta talk bout my mama?"

Mook told his mother he was coming in a minute as they all shut themselves in his room. The boys quickly counted up all the baggies they had, calculating how much they would make after giving Mr. Chou his cut. Desmond joked that he didn't want to give the old man anything after pulling a gun on him but Mook reminded him of what Mr. Chou said. The eerie thought of an old Vietnamese gangster hunting your whole family down for stiffing him on a few hundred dollars was too much to handle. Desmond instantly retracted his statement as he watched Mook put all of their weed in a large duffle bag and hid it in his closet. Ronald knew some of his dad's old running partners that dabbled in street hustling and told his guys he would get in contact with them tomorrow.

Things started to look promising for Ronald after his first package of cannabis sold out in less than two days. The high-quality product Chou had him selling was too easy to sell because it sold itself after a customer would see it. Bright green bud with specks of rainbow colors was like a sparkling diamond to a "Weed head" and the boys had salesmen attitudes to go along with it. The fact that a 11-year-old kid was selling them weed was hilarious to most people and they very seldomly had issues with anyone trying to rip them off. Chou sold them all real 9mm pistols after their second time coming back to him for a re-up,

"You need real protection. I not always be around to protect you."

"Whacha talkin' bout Mr. Chou?"

"My people see you, my people watch over you boys. Protect my money."

"Mr. Chou, we don't need nobody watching us, we good, ya heard me."

"I hear you all the time. Why you keep asking me that? Ya heard me."

Right then, Ronald and his crew caught on that Mr. Chou was a bigger deal than they thought. The designated leader of the crew wanted in on some bigger more profitable task, but Chou turned down Ronald's request. The store owner loved the kid's ambition but felt he wasn't old enough for the grown man task he was asking for. Ronald respected the old man's decision and patiently waited because he just knew his moment was coming.

YEAR 2011

Business with Chou was going really good, the boys were making more money than they ever had and the experiment the old store owner thought up was working out perfectly. As always, Desmond put together a crazy scheme of his own to make them some more money and Mook was all in. He ran the idea by Ronald,

"Say son, these whitefolks outchea buyin' up these houses in the hood and I know they got money. We creep up in the house when they gone and clean they ass out. I seen one bitch had a Princess rolly on walking this ugly ass white dog one day, she look like money."

"Nigga, how she look like money. Money green. She was green walkin a dog?"

"Dis nigga got jokes. You know what da fuck I mean. You in or out? Me and Mook tryin to get dis money."

"Nigga, you know I'm in."

Ronald thought it through and figured it wouldn't hurt trying out a few houses to see how much they could make off of them. He seen the neighborhood was changing, people that didn't look like him were moving into freshly remodeled homes and the young entrepreneur assumed they had money to lose. Mook had already scoped out two houses in a neighborhood close to the New Orleans Fairgrounds, that recently got new tenants. Desmond was ready to go in for a quick smash and grab, but Ronald told them they needed to wait until they could make sure no one was home. The instigator was getting tired of Ronald always being "Mr. Careful" all the time and felt he was holding the crew back. Mook was comfortable with how things were going so he didn't have any gripes with Ronald being cautious all the time. The crew voted and Desmond was outnumbered two to one, so they had to wait on the perfect time to break in the houses.

Olivia had just got back home from Slidell after making a run for Papa Sha. As she made it inside the smell of a home cooked meal was waiting for her at the front door. Olivia's early training with her daughter in the kitchen was hard at work as the baby of the family was cooking dinner. She seen Darlene standing by the oven with mittens on,

"Wha cha doing in here baby girl? Where's yo big head ass brother?"

"Hey mama, I was baking some chicken for us. Ronald, Mook and Dez took the bus to one of they friends in the East."

"He always running the streets with them raggedy ass boys. He bet not get his self in trouble out there."

"Mama, they just be chillin. They ain't doin nothing out da way."

"Dee, we talking bout Ronald here. You don't always have to cover for him. He's always up to something."

Olivia knew her son was into some illegal shit but the money he leaves for her keeps her quiet. All their bills were kept up to date, the refrigerator stayed with food and Olivia didn't have to make so many delivers for Papa Sha. She was a little scared for her son, but she also knew her little Ronald wasn't little anymore and he had his father's drive in him. Olivia sat at the table watching her daughter move around like she was a professional in the kitchen and just admired how grown she had become. Even though Darlene was just 10 and Ronald was 12, they both portrayed a much more mature attitude than their ages. Olivia knew her kids were pretty much taking care of her and not the other way around. Her addiction was still somewhat a factor in her life but keeping busy with making runs and the occasional

"John" here or there slowed down the pill popping. Olivia loved her kids dearly but the desire to get away from her troubles with a pill or two was a vice she just couldn't shake. She was sitting at the table enjoying a good conversation with her daughter when she got a text from a client that wanted some "quality time". Olivia didn't want to leave but she knew the money was good,

"Baby, I gotta go make anotha run right quick, I'm a be back."

"Ok mama, be careful please."

With Ronald doing his thing and her mother always gone, Darlene had become accustomed to being home by herself. As much as Olivia tried to hide the fact away from her daughter, Darlene knew her mother seen a lot of different men. Just like Papa Sha would, some would be so bold that they would come to the house looking for her. It was one of the main reasons Ronald stayed away from the house as much as he could because he didn't want to see men lusting over his mother. That was an issue Roger made sure never occurred when he had control of the business but since he was no longer there, things ran amuck. Ronald would make sure to always tell Darlene that she never needed a man to give her money because all they would ever want was sex in return. The young female understood how overprotective her brother could be and knew he only had good intentions for her wellbeing, but Darlene had a mind of her own. She knew she never wanted to be like her mother but the attraction to the "bad boy" persona was overwhelming for her. Darlene was just mindful that if she was to ever get a boyfriend, she had to hide him from Ronald like a prized jewel.

The boys made it to Chou's corner store in the East for another re-up but were surprised at all the people that were in front of the store. The small parking lot was completely decorated with banners, streamers and balloons all over. There was four lines of people that lead up to two barbecue grills in front of the store and a DJ playing music for everyone to enjoy. All the times they had been back to Chou's store they had never seen so many people there before. The bright yellow sign over the front entrance read "Reopening Anniversary" but when Desmond tugged on the handle the doors were locked. A young teenage girl seen the boys trying to get inside,

"Mr. Chou locks the doors during his parties. Don't want a lot of in and out, somebody might get sticky fingers."

"Nah, we comin' see Justin."

"Oh, lil cutie. He over there with Mr. Chou at the corner."

The girl pointed over to two police cars that were parked across the street, with four officers standing out talking with Justin and his father. All three of the boys looked like stone statues staring over at Mr. Chou laughing with four uniformed policemen. They slowly walked over to the edge of the street but didn't want to cross as they tried to get Justin's attention. Mook was ready to bolt and Desmond's feet was stuck to the sidewalk in fear, but Ronald was curious as to how composed Mr. Chou was with police around him. Knowing the amount of work they've done for Chou, knowing the risk of being caught by the lawmen and yet Chou carried a carefree smile. Ronald wanted to learn from the old man dearly but first he needed to get what he came for. Justin had finally seen the young crew and walked over to them,

"Man, why you didn't come ova?"

"That's da muthafuckin' police ova there and I got 600 dollars on me."

"And? That's my pops people, they doing a detail for him for the party."

"Dey know yo pops moving weight?"

"Man, y'all crazy. C'mon, we can go in through the side."

Justin shook his head laughing at the comments and questions, as he walked the crew to the side door of the corner store. Even in the midst of his friendly conversation with the four law officers, Chou kept a watchful eye on his son as the four boys walked in the building. He trusted no one, not even people that worked with or for him and Ronald's crew was no different. Chou signaled to one of his neighborhood goons to follow behind Justin just to make sure his son was safe. Mook noticed the guy standing at the door and joked with Justin that Chou always got somebody watching over them. The son of the Vietnamese gangster showed a facial expression of aggravation that his father always had someone watching over him like he was a child. Justin was 16 years old and like most teens his age felt he didn't need any guidance or guardians watching him all the time. It annoyed him so much that his father still treated him like he was a kid but trusted him enough to handle distributions to the numerous street runners Chou had. The guys handle their business transaction with the reup and Justin felt like being defiant towards his father for being so shielding. He offered to take the crew for a joy ride home instead of them catching the bus. Chou taught Justin how to drive when he was just 11 and the teen had his own car at the age of 15 but the watchful father always had someone with his son on rides. While his father was busy being a host to the party he was giving, Justin took the opportunity to sneak away with Ronald and his partners. Ronald had no idea that Chou didn't want his son associating with them on a friendship type basis, that the only contact they would have would be strictly business. The Vietnamese store owner knew the boys were still young and reckless which could bring attention to themselves. Chou didn't want his son to get too attached to the juveniles and they end up getting caught or getting him caught up in their activities. Justin was bringing the boys home when he got a call from his dad,

"I'll be right back. Dropping Ronald off at home."

"What I tell you?! What I say?!"

"Damn, I'm a be right back."

Ronald stayed silent while his ride was talking with his father but could hear Chou's anger over the phone. After Justin ended the call he told the boys that his father was just being overbearing and always wanted to know his every move. The crew kind of understood Justin's agitation and all started to tell their stories of tyrant like parents. Chou's son did the one thing he didn't want him to do and that was build a connection with Ronald's crew. The quick 20-minute ride to drop the boys off turned into an hour and a half as they just enjoyed each other's company. Justin found some friends that finally understood him.

Justin was dropping the boys off at home when he drove pass the New Orleans Fairgrounds and Mook mentioned to Ronald that they had just passed up one of the houses he been looking at. They all surveyed the house as the car went down the street and Justin was a little curious as to what had their attention so badly. Ronald didn't want to share the idea they had with the teen, but Desmond could care less. All their plans spewed from his lips like a running faucet and Justin was all ears. He liked their plan and even offered to be the driver for them after they gathered enough loot from the house. As Chou's unruly teen parked in front of Ronald's home and they went over the meticulous idea the young leader came up with. Ronald was game about the break-ins, but he was more concerned about not getting caught and he stressed to everyone in the car that no one could be home, or they won't do it. Mook had already peeped out that the residents leave early in the morning and don't come back until in the evening,

"10 o'clock would be the perfect time to hit'em. We just gotta sneak in through the back."

"I can wait in my car up the street and when y'all ready, call me. Load up real quick and we out."

"Sounds like a plan Lil Cutie."

"What?"

"Haha, that's what ole girl called you at da party. You know, da one sitting by da DJ. You need to holla at her cause she was fine."

"Say bruh! Focus. I ain't tryin to get caught up."

"Okay. DAD, this nigga."

After Desmond got out all his jokes, Ronald continued with the plan, in their heads it was a fool proof idea and they were all ready as everybody exited Justin's car. Ronald walked up to his porch as he watched the newly added member of his crew drive off along with Mook and

Desmond walking home. He stepped inside to the wonderful smells of a home cooked meal and just knew his mother must have taken time out of her busy schedule to cook dinner. Ronald walked in the kitchen to his baby sister pulling a pan of baked chicken out of the oven,

"You cooked? Oh, this bout to be nasty."

"Nigga you ain't gotta eat."

"Damn, I was just playin."

"Whateva. You hungry?"

"Hell yea."

"Den fix ya plate. I ain't yo maid."

Ronald laughed at her sly remark as he asked if their mother was home. Darlene told him she had to go meet someone and that they didn't need to wait for her to eat. Olivia's only son was frustrated that his mother wouldn't be home to share another meal with them that night. It had become a normal thing that Olivia not be home at night or even spend a day at home with her kids. Darlene started dishing up two plates for both of them and her big brother went to the fridge to get something for them to drink. The Sweed kids sat down at the table, said grace and enjoyed the meal Darlene prepared while the baby of the two told her brother about her day. It was truly a break from the everyday chess game Ronald played out on the streets. At home he didn't have to worry about looking over his shoulder, he didn't have to worry about being robbed or even being chased by police. Home was his safe haven and he relaxed as he enjoyed his little sister's company. After dinner Darlene was washing the dishes while Ronald helped put up the food, but she struck a nerve when she asked about Desmond. Ronald didn't like the fact that his sister was blushing about the "daredevil" Desmond and expressed it,

"What da hell you cheezin' foe? You can stop thinkin' bout da nigga, that's what you can do."

"Dang, I was just askin' bout ya friends. He is yo friend, right? Ro you not my daddy so stop trying to be."

"Whatever. Just keep the nigga name out ya mouth."

The pleasant evening ended with Darlene storming off, leaving her brother in the kitchen to finish cleaning up. Ronald knew he hurt her feelings, but he didn't want his little sister getting close to someone as dangerous as Desmond. The life his mother had and still has was a life he didn't want for his sister.

Olivia arrived at a house in the middle of the French Quarters off of Bourbon Street to meet her date for the night. She walked up to an old fashion French style home that was adorned with hunter green shutter doors, antique gas fed porch lamps and pale white painted brick walls. The smiling gentleman waiting for her at the door reached out for her hand as he helped her up the three steps that led into the home. Except for the original wooden floors, inside was far from old fashion with modern furniture and elaborate changing color LED lighting. Just like most of Olivia's high paying clients Bradley was a well-off businessman that enjoyed sexual pleasures from time to time to relieve an urge. He paid three times as much as a normal trick because the thing about Bradley was, he was into dominance and submission. Olivia knew Bradley liked to tie his women up and have his way with them until he climaxes from the events. On the outside he was a complete gentleman, sweet as candy but behind closed doors Bradley was devilish and enjoyed tantalizing tortures. He asked her if she wanted something to drink and Olivia smiled,

"I'll have whatever you having baby."

"I don't know if you ready for this here. I'm drinking nothing but Absinthe shots, I don't know if you ready to party with the Green Fairy."

"Sounds like we partying tonight."

Bradley poured her some of the neon green alcohol in a cold shot glass and Olivia slammed the drink back, the 110 proof burned its way down her throat. The threshold was crossed and Olivia seen no sense in stopping as she asked for another shot while unbuttoning her top for Bradley. She sipped the next shot he gave her because she was still recovering from the first one as Bradley peeled her blouse off of her. Olivia's soft skin mesmerized him as he slowly caressed her breast in his hands, her see through lace bra kept him from touching her erect nipples. He reached behind her to unhook the clasp holding the brassiere together and the weight of Olivia's breast dropped as they jiggled for him. She could tell he was fully aroused as the bulge he had, tightened the front of his pants. Olivia stroked the enlarged muscle through the clothing while Bradley took his time to undo the buttons on the side of the skirt she was wearing. The skirt fell to the floor revealing lace panties that matched the bra top she had on and Bradley rubbed her plump pussy print with two of his fingers. The erotic level between the two literally raised the temp in the room or maybe it was the alcohol sweating through their pores. Bradley had gained his fill of the soft touches he was receiving from his erotic muse as he reached up and wrapped his hand around Olivia's soft neck. He squeezed his large palm until her caramel skin tone reddened around his fingers and Bradley stuck out his tongue to lick her lips,

"You ready?"

"Yes daddy."

Still with his fingers tightly clamped around her neck, he walked her to a back room, the heels of her "Red Bottoms" clicking on the wooden floors. In the room stood a large handcrafted wooden board with restraints affixed to it, the board reached from the floor to the ceiling, stained and lacquered the same color as the floors. He backed Olivia into the board, raised her hands up as he strapped the restraints around her wrist and kissed her neck. The soft touches from his fingertips was just a prelude to what was to come next as Bradley raked his nails against her skin. His movements were slow but precise like a tiger on a hunt as he nuzzled against her breast, licking her nipples and hardening them with every touch. The two shots of

Absinthe Olivia took earlier began to take effect as her body started to relax in the leather restraints holding her wrist and her anticipation for what is to come next no longer heightened her heartrate. Artificial lights no longer lit the room as tall white wax candles burned and Bradley brought one of the candles to Olivia. Believing she's about to feel the sting from the melted wax resting in the candle, Olivia braced herself, but her suitor only placed the candle at her feet. He then went to a small table covered in a cloth, he removed the fabric from the table and picked up several items off it. Olivia couldn't see what he had in his hand until he was right in front of her as he released a handsome smile and showed her the handful of clothespins. He pinched both of her nipples so that he could close the pins on them and then he began to pinch her skin with a few others. The stinging from the clothespins had Olivia completely focused on her nipples but then her attention went to where Bradley was caressing next. His hand reached inside her panties, cuffing her waxed pleasure pocket and his middle finger found its way between her soft plush lips. Her clitoris jumped to the soft rubs from his fingertip and the slight slips inside her walls,

"You like that?"

"Yes daddy."

The moisture built up with every stroke from his finger until she dripped in his hand but then Bradley stopped. He pulled a small pair of scissors from his pocket, cut the sides of her panties and they fell off of her exposing her precious pearl. Bradley then pinched her clit as he clamped a clothespin to it, the sting sent chills through Olivia's body. Strapped to the large wooden board, Olivia was helpless to whatever Bradley wanted to do to her and he continued with his taunts as he picked up the candle from the floor. He unbuckled his belt and removed his pants while he pressed his body against hers. His hardened manhood pushed up against her, pressing the clothespin more on her clit but then Bradley raised the candle over their heads. He slowly poured the hot wax from the candle and it splashed on their skin, sticking as it cooled off. Every splatter of the wax stung something serious as Olivia held back her screams but the more he poured the more pleasure he encountered. The wax seemed to meld their bodies together as it cooled on their skin but then a hot stream of wax reached down to where Bradley's man meat was resting against Olivia. The sting splashed on his shaft and his creamed excitement exploded out as he shivered in front of

Olivia in pleasure. She leaned her head forward, kissed his lips as she whispered,

"Now that's what I came here for daddy. You like dat?"

"Yes."

Ronald woke to his sister calling out his name from the front room. He walked in to Mook and Desmond waiting for him,

"Damn dawg, you still sleep. It's time to get it, Jay outside waiting on us."

"Where y'all going?"

"None of yo damn bizness. Fuck I tell you."

"Fuck you Ro!"

Ronald's crew was stuck like deer in headlights as the siblings argued and he grabbed his things while walking out the door. They all got in the car with Justin, and they made their way to the house they were about to hit. The crew had their game faces on as the driver stopped at the corner to let them out. Ronald told Justin he will text him when they're ready. The boys casually walked up the sidewalk like normal, looking at every car that drove pass them, making sure no one was watching them. They made it in front of the house and like they planned, no one looked like they were home. Desmond darted down the alleyway on the side of the house as Mook walked up to the front door and rang the doorbell. Ronald kept walking as if he was leaving them, but he actually was looking to see if anyone was on the other side of the house. Mook knocked on the door again as he looked over his shoulder at Ronald standing on the sidewalk waiting and then Desmond opened the front door. The hellboy of the crew had pried open the backdoor that led out to the backyard. The two boys rushed in the house as they quickly closed the front door and commenced to look around for anything valuable. Ronald concentrated on the living room, as he shuffled through things grabbing a laptop along with some other expensive electronic gadgets. Desmond went straight to one of the bedrooms where he found some pricey jewelry, another laptop and 800 dollars in a nightstand. Mook found himself in a dark room with no windows, but as he tried to feel around, he realized he wasn't in there alone. A deep growl from a large animal filled the air of the room and Mook made a beeline straight out into the hallway,

"Man, somebody in here!"

"What?"

"Somebody in this room!"

Ronald looked up from stuffing items in a backpack he had to seeing Mook frantically running down the hall towards him. Directly behind his partner was a large black and brown image running on four legs, breathing heavily. The two boys immediately jumped on top of a large wooden dinner table as a shiny black Dobermann Pinscher rushed to the edge of the table, snapping at them. Screams and scuffles from the boys trying to get away from the dog alerted Desmond as he ran in the front of the house to see his friends on the table. When the dog seen Desmond, it chased him back in the room he came out of, and the frightened juvenile shut himself in there. Mook tried to get down from the table, but the enraged animal's attention went right back to the intruders on the dining room table. They were trapped in place with a beast that had no other concerns but to bite the first person it could sink its teeth into. The animal's growls and screeches from their sneakers on the wooden table was the only sounds that could be heard. Every time one of them would move the Dobermann would snap at them, just nearly missing them.

Ronald remembered that Justin was waiting outside for them and reached in his pocket to call for some much-needed help,

"Say dude, I need you to come open this front door! This big ass fucking dog got us stuck in the house."

"What?"

"Come open da fucking door! Shit!"

It was as if the animal could understand what Ronald was saying on the phone because it walked straight over to the front door of the house and waited. There was loud banging on the door and then it opened up but the image the boys wanted to see wasn't standing in the doorway. Standing in the front of the house with guns drawn was three New Orleans police officers, in which one of them the dog was very familiar with because it sat still at his feet,

"Good boy Gator, good boy."

The officers commanded the boys to get down from the table as another officer found Desmond hiding in the closet of the bedroom, dragging him to the front. The boys were handcuffed as one of the officers looked over the damage they created,

"Y'all really picked the wrong fuckin house to rob, I can tell you that."

Ronald took a moment to look around the home and noticed the uniformed officer standing in front of him was the same man in the photos on the wall. The policeman was alerted by the silent alarm Desmond unknowingly set off when he broke in the backdoor. One of the officers offered to beat the boys with his night stick for vandalizing his comrades' home but the lawman declined. The policemen snatched the boys up by their shirts as they walked them outside where three more officers were waiting next to squad cars in front of the house. The entire street was blocked off with police units parked in the middle of the street and Ronald could see Justin a block away staring with fear in his eyes.

Tears began to roll down Mook's face as the policeman sat them on the curb,

"I can't go to jail. My pops gone kill me, I can't go to jail."

"Shut up!"

"Man, my mama gone beat my ass."

"Shut. Da Fuck. Up."

Ronald tried to keep his crew calm while the police walked around looking over everything. He himself was scared to death but he didn't want the police to know he was scared. He didn't want to show weakness. Desmond looked around at all the police that were walking around and started laughing. The other boys wondered what was so funny because they didn't see anything amusing about being arrested. Their unorthodox partner explained to them that he has over two grand saved up in a shoebox in his closet and he's about to go to jail for a 200 dollar gold watch. The boys all started thinking about the money they had saved up from the corner deals they've been doing for the past year. They found it hilarious that they were going to jail for trinkets they could have bought with their own money. Ronald shook his head in disbelief that they were being arrested for home invasion and not for distribution. Their chuckles all stopped when the owner of the house stormed in front of them yelling,

"You muthafuckas busted up my backdoor! I wish Gator woulda bit yo ass. Ain't nothing worse than a fuckin' thief."

"Man look, I thought this was my homeboy's house. I saw da door broke and I went in to check…"

"Shut da fuck up!"

The boys were silent as the angered officer vented his disapproval while he picked each one of them off the curb and put them in the back of his squad car. The easy part was over for them, now it was time for them to go to the station and call their guardians. The ride to the station was long and it really gave all of them time to think. They weren't thinking of a way to get out of the trouble that they were in, rather the wrath they were about to get. The actual charge being added to his clean record was the least of Mook's worries but thoughts of his parents' disappointment in his actions was all that battered his spirit. Desmond been in the system for school fights and verbal assaults before but nothing like this. He was afraid of what his mother was going to do once he called her. Ronald knew exactly who he was going to call, and it wasn't his mother. He also knew he was going to get an earful of chastising in the process. The police cruiser pulled up to a large grey building with red bricks outlining the corners and a 10-foot archway that read "Intake" across the top. The car stopped in front of two rust-colored doors that swung open with two huge police officers that look like they should be on someone's football field instead of being law enforcement. They forcefully opened the back doors of the squad car and snatched the boys out,

"So, these the lil shits that broke in yo house. Oh, this boutta be fun. Get yo bitch ass inside!"

The officers walked the boys down a long white hallway that had a dark green line painted down the middle and sat them on a steel bench that was positioned across from an information desk. Fear began to set in as two men in orange jumpsuits with the letters "OPP" on the back walked up the hall, sweeping up dirt in their dustpans. The two inmates had the look of failure on their faces as they sluggishly walked the halls cleaning up behind the cops that paid them no mind. Ronald looked around the building and realized he did not want to be there anymore as he asked the officer at that desk can he make his phone call. The large policeman looked over at them,

"Boy if you don't shut the fuck up!"

Desmond nudged his partner and shook his head no in an attempt to keep Ronald quiet, but the leader of the bunch wasn't having it. The young Sweed boy understood the scare tactic of having them wait for the unknown, scaring them with big men in their face and told not to move or talk. The officers didn't scare him one bit and the idea of being put in a cell wasn't the problem at the moment. Ronald was feeling claustrophobic being handcuffed to the steel bench that was bolted to the floor and he needed to get loose immediately. The fact of not being able to move was driving him nuts and he knew if he made enough noise one of the officers would come get him. The antsy 12-year-old began to fidget and get upset,

"Man, fuck that! I want my phone call, ya heard me. You gotta give me my phone call!"

"Boy, who da fuck is you? You get yo call when I tell you you get yo call. But since you wanna be Mr. Loudmouth, you gone be the last one to make a phone call. Ya heard me."

"Fuck you!"

"Nah lil nigga, fuck you."

Ronald thought his plan to get from the cuffs was all lost but then another officer walked up and took him from the bench with his friends. The lawman pushed Ronald in a windowless room, closed the door behind him and told the young boy to strip. Terrified of what was about to happen,

Ronald stood still, petrified that the man was about to hurt him. The officer shouted again for Ronald to remove his clothes as he handed him a small orange jumpsuit to put on. As uncomfortable as it could have been, the frightened juvenile did as he was told and took all of his clothes off. The officer instructed Ronald to put the jumpsuit on, place his clothes in a large plastic bag and then walked him to another room down the hall. The youngster stood at a frosted glass door waiting for the officer to bring him in. He looked down the hall to see his friends still cuffed to the steel bench, it was the last time he would see them that day. The officer walked Ronald in the room, up to a large computer screen and placed Ronald's hands on the table in front of him. The young lad's fingerprints popped up on the screen and then the policeman told him to face forward as the camera over the computer screen took his picture. Ronald's identification was officially in the system and the officer grabbed the collar of the jumpsuit escorting him to a desk in the room,

"Ready to make your phone call now? Sit yo punkass down."

Darlene's nerves were completely shot as she sat in the passenger seat of Eve's car while they headed to the police station to get Ronald. The youngin' didn't call his biological mother with his first and only call but the woman that treated him like a son. Eve drove up Broad Street pissed to the highest at Ronald but concerned for his welfare after hearing about the house he broke into. She knew one thing about the police of New Orleans, they watch over their own and if one is hit hard, they all are. They had no quarrels about retaliation and Eve was just scared for her little man's safety in lock-up, where they had him. Darlene knew her brother was up to no good, but she never thought he would get arrested or committed a crime like this one, so careless. Eve herself was being careless, running red lights and speeding through traffic as she got close to the station,

"I can't believe this little boy. What the hell was he thinking? I swear, if the cops ain't beat his ass, I'm a beat the shit outta him when I see him."

"You think they beat him up?"

"I don't know baby. I'm just talking out da side of my head."

Ronald's little sister just wanted to see her brother's face as they parked in front of Orleans Parish lock-up on Gravier Street. The two worried family members walked in the front to the information desk and Eve asked one of the officers of Ronald's whereabouts. The officer told them to take a seat, where a woman and a gentleman were seated. Darlene's eyes darted back and forth, as every sound she heard in the building caught her attention. Fear had engulfed her completely and Eve held onto her hand in an attempt to calm her. The lady sitting close to them looked over at Eve and asked if she was here to pick up her son, she looked to the floor as she nodded her head yes. The woman held the same shameful expression on her face as Eve when she looked over at her, it was then when Darlene recognized the two as Mook's parents. The young girl whispered to Eve,

"That's Mook mama and daddy. If Mook got arrested so did Desmond. Where is his mama at tho?"

"Shh…"

Right when they couldn't wait any longer, the olive-green double doors to the left of them swung open and an officer walked Ronald out. The law officer then escorted Ronald and Eve to the information desk where they had to sign some release forms. As she watched her adoptive son print his name on the paper, tears rolled down her cheek, happy that he was in one piece and safe. Ronald couldn't look Eve in the eyes as she talked to him standing at the desk. He looked over at Mook's parents and asked the clerk where his friend was. The only response Ronald received was sarcasm,

"Worry bout you and sign these papers, lil boy."

The rebellious pre-teen wanted to lash out at the officer but knew it would all end bad for him if he did. Eve could see the frustration on the young man's face and consoled him like she did when he was little by rubbing the back of his neck. The feeling brought back memories of a happier time and Ronald calmed himself. As Eve was signing her portion of the paperwork the clerk informed her that they usually don't release juveniles to anyone but the parents or guardians. They made an exception that an adult could pick them up because the charges were dropped against Ronald and Mook. Eve was curious and asked why the officer had the charges dropped. The information clerk replied,

"Girl, I don't suppose to tell you but the third boy, Desmond Price, took the charge. He said that he broke in the back door and Ronald here and a Jason "Mook" Lewis ran inside to stop him. Either they some good friends or that boy one hell of a friend to take the whole charge."

YEAR 2012-2013

The year was going good for Ronald, he made it to 13, he was in his last year of junior high and his weed clientele kept growing by the day. He was the man in school, no one really tested the one everybody called "Pitbull", but Ronald made sure his buddies got the same respect. After staying a few weeks in juvie because his mother wanted to teach him a lesson, Desmond was released on 6-month probation for the home invasion. Mook's parents were stricter on him than ever, school or home and no hanging out in the streets all the time except for the weekends. The boys minded their manners, other than Ronald hustling on the streets to outsell any corner boy in the area. The element of gang activity began to become a big factor, boys Ronald's age walking around with colored bandanas hanging out their back pockets. The scene brought back ill memories of his brother and how Brock never got the chance to reach the age he is now. The thing Ronald liked about his crew was that they all had the same mindset that they didn't need gang colors or an organization to feel important. Just like in Houston, Ronald let it be known that he nor his crew was going to join any gang but unlike in H-Town they were challenged on it. Desmond would get in constant fights, walking home from school, with guys claiming he was on their turf and Ronald along with Mook would come to his rescue all the time. Gang life wasn't for them and they let it be known. A sense of respect was finally given to the boys from one of the gang's OG after a brawl broke out between Ronald's crew and some young thugs that tried to intimidate them. Ronald stood his ground with the gang and didn't allow them to push him or his friends around. The leader of the group seen that it would be better to get along with the boys than to create tension. Tension that could eventually call for the cops to get involved in their activities and stop cash flow.

Times were changing for Olivia also because she knew her body wasn't going to stand up to the girls working the streets and the escort scene. Being 34 made her a senior to the girls that guys were looking for when they called for a "lady of the night". Olivia sought out a new profession and it involved her going back to school for it. She began nursing school because it was always something she desired plus she could still make runs for Papa Sha in between schooling. The gangster made sure to keep her on a short leash because he wanted Olivia to always need him, but she was determined to get from under his hold. Papa

Sha would sometimes have Olivia do escorts for him as a seasoned vet to keep her making him money and as a result of him cutting Jazzy loose. Jazzy's loudmouth and arrogance had ran its course with Papa Sha along with Dracko. They saw fit to send her on her way before she ended up in a swamp face down like they would do anyone else that crossed them. Jazzy didn't take kindly to the segregation, but she knew the Haitian gang wasn't one to mess with. Olivia understood that too, hence her cooperation with Papa Sha and his antics. She even tried to convince him to help her with nursing school,

"C'mon now Sha, if I stick with this maybe I can get in good with some pharmacists. Get you some of those top-grade pills out there, think about it."

"Na cher, you my numba one gurl. My favorite rydah. Me don want no one moving me pistols but chou. You read doctor book when you cum back."

He laughed as he suggested Olivia have Ronald drive the car for her while she studied her nursing courses. Olivia was set that her son would not work for Papa Sha ever. She turned down the suggestion as she continued to make his delivers so that she could bring in some kind of money. The mother of the Sweed kids was trapped in a tight predicament under Papa Sha's thumb but her option to pass through nursing school was her way out. The Haitian gang leader had plans to have the entire family working for him, he just had to get to the little man of the house.

The boys connect Mr. Chou stayed supplying them with premium chronic to sell but disliked the fact that his son Justin was so entangled in a friendship with them. It was hard for Chou to control a boy that was 17 at the time, that was just as stubborn as he was, but Chou's angel was his daughter. Allison Chou was 15 years old, loyal to anything involving her family, smart as smart can get and a daddy's girl. When it came to balancing the books, it wasn't Chou who looked them over, Allison was a mathematical genius. She could crunch numbers like nobody else from an early age and Chou trusted her with all his money along with all of his inventory. Mook found Allison extremely gorgeous, but she wouldn't give him the time of day anytime he would come over to the store. Ronald would warn him,

"Man that Chinaman gone chop yo dick off and feed it to you with some duck sauce. Keep trying to holla at his daughter and watch what happen."

"Shid, that little thing sexy. I'll take my chance."

They met up with Justin for their usual pick up when Ronald seen one of Papa Sha's goons sitting in the car in front of the store. He could tell it was a Haitian gang member from the flashy silk Versace shirt along with the miniature blue and red Haitian flag hanging from the rearview mirror. The boys paid the tough guy no mind as they walked in the store but then bumped into Dracko standing at the counter trying to intimidate Chou. Ronald and his crew went to intervene, but Chou gestured for them to head to the back where Justin was. When Dracko seen Olivia's boy his eyes lit up in surprise, but he said nothing to Ronald or his little crew walking with him. When the boys walked through the plastic curtain that led to the back storage, they walked into Justin pointing a sawed-off double barrel shotgun in their direction. Frozen in fear Ronald's crew didn't know what to think. Then Justin explained to them that his dad told him to wait back here and if anyone other than family comes back by him to shoot. Chou's boy confessed to them that they've been getting harassed by the Haitian gang members for a month now. Justin was scared that his dad would get hurt if he didn't work with the gang, but Ronald comforted his friend,

"Pops ain't gone let them clowns fuck with him too long, this his city."

"Yea, but dem fools crazy."

"Yeah they crazy but dey know not to fuck with him."

Ronald still couldn't stand anything associated with Papa Sha and his gang as he told Justin he would help the family anyway possible to get rid of the nuisance. The young man appreciated his friend's offered help as they transferred money and inventory between one another. The boys were all loaded up and they headed out of the store as Ronald seen the concern on Mr. Chou's face. The store owner was worried that his little prodigies would run into trouble catching the bus with product in their backpacks, so he told his son to drop them off as he handed him an object wrapped in a towel. The boys all jumped in Justin's car as Desmond shouted,

"Shotgun!"

"No fool, this my dad's UZI he keeps behind the counter."

"Nigga I was talkin bout da drive. What UZI?"

Justin unwrapped the object resting on his lap that Chou handed him, and it was a shiny black UZI machine gun.

Desmond laughed but marveled at the exquisite firearm sitting in his friend's lap. Justin drove straight to Ronald's house to drop them off as he talked to them about Dracko. How he had been coming over every few days. Trying to convince Chou to go into business with them. Chou didn't like how the gang members came at him with their threats, but the Haitians didn't know any other way to be but intimidating. Ronald couldn't think of any way of getting rid of the pest that had become a headache for Mr. Chou, but he knew the old man was going to think something up. As the boys got out the car, Chou's problem became their problem when Mook seen Dracko and Papa Sha sitting in a car up the street. They all knew it wasn't going to be long before they all were approached by one of the Haitians.

Ronald walked inside to his mother sitting in the living room studying hard on an assignment for her nursing class. He was proud of the complete change she had made and encouraged her every chance he got. Olivia was so deep into her studies that she didn't see her son come in the house and was surprised when he placed a shrimp poboy in front of her. Ronald had got a few sandwiches from Chou's store for the whole family and sat in the kitchen quietly eating his with his sister. They all enjoyed their meal while Olivia was heavy into her studies but then there was a knock at the door. Ronald went to answer the door and opened it to Papa Sha's fiendish grin. The young teen told the gangster that his mother was extremely busy and couldn't come out. Papa Sha smiled as he shook his head,

"No little one. Me cum see you."

"Fa what? We ain't got nothing to talk bout."

"Nah, we do. We have much to discuss. You work for old man Chou, don't lie to me. Me boys see you there. You and yo crew. You travel all the way to the East for product and you not cum to me first? I thought I was family, Uncle Sha and you work for the Chinese man?"

"Say man, we was never family. You didn't like my daddy and he definitely didn't like you, so get off the gas with dat. And Mr. Chou not Chinese, he Vietnamese. Get ya facts right."

Papa Sha didn't take Ronald talking to him like he was a peasant and began to get aggressive as he stepped to him. He began to tell the teen that he and his crew members will push his pills on the street like they do with Chou's premium chronic. Ronald resisted the offer and then Papa Sha threatened Ronald with more than words as he revealed the handle of a large pistol in his waistband. Before Ronald could respond to the threat, Olivia came to the front door and pushed her son inside,

"Sha what are you doing?!"

"Just talking Che, just talking."

The hood smiled as the mother begged for him to leave her son out of his business dealings. Papa Sha didn't say a word as he stepped off the porch smiling his usual evil grin, got into the car waiting for him and it drove off down the street. Olivia rushed inside with fear in her heart for her child as she asked Ronald what Papa Sha wanted with him. Still mad that the gang leader came at him, Ronald replied,

"Nothing."

"Ronald don't tell me nothing. Sha don't come around for nothing."

"It was nothing Ma."

He went to his room and began texting his friends about what just happened. Mook's reply was that he had a feeling that one of them would get approached because he seen

Papa Sha talking with Dracko in a car when they got dropped off by Justin. Ronald didn't know what to do but he knew he didn't want anything to do with Papa Sha or his gang. Desmond on the other hand was excited because he thought Papa Sha was the type of thug he wanted to be as he texted back,

"C'mon now. Papa Sha with da big dawgs. I'm tryin to have deez hoes thirsty my nig."

"Mane if you don't get yo virgin ass on somewhere."

The two boys were arguing back and forth through text messages while Ronald stressed about Papa Sha because he knew the criminal would end up doing something. He had confidence that Mr. Chou could handle himself, but Ronald wasn't sure about himself being able to stand against the gangster. He was sure about himself in taking care of business dealing on the corners, but Ronald didn't know if three 13-year-olds could stand up against a whole gang.

The next morning Mook showed up at Ronald's door with a package from Dracko and the youngster was scared because the gang member told him he had to sell the product or else. The irritation could be seen all over Ronald's face as he snatched the bag from Mook's hand. They went to his room to see what they had to sell but were stopped by Olivia who had a strange suspicion the boys were up to something. Ronald attempted to blow pass his mother, but she stopped him in his tracks,

"What's in the bag Ronald?"

"It's nothin mama."

"I don't wanna hear that shit!"

"Fa real mama it's nothin. Mook just came over to show me something real quick."

The boys rushed off to Ronald's room to see what Dracko gave them to sell. They opened the bag to find two large prescription bottles of Percocet and instantly Ronald closed up the bag as he told Mook he couldn't keep the pills in his house. The young teen was scared his mother would find them and relapse back into popping pills again. Mook told his friend he couldn't keep them either because ever since his arrest his parents been questioning his every move and knew they would find them. They decided that their only option was to bring it to Desmond's house until they knew what to do with the product. After sneaking pass Ronald's mother, the boys headed to Desmond to get him to store the pills until they could sell them to someone. Mook was nervous because of how Dracko came at him, in front of his home. The fact that the gangster knew where he lived was disturbing for the young dealer especially because how careful he has been. Except for their buddy Justin, the boys made sure no one knew where they lived for the very reason that came walking up to Mook that morning. They got to Desmond's house, but the outside of the home didn't say that a drunkard and a young drug dealer lived there. The small patch of lawn in the front was immaculate, like a freshly vacuumed green carpet. The white wooden porch was so clean that you could probably eat off of it and windows so spotless you could see your reflection in them. Desmond's mother wasn't the usual drunk that falls asleep after a day of heavy drinking. The more she drinks, the more she cleans and from the sight of how well put together the house was she drinks a lot. Desmond seen his buddies walking up to his house and came outside to greet them, their faces said nothing but trouble. Ronald looked up and down the street to see if anyone was watching them,

"We got a problem."

Chou was at his store going over the inventory with his daughter Allison when Ronald walked in with his clique. The boys told him about the encounter they had with the Haitian gang and were in need of his advice. Chou had nothing for them because he was dealing with his own issues with them also. Discouraged that they were under the foot hold of Papa Sha's tactics, Ronald and his crew went to leave. On their way out, Allison stopped them with a little advice of her own. She told them to try and sell the pills in Papa Sha's territory, then get someone to rob them of the pills. Allison figured if the boys looked vulnerable to Papa Sha, he won't look for them to sell for him anymore. Ronald thought it was a stupid idea, but he was desperate,

"That don't make no sense Allie. Anybody that know us know we ain't going down easy and you definitely not just gone rob us and get away with dat shit."

"Ok, it's either that or you stuck pushing for that Caribbean buffoon. Pick ya poison."

Just because it was his crush saying it, Mook agreed with her as he tried to convince Ronald to go along with the idea. Desmond was down for whatever as he told Allison they were going to need someone from Chou's crew to do the robbery, it had to look like an outsider. Chou's young female mastermind told them she would get the right people for the job and let them know with a text, so they wouldn't be caught off guard. Ronald was reluctant to agree to the plan, but he had no choice. The boys headed out to make it back home when Mook took a shot at approaching Allison,

"Allie, when we gone hook up? I been digging you for a minute nah. Nigga just need one chance."

"Little boy, if you don't go somewhere. I would end up hurtin' you. Do you even know what to do with this thing?", replied to Allison as she reached down and grabbed a handful of Mook's crotch.

The young teen was completely loss for words as Allison held his manhood in her palm with a smile on her face. His boys bust out laughing because of it and pulled him away as to save him from any humiliation. Ronald told Allison he will keep in touch with her, and the crew left to head back home. The boys waited on the bus to arrive to take them back home. Ronald and Desmond were clowning around cracking jokes on each other, but Mook stood quiet staring out in space. Desmond started messing with Mook, teasing him about Allison but the words seemed to fall on a deaf ear. Ronald nudged his friend trying to make sure he was okay, making sure he wasn't embarrassed by what Allison did. Mook just stared out across the street at Chou's store,

"Dawg, she grabbed my shit. She was holding my dick in her hand. Dat shit felt good."

"Nigga, you stupid."

A few days had passed since their little talk with Allison, and she had finally texted them that she had somebody for the stunt they were about to pull. The boys were all set to pull off the made-up robbery as Desmond clowned around performing how he would fall down when the robbers show up. Mook even got into character stating how he's going to start crying in front of the muggers when they arrive. They all thought it was funny, but Ronald told them that they had to be convincing because Papa Sha's corner boys would be in eyesight of them when it happens. The Haitians had to believe it was real and not pretend or the whole thing would be for nothing. They went to their normal hangout spot where they've sold almost half of the pills already, the area was teaming with pill popping addicts. The spot was an old run-down playground that the city forgot about, but the neighborhood thugs would sell their products there and occasionally play basketball. The park sat in the middle of the block with a main boulevard on one side, a line of shotgun houses on the other and an old chain-link fence around it. Anyone standing at one side of the park could see clear across to the other side, if they look pass the basketball court, slides and swing sets. It was a nice spot for a pusher because an assortment of dope fiends frequent the area, lounging on the bleachers or sleep in the park restrooms. The hoodlums actually respected one another in not stepping on each other's toes. If one sold pills, the other sold crack, if one sold weed, the other sold heroin. It was an addict's paradise. Every paradise didn't come without its uncommon scuffle or argument between dealers feeling slighted by another and the random sounds of gunfire could be heard but not often. Ronald along with his boys were in position and just like Allison told them it would happen, it did. Two hooded goons popped out of nowhere with pistols drawn and demanding everything out of the boys' pockets. Ronald tried to make the robbery look believable as he began to aggressively talk back to the hooded robbers,

"Nigga this Papa Sha shit! Y'all know who da fuck dat is?"

"I don't give a fuck who it is. Gimme da shit, bitch!"

His aggressive behavior backfired as one of the gunmen struck Ronald in the face with the side of his gun, cutting him right under his eye on the cheek. Desmond immediately fell to the ground truly scared because at that point the robbery felt too real. Mook's waterworks began for the same reason his partner was on the ground, complete fear as the barrel of a gun was placed on his forehead. The robbery felt too real for them and the gunmen weren't playing any games as they ordered the boys to empty their pockets. The other dealers in the area could see the offense taking place but none of them intervened as they watched from a distance. The boys plan was going perfect but right before they could reach in their pockets to give their accomplices the pills, bright red and blue lights filled the night. The scene was too familiar for the boys, and they knew the police were right on top of them. The two gunmen darted off, jumping the nearby fence and sprinting through the neighborhood in an attempt to lose the police. Ronald and his crew all fell to their knees with their fingers locked behind their heads because six officers were right on top of them. The whole park was raided, with several dealers and addicts arrested in the process, including the teens. The boys were handcuffed, thrown in the back of squad cars and carted off to central booking. Once there the arresting officer laid out all the stuff they confiscated off of the teen dealers. The intake officer started naming off all the items,

"Two 9mm handguns, three cell phones, one with a cracked screen, six hundred fifty-two dollars in cash, 10 baggies of marijuana like substance, one pack of spearmint gum and 75 pills of Percocet. Y'all gone and cancel Christmas cause you ain't going nowhere no time soon."

Mook couldn't even cry this time around because he was pissed that he had gotten arrested trying to get over on Papa Sha. The thought of hearing his parents chastise him again drove him to the edge of aggravation. Desmond just knew his mother was going to leave him in prison because of this arrest and Ronald sat quiet without an emotion to show. He mentally was playing out the whole situation in his head and trying to figure out what went wrong.

A week had passed since their arrest and today was their court date, but they were not ready for what the judge had in store for them. The boys were questioned several times earlier about the pills, marijuana and guns, the officers wanted to know where three 13-year-olds acquired the items. All the boys stayed silent about it as they all took the charges of possession with intent to distribute. They knew if they told them where they got the pills, they would eventually have to tell the cops where they got the weed and guns. They desperately wanted to get Papa Sha out of their hair but didn't want to betray Mr. Chou in the process. The code of silence was strong with them, and nothing could change their minds on the matter. They were all kept in separate parts of the parish prison, never seeing one another until their actual court date. The boys were shackled and walked into the courtroom one at a time by a court bailiff. The courtroom was massive with a crowd of people sitting in there, the bailiff sat them down in a sectioned off part of the room and the court appointed attorney came over to talk to them. The young female attorney looked as if she just passed the Louisiana Bar Exam yesterday, but confidence was in her tone as she spoke to them. She told them that she is going to try to get them on probation because of their age and that it was their first time being arrested for narcotics. The lawyer really sounded like she knew what she was doing, and the boys agreed with everything she said including pleading guilty to the charges. She told them the judge proceeding over the case was hard on drug dealers but believed in reform and was fair. As the lawyer talked Ronald scanned the room and all the words coming out of his attorney's mouth turned muffled when he seen his family sitting in the courtroom. Olivia's eyes looked as if she had been crying for days. Darlene carried the weight of the world on her shoulders as she looked at her brother in the bright orange jumpsuit. Mook looked through the crowd of people to find his mother with eyes full of tears and his father with nothing but disappointment on his face. Desmond's mother looked as if she was completely disgusted being there but her hands wringed in her lap as her knee nervously bounced. The entire courtroom stood as the judge stepped out of his quarters, sat at the bench and started the trial. The prosecutor began with their rant about the boys being harden criminals and that the courts shouldn't release them back into society until they paid their debts. The state's attorney then gave testimonies after testimony of evidence that the boys had been selling on the corner where they were arrested for weeks. The police had been conducting undercover surveillance on the park for a month after a tip that there was heavy drug traffic going on at the park. Ronald was shocked when he seen police video of them selling on the corners and Mook couldn't do anything but put his head down. After the prosecutor finished the teens attorney debated her point in the case, painting the boys as innocent children that got caught up with the wrong crowd. She mentioned how Mook was on the A-B Honor Roll, how Desmond never missed a day of school and even mentioned Ronald losing his brother along with his father to street crime. The lawyer was swaying the judge in her favor until he came across an arrest three months ago that involved all three of her clients. The judge stopped the attorney,

"Counselor everything you're saying sounds like a model citizen that as you said got caught up with the wrong people. There's one little tidbit of information you failed to mention though. The fact that these three young men were just arrested less than a year ago for burglarizing a New Orleans Police Officer's home. Now that right there doesn't catch me as someone that just made a mistake. Sounds like the making of a career criminal to me but I could be wrong."

"Your Honor, these young boys are victims to a society that has forgotten about them, and a second chance could be wat turns them around."

"Counselor your turn is up in this matter."

The attorney was stunned, and the boys knew pleading guilty was falling apart for them as the judge began giving the court more of his views on the matter. Ronald had zoned out looking at his sister's face, thinking about how he let her down as a big brother. It was as if the room went quiet for him and he thought back to when he was young when his father and brother were alive. He thought about if he never started stealing from corner stores or stealing out of cars, what he could have done different. Ronald was ready to accept whatever punishment he was about to get but when he heard the judge say five years in Orleans Parish Prison, his heart sunk. He turned to look at his mother and she cried out in pain. Mook's mother almost fainted if it wasn't for his father holding her up and Desmond's mother walked out the courtroom as soon as she heard the judgement. The boys sat there deflated in their seats as the attorney tried to tell them she was going to appeal for them. Desmond stood up angered as he shouted to the bailiff,

"Take me back to my muthafuckin cell man!"

Time went by quick for the boys as they spent their first year in an open dormitory like setting in the prison. It was full of juveniles in their age range, from all areas of the city and beyond. The teens figured they could survive doing four more years there but then the sheriff deputies began to clear out residents in the dorm. They started to disperse the juveniles to other parts of the prison in two-man cells as they cleared out the dormitory for newer intakes. The boys were uneasy about the move, but they knew if they kept their mouths shut and didn't start a fuss like the other teens they wouldn't get "the Yellowpages". The Yellowpages was a brutal punishment made up by the captain of the prison in which they made a prisoner hold a large phonebook to their chest while a deputy punches it as hard as he can five times. If the prisoner drops the phonebook or falls to the ground before the deputy is finish another five punches are added. The punishment was extremely painful, and most could barely survive the blows, it also barely left any marks or bruising. Ronald and his boys made sure not to make any arguments about having to move. They cooperated with everything the officers were telling them. They were all brought to the same section of the prison and separated in different cells, but they knew they would see each other in the common areas. Ronald was partnered with a 19-year-old that was on his way out of the juvenile section of the prison and was heading to the adult side. Jacoby was in jail for three counts of first-degree murder, and he was just finishing his 4th year of a 99-year sentence. Looking at him a person couldn't tell Jacoby was even capable of killing a man let alone three, but he was a certified killer in the streets. Ever since the age of 13, Ronald's age now, Jacoby was a hitman for the CTC gang out of the lower ninth ward. CTC gang stood for Cut-Throat-City gang and the youngster was good at what he did. Because of his small stature, most guys didn't pay attention to him but by the time they realize who he was it was too late. The young murderer was locked up for three killings but in actuality he had several bodies under his belt. The judge threw the book at him merely because he showed no emotion whatsoever in court, calling him a monster of civilization that needs to be put away. Ronald walked in the cell with his head high and chest out, attempting to make himself look bigger as he carried his belongings in his arms. Jacoby was sitting down at the steel desk in the room and chuckled,

"You ain't gotta put on a front fa me lil man, you good. You got da top bunk."

"Ok."

"What's ya name lil man? Where you from?"

"Ronald but people call me Pitbull and my friends call me Ro. Grew up in the seventh ward."

"Oh, I got me a ole Hard Head in here. Name Jacoby but everybody here just call me Coby. Lower ninth ward over here CTC baby. We ain't gone have no problems huh? Just clowning man. Cop a squat get yaself comfortable, we ain't going nowhere. Ro or Pitbull? Nah, that don't fit at all. What's yo middle name?"

"Levi."

"Levi? Yeah now that works fa me. From now on yo name Levi. Shit kinda gangsta. Biblical even."

The two got to know each other, didn't really hang in the same circles but found out they knew a lot of the same people. It was funny to them that they both knew Mr. Chou in the East and neither liked Papa Sha or any of his members. Levi seen potential in being cool with his new cellie.

Desmond found himself bunked with a scrawny guy by the name of Stoney, who was so happy to have a cellie. Stoney took Desmond's things and helped him put them away as he asked him a bombardment of questions about where he's from, who he knew and how long he was in for. The new arrival was a little skittish towards the overzealous roommate, but Desmond went along with the conversation. His key goal was not to ruffle any feathers and if that meant answering a long survey of questions, he was going to. The conversation felt a little strange to Desmond, but he went with it as he started asking questions of his own,

"So what they got you in here foe?"

"Me and my girl was fuckin' around and her mama caught us and got to trippin'. They hit me with a sexual assault charge because they say she a minor. Most guys don't like to say they in here for a sex crime, but it was all consensual with us, shid. Guess her mama got mad and called the cops on me cause she musta wanted to suck my dick too."

"That's fucked up. Got you caught up in the system on sum bullshit."

"Exactly! You got a girl out there waiting on you?"

"Nah, I was too busy gettin' in that work on the street. I ain't have no time for no female."

The boys were talking about things they liked and didn't like along with what they were going to do when they get out. Stoney was 15 and told Desmond he had to serve 3 years in prison for the crime they arrested him for, but he was trying to get released early on good behavior. Desmond said he was trying to do the same thing, his new cellie informed him the best way was to get enrolled in the school programs. Stoney gave him all sorts of information on the subject, and it was truly appreciated by the young teen. They chilled in their cell, eating a few snacks Stoney had stored up from his commissary as Desmond's cellmate told him about everyone in D-Block where they were.

Mook's experience with his new cellmate was completely different from his friends in fact the teen didn't like his roomie one bit. A fat stocky 16-year-old kid by the name of Marques literally pushed his weight around as he barked out his rules of their cell. Marques was serving a 15-year sentence for Grand Theft Auto, Vehicular Manslaughter and he had a bad case of OCD, in which everything had a place. Mook was the type to drop things and leave them where they are, so rooming with someone like Marques was an issue. He compromised with Marques' long list of rules because getting into a fight with his cellmate was not on the list of things Mook wanted to do. After getting all his demands out, the heavy-set foreman of the cell laid on his bunk and read through a car magazine he had. Mook tried to get to know his cellie but his replies were short and abrupt. The new cellmate had had enough of the tough guy act when he uttered,

"Say man, I'm just trying to be nice here. We gotta share this small ass fucking cell together and I thought we could be cool."

"Look I ain't trying to make no new friends or be fuckin' besties in this bitch. I just wanna mind my fuckin' bizness, do my fuckin' time and get up outta here."

"Dawg, I'm trying to do the same damn thing, but we stuck in this room with each other for at least four years or until one of them officers switch us out."

Marques thought about what his new bunky was saying and agreed that they should get along since they would be locked up together for most of the day. The big boss still wanted his cell a certain way, but he became a little more hospitable with his new roommate. They started to find out they liked a lot of the same things in cars and they both laughed when Mook told Marques about his encounter with trying to boost a Hummer from outside a nightclub,

"Nigga, a Hummer? For real?"

"Yea, dat shit was stupid big trying to speed down Canal street."

"Da fuck."

It was dinner time and the entire D-Block emptied into the dayroom area where they had their meals. The crew had finally linked back up together with their perspective cellmates close around them. Jacoby and Marques knew each other because they've been in the same section of the prison ever since they arrived, Stoney was the outcast of the group because the boys knew why he was there. Desmond felt some kind of way behind the other boys singling Stoney out of their conversations or blatantly ignoring him all together. He addressed them all sitting at the table,

"Say mane, we all in here doing our time and we gotta see each other every damn day. Yea he fucked up just like all

of us but don't hold it against him cause of da fuckin'
charge. It was his ole lady, not like he went out and raped
somebody, fuck."

"You need to pump yo brakes lil man."

Mook pulled his homie to the side to have a talk with him,
Levi stayed seated as he finished his food and Jacoby along
with Marques just shook their heads at Dez's remarks.
Stoney seen he wasn't wanted at the table and left to go sit
in the TV area. Jacoby took the opportunity to tell Levi that
no one really deals with Stoney. Not because of his charge
but because of the nature of it and that Levi needs to keep
an eye on his friend. The thing Stoney failed to tell
Desmond about his sexual assault offense was that the girl
he claimed was his girlfriend was just 11 years old, while
he was 15. He was hired to babysit the girl while the
mother was at work on the weekends. The mother of the
child caught them performing oral sex on each other one
day when she came home early and called the police
immediately. After an investigation the police had found
out that Stoney had brainwashed the little girl into
believing they were in a relationship and that her mother
was jealous of her. It later came out after his arrest, several
other minors including boys stated that Stoney had

performed or had them perform sexual acts with him. Levi looked at Stoney in a completely different light and was scared for his friend's safety, sleeping in the same cell with a predator. The boys had all finished their dinner as everyone just chilled in the dayroom looking at TV or the common areas playing games. Levi took the time to write his little sister, he tried to write her a letter once a week just to touch bases with her. The idea of him being locked away for four more years and Darlene having to fend for herself was nerve racking for him. He even reached out to Justin to check up on Darlene from time to time just to make sure she didn't need anything. Justin was more than happy to look out for Levi's little sister especially after hearing how they got caught. Levi had finished writing his letter and join his crew in front of the TV as they watched an action movie on the screen. He wanted so much to tell his friend about Stoney, but Desmond would get real defensive when questioned about his cellmate, so Levi left it alone for now.

It was almost lights out time and all the residents began going to their cells before the guards started ordering them to. Levi told his boys he'll see them in the morning for breakfast and Mook clowned him with,

"Nigga stop all that friendly shit. Go to sleep fool."

"Good night John Boy!", laughed Desmond as he went to his cell.

Levi still felt apprehensive about his friend being trapped in a cell with a beast of prey like Stoney. Jacoby told him to just wait until the morning, talk to a guard to see if they could move him to a safer cell and that everything would be cool. The concerned friend figured that would be the best option and went to his cell. Desmond had climbed up in the top bunk to get himself ready for bed and Stoney offered him a special juice box from his commissary. What made the juice box so special was that Stoney had figured out how to make prison hooch with it and Desmond happily gobbled it up with him. After a few laughs for the night, all the lights in the cell block went out except for the ones right over the walkways for the guards and Desmond giggled himself to sleep. He was in a sound sleep but was suddenly awaken by someone grabbing him by the ankles. With a quick pull, Desmond flew out of his bed and landed on his back on the concrete floor. He could barely see the image towering over him, but he could tell it was Stoney.

Desmond attempted to get up, but the shadowed figure sat on his chest and began choking him. The victim tried to fight back but he was overpowered by the sheer strength and the python like squeeze from his attacker. He tried to keep his eyes open, but the choke hold dizzied him to almost pass out. Stoney then stood the limp bodied Desmond up, stuffed a dirty sock in his mouth damn near choking him again and bent him over the steel table in the room. With one hand clasped around the teen's neck, he quickly removed Desmond's underwear, pulling them to his knees. He then spat in his hand, caressed saliva on his hardened manhood and pushed himself inside of his victim. Desmond's screams were muffled by the sock, with his face smashed into the table. Stoney defiled every ounce of innocence the teen had left in him. The act was completed and Stoney climbed himself back into his bed like nothing happened. Desmond fell to his knees in pain and total disbelief of what just took place, he knew he was in some real trouble. Stoney laid there in his bed with a big smile of relief on his face as he informed his bunky,

"You open ya mouth about this and I'm a fuck you up fareal. Now get ya some sleep, tomorrow Saturday. We get French sticks and sausage on Saturdays. Phew, that was good good."

A week had went by since the guys arrived in their new cell block and everyone was pretty much cool with their surroundings except for Desmond. The assaults from Stoney had become a reoccurring thing almost every night and the young 13-year-old had become coldhearted to everything. His will looked as if it was completely depleted, lacking all life as he went on with the everyday goings and comings of the day. Mook could tell something was wrong with his friend but couldn't put his finger on it. The guards had taken the D-Block residents to the gym for a little fresh air recreation and to stretch out their legs. 80 inmates all rushed to the outside gym, to play basketball, lift weights and jog around the track for some exercise. Mook tried to perk his buddy Desmond up by tapping him on the butt like in a basketball game,

"Tighten up bitch!"

"Da fuck wrong with you! Muthafucka don't touch me like that!"

"Damn dawg, I was just clownin with cha. My bad."

Mook backed off as he looked at Levi, who noticed how his friend jumped at the fact that Mook touched him. They watched as Desmond went off by himself in the corner of the gym, they tried to get him to come sit with them, but he refused. The two friends didn't know what to think, assuming Desmond was growing old of their friendship and was just distancing himself from them. Jacoby had seen the type of mannerisms Levi's friend was demonstrating before and knew it was all because of one person. He didn't know how to tell them, but he knew they needed to know what was going on with their friend. Jacoby sat them down with Marques as he told them,

"Say my nigga, ya boy been touched and I don't mean in a good way, ya heard me. He been acting real stand-offish cause dat muthafucka Stoney been pushin' his shit in. You see how his back is to da wall and he can see everybody? It's not dat he don't wanna be around y'all, he just can't trust nobody right nah."

"Man, stop playin'. My nigga Dez ain't with dat kinda shit."

"We ain't neva say he was with da shits. Just sayin' dat muthafucka gotta him, fareal and y'all just need to be mindful of it. A nigga don't like to be touched right nah, ya heard me."

Levi was heartbroken and had heard enough as he went over to his friend. Desmond was crotched down in the corner of the gym watching every soul that walked by him when his neighborhood friend walked up. Levi didn't say a word, just sat next to his friend and watch the other residents go about their day in the gym. He could literally feel his friend's pain in the air, the look of pure agony in his eyes and the slight shiver in his body was hurtful in itself. Levi didn't know what to say that would make it all better for his friend emotionally or mentally. But his mind was racing with ideas on how to make it right physically. Mook walked up to the two sitting in the corner, asked if he could join them and Desmond tapped on the dirt ground with his hand. Levi laid his hand on Desmond's shoulder and the young teen flinched; it was like a knife to his gut to see his buddy that messed up. He vowed to him right then,

"He will never touch you again, I promise you dat shit."

Everybody was back in the cell block, talking, looking at TV and just relaxing for the day before the dinner trays arrived. Levi's mind wouldn't stop churning as he thought up different ideas of how to just ambush Stoney, beat him to a pulp and leave him in the middle of the dayroom area. He even thought about catching him in the showers and beating him with a bar of soap stuffed in a sock. The thoughts of different ways of assaulting him were endless until he seen Desmond sitting at the table defeated just scribbling on a sheet of paper with a pencil. Levi knew exactly what he was going to do and asked his friend to give him the utensil. The calculating teenager used the predator's urges against him as he began to write a note to Stoney. The guards came in with the dinner trays and everyone got in line for their meal, the hunt was on, and Levi made sure he was standing behind his prey. It was like a lion stalking a gazelle in the savanna in the act of Levi eyeing down his victim. When Stoney grabbed his tray, Levi took the chance and handed him the note discreetly. The shock on his face told the story as the two locked eyes and Stoney walked off to eat his dinner. The crew all sat together at one table as Levi ate his food making sure to stare at the horny rapist across the room on several occasions. Mook could tell his friend had a serious thought bouncing around when he asked,

"Nigga wha cha got brewing, cause I can tell when you up to something."

"I just need you to make sho I'm not disturbed when I move."

"Nigga say less."

Stoney had finished his dinner and took time to read the note Levi wrote. As his eyes glanced over the letter an evil smile appeared on his face and right then the one Jacoby renamed Levi knew he had set a perfect trap. His victim got up from his table to dump his tray and glanced over at Levi gesturing for him to follow. Stoney casually walked up the steel stairs to the walkway that lead to his cell and looked to see if Levi was trailing behind him. Desmond's friend made sure that Mook was close by to deter anyone from coming close to the cell he was going to. When Levi arrived at the door seal of Stoney's cell, he seen the perverted predator waiting for him on his bunk. It turned Levi's stomach thinking he had to get this close to him, but it was the only way his plan was going to work. He sat next to Stoney on the bed as the horned devil stroked Levi's thigh,

"Shit, I didn't know you was interested. I woulda been took my shot at yo chocolate ass. So wha cha wanna do?"

Levi remained quiet while he dropped to his knees in front of Stoney, spreading his legs open while pulling down his victim's pants. He pulled his man meat from his underwear and began to stroke it when Stoney told Levi that he likes how Desmond sucks his dick. The agitated teen clamped his hand around the hardened appendage while fondling his fingers up and down. The rage inside built up to a boil in Levi as Stoney laid his head back to enjoy his oral pleasure. He didn't see his attacker reach down in his sock to pull the pencil out that Desmond gave him. Levi grasped it tightly in his hand and with one hand gripped around Stoney's penis, he swung his closed fist at Stoney's neck like a punch,

"Bitch!"

The sharp pain caught him off guard, but the spray of red blood told him that he was stabbed. He looked up at his attacker with fear in his eyes and the rage was finally seen in Levi as the assault ensued. Two more quick jabs to the throat followed, then two more to the stomach as Stoney attempted to get up to defend himself, scared for his life. Levi pushed the sufferer back down to the bed as he continued to force the pencil through Stoney's flesh repeatedly, every hole releasing pools of blood. The blitz of pencil strikes stopped as Levi stood over his victim. He watched him gasp for air through the gurgling sounds of bubbles popping in the thick layer of blood pouring from Stoney's neck. The body fought to survive but the injuries were too great to recover from as the scared look on Stoney's face faded away to his death image. The predator had fallen to become the prey to a much more powerful adversary and Levi walked out of the cell like nothing happened. Mook immediately seen the blood splatter on his friend and rushed him to the showers. Luckily no one really paid attention to the two as Mook turned the hot water on Levi and it rinsed it all away down the drain. He stood there in the spray of the shower head as the water hit his body and Levi couldn't believe what he had just done. Killing a man was not in his plans that day but he felt it was something that had to be done for the safety of his dear friend. Mook couldn't tell because of the water but the last bit of rampage that was in Levi poured from his eyes in the form of tears. The teen felt a sigh of release as the water washed away all the anger he had built up in him. His friend came with a change of clothes as Levi stepped out of the shower. They stuffed the soiled clothes he had on at the bottom of a dirty clothes hamper next to the shower room. The two made their way back with the general population of the cell block and the area was in a chaotic frenzy. Guards were darting around the block looking for any clues as inmates talked about what was going on. Mook tapped one guy on the shoulder to ask what was happening and why the guards were searching everyone's rooms. The inmate replied,

"Man somebody done stabbed that bitch Stoney ass up. Had dat muthafucka leaking in his cell with his dick out, ya heard me. But that's what that muthafucka get, fuckin baby rapist."

Levi looked over at his friend Desmond and complete admiration for what he did for him was all over Desmond's face. The demon was finally slayed and Levi was the hero in Desmond's eyes.

YEAR 2014

It's been two years since Levi was sentence to five years in prison and Olivia was feeling his absence. Not just physically like his sister was but financially too and it began to wear down on the single mother. Earning her bachelor's degree was harder than she thought but it was all worth it when she got a job offer at a small clinic. It was Olivia's first step to getting from under the pressures of Papa Sha and his demands. The clinic she worked at gave Olivia purpose because it was strictly for low-income families, and it made her feel as if she was giving back to the community instead of taking from it. In just six months of being there she impressed the head doctors so much that she rose up in rank with the nurses there. Doctors began trusting her with their appointments, documents and lab work for the clinic. Olivia felt she had finally made it, not that her life before wasn't financially rewarding but now she doesn't have to creep around corners or look over her shoulder. She still felt the pinch from her son not being there, but it was tolerable to deal with. The housing authorities found out that Olivia had a well-paying job and took her off of section 8 so her rent increased, taking more money from her than she could handle. The strain of making more money weighed on her and Olivia found herself back to asking Papa Sha for deliveries in her spare time. The thug was tickled that she came back to him,

"Nah che, you know me want dee best for you and dat pretty gurl of yours. Leave dat dirt clinic, working for me not dat bad. You know this. I take care of my people. When that boy get out, you have him cum work for me too, yeah."

The thought of her children working with Papa Sha was one thing Olivia was not comfortable with as she told him no, but the Haitian drug lord was persistent. Papa Sha's vendetta against everything that Olivia's late husband created was what drove him. He wanted to destroy the image of Roger and if it took him to get the Sweed kids under his wing than that was exactly what he was going to do. Olivia had become the pawn piece that Papa Sha moved around so that he could get to the pieces of the puzzle he really wanted. The mother of the children was just standing in his way and the hood rich criminal was thinking of a plan to get her out of the picture.

Darlene was walking home from school, the 13-year-old was coming into her own, becoming a young woman. With her mother mostly gone working at the clinic or making runs for Papa Sha and her brother gone for another three years, Darlene started becoming more mature by the day. Without Levi around watching her every step and running off any or every guy that looked her way, Darlene had freedom. She figured by the time her brother does come out of jail, she'll be too old for him to try and shelter her from every male in New Orleans. Texting boys and the occasional conversation at school was all entertainment for Darlene, she still prided herself on keeping good grades like her father always wanted. Darlene had one boy she was interested in but like all the other boys that caught her attention, he was a true bad boy. Shabazz was a dreadlock little baby gangster that hung around with some gang members in the 7th ward but wasn't a member, more like an affiliate. He kept their colors on him all the time and sometimes even accompanied them committing a crime or two. Darlene was infatuated with the bad boy persona and Shabazz was attracted to the good girl aura she had. The two would stay on the phone for hours just talking about whatever came to their young minds. Shabazz knew about Levi, heard the stories about him and knew how protective he was over Darlene. The biggest rumor going around about Levi was that he stole his neighbor's car to drive across the river to Westwego to kill a boy for flirting with his sister. All the stories didn't scare Shabazz away, if anything they drew him in more. Darlene had made it home to her mother leaving out again as always,

"Baby I'm a be back later tonight. No staying up late. You got school tomorrow."

"I know mama."

"And nobody in my house either."

"I know mama."

Olivia drove off and the first thing Darlene did was text Shabazz to get him to come over. The young teen was as rebellious as her brother was and just as sneaky when she told her beau to come to the back door because she didn't want her nosey neighbors seeing Shabazz walk in through the front.

Olivia had a package she had to pick up for Papa Sha from Destrehan that needed to be in Slidell the same night.

She knew the drive was going to take all day and headed out early so that she could be back before bedtime with her daughter. Olivia couldn't stand having a real 9 to 5 job and still having to do side hustles for Papa Sha to make ends meet but she did them anyways. She knew the Haitian wanted nothing more than to have her entire family working for him and she did everything possible to not let that happen. The drive from the 7th ward to Destrehan was long enough but the traffic made it even worse as the I-10 was like a three-lane parking lot. Olivia creeped through traffic, trying to think up her next plan to get away from Papa Sha or at least something that would have him paying her for a service. She thought about boosting some of the pills from the storage locker of the clinic she worked at, but the doctors kept a strict inventory of all the products in there, one thing missing would mean trouble. The thought of losing a good job was definitely not what she wanted to do but staying caught in Papa Sha's clutches was suffocating her. She had finally got to her destination, a small trailer park in Destrehan, where this old Cajun came out to greet her. He was the typical stereotype of what a person envisions when they hear someone talk about a Cajun out in the swamps. Dingy blue overalls that partially covered up what use to be a white undershirt and some boots that look as if he walked through every mud puddle possible. What topped it all off for Olivia was the strong accent,

"Nah che, you prettier than da first pot of a seafood boil during crawfish season, nah."

"Thank you."

"You must be here for the island boy. We don't see pretty like this all the time, no we don't."

"Stop it, you gone make me blush."

"Blushing ain't nuthin' but ya face tellin' da truth."

The friendly Cajun walked Olivia to the back of his old pickup truck parked in front of his trailer. The mobile home was a sight to see, hanging on by a thread of hope with tattered siding, dirt thrashed windows and resting on a stack of cinderblocks. Olivia's eyes couldn't leave from staring at the screen door that kept swinging in the wind, slamming against the door seal of the trailer. She was startled when the courteous Cajun jerked the tarp off the back of his truck revealing two large duffle bags that were bursting by the seams with automatic rifles. The Cajun grabbed the bags and started bringing them to Olivia's car when she seen a large box with a pharmaceutical company's name on the side. She knew the guy wasn't nowhere near being a pharmacist and then she seen the box was a case of promethazine,

"You selling that box of goods too?"

The local laughed as he asked her if she wanted the box because he didn't have anyone to buy it and considered it as a lost. A lightbulb sparked as Olivia told the guy she would happily take the case off his hands and gave him her personal cell just in case he come across anymore. He told her he comes across all types of pharmaceuticals at the shipyard he works. Laughed that now he'll make sure to get a few boxes now that he has someone to buy them off of him. The friendly guy sealed the deal with a handshake and kissed Olivia on both cheeks as he walked off to the steps of his trailer, waving her off. She made her way to the Interstate so that she could make the drop in Slidell, but Olivia was excited about the added prize she acquired. When she peeked in the box sitting on her front seat, Olivia counted 15 unopened bottles of syrup. Looking at the bottles she knew she could make close to 45 hundred dollars off the case and knew exactly where she was going to bring it. Olivia still stayed in contact with the guys that use to buy product from Roger and knew they would love to take the case off her hands. She had finally found a way from under Papa Sha and things were looking up for her.

Darlene was at home by herself watching TV when she heard a knock at the front door, pissed that her beau didn't listen to her instructions, she swung the door open. Standing on the porch with the most calming smile was Eve coming to visit, Darlene was surprised to see her,

"Eve!"

"Hey pumpkin."

"Hey!"

The two hadn't seen each other in a few years and instantly hugged in a tight embrace. Eve heard through a mutual acquaintance that Levi was in jail and she had to come check on the only family she knew in New Orleans. They sat on the porch catching up on old times because the last time Eve seen Darlene, she was maybe 10 or 11. The young teen sitting in front of her was far from the little girl she remembered and Eve was so proud of the little woman she became. Darlene told Eve about Olivia going to school to become a nurse and how she had a nice job at a clinic. Knowledgeable of how her mother makes extra money Darlene mentioned that her mother still works for Papa Sha sometimes. Disappointed that Olivia was still dealing with the slick Haitian, Eve defended her old friend all the same,

"One thing you gotta learn baby, don't tell everybody ya family business. Ya mama doing what she has to do to take care of you."

"But it's you, you family."

"That's besides da point baby. I'm just telling you because I don't need you telling the wrong person. What happens in house, stays in house. Remember that, ok?"

"Yes ma'am."

Darlene understood what Eve was trying to tell her and promised to keep family business with the family. Eve playfully changed the subject as she asked the little one about a boyfriend. Darlene's chocolate face glowed and shined red as she denied any boyfriends to her makeshift stepmother. Eve looked at her baby girl with disbelief on her face accompanied with a smile while the teen stumbled over her words. Just from her reaction, the family friend knew there was a boy in the picture but like everything else, Eve never judged or reprimanded Darlene. She gave her some sound advice on boys and how to protect herself other than just physically. Eve knew Darlene was young minded when it came to boys, she knew at her age her hormones were high and a young man would take advantage of that if she wasn't careful. The young teen listened as if she was in class to every word coming out of Eve's mouth, taking mental notes of the whole conversation. It was a conversation her own mother never really had time to have with her and a conversation she knew she couldn't have with her brother. Eve gave her the raw and uncut version, holding back no punches as she "schooled" the teen. The senior on the porch had her fill of her teaching moment and asked about Levi,

"So how is that big head brother of yours doing? Do you get a chance to talk to him any?"

"He use to write me at least once or twice a week but lately the letters been coming maybe every two weeks. He said in one letter that the reason he doesn't call is because he doesn't want us to pay for them."

"I'm a take care of that. I know somebody that works for the Sheriff department that owes me a favor."

"A favor?"

"Baby girl, you gotta always keep one in the pocket for safe keeping. I'll teach ya dat later."

Eve had become a headliner in the gentleman clubs around New Orleans and her connections covered men from all walks of life. She called a guy on the phone while she sat next to Darlene on the porch and the teen seen another side of Eve. Sassy, sweet, dominatrix like and the conversation was controlled with her tone, the youngster was watching a pro in action. In less than ten minutes, Eve had convinced the guy to meet up with her so that she can give him a phone to give to Levi so that he could call his family from prison. With a fake kiss through the phone, she ended the call and smiled at Darlene with a cute smirk,

"Just that easy. That big head boy betta call me too. Let'em know that when he calls."

Levi's baby sister was so appreciative for what Eve was doing. The sweet stepmother of the Sweed kids was about to leave when Darlene's boyfriend arrived, the shock on the teen's face was hilarious to Eve. Shabazz stood there unknowing what was going on as Eve walked pass him and Darlene stumbled over her words again. The loving adult got in her car as Darlene attempted to explain herself,

"He just my friend. We gone stay on the porch, we are not going inside."

"Girl the way yo face lit up when you seen him, that ain't just a friend. He cute though. Make sho y'all stay on that damn porch too. I ain't playin' with you."

"Yes ma'am. Love you."

"Love you more pumpkin."

Olivia was almost to her destination in Slidell, but her mind was on the new profitable venture she was about to embark on. She talked with some guys in the East that her husband use to deal with back in the day and they were all game about doing business with her. Olivia set up a meet with them and the guys told her they had a buyer that would be able to take half of the bottles off her hands. She couldn't believe she was going to make half or more of what the bottles were worth. Olivia drove up a low-lit street with abandoned houses at every other lot, cars that look like they were stripped to the bone and vagrants walking the block. She pulled up to the house she had to make the drop at and the visual she seen wasn't pleasant. A fenced in rundown trap house that had flood lights at every corner of the roof, a ragged porch that looked like it couldn't hold one person on it and three huge pit bulls roaming the yard. Not sure what to expect, she tucked a chrome .38 in the back of her waistband after she put the car in park. Olivia got out of her car looking around for anything suspicious, the sounds of the dogs barking at her echoed down the street and the front lights inside the house came on. The door swung open to the house as Olivia reached for the duffle bags in the trunk and a person yelling came from the porch,

"Hike!"

The sight of three former highly aggressive pit bulls sat down immediately without a sound coming from their mouths and sitting at full attention. Olivia couldn't believe what she was seeing and then the encounter got stranger. An image walked from the shadows of the house but when they stepped into the light, there stood a manly white female in a white tee and some jeans. From her neck to her ankles, she was covered in colorful tattoos and a razor-edged taper fade only a professional could pull off. Knowing she was not what her delivery person was expecting, the woman cracked a smile as she opened the gate to the fence to let Olivia in the yard. Still afraid of what the dogs would do, Olivia kept her eyes on them as she stepped pass the gate,

"You Sam? They not gone try and bite me huh?"

"Yup, that's me. You gotta be Sha girl. These crumb snatchers know not to move, trust. They do as much as stand up and I'm a punch da fuck outta dem."

"You had them trained real good."

"Girl, I trained these muthafuckas myself. I ain't trustin' nobody with my babies."

Sam walked Olivia inside so that they could take care of business in private. Right before closing the door the homeowner shouted another command and the dogs got up from their seated positions to roam the yard like normal. Inside the home was like night and day compared to the crumbling outside. A plush leather sectional, shiny hardwood floors, a 70-inch TV hanging on the wall and a plethora of other immaculate items throughout the home. A young large breasted blonde, smoking a blunt came up to Olivia and asked her if she would like something to drink. The visitor declined as she laid the duffle bags down in front of Sam sitting on the sofa. The owner of the home pulled the blonde close to her, kissed her on the lips and whispered to her to go get something out of the bedroom. Olivia assumed the blonde was Sam's girlfriend but then a seductive red head in nothing but some boy shorts and a loose top walked out the kitchen to curl up next to Sam on the sofa. The gun buyer pleased with the inventory of weaponry she just received leaned back and put her arm around the female next to her. The busty blonde gave Olivia a backpack from the bedroom with a smile and Sam got up to walk her to her car. Since she was walking with their master the dogs paid Olivia no mind as she casually went about her way. Sam was curious and had to ask,

"Why you work for that fool Sha? He a asshole foreal."

"Just trying to make a little extra that's all."

"Shid, if you want to, you can cum work for me and maybe I can make you feel safer than that .38 in yo back pocket."

"What?"

"Baby girl don't front. I got cameras all on this house. Shit, I seen when you parked you tucked it in."

"Hey, a girl gotta be careful all the time."

"Nah, you good ma. Ain't nobody gone fuck with you round here. Not round me. You be good aight."

"Alright nah, Sam."

After leaving Slidell, Olivia called her soon to be partners to let them know she's getting close. She thought about what Sam said about Papa Sha and couldn't agree more that he was an asshole. Her meeting tonight was to get away from any and everything he's connected to. Being able to start her own little business pushing lean and whatever else the Cajun could get his hands on was key to that goal. She knew the risk that if she was to get caught it would result in jail time and even losing her license as a nurse. The possibilities outweighed the risk for Olivia as she turned on Morrison Rd and headed towards her new partners apartment. The apartments she pulled into was known for heavy drug traffic and most of the time police left the area alone because it was as the chief of police would say,

"Too much of a hassle and too much of a risk for his men."

The management of the apartment complex tried to keep things in order with security guards, but the area was teaming with drug dealers. Even though there was a good bit of criminal activity going on in the apartment, it was far from a rundown establishment; the place was kept neat and tidy. Olivia knew the guys from past encounters when she was with Roger. She trusted them, so to see a few fellas hanging out in front of the complex wasn't nothing unusual for her. She walked up the steps to his door with eight bottles of lean in a tote bag she had and waited for him to answer after she knocked. Olivia could hear music blaring from behind the door and she could see movement through the peep hole. She knocked on the door again thinking maybe he didn't hear her the first time when three men came walking up the steps. Focused on the door Olivia didn't pay attention that the three guys walking up the steps drew guns from their pockets and was coming straight towards her. Once she realized it was too late, and she had two pistols pointed at her face while another guy attempted to pluck the tote bag from her hand. Olivia had a death grip on the straps, refusing to let go as one of the guys pressed the muzzle of his gun on her forehead. Frustrated with her ignoring his orders the guy smacked her in the side of the face with the gun, knocking her to the ground,

"Bitch, I said let it go!"

With excruciating pain over her eye and blood dripping down her cheek the only thing Olivia was concerned about was not losing a hold onto the bag. She refused to let over two grand worth of product just walk away from her that easy. She just knew if she held on a little longer her friend would come to the door and rescue her. The guy tugged at the bag one more time while the other put his gun to the side of Olivia's head telling her to let go. Right when her grip began to loosen, she seen out of the corner of her eye her friend's door open and she knew she was safe. The three guys stepped back as the apartment door opened and Olivia's friend knelt down in front of her with the calmest voice,

"Let the bag go Liv, it ain't worth it. Give it to me."

She looked up at him as he pulled the bag from her hands and walked back in his apartment with the three guys following behind him. Olivia never imagined an old friend would do her that dirty, but he did, and it was nothing she could do about it. She brought herself to her feet and staggered along to her car, still dripping blood from her forehead where she was struck. The parking lot had a wavy haze to it as she made her way to the car but then the sound of rushing footsteps could be heard coming down the stairs. Olivia presumed the robbers had just realized all 15 bottles weren't in the bag and were coming for the rest. She rushed to her car as fast as she could, opened the door and immediately started the engine to get away but one guy reached in as he grabbed a handful of her hair. The other guys tried opening the other doors, but they were already locked as Olivia put the car in drive. Her screams could be heard throughout the complex as her assaulter tried to pull her from the front seat. Olivia slammed her feet to the gas pedal speeding away, but that one determined aggressor held tight to her hair, running alongside the car. He pulled and tugged trying to snatch her from her vehicle by her hair until Olivia drove on the side of a large pickup truck and ran him into it, knocking him off. She dashed out of the apartment complex parking lot not even thinking of looking back as her tears mixed with the blood on her face. Olivia no longer thought about the pain on her forehead, all she felt was defeat as she made her way home and considered what her next move would be.

Year 2015-2016

It had been three years since Levi was locked away for possession and distribution. He and his crew got some good news a month ago from the lawyer that overseen their case in court. The attorney worked her magic and got them an early release from prison, Levi couldn't be any more pleased with her work. Mook was the first of the group to be sent home and he cried like a baby when he took his first step on the sidewalk by the prison. His parents were relieved to have their son back home with them and his father had already gotten him a job at a grocery store. Levi was the next one up to leave and Darlene hugged the air out of him when he walked out from the holding cell. She and her mother had come to pick him up from the Parish Prison, Darlene was overwhelmed that her brother was back with her. Levi knew he never wanted to return back to prison and was determined to change his life around. After hearing about the job Mook got he contacted Mook's father in an attempt to grab a job himself. Desmond leaving the prison was nothing like his counterparts, no warm welcomes, no one there with a big smile on their face and no ride home. In the three years Desmond was in prison, his mother fell ill with liver cancer. She was holding on only to see her son's face at a hospice close to their home in the 7th ward. The troubled 16-year-old got into a cab and rushed to be by his mother's side but when he arrived the head nurse sadly informed him that she passed away that morning. With nothing left Desmond fell into a deep depression because all he knew was his mother and living with his uncle was nothing nice. His uncle was ex-military, strict, meticulous and always told his nephew that as soon as he graduates he's joining the military. The idea of joining the military was nowhere near what Desmond wanted to do with his life. The next few days the boys always made it a point to spend time with Desmond after their shifts at work. They knew the upcoming funeral was going to be hard on him and they just really wanted to kick it with their buddy in an attempt to make him feel better. In her will Desmond's mother left him the house but gave his uncle full custody of him until he made eighteen. Levi would make jokes trying to make his friend laugh,

"Nigga when you make eighteen, tell'em he gotta go. Wait, ain't dat muthafucka like a Navy Seal or something. He might beat yo ass, you know you can't fight."

"I will hit that muthafucka with a broom stick. He bet not put his hands on me, big muthafucka."

"Nigga, you ain't gone do shit. He gone have you in the Army like, 'left, right, left' looking ass."

"Fuck you dawg."

"No. Fuck you Private Dizzy Dez."

Desmond truly appreciated his friends, loved them like they were his blood brothers and they held the same love for him. His uncle knew about some of the activities the boys engaged into in the past, but he didn't hold it against them because he measured it to them being young and learning. Mook's parents weren't so understanding and reminded him every time of his prison stay. Levi's mother was just glad to have him back home but, the teen felt he had to do more than just be a presence for his little sister.

Doing the right thing for a change was harder than it looked for Levi and Mook. Going to school, going to work, checking in with their parole officer and staying out of trouble all had its challenges. Levi had no issues with going to school, he actually liked learning. His teachers were extremely helpful when he needed it and to be around some pretty females his age was a plus. Levi's problem was the hard work he had to do at the grocery store for the small check he received in return. When a person becomes accustomed to bringing home a thousand dollars every other day to barely clearing three hundred every two weeks, they get frustrated. Levi's main goal was to provide for his family, to help his mother out the best he can and to keep his baby sister in designer clothes. His teenage mind couldn't see pass that and bagging groceries wasn't cutting it for him. On the other hand, Mook was content with pushing carts and bagging groceries as a source of living, it kept him out of jail. It didn't hurt that both of his parents worked and he was always able to go to them for extra cash. The boys were pushing carts when they seen two familiar faces pull into the parking lot. Justin and Allison both were surprised to see the duo having a "common man's job", working for a living. Mook seen the beautiful girl he use to have such a crush on three years back and the feeling was still the same but this time he didn't show it as much. Levi was a little embarrassed that they seen him doing manual labor, but he kept his head up,

"What's good boi? Hey Allie. What y'all doing round here?"

"Man, we just chillin', stopped over here to make some groceries."

"Fasho. How Pops doing? Sorry I ain't been around. A muthafucka had to get a job so my P.O. could stay out my ass."

"Shid, I understand. You look good."

 The boys had pushed the carts up to the front of the store as the Chou siblings walked in. Mook couldn't help but to follow Allison's every move with his eyes as she walked into the store, she was absolutely gorgeous to him. Levi joked around with his friend, teasing him on the fact that he was scared to step to her. The boys were sitting on the side of the building taking a break when their micromanaging boss came out to tell them they needed to go back in the parking lot to get grocery carts. Levi noticed it was only a couple of carts out in the lot and told the manager he'll wait til there's more. The manager took it as the boys ignoring his orders,

"Y'all can go get the carts or y'all can leave. I can always find somebody else to do it."

"Damn, it's like dat?"

"Yes, it's like that."

The manager knew they needed the job in order to stay in good graces with their parole officer and always seemed to use it to his advantage. Levi looked at him with so much irritation on his face because the manager knew his situation and knew Levi needed the job. Mook told his buddy he would go get the carts and rush out while Levi stood back listening to the manager attempt to scold him on following directions. Levi was at the end of his rope with the manager and was about to do something that would more than likely get him fired. Fist balled with fire in his eyes, Levi was about to lay the manager out in the middle of the street when Justin called his name. The store runner had no clue that he was just saved by a customer as Levi walked off to his friend. Mook helped Allison put their groceries in the car while Justin talked to Levi about getting back on his feet,

"My pops left two of the shops to me and Allie. We need somebody to help us run the stores and maybe you could get back in the game."

"Man, I don't know bout dat. My P.O. watch my every move."

"Muthafucka, I'm not saying get back on da corners, that's kid shit. I'm talking bout, running da store and if somebody need product you handle it. Trust me, my pops do more than just push herb."

Levi thought about it and told Justin he would be in touch with him soon. Mook had a nice conversation with Allison and she actually seen he wasn't the little boy she remembered. He had finally talked her into going on a date with him and Levi's friend couldn't be anymore excited as they watched the Chou kids pull off. The idea of working for Chou again pondered in Levi's mind as Mook rambled on about what he wanted to do and where to go with Allison,

"Shid, I might bring her to dat new Creole seafood spot on Annunciation street. Or or, I could take her to the Trolley Stop on St. Charles, yeah."

Ever since she was held up by who she thought was a friend, Olivia had been on edge, watching her back constantly and trusting no one. She still worked at the clinic but the habit of sneaking pills out of the supply cabinets for her own personal use had become a regular occurrence. Olivia had fell off the horse, but she was a functioning addict. She would pop her pills like a person would take a glass of wine after a long day's work. Olivia stayed busy, working at the clinic and running delivers for Papa Sha. Pick-ups with the Cajun in Destrehan and keeping in contact with her new friend Sam out of Slidell. After hearing about the robbery, Sam had taken it upon herself to right the wrong Olivia went through. Two of the guys were caught in a drive-by while the main guy that betrayed Olivia simply disappeared off the face of the earth. Sam never told Olivia what happened to him, only saying Atchafalaya River had a new resident and that he would never back stab another soul again. She was still haunted by ghost, watching everyone else like they were going to do her wrong somehow. The one good thing for her was that her son was back home and after Levi heard about the situation his mother was in, he was extra protective. Olivia loved the fact that he was home at night, not running the streets like he use to and helping around the house when needed, Darlene not so much. The young teen loved the fact that her brother was out of prison, but his presence became a deterrence for her boyfriend Shabazz. Levi had realized that he couldn't keep boys away from his sister, but the suitors knew, can't just anyone show up. Darlene's big brother didn't tolerate corner boy or gang banger mentality around his little sister. He knew most of the boys she was dealing with weren't the typical schoolboy, but they knew they needed to come correct and respectful around him. Olivia and Levi had a feeling Shabazz was heavy in his gang affiliation, but the teen didn't show it when he was around them. Shabazz wasn't scared of Levi, but he heard the stories. He knew he would have a serious problem on his hands if Levi thought Shabazz got Darlene in any kind of trouble with gang activities. They had a clear understanding for one another.

Allison had finally broken her stance and accepted going out on a date with Mook. She had seen something different in him and was curious to see more. Mook kept his composure and played it cool as he was ecstatic to finally get the chance with his crush. She was an exotic treasure to him, nothing like the girls he's been use to around his neighborhood. Mook didn't know if it was the fact that Allison wasn't like any of the other black girls he's talked to or the idea of dating a girl of a different race.

All he knew was that he wasn't going to mess up this chance to open himself up to new things. He had talked his dad into letting him take the car on his own for the date night and promised his mother that he would be careful. It was as if he was going to his senior prom the way Mook meticulously planned out every moment he would have with Allison. From the clothes he wore to the places he wanted to take her, Mook had it all planned out in his head. The time had come for him to leave as he headed out and his buddies were waiting outside for him. Levi and Desmond were chilling on Levi's porch as they shouted for him from across the street,

"Aww shit! Nigga all dressed up for his funeral. Chou gone pop yo ass when you show up to pick up his daughter."

"Nigga you stupid."

"Man look, I'm just trying to help you out. You know Chou don't play behind his Princess."

"Man, we just going to a movie and dinner."

"Nigga you know damn well you tryin ta fuck! Stop playin with me. Ole duck ass."

Mook just laughed at his best friends clowning him and got in the car to meet Allison. His nerves had calmed, and he was ready for an interesting night out. It felt like it was taking forever for him to get to his destination, but it gave Mook time to think up the right words to say. He knew old man Mr. Chou was very protective over his baby girl and he didn't want to say the wrong thing in front of him when he picked Allison up from their house. Mook finally drove up to the Chou's house and Allison seemed to walk right out when he parked in the driveway. He walked up to greet her and meet Chou, but the anxious female was going straight to the passenger side of the car. When Mook asked if they were going inside to meet her father, Allison laughed and reached for the car handle,

"Dude, you met my dad years ago. You know who he is, he know you. Can we go get something to eat? I'm kinda hungry, I'm just saying."

"Oh, okay. I guess we going then."

Mook chuckled to himself as he went to let Allison in the car so they could be on their way. He realized he was thinking too much into the date and all he needed to do was enjoy himself with Allison.

Desmond was still chilling with Levi on the porch talking about Desmond's uncle and his military style schedule he had laid out for his nephew. The motherless teen couldn't stand the fact that his uncle was declared his guardian. It was more of a rebellion against all the doing the right thing in Desmond's eyes, but Levi made a good point with him,

"Round, we gotta be on our P's and Q's right nah. P.O. not playin' with us and you know 12 definitely not playin' with us. We can't make no ripples. Just do wha cha gotta do but Justin looking to have us workin' in the stores fa him. Fam, just hole out a lil longer."

"Easy fa you to say. Ya mama ain't waking you up at 4 in da fuckin' mornin' ta workout. Den this nigga can't cook man! All his food blan as fuck! It's called salt and muthafuckin' pepper nigga!"

"Nooooo. Food be garbage?"

"Man, like dog food garbage. How you fuck up Ramen noodles? Like fareal."

Levi couldn't help but to laugh at his friend, but Desmond was so serious about the situation. The two neighborhood friends chilled on the porch, talking about whatever came to mind when Shabazz walked up to the house. Levi still had his objections to the youngster, but he held his tongue in the matter as he greeted the young teen walking up to him. Desmond had no problems with the young boy as he dapped him off like he would anyone else. Darlene's big brother shook Shabazz's hand and asked if Darlene knew he was coming. Shabazz snickered at the question,

"Yeah big bro, I just talked to her. Can I go inside or do you want me to wait out here?"

"Nah, go head lil nigga. You good."

He eyed the youngster down as he walked through the door and let out a sigh as he heard Darlene's smiling voice call out her boyfriend's name. Desmond could see the frustration on his friend's face but let him know that he couldn't change how Darlene feels about the boy. Levi expressed to his partner that he just didn't want his sister around certain kinds of guys because he knows the dangers of being around that kind of element. Desmond understood where he was coming from but let his friend know that the more he tries to keep her away from something the more she's going to be drawn to it. The big brother didn't want to say his friend was right, but he knew what he was saying was true. A dark green sedan pulled up in front of Levi's house with three guys in it that Levi nor Desmond knew. Uncertain about who the guys were, Levi made sure his throw away 9 was right where he tucked it in the chair's cushion on the porch. The two friends didn't have to say one word to each other, their eyes said everything they needed to say, and they were completely on guard for whatever happened next. The front door swung open to the house and Shabazz darted out to the car waiting for him with Darlene close behind. She wanted to go with her boyfriend, but Shabazz stood at the back-passenger door,

"Nah, you good. I'm a be right back, I promise."

"Nigga, c'mon", shouted the driver.

Darlene pouted like a spoiled 3-year-old as she watched the green sedan speed up the street to the corner. She started walking back towards the porch where Levi and Desmond were sitting when a barrage of gunfire erupted in the neighborhood. The sound froze Darlene where she stood in fear. The older teens leaped into action as Levi held a tight grip on his pistol, pointing in the direction of the fireworks and Desmond covered Darlene as he held her down close to the house. Knowing his sister was safe with Desmond, Levi made his way down the street where two dark colored trucks sped off leaving a smoking bullet riddled green sedan sitting in the middle of the street. All the windows were shot out, the doors of the car looked like swiss cheese, all the tires were flat, and blood was dripping everywhere. Just looking at the sight, Levi knew there wasn't a living soul in the car, but he had to make sure as he slowly walked up to it. He tucked his gun in his pants the closer he got to the vehicle and took a peek inside. The two guys in the front were as dead as dead could be, with multiple bullet holes in the head but the gurgling sound of someone in the backseat caught Levi's attention. Shabazz reached out to him as he tried to breathe but the thick pools of blood pouring from the gash in his neck made it impossible. The young teen was drowning in his own blood as his lungs filled up with fluids, but Levi was there for him in the minutes he had left. He could hear sirens getting closer to the area as Levi applied pressure to Shabazz's neck, trying to stop the bleeding. It was nothing like the movies Levi seen on TV because blood was spewing between his fingers, dripping down his hand and it felt like it was taking forever for help to come. Shabazz looked terrified as he tried desperately to take a breath, but he couldn't and his body began to convulse. Levi tried his best to hold him down, but it was too much for him to watch the young boy die in front of him. He looked away down the street as he just held his hand on Shabazz's shoulder and the jerks of the teen's body slowly calmed to nothingness. Levi knew right then that his sister's boyfriend had just died in his hands,

"Fuck!"

Olivia had no idea what happened down the street from her home because she was dropping off some product to Sam in Slidell. They were talking about the recent litter of pitbull puppies Sam's dogs just had and Olivia's business partner offered one of the puppies for the kids. Olivia thought it would be good for the kids besides the big hazel-colored eyes on the charcoal grey puppy at her feet was irresistible. Sam had trained the puppies just like her own dogs, so Olivia knew she had a true guard dog that was gentle by nature. She was being escorted back to her car by Sam as always but this time with a four-legged companion. Olivia got in her car and seen she missed three calls along with a text message from Eve but thought nothing of it. She left Sam's neighborhood and before she could get on the freeway to head back home Eve called her again. The next few seconds brought back so many bad memories for Olivia as she listened to Eve,

"Liv wherever you at, you gotta come home now. The kids are fine but there was a drive by down da street from ya house and Dee's little friend was shot. Po baby is all shook up."

"Eve, no."

"Liv, da kids are fine trust. Just get home."

The thought of her kids being that close to the chaos that occurred up the street terrified Olivia. The engine of her car screamed as she pushed the gas pedal to the floor and dashed between cars on the freeway. She knew her children were safe with Eve. But flashes of Brock's death attacked her memory as Olivia listened to every word that came out of her friend's mouth. The situation got really scary for both of the women when they found out that one of the victims in the car was Shabazz. They knew Darlene went with the young boy everywhere and she could have easily been one of the victims up the block. Olivia was desperately trying to get home,

"Is my baby ok? Where is Ronald? Please tell me he wasn't caught up in that shit."

"Dee done closed herself in her room, I'm just giving the baby some time. Ronald didn't do anything wrong. If anything, he just being his protective self, sitting in the hallway by her door, waiting for her to come out."

"Good, I can't take that boy getting into anymore trouble. My poor baby girl. She really liked that boy."

"I know."

The mother of the Sweed kids was approaching her home when she seen NOPD presence at the next block still investigating the scene for any clues as to who committed the crime. A chill shot through her body with thoughts of what if battered her mind but it all went away when Levi opened the front door. He walked outside to greet his mother and Olivia snatched Levi in her arms. The hold she had on him was so tight that he could barely breathe but when he looked over her shoulder, he seen a nice surprise. In the fearful excitement in trying to get home Olivia forgot she had the adorable pitbull puppy with her. Levi opened the door to his mother's car and the precious canine rushed out zig zagging around Levi's legs.

"Friend of mine gave him to y'all as a gift."

Levi picked the little bundle of animation up as he followed his mother inside and knew exactly who needed the fur ball the most. He didn't even say anything to his baby sister as he opened her bedroom door, only to sit the grey puppy down in the room. Darlene didn't see the animal standing in her room, as her head was down and her eyes flooded with tears. The animal's instincts kicked in that the human in front of him needed consoling and he snuggled his nose at her feet. The troubled teen looked down at the big hazel eyes looking up at her and picked the puppy up, hugging him as he nuzzled his head under her chin.

A week had passed since Darlene's boyfriend was gunned down just up the street from her home. Followed by several questioning moments with NOPD, only because people seen him there, Levi was cleared by the police of any wrong doings at the shooting of Shabazz and his friends. They found out that it was a rival gang that followed the green sedan and ambushed them at the corner, but no one could identify the shooters. The puppy her mother brought home that day became the saving grace that kept Darlene sane, because of his mannish mannerisms the

Sweed kids named the grey pit Debo. Every time someone had food Debo would sit in front of them and stare them down until they gave him a piece of whatever they were eating. The pitbull was a joy to be around with his silly antics but at the same time Debo was highly protective over Darlene and Olivia. No one could be in arms reach of the females of the house without the four-legged security guard in eyesight of them at all times. Levi loved the fact that Debo was so watchful over his family. Especially after starting his new job with Justin at the corner store, he knew someone was home to look after the two women he loved so much. Levi and Desmond were back in the mix, moving product through the city but this time they didn't have their buddy Mook with them. While Levi worked Justin's convenience stores with Desmond, Mook stayed pushing grocery carts at the neighborhood grocery store. He didn't like the job, but he felt it would keep him out of trouble staying away from the temptations of going back to hustling on the streets. Levi along with Desmond tried to talk Mook into getting with the program,

"C'mon, son. It's not like befoe. We workin' behind the counters and stockin' the stores. Now if somebody come in needin' some extra, we make sho they legit and take'em to da back. Shit too easy. No mo corner boy shit."

"Nah bruh, I can't do it. I ain't trying to go back to jail."

"So you tellin' me, you cool with makin' 9 funky ass dollas a hour, walkin' in the fuckin' heat all damn day? Instead of being in the A/C, chillin'? C'mon nah, that don't even make sense."

"I'm good, fareal."

Maybe it was the pressures from his parents pushing him to be a model citizen because he was still under their roof. But Mook was unmoved on his decision not to join his crew this time. Desmond was all in, working doubles sometimes just to stay away from home and his uncle. What his boys didn't know was that Desmond was still traumatized over what happened to him while he was in jail. Thoughts of being trapped in a room with another man sickened him to his stomach and it didn't help that his uncle was always on his case about something. Desmond kept it to himself, covered it up with jokes and smiles but deep inside he was going through some serious PTSD. Flashes of Stoney haunted him and nightmares of that night occurred regularly. He and Levi hustled hard for Justin at his stores, making Mr. Chou proud that he decided to allow them to work there. Even though Chou gave the stores to his children, he still had a hand in the operations of it and watched over the moving of product. The young men found out quick that they only seen a portion of what was moved out of the corner stores, high quality cannabis was only ten percent of the products Chou was pushing. After a few days at the shops, Levi realized why Papa Sha was so pressed to get in on working with the Asian Drug Lord. Chou dealt everything from weed and pills to guns and bulletproof vest and everything in between, nothing was off limits with the right price. If the old Chinaman didn't have it, he sent his clients to someone that did for a finder's fee. He had his hands in a little bit of everything, from labor workers to whole construction sites. The mayor may have had the clout of running the city in the eyes of the government, but Mr. Chou owned the city and half of the police force that patrolled it. Levi kept his ears open for any tidbits of knowledge and watched every movement of the old man.

It was Desmond's day off from work and he passed over by the Sweed's house to check on Darlene like he did every other day ever since that traumatic afternoon. He knew what it was like to lose someone that meant a lot and Darlene looked forward to his visits. They usually just sat on the porch and shoot the shit, but Darlene wanted to take Debo for a walk this time, so they made their way through the neighborhood. The well-mannered canine led the way as the heavy chrome colored chain jingled in the air as he walked the sidewalk with the teens. Darlene found herself more and more intrigued with everything about Desmond, but she felt because he was her brother's friend, he wouldn't give her the time of day. Desmond noticed Darlene's maturity was well beyond her age and she was extremely attractive to him, but Levi was the defining factor that kept him from going any further than friends. They made their way to a nearby park where they took a break on a bench in front of the children's playground. Darlene took the opportunity to express herself while they were alone,

"Dez, I really appreciate everything. I really look forward to our talks."

"Hey, you doing me a favor. I ain't gotta be in da house with my annoyin' ass uncle."

"He can't be that bad, is he?"

"Girl it's like being in prison but you get to sleep in your own bed. You and Levi got it easy, y'all mama don't ask that much fa y'all to do. Dat nigga ignant and nosey as shit.

Why you sleep so late? Why you up so late? Why the TV on? Why the lights on? Muthafucka damn. Can't wait til I turn 18 cause he gettin' the fuck out, fareal."

"Boy, you stupid."

Listening to Desmond gripe about his uncle made Darlene feel a little better about some of the demands her mother had for her. His joking around also gave her a settling relaxed feeling that she could tell or ask him anything. The maturity Desmond began to notice came out when Darlene asked him if he was seeing anyone on a relationship type basis. After he beat around the bush with his answer, he could only come up with a few girls he only had small encounters with, mostly one-night stands. The following question threw Desmond for a loop when Darlene asked him if he ever broke a girl's virginity before. It wasn't a conversation he wanted to have with his close friend's baby sister and Desmond laughed it off telling her it was time to head back. As they left the park, Darlene began to open up about how she was going to let Shabazz be her first,

"Me and him talked about it a few times but the furthest we got was just kissin' and some rubbin'."

"Rubbin'? What da hell you mean, rubbin'?"

"You know what I mean. Don't act like you ain't ever do it."

"Ok, Ion wanna talk bout this no mo. Next subject."

"No but fareal, I really wanted somebody that cared for me to be my first and Shabazz was that person, but I guess that won't happen."

"You have all da time in da world to find dat person. Can we change the subject now? I really don't wanna talk about you and your virginity."

"But I wanna talk to you about it. I can't talk to you about it?"

Darlene released an innocent grin when she was about to ask Desmond another question, but he was saved by a phone call from Levi. The relieved teen quickly answered the call as if it was a life preserver from the risqué conversation Darlene was trying to have with him. The first thing to come out of his mouth was that he was with Levi's sister, taking Debo for a walk. Levi didn't care about the small talk because he was all about business at this point. He ran into an old friend at the Chou's convenience store that was looking for work and the ambitious Levi seen a potential corner boy in the works.

Levi was stocking some items at the store when four young boys came in but just from their odd habits the store clerk knew they weren't in there to buy anything. As he went behind the counter, Levi watched the young boys move about in the store but kept a close eye on one because he looked very familiar. All four of the boys had a handful of stuff from cold drinks, chips, cookies, candy and one even had a quart of motor oil. Levi chuckled at the amateurs that thought they were about to run off with the handful of goodies they had but the store clerk had a surprise for them. What the youngsters didn't know was that the front doors to the corner store had magnetic locks that could be activated behind the counter, preventing anyone from leaving the store. The boys met up at the counter as if they were ready to pay for all of their stuff and the ringleader asked for a pack of Swisher Sweet blunt wraps. Levi laughed because he knew when he turned around to get the wraps, the quartet was going to make a break for it. Just like he thought, as soon as he reached for the packet the boys sprinted towards the door but were met with a brick wall when the door failed to open. One boy kicked at the door handle trying to get it to open but the magnet locks were way stronger than his kicks. Levi leaned over the counter,

"That ain't gone work. Now bring y'all lil asses here. Bad ass muthafuckas."

"Man, open da fuckin door!"

The young dreadlock thug tugged at the door trying to break himself free and Levi finally realized where he recognized him from. Shocking all the boys he shouted out Kareem Daniels' name. When the four little criminals heard that the cashier knew one of them, they froze. Kareem didn't know who the store clerk was and pulled at the door trying to escape but Levi's ultimatum convinced his accomplices to push him out the way. The request that all of them could leave if Kareem stayed behind sounded a lot better than all of them getting arrested. The 11-year-old Kareem was reluctant to stay but curious at the same time as to who the cashier was. The agreement was made, and Levi turned off the magnetic locks as Kareem took a seat next to the coffee machines. The other three youngsters bolted out like the police was chasing them and the young Kareem watched as they ran off with agitation in his eyes. He figured he was about to hear a lecture on how he's wasting his life and that he could be doing so much better than shoplifting. Kareem sat back preparing to ignore everything Levi was about to say but was surprised at what happened next. Levi started calling out the pre-teen's siblings to him and made him remember who he was. The last time Kareem seen Levi, he was a toddler, and a lot has changed for the young man since then. The Daniels' household wasn't all peaches and cream how Levi remembered it. Delores Daniels refused to receive any kind of assistants from the government and being a widow with four kids was somewhat a strain. Her dead husband's retirement was just enough to keep a roof over their heads but nothing else, so Delores cleaned hotel rooms in the day and served drinks at The Zulu Club at night. The lack of guidance at home led to both of the twins becoming teen moms and adding to the mouths that needed to be fed in the Daniels' home. Kareem along with his older brother Cedric turned to hitting licks in order to make some extra cash. Thoughts of insulting his father's legacy resulted in Cedric slacking off from the simple robberies he was involved in, but Kareem continued on his spree of crimes. The young boy's demeanor reminded Levi so much of how he use to be and he knew Kareem needed structure before he ended up in prison. He thought about how Mr. Chou took a chance on him by bringing him into the game and wanted to do the same for the youngster. With Mook stepping away from the hustle for now, Kareem became a perfect fit for someone that was hungry to make money. Levi quietly became Kareem's big homie,

"Say lil man, I'm a front you this premium QP, bring me back $800 and then reup and we good."

"Why you looking out for me like this? I was tryin to run off with yo shit."

"Cause I know yo people and they been nothing but good to me. Besides, if you woulda got sporty with me I probably would have whipped yo ass. Also don't fuck round with dem lil niggas you was with earlier. You see how they left yo ass, don't need nobody like dat in yo circle. Yo team gotta be like family my nigga."

"But what if I just take yo QP and bounce."

"Then I'm a bounce yo ass up and down these streets. Lil nigga, I know where you live. Da fuck."

"Oh yeah, my bad."

Eve came over to check on her adopted family with a trunk full of gifts for the teens she considered her godchildren. She knew the kids' school year was about to start soon and took it upon herself to furnish their entire wardrobe. Olivia couldn't believe what her friend had done,

"Girl you didn't have this to do. Stop spoiling these kids."

"They my babies. My boy Ronald got his last year of high school, so you know he gotta be fiya and my Princess is a Sophomore this year. She gotta show up and show out on dem hoes. I will spoil them as much as I want to. Ahh!"

"Eve, you a mess."

Darlene ran outside to help her Nanny with all the bags in her car she had for her and Levi. The teen happily tried on the designer clothes while modeling for her mother and Eve. The two good friends were waiting in the living room for Darlene to come out with the next outfit she was trying on for them when there was a knock at the door. Thinking Levi had forgotten his key again, Olivia opened the door without even asking who it was. The front room of the house rumbled from the deep growl Debo let out when he seen Papa Sha and Dracko standing at the doorway. The protective pitbull walked up on the side of his master like the guard dog he is and stared down the two men he didn't recognize. Olivia gave the command for her guardian to calm himself and he did just that but stayed focused on the two strangers. With his infamous evil grin Papa Sha looked down at Debo,

"Good bitch."

"A bitch is a female dog, this a boy."

"Who said I was speaking to the dog, che?"

"What da fuck you want Sha?"

"No invite?"

Olivia stood at the door confident with her dog at her side and waited for Papa Sha to give the reason for his unwanted visit. He told her he needed her to drop off a package for him and that it needed to be done before night's end. Reluctant to complete anymore jobs for the Haitian gangster, Olivia made up an excuse that she couldn't have the drop done by his timeline. She figured they would leave but Dracko stepped up and insisted that the delivery be taken care of right now. Olivia had been doing pretty well for herself without the occasional drop-offs and pick-ups for Papa Sha, but they were persistent this time. She felt a little weary about the run he wanted her to do and Olivia still had a feeling Papa Sha had something to do with Roger's arrest years ago. Eve wanted nothing to do with what was going on and went to excuse herself from the company her friend was keeping. As she got up to go check on Darlene in her room, Papa Sha made a comment to her,

"Aww che, you with company. She go with you to deliver. Make it what you call it? Girl's trip. Or maybe she wanna stay with me. We have nice fun."

"Boy if I gave it to you fa free, you couldn't afford it. I'm not da one."

"Bel anfom toutbon."

"Whateva you said, ya mama."

"Girl, he called you a pretty sexy bitch."

"Whateva. Liv, I'm going check on my baby girl."

Eve walked off as Papa Sha's eyes followed her as he held his devilish grin towards her and Dracko handed Olivia a duffle bag. The Haitian gang leaders stepped off the porch and got into a Jeep parked in front of Olivia's house as Levi was coming home from work. Agitated to see them the man of the house just walked pass the Haitians as he walked inside. He could see the worry in his mother's eyes as she watched the Jeep drive off down the street. Levi had some plans in place to bring more money into the household, but he needed a little more time to set it up. He couldn't stand that his mother worked for Papa Sha,

"What da hell he wanted mama?"

"Nothing baby, I got it."

"Mama let me help you."

"Nah, I'm good. I got this one baby. You focus on work and stayin out of trouble. I don't need you involved in anything Sha got goin on."

YEAR 2017

Things been going as good as it could in the Sweed home with everybody succeeding at their own thing. Olivia finally separated herself from the hold Papa Sha had on her with the help from the partnership she had with Sam and the Destrehan Cajun. Levi looked like a real boss in Mr. Chou's eyes with the recruitment of Kareem, who hustled hard for the business. Darlene came into her own and became her own little woman but the infatuation she had for Desmond kept him nervous around her. He tried to keep his distance, but it was hard to do that when he was always at the house chilling with Levi when they weren't at work. Desmond still was uncomfortable being alone with his uncle in the house so he stayed away as much as he could. The decision to always find himself at Levi's house had its pros and cons. Darlene would take opportune times when Levi wasn't around or wasn't looking to make moves on Desmond. It was as if she was stalking him like prey, but Levi's homeboy was falling susceptible to the very attractive Darlene. She definitely wasn't a little girl anymore even though she was only 16 but Desmond was just two years older than her. He found himself looking forward to going by the Sweed house to see Darlene there and when she wasn't there making up an excuse to leave.

Olivia was at work when one of the desk clerks called her to the front for a visitor asking for her. When she arrived, she noticed Eve waiting in the lobby for her with a plastic bag in her hand,

"What's wrong? Wha cha doin here?"

"Damn, I can't just show up with two po-boys from Gene's for my friend for lunch?"

Olivia hadn't had lunch yet and welcomed the gesture as she informed her supervisor that she would be stepping out for her break. The two went outside to a covered patio area by the clinic and sat down to enjoy their meal. They started laughing about how far they have come from where they use to be. The two still had a lot of street hustle in them and weren't completely legal with everything they did but they weren't beating the pavement anymore looking for their next John either. Olivia ran her operation how her late husband did his, but her trust level was low with any and everybody. She wasn't a kingpin, but she was her own boss and a true supplier to the streets with her continuous supply of syrup. Sam even cashed in with her on making sure the shipments kept coming and the Destrehan Cajun always came out in the clutch with premium stock from the shipyard. Eve on the other hand was still shaking her ass on the pole but was considered the headliner in the clubs. She worked the exotic club scene like a pro and she also had a prestigious clientele that paid good money to have private performances. The two women felt they had made it with what they were dealt and made good with it but in the back of their minds knew it couldn't last forever. Olivia talked about one last score or one big lick that would set her for life and Eve even mentioned retiring from dancing. They pondered over their next move as they finished off their lunch and the two were virtually unstoppable when they put their minds together.

Kareem was back at the shop for a reup like clockwork and Levi couldn't be any more pleased with the hustler he had become. Justin was in the back-storage room packing up Kareem's order while Levi and his protégé kicked it up front. The two childhood friends were going down memory lane as Levi told Kareem about when the families lived across the street from one another. The baby of the Daniels children never really got a chance to get to know his father, so every story was enlightening to hear. The two were laughing when a female walked in the store and immediately caught Levi's eye. The young woman had a sassy flare about her that drew a person in when they seen her. The eyes was what trapped Levi in her spell but then he realized who she was when she began to talk to his potna,

"Reem, I ain't yo damn chauffeur. I got stuff to do. C'mon."

"Damn Shay, I'm comin."

"Shalay Nicole Daniels."

"So you gone call out my whole name? And who is you?"

"That's cold. You really don't recognize me? Levi…I mean Ronald Sweed. I use to live across the street from you."

Shalay smiled when she recognized the handsome store clerk standing in front of her. She hadn't seen Levi in a few years and from the image that was smiling back at her, he had truly changed. The two simply forgot all about Kareem standing there with them as they engaged in a deep conversation, catching up on old times. Levi took it upon himself to give Shalay his cell number and joked with her that she better use it. Kareem had had enough of the romantic reunion between the two and was happy Justin came from the back with a backpack for him. Shalay wasn't stupid by far and didn't have to see what was in the backpack to know that it wasn't schoolwork. She stayed silent for the moment but the look on her face let Levi know she's far from clueless as to what just happened. The store clerk walked the Daniels out to their car as Levi asked Shalay when he would see her again,

"Now that I know this where Reem always runnin to, probably real soon."

"We ain't gotta wait til Kareem come over here. How about I come over after I get off work?"

"What time? I gotta go pick my son up from nursery at 3."

"Bet. You hit me up when you get back home."

Eve was dropping off a rubber band wad to Olivia for the last package she got from her. Working the club scene helped her clear out any and everything she would sell for her close friend. It was more of a partnership when it came down to selling product for Olivia and Eve came across a guy that could move them all to a legal way of living. The guy's name was Dante and he seen that Eve was the perfect advertisement for the new product he was trying to get out to the public. The exotic dancer made it her business to market herself to the point where every guy wanted her breast stretching out a t-shirt with their logo on it. The entrepreneur was starting a CBD wellness shop in New Orleans and Dante had plans to make it a franchise. He figured Eve would be the best way to get the word out since she was already dabbling in the cannabis field, selling dime bags in the clubs she worked. The businessman offered her a proposition to sport his logo stamped clothing and 10% of the sales she bring in. Her creative juices began to flow as she thought of ways to get her day one involved in the opportunity. Dante wasn't looking for a business partner in that sense but when Eve suggested he have a sponsor for upfront expenses, he couldn't turn it down. Eve ran the idea by Olivia,

"We just gotta get him in a building cause Ole boy selling shit out da trunk of his car like he pushin his only mixtapes."

"Girl you think da shit gone sell? I'm seeing a bunch of dem CBD stores and shops poppin up around here. What make his any different?"

"Cause he got dat loud. Bitch he opened up a bag and I coulda swore it was da real shit and most of da time he sells out."

Olivia thought about it and agreed to the deal because she wanted to eventually get away from hustling. In the beginning she thought she would be a street hustler all her life and was completely fine with that decision. Olivia now sees that the lifestyle she chose had a shelf life and it was running out for her. The two hashed out a plan to get the ends to finance Dante on getting a shop he could start his Hemp Wellness Dispensary. Eve was stoked about the business venture and Olivia was ready to dip her feet in something new that wasn't illegal.

With Levi starting to spend a good bit of quality time with Shalay and Mook on his hiatus always with Allison, Desmond found himself on his own. He connected with some guys he sold pills to that liked to party almost every night and it became the perfect replacement for missing his home boys. Long days at the Chou stores, followed by wild nights and a different female every night, Desmond kept himself occupied. His occasional visits to the Sweed house kept Darlene interested in him but the abundance of females that were into popping pills and letting Desmond have his way with them was way more intriguing at times. It got around quick that he was the man to go see if a person was looking for that medicated high. Plus he had no problem partying with them. Because he was 18, his uncle left the house to him and moved to Baton Rouge, so Desmond was too free to roam as he pleased. Blurred psychedelic nights turned into him waking up next to some soft naked bodies of the opposite sex most nights. Desmond had become accustomed to drunken sex on the regular but sometimes he had to explain to a groggy female that just woke up next to him what happened and where she is some mornings. His adventurous stories at work kept Levi and Justin wondering if he would ever slow down but the money coming in was too plentiful along with the women.

Desmond would easily clear 500 a night just selling Xanax, Percocet, Ex or whatever he could get his hands on in the storage room at the shop. The boys had become very trustworthy with Justin and Mr. Chou so if they left with a package or made themselves a package to sell the Chous knew it would get done. Along with Kareem pushing premium chronic on a regular and Levi having a few guys controlling the out put of coke in the East, Desmond had the pills' market on lock. He had a handful of runners that sold all over the city and bordering cities, the city of Chalmette became one of his top buyers. Desmond didn't get addicted to the pills like his clients did but he did get addicted to the lifestyle of it all. His circle got out of control on some nights looking for girls to take advantage of but instead of getting them back in line, Desmond went with the flow. It became a sense of hunting for his crew, finding unsuspecting women, spiking their drinks and running trains on them in nightclub bathrooms. The more willing suspects were brought to rundown hotels where they would be pushed to complete all sorts of sexual favors for a free pill or two. Recording sex sessions on their IG and SnapChat became an everyday thing for all of them. Levi would preach to him,

"Say round, don't getcha self caught up. You memba that football playa got caught up, he was damn near doin the same shit you doin now and he serving time time."

"These hoes letting me bust in they ass for one damn perc my nigga. I had a threesome with this white bitch and her country ass cousin the other day. These hoes wanna fuck, I'm just givin dem some ex and dick to go with it."

"Nigga, you wild."

"Shid, dey letting me. You want me to say no?"

Levi tried his best to warn his friend of the dangers of his actions but Desmond was too wrapped up in the sexual web he was in. The concerned friend couldn't do anything but allow the neighborhood home boy to learn on his own, he was too far gone. They stayed with the program bringing in stacks and bands for Mr. Chou, the operation was seamless.

Mook had just got off of work and like clockwork Allison was waiting outside for him. The two had become a cute couple but not without its issues. Allison ran two stores for her father along with running the under the table business and Mook was still bagging groceries at the store his parents had him working at. She didn't have a problem with his job, but her boyfriend was in his feelings about it. Mook didn't care for the fact that his woman was the bread winner in the relationship, but he also knew he couldn't compete with her income. Anytime they would go out, Allison fronted the bill with no problem because she understood her man's situation, that sometimes he couldn't afford the places they went to. Mook on the other hand always saw a problem and it would turn into an argument for no reason. The couple was heading up the street from Mook's job when Allison suggested that they go grab a bite to eat,

"Baby, you hungry? I know you been busy at work and yo breaks be short."

"Nah, I'm good."

"Baby, I gotchu."

"Fuck you mean? I can buy my own damn food. I ain't fucking hungry."

"Muthafucka I was just offering to get us something to eat. Yo ass can starve."

The rest of the ride to Mook's home was silent as Allison drove up the street. She stopped in front of the house and Mook exited the car without even a kiss goodbye. The strain on the relationship was real and the longevity of it was coming to an end.

YEAR 2018

Olivia started her hustle on getting the funds together so that Dante could open up a permanent spot for his CBD wellness store. The task wasn't easy, but she was almost near her goal and Eve was right there along with her other partners helping her out. Sam got in touch with her uncle in New Orleans who was a realtor, and he found the perfect place for Dante's shop. The cannabis distributor had no idea that his business was about to take off the day he met with Eve, but everything was moving in their favor. A meeting was set up to see the property and Dante wanted his business associates there, but Olivia wanted to stay a silent partner. It wasn't that she didn't want to see the place for herself but that she was being extra cautious with everything. Olivia knew Papa Sha had eyes everywhere in the city and with the new Jamaican CBD salesman starting to gain recognition the Haitian gang leader would be close by. She told Dante about Sha,

"Look, homie is real conniving and if he doesn't get his way, he will try everything to ruin yo shit. It's like he has a vendetta against me, and I don't want to spoil anything from you getting this shop."

"No worry yo self, dim Haiti boys tink dim real Shottas. Dim boys know nothing. I got this. Thank you love."

He thanked her for all that she had done for him in getting this far with his business and made his way to meet with the realtor. Olivia didn't know it at the time, but Jamaicans and Haitians had a type of love hate kind of relationship with one another. So the fact that Papa Sha was a problem for her, Dante became a true ally to her and had no issues with addressing Sha if the event occurred.

Levi and Desmond were at the shop going over inventory when Mook came through, but it wasn't for a friendly visit. The third wheel of the crew had an issue he most definitely had to deal with but didn't know how and his boys were the only ones he could think of. In the midst of the pointless arguments Mook and Allison had with each other, he found comfort in one of the cashiers he worked with at the grocery store. The peacefulness with the clerk turned into more than just conversation with Mook. Little did Levi or Desmond know, but the reason he was standing in front of his friends with worry all over his face was about to be explained. Desmond could tell something wasn't right how his potna was pacing,

"Nigga, you good?"

"Nah my nigga. Shit is not good."

"Well, spit it out. Shit."

He then went on to tell his friends about a cashier named Jasmine who he got really cool with. Jasmine knew Mook was dating Allison because he told her all their problems anytime a disagreement arose, and the young female became his comfort zone. The relationship went from a friendly text asking, "how you doing" to emotional text saying,

"I really need you in my life."

The status of their friendship moved so fast that Mook didn't realize he was caught up in Jasmine until he was unbuttoning her jeans in the storage room they snuck off to. The two secret lovers had several sexual encounters at work that only went as far as oral pleasures between them. The actual climatic moment was one night Mook told Allison she didn't need to pick him up from work because he would be helping close the store. Just like Mook's girlfriend, Jasmine had her own car and offered to bring her co-worker home after a late shift. They were so in tuned with each other that a short drive to Mook's house from the store turned into a slow cruise through the city that neither one of them minded. The drive paused under a large oak tree on a long dark road and the only lights could be seen was from Jasmine's car radio with the occasional passing of lights from moving cars. The two couldn't control themselves as the engagement fogged out all the windows in the car and they meshed into one that night. The actions of that evening brought forth an innocent baby growing in Jasmine's womb and now Mook has to explain it all to Allison. After listening to his friend's story, Levi burst out laughing,

"She gone fuck you up. Then she gone tell her daddy and he gone fuck you up."

"Nigga that ain't funny. What I'm gone do?"

"My nigga, getting yo ass beat ain't never funny but it's gone happen bitch."

"Dawg, I'm serious."

Desmond was next to Levi weak laughing at their buddy but then they got silent when Justin walked in the back where the group was. Being the older brother to his girlfriend, Mook knew he didn't want to explain anything to Justin right now. The stressed-out future father made up an excuse to leave and Desmond walked his friend out to the front. Levi stayed behind to keep Justin occupied so that he didn't hear any of the disturbing news Mook had to tell Allison. Once they were outside the convenience store the joking went off to the side and Desmond let his friend know that he would support him with whatever he wanted to do. Desmond put his arm over Mook's shoulder,

"Say fam, if you wanna bring ole girl to the clinic to get it fixed, I got you. If y'all wanna keep it. I got you. If you wanna just hide from Allie, you know you got a place to go."

"Dawg, I just wanna keep this shit under wraps, fareal. Like just keep it a secret for a while."

"Yeah, secrets should always stay that, a secret. But yo secret will be breathing fresh air in like 9 months my G."

Darlene was home from school studying for an exam when there was a knock at the door. With her mother and brother both at work, she answered the door with Debo at her side. The always protective pitbull's nub of a tail viciously wagged as he seen it was Kareem standing on the other side. Darlene's face showed her thoughts as she asked,

"Reem what you doin here? Ronald at work."

"Nah, I texted'em earlier, he said he was on his way."

"Oh, you can chill and wait fa him."

Kareem walked in and took a seat on the sofa as Debo sat right in front of him wanting for a scratch behind the ear. As the guest played around with the family pet, he noticed Darlene was deep into her studies and didn't look up once. Even though she was draped in an oversized hoodie along with matching jogging pants, Kareem noticed how attractive she looked and couldn't help but to give her a compliment. Darlene shook her head as she smiled at the young teen's comment and told him she was out of his league. The ambitious teen took it as a challenge as he walked over to where she was sitting and replied that he was far from anybody she had ever came across. Darlene closed her textbook,

"Little boy, I would eat you alive. You couldn't handle all this chocolate if I hand fed you."

Before Kareem could rebuttal her comment, the click clacks of Debo's nails on the hardwood floors shuffled to the front door and Levi walked in from work. Darlene released a smirk as Kareem walked off to talk with Levi about some things he heard in the streets. She watched the guys walk back to Levi's room and thought it was cute how Kareem kept looking over his shoulder at her.

Levi walked Kareem in his room and started kicking off his tennis shoes as he pulled his uniform shirt over his head. Thinking about how Mr. Chou's operation runs, Kareem couldn't help but to mention the little things he noticed,

"Dat Chinaman be havin y'all look legit when you at work, uniforms and all."

"Shid, that's how he stay in business. Ya heard me. If shit look straight, ain't no reason to be snoopin around tryin to catch somebody slippin. You got my shit?"

"Yea, I got a band fa ya right now and I'm a need to reup with ya. But I need to talk to you bout some shit being said. Ya heard me."

Levi sat on the end of his bed as Kareem told him about a conversation he overheard between two teens at school. One of the teen boys were pissed about his sister being stranded at a hotel and having to call her parents to come get her. The girl had confessed that she was at a party with some friends and a guy gave her some ecstasy. She didn't remember most of the night, but she remembered waking up with the guy on top of her in a strange hotel with two other guys. Kareem said that what really made the teen mad was not that his sister went to a hotel with some random guys but that they left her there. What Levi's protégé said next had him scared for his neighborhood friend Desmond. The teen kept saying that his father was looking for a black guy by the named Dez. Levi wasn't too worried about that until he heard that the girl was a Vietnamese teen out the East and he knew the Vietnamese community was close knit. Kareem then stated,

"Dude said his pops was goin talk to his uncle bout it too."

"Please tell me his uncle ain't who I think it is."

"I think so, cause he said his uncle run the corna sto on Haynes."

"Fuck!"

Levi knew if Chou gets to Desmond before he does, his friend would never see the light of day. He told Kareem they needed to find Desmond and try to convince Chou not to kill him. The two set out on a rescue mission that had several ways it could go, depending on how either party reacted.

Eve and Dante had just finished signing all the paperwork for the lease agreement to the new shop Dante was going to run. They were kind of excited to see everything was working in their favor but then the dark cloud named Papa Sha met them at Dante's truck. That same annoying arrogant grin of Sha stared the business partners down as Eve's eyes rolled to the back of her head avoiding to look at him. Dante's chest poked out a bit as his focus was on Papa Sha standing in front of him and his Lieutenant Dracko leaning against the owner's truck. Papa Sha could see Dante was amped for battle,

"Easy, easy rudeboy. All puffed up like a Frigate. Me just here to congratulate me island brother."

"You are no brotha to me but thank yuh."

"Now dat offends me. It could fall in your favor to have me as your friend rudeboy."

"Me need no friends like you."

"Really? Now dat hurts."

Dante ignored Papa Sha's statement as he opened the door to his vehicle for Eve to let her get in his truck. He walked over to the driver side of his truck where Dracko was standing and the deep soul piercing look the gang member got from the agitated Rasta moved him out of his way. The engine of the truck revved as Dante put it in drive to pull off and he looked the now upset Papa Sha in the eyes, giving him the same grin, he approached them with. Eve released a sigh of relief as they went down the street and she asked Dante if he was okay. The new store owner laughed as he replied,

"Fuck boys can't intimidate me. Me clan chew dem up like plantains. I'm gud me love, I'm gud."

"He called you a Frigate, what's that?"

"Him tried to be funny. Frigate bird is an island bird in the Caribbean that puffs up its red chest, makes him look big. But he not know, I'm true Rasta! Rasta fear no man but him scary and I don't trust scary. A scary man is a reckless man."

Eve seen a side of Dante she wasn't ready for but was mildly attracted to it all the same. The two made their way to Olivia to give her the good news on the new shop. Eve sat in the passenger seat, confident that the man driving would be her protector if a circumstance would arise that needed his attention.

Time was pressing on Levi and Kareem to find Desmond before Mr. Chou or the father of the girl that was taken advantage of at a party. The boys caught an Uber to the corner store, trying to find Dez and ran into Justin working behind the counter. Nervous that Justin would ask where Desmond was, Levi made up an excuse that he needed to pick up a package for Kareem as he rushed to the back of the store. The shop operator thought nothing of it because it was a normal event for Levi. When he came from the back with a grocery bag for Kareem, Levi asked Justin if he could borrow his car to drop Kareem off at home. Justin tossed his co-worker the keys to his car,

"Say man, please bring my car back in one piece. You know yo ass got a heavy ass foot."

"C'mon now, you know I gotchu."

They got in the car to leave and Kareem told Levi he had finally gotten in touch with Desmond through a text. Desmond was waiting for them at Levi's house, the Sweed boy was relieved his friend was somewhere safe for the moment. They sped up the freeway to get back to the 7th ward from the East. Levi didn't want to get Kareem anymore involved than he already was in the situation that Desmond was in, so he dropped him off at home. As Levi headed home he tried to figure out a solution his close friend got himself into. He was in front of his house when Justin called,

"What's good son? I just dropped lil man off. I'm a be there in a minute."

"Say Levi, I need you to be straight up with me. You with Dez?"

"Nah, why what's up?"

"I like you Levi, please don't lie to me. I know you and Dez like brothers."

"Man, what the fuck you talkin bout."

Mr. Chou then took the phone from his son and the cold calculating tone of voice Levi heard sent fear through him for the first time in his life. He sat in the car as Chou gave him a life altering decision to make. The now soft-spoken Asian drug boss gave Levi two options to choose from and both were deadly, but one didn't include his entire family. Levi tried to reason with Mr. Chou stating that he and Desmond would work off any amount he came up with, but Chou wanted nothing to do with that. Chou calmly stated one more time before ending the call,

"Either you bring Desmond to me or I have my people come bring you and your entire family to me. You will watch you mother suffer. Olivia, right? Then you sister Darlene suffers and then after they die, I make you suffer. He not you blood brother, it not worth you family life. Bring him to me in one hour or I come looking for you family."

Levi had no choice but to bring his neighborhood friend to meet the Angel of Death or face the same fate for trying to run. He slowly got out of the car as if his body was drained of any energy, dreading looking Desmond in the eyes. With no other option to how the night could end Levi walked into the house to see Desmond and Darlene sitting on the couch talking.

What Levi didn't know about Desmond and Darlene was that they had been secretly seeing each other for a few months now. Desmond was tired of sneaking around trying to see his woman behind his friend's back and finally wanted to tell him. Darlene was on the exact same page with him because she loved Desmond with all her heart. Outside of the street hustling, Desmond was kind, sweet and gentle with her, everything her father was. He had become her first when they consummated their relationship one evening when no one was home. But being young and unprotected brought on a whole new revelation to their relationship. Darlene was a few months pregnant and began to show, the two knew the time had come that they bring their affair to light. Nervous that her brother would blow everything out of proportion she mentally prepared herself for his over protectiveness. Desmond was on edge because he knew how Levi felt about his sister and knew he might end up in a fight with his good friend. As they waited for Darlene's brother to arrive, the couple lovingly went over baby names and the mother to be was set on Desmond Junior if it was a boy. Desmond felt it was going to be a girl though,

"Baby, if it's a girl her name has to be Diamond because she gone be my precious gem."

The wait was over, and their hearts began to race as they heard keys open the lock to the front door. Desmond sat up on the sofa as Darlene hands instantly laid on her stomach, calming the jitters of her unborn child. Levi walked in with getting Desmond out of the house and back to Mr. Chou on his mind. He was moving frantically through the house when Darlene asked him to take a seat,

"Dee, I ain't got time. We gotta go handle something right quick."

"Fam sit down I need to talk to you."

Levi reluctantly took a seat and listened to the two speak as they poured out their hearts about one another. Darlene couldn't help but to let out an innocent smile when Desmond declared his love for her to her older brother. The conversation was like a boulder settling in the pit of Levi's stomach as he could see how they felt about each other and knowing what he had to do. It wasn't until he heard Darlene say five words that killed his spirit,

"Levi, I'm having his baby."

Levi really couldn't say anything to them and got up from the sofa. He told Desmond they needed to go meet with Mr. Chou and hash out a problem at work. Desmond didn't know about the girl that ID'd him as the one that took advantage of her and Levi couldn't open his mouth about why Chou really wanted him at the shop. The ride back to the store was uncomfortable for Levi because at this point, he was saving his family but destroying the trust his sister had for him. He knew if Desmond didn't come back with him, Darlene would blame him for everything. Justin had texted him that they needed to enter the shop from the back door and when they pulled up to the back of Chou's store Levi couldn't look his friend in the eyes. Thoughts of Desmond's child never knowing who he was broke Levi to the core. Only because he knows what it feels like to not have a father around when he really needed one. They got out of the car and walked to the back door that only had one bright light focused on the exit sign above it. Desmond unknowingly knocked on the door to his demise and it opened to Justin standing next to his father Mr. Chou along with another Asian guy in a low-lit storage room. When Levi stepped in the building, he realized that they were walking on a large heavy plastic sheet and he instantly knew the outcome wasn't good. He looked over at Desmond and a big Mexican punched Levi's friend in the stomach, dropping him to the floor. Levi shouted,

"Wait! I can fix this! Wait!"

"Levi, walk away. There's only one way this could be fixed and you don't want to be here."

"Don't do this!"

"Walk away."

Levi felt he had let his whole family down as sounds of his close friend being beat filled his ears but then Levi saw the finale to the beatings. As the exit door opened the bright light from outside shinned on two blood-soaked plastic sheets rolled up. Levi knew those two bundles could only be two bodies and Desmond was the next bundle to join them. He knew he would never see his friend again. Justin told him to take his car and he'll come by to pick it up but that he needed to leave. The pain of losing someone so close to him tore Levi up but saving his family from that torture was all that alleviated it.

Levi couldn't go home and face Darlene after what just happened, so he went sat at the shoreline of Lake Pontchartrain. He didn't cry when his brother died, he didn't shed one tear when he heard the news that his father was killed but Levi couldn't control the pain he was feeling at the moment. Tears blurred his vision as droplets rolled down his face, falling onto his shirt. It wasn't the fact that he was losing someone close to him but the idea that someone close to him was being hurt because of something he felt he could fix. Levi knew Darlene would fault him for Desmond's death and he prepared himself for that burden he would have to carry. He didn't know what to do next, but he knew he had to be there for his little sister. A call from Kareem changed everything,

"Hey brother-in-law. Congratulations!"

"Dawg, what you talkin bout?"

Kareem thought Levi had heard the news already and apologized for spoiling it for him. Still confused on what was going on, Levi asked again what was going on. The young teen told Levi to check his text messages and he seen he had three text from Shalay. One of the messages from Levi's girlfriend was a picture of a positive pregnancy test stick with a heart emoji on it, things had just got a lot more difficult.

YEAR 2019

The year started off with nothing but pains for Levi, it looked as if he was on his own. Mook and Allison broke it off after he told her about Jasmine expecting his first child. Levi's last close friend distanced himself from the life he was living in an effort to be a better person for his child. After Desmond went missing Darlene moved out with her newborn baby girl Diamond into Desmond's house. Levi only seen Diamond once before his sister moved out and the last thing she said to him was that she never wanted to see him again. He would leave money in the mailbox at the house every week for her, but the envelopes would always find its way back on the doorstep of Levi's home. Along with the family issues he was having, Levi was constantly under a watchful eye when he was at work. It had seemed that Mr. Chou had lost trust in him and placed one of his henchmen at the stores while Levi was there. The thing he didn't know was that the Asian guy he seen with Mr. Chou on that terrible night Desmond was killed was Chou's older brother. The uncle to Justin was more than just a Vietnamese American citizen but a high-ranking member of the same gang Mr. Chou was part of. It wasn't that Chou didn't trust Levi but that his brother made him place the Asian goons at the stores just in case they get word that Levi wanted to retaliate on his friend's death. The one highlight to everything going on in Levi's life was the birth of his daughter Ronnisha but even that situation had its trials. Being a mother of now two young ones, Shalay shied away from the fast money, danger and drama that came with dating a street hustler. She told Levi if he wanted to be with her, he had to step away from the life he was living, the only thing was it was all he knew.

Dante had become well established with his CBD wellness store in the community and business was doing really good. His business partners were benefiting from the sales also and Olivia felt she had finally made it. She hadn't completely abandoned the lucrative hustle she had going but she did scale back from the massive amounts she was pushing out. Eve and Dante had something going but backed away from each other because they didn't want to mix business with pleasure. It was easy for Eve to step away in order to keep business flowing but Dante not so much. He would catch himself wanting for her and acting on his needs,

"Yuh look gud today baby gyal."

"Boy stop it. I just left the gym and I look a hot mess."

"Yo empress, yuh look good anyways."

"Stop it. I'm here to go ova da inventory with you."

"Bumboclot! Alright, alright."

The two went to the back room to log all of the inventory up from the last shipment while Dante's workers watched over the store. The men weren't actual workers but brothers of the same beliefs as Dante, true Rastafarians that stood in as his muscle. After his grand opening Dante had a few encounters with Dracko hanging around the store but nothing major. He called for his brothers to watch out for the store and they were more than eager to step to a Haitian that thought he was better than them. Unlike most CBD stores that popped up in the city, Dante had most of his products imported from his homeland. It was a little more expensive, but Olivia had no problem fronting the bill because the quality was far beyond anything in New Orleans. If Olivia was the executive producer of the business and Dante was the actor, Eve was the director of the whole operation. She made sure all the numbers were right, that the store stayed in pristine condition and every customer was treated like family when they walked in. Eve knew the benefits of creating an experience when it came to customer service and she was a pro at it. Her drive to make the shop a success was partially what attracted Dante to her, second to her exquisite beauty. Eve was going through some boxes of CBD oils when she had to bend over to pick up a box from the floor. The site of her grey tights hugging her round ass with a protruding camel toe poking its way out sent Dante over the top,

"Geezam! Jah take me now. Gyal you beautiful."

"Stop lookin at my ass. What I tell you?"

"Me sorry. Me apologies. Yuh pum pum fat!"

"Dante! Focus."

"Ya mon!"

Months had passed and Levi still couldn't get the image of his friend on the floor in the back-storage room out of his head. Not truly knowing the whole story, his sister continuously blamed him for Desmond's death and his mother sometimes questioned her son about it. Levi knowing it was the only outcome that didn't involve his family facing the same fate as his late friend, he kept everything bottled inside. Making new friends was out of the question for him because he didn't want to go through losing anyone else. Kareem was still hanging around, making pick-ups and keeping Levi up to date with his baby girl Ronnisha but that felt more like business than a friendship. Justin felt bad about how the situation went down with Desmond, but Levi understood he couldn't go against his family. The whole ordeal was pressing Levi and all he wanted was an out, but he had been hustling for so long it was all he knew. Kareem had come over to drop off some money for a reup and one of the goons reached out to take the overstuffed envelope from him,

"I'll take that."

"Nigga who is you?"

"It's cool Reem, it's cool."

"Nigga, I only deal withchu. Ion know dis muthafucka."

Levi pulled Kareem off to the side to talk to him as he took the envelope from him and handed it to the security guard.

The youngster kept an eye on the guy as he walked to the back. After calming the little hustler down, Levi asked about his daughter and Shalay. The two talked for a minute before the muscle came back with a backpack for Kareem,

"Here, you delinquent ass nigga."

"This delinquent ass nigga supportin yo paycheck, ya fuck boy."

"Reem, chill."

"Dat nigga startin with me."

"Aight bruh. You good? You got ya shit? Gone bruh."

"I'm good. I'll holla at chu later."

Levi couldn't do nothing but shake his head at the feisty young bull he trained to not take shit from no one. He looked over at the makeshift guard who was completely in his feelings after a 14-year-old kid read him like a book and just laughed to himself. Levi's day had a bright spot thanks to Kareem and his antics.

Papa Sha seen that the newly opened CBD shop was off limits after reports that it was well protected by Dante's Rastamen, so he set his eyes on an old spot he wanted to claim. The Haitian drug lord went to visit one of Chou's stores to have another talk with him, but Mr. Chou wasn't there. When Levi seen a black Mercedes bearing the blue and red Haitian flag, he knew nothing but trouble was behind it. Papa Sha stepped out of the vehicle, in his silky Versace with matching shades and shoes, smiling as always. Levi looked over at security and told him to go get Justin because he knew the guy outside wasn't here to buy anything. The store clerk wrapped his fingers around the handle of the Mac 11 tucked under the counter and just stared down the men walking in the store with the gangster. Justin rushed from the back with his security guard right behind him,

"Can I help you?"

"Yeah boy, get ya daddy."

"He's not here and I'm in charge. Can. I. Help. You."

"Haha, the pup done grown up on me. Yeah. Well I believe it's time for us to talk. Private. Just you and me. Yeah."

"I don't think we have anything to talk about. The same answer my father gave you is the same answer I'm a give. Now if that's all you wanted to talk about, you can leave."

"Such a shame. Such a shame, I tell you."

Papa Sha let out his signature smile, turned around and walked out of the store to his car. Levi knew the results of that brief conversation was not going to end well with the Haitian and told Justin he needed to let his father know about it. Cocky in his own arrogance, Justin dismissed his employee's advice and just went back to his office thinking he handled the situation.

With her daughter living in her own place now, Olivia made sure to check on Darlene every day to make sure she didn't need anything. She knew she raised Darlene to be completely independent on every level but being a mother, Olivia had to see with her own eyes. Darlene was sitting on the porch watching her baby girl Diamond playing with her dolls when Olivia's car pulled up. She had cut her brother completely from her life, but her mother was a lovely sight to see when Olivia stepped on the porch. Picking up her granddaughter with nothing but joy in her heart, Olivia covered little Diamond's face with kisses,

"What maw maw baby doing?"

"Hey mama."

"Hey my baby, how you doing?"

"I'm good, just relaxing before I drop her off at the sitter and head to work."

"I can watch her."

"Yo son still live there? If so, then that's a no."

"Baby how long you gone blame him?"

Darlene gave her mother a blank stare and Olivia knew it was a lost cost to try to convince her daughter to change her mind. She just sat down and enjoyed the time she could spend with her granddaughter. Olivia didn't know the whole story of Desmond's disappearance and the only thing Levi would tell her was that his friend messed up, but he had no parts of it. She understood the street life, being a product of the lifestyle herself and her only son absorbed into it too. Olivia wanted nothing but her family to go back to how it was when they were little and innocent but that was far gone. She tried to explain the situation of Desmond to her daughter by comparing the life she lived with Darlene's father. It was too hard for the Sweed girl to believe that her brother had no participation in the love of her life missing. Olivia could see getting Darlene to understand her side was pointless and let it go as she enjoyed the time with little Diamond. The young mother went inside to get ready for work as the new grandmother played with the baby and got her dressed to go to the sitter. When Darlene was all set to head off to work Olivia gave her daughter a little bit of guidance before heading off herself,

"Baby I understand you're hurt and no one can tell you how to feel or how to heal. Family is everything. Don't let your brother close his eyes without y'all coming back together. Cause once his eyes are close, you don't want any regrets. Baby I love you and my lil Diamond. Y'all fix this. Please."

Allison bust through the front door like a SWAT team would a drug house and made a beeline to the back office. Levi attempted to speak to her, but she shot pass him as if he wasn't standing there. Slowly making his entrance right behind her was Mr. Chou's older brother and unlike Allison his eyes were focused on Levi. The store clerk could feel the Asian boss follow his every move as he asked the security guard a few whispered questions. Levi tried his best to listen to what they were talking about but couldn't without looking obvious, so he kept to himself. Allison called for her uncle to come to the back office with her and Justin, she looked at Levi with a brief smile but gestured he keep an eye on the front door. He knew something had to be up, but Levi needed to know what was going on and made an effort to get the silent goon to break his silence. Levi casually made a comment,

"Man, shit must be serious if three bosses here at once. Allie usually talkative but she was straight business today."

"Ion suppose to be tellin' you shit but Allie store got hit this morning right when they opened. They pistol whipped the dude until he opened the office where the product was locked up."

"They ain't take no money, just product?"

"Nah, just that. Left the register full. Dude said it was three black dudes, two of'em had dreds but all of'em was masked up."

"Why he opening up by his self? Mr. Chou always had two of us open a store up."

"The female that was supposed to be there showed up right when da three dudes was leavin and they slapped her to the floor on the way out when she walked in."

The whole scenario didn't sound right to Levi or the hired gun, but they kept their comments between each other and let the three Chous figure it out. Right when it couldn't get anymore serious, Mr. Chou walked in with fire in his eyes and stormed to the office. He looked over at Levi and told him to close the store up early before going in the office. As he counted the money in the register, Levi could hear his boss man shout at everyone in the office in a Vietnamese dialect. His eyes got wide as he could hear Justin and Allison chime in, but their father didn't sound like he wanted to hear anything from them. The security guard just stayed quiet as he listened to the loud conversation coming from behind the closed door of the office. The guard overheard Mr. Chou saying the same thing that he and Levi were just talking about and it didn't sound good. The curious cashier looked at the stores' schedule to find the girl's name that was supposed to open Allison's shop. After a quick search Levi found the girl's IG and Snap Chat but what he saw in her videos kind of incriminated her. A video of her in a car with three of Papa Sha's crash dummy henchmen that fit the description of the guys that robbed Allison's store caught Levi's attention. Images of drugs, guns, money and ski mask flashed across the screen as one of the dreadlock thugs shouted,

"Hitman clique, ya heard me. Don't get caught slippin'.'"

Levi knew right then and there that the entire robbery was a setup but also knew the retaliation for the act would be deadly. Because of how they treated the situation with Desmond, not letting him correct the problem, Levi didn't want to get involved. The only thing that ate at his conscious was his loyalty to Mr. Chou, so he stepped to the office door and opened it with the video playing,

"Dis da main reason I don't have any of these social media shits. Look like ya girl was hanging with dudes da night before they hit y'all. We get to her, we get to dem."

"Levi, I need you to take Allison home and stay there with her. Understood?"

"Daddy stop treatin' me like a damn baby. That was my store they hit. My shit they stole. I trusted that bitch. I need to be there."

"Allison go home."

Fourteen years had passed since Olivia had what she thought was a wonderful life but now in her eyes it had fallen apart. She lost her oldest to a senseless crime and the one she considered her quiet kid done turned into the street hustler his father used to be. To make matters worse, her baby girl seemed to have pulled away from having any dealings with her family. Olivia sat in her living room in the dark, missing the sounds of her kids running through the house and most of all Roger because she knew he would fix everything. She sunk into the sofa going down memory lane with thoughts of what if and the pains of the now began to weigh down on her. Just wanting to hear her children's voice, Olivia reached out to Darlene but the youngest of the Sweed kids didn't answer the phone for her. She then dialed Levi's cell and he answered but his conversation came across a little rushed as if he wanted to get off of the phone with her. Olivia felt it was her place to try to mend the shattered relation between the two siblings in an effort to get her family back to some sort of normal. She asked Levi when the last time he spoke to his sister and his reply disturbed her because they use to be so close. Olivia knew the reason why Darlene cut her brother out of her life, but she wanted to understand Levi's side of the story. Every question she asked him was met with open statements that didn't give Olivia anything. She was tired of beating around the bush with Levi,

"Ronald, I need you to tell me the truth and no word play."

"Mama look, I don't know how many times I gotta say it. I didn't touch that dude. All I did was what I needed to do to keep my family safe."

"Well you need to tell her that."

"That girl don't want nothing to do with me and I'm good with that. As long as her and Diamond safe. Mama, I gotta go. I'm a see you later."

Levi ended the call with his mother while she was still trying to get him to rethink reaching out to his sister. Olivia was talking to a blank cell phone screen when she realized her son had hung up with her. Feeling lonely with no one in the house but Debo, she went through her contacts on her cell and called up her fuck buddy. Bradley use to be one of Olivia's regulars that turned into a regular stress reliever for her when the urge arise. It started out as an occasional pills and penis kind of thing, but Bradley didn't like when she would call him high. He told her that he enjoys her company when she's herself and that pills had her as a completely different individual. Olivia complied to his request and went cold turkey off her addiction while gaining a new one, the only side effects it had was total relaxation. She had already mastered the ability of not catching feelings for no man and he wasn't any different. They both satisfied a need for one another; she admired a grown man with the stamina of a teenager and he was drawn to a sexy sassy female that knew what she wanted,

"Hey, wha cha doin?"

"Nothing just chillin."

"Good. Bring dat dick. I need my back broke in."

"Girl you stupid. On my way."

Levi did as he was told and brought the agitated Allison to her loft on Tchoupitoulas Street. She really didn't want to go home but her father wasn't taking anything less than her obedience at this point. Levi tried to explain to her the dangers Mr. Chou was trying to keep her from, but Allison wasn't in the mood for listening to reason. She debated with Levi,

"I can run the numbers in the books, make deals with some undesirable ass people and even conduct some meet ups but I can't defend my own shit?"

"It's not he keepin you from defending yo shit. Ya pops just trying to keep his baby girl safe."

"I'm not a fuckin baby!"

"Trust me I can see dat."

"So, explain to me why I can't go confront the bitch that set me up? I fuckin taught her everything, showed her da game and dat muthafucka clowned my ass."

Levi was curious as to what the thieves got away with and was jarred to hear Allison lost 2 kilos of heroin along with 2 pounds of weed. She was supposed to make the drop to a client from Texas that came in town to do business with the feminine Chou mainly because of her sex appeal. Levi had no words for the amount of money that was stolen from them and understood why Mr. Chou was so pissed. He parked the car in the garage attached to the apartment complex and walked Allison in. Levi knew the Chous were living the good life but never been to any of their homes before. Walking into Allison's place was a culture shock for him because she was just 2 years older than he was and didn't expect a 22-year-old to have a place like she did all to herself. A lavish loft style apartment with hardwood floors, marble countertops, plush leather seating and all the amenities a person could ask for. Levi stood in the living room area just looking around fantasizing about how his first apartment would be when Allison told him he didn't have to stay and babysit her. Levi replied,

"Yo daddy told me don't leave until he calls me and I ain't budgin, ya heard me."

"Well sit yo ass down. Standin there like a damn statue. You hungry?"

"I can eat."

"Shid, can you?"

"Girl stop playin with me."

"I been at work all day, I want some food."

"Oh, you was talkin bout food. Oh ok."

Allison laughed as she went to the kitchen and started pulling stuff out of the fridge. Levi sat on the sofa wondering how his boy could walk away from the lifestyle Allison was living to shack up with a minimum wage female. He asked her if Mook ever tried to contact her after they broke up and Allison pretended as if she didn't know who he was talking about. Levi chuckled at how Allison put the whole relationship behind her as if it never existed but then she put him on the hot seat. She began asking him about his relationship with his baby mama, but Levi didn't act like it never happened like her and Mook. He couldn't act as if the relationship never happened because they had a little soul by the name of Ronnisha. But the mother of his child wasn't sharing visits. Allison had no children of her own so she didn't know the pain Levi was feeling but could see it all over his face. Levi quickly changed the subject because he could hear and smell hot sausage cooking in the kitchen where Allison was. He walked in on his host putting together two hot sausage sandwiches,

"Oh you trying to show out. I thought you was gone warm me up some leftovers or something."

"Boy please, this ain't nothing. I cooks. Besides I likes to eat."

"You do?"

"Oh, now you wanna play."

The two took a seat at the large island in the middle of the kitchen and enjoyed the meal Allison prepared. Levi took the opportunity to ask Allison some questions he had about his friend Desmond's demise. She really didn't want to talk about it but felt Levi needed to know the truth. The young woman Desmond had ran into that night was her younger cousin who liked to go to parties she wasn't suppose to be at, being that she was only 16-years-old. Allison told him that her cousin went to the party where she met Desmond for the first time and he gave her some ex. He talked her into leaving with him to go to another party, but they ended up at a hotel where Desmond and two other guys ran a train on her, then left her there when they were finish. Levi couldn't believe his friend would do such a thing, but Allison stressed that the whole story was true and Desmond confessed to her uncle about it. She told him that her uncle wasn't mad that Desmond had sex with his daughter because she had lied about her age and was very promiscuous. Her uncle was pissed that Desmond left his daughter in a deadly rival's territory stranded where she could have been killed and that was the reason for his actions. Thinking about his mother and sister, Levi imagined he would react the same way if it would have been him. After the long talk they both went and sat in the living room to watch some TV as Levi waited for an all-clear call from Mr. Chou. The two adults found themselves relaxing on the sofa enjoying a good thriller movie when Allison got really comfortable with Levi. She snuggled up against him as she stretched her legs out on the plush leather furniture. Levi himself was a little on the uncomfortable side as his boss' daughter rested her hand on his inner thigh. Trying to control any impulses that would enlarge his manhood, Levi concentrated hard on the movie in front of him and blocked out the highly attractive woman laying against him. As the movie went on, Allison's hand began to voyage up and down Levi's thigh, sending shockwaves through his body. His brain was telling him to get up, but his body wouldn't let him as his eyes glanced over Allison's soft cream-colored thighs. Thoughts of just ravaging her body flashed in his mind but Levi's self-control was holding on as strong as it could. The battle that was going on in him was epic and the sinful side was losing as the young man sweated out thoughts of a sexual encounter with such a beautiful woman. He felt he was gaining control, but it was all for nothing when Allison felt a nudge on her arm from his growing appendage between his legs. She reached over and began caressing the steak that started expanding in her hand as she whispered,

"I don't know about you but I'm a need some of this."

"Hole-up."

Allison unzipped his jeans, reached in and pulled out a hardened vein filled tool that literally moistened her vaginal walls from the sight of it. She began stroking it, but her hand barely wrapped around its thickness as it stood at attention for her. Levi couldn't believe they were engaging in the act, but his hands took over his mind as they reached over to play with Allison's small B-cups. Her nipples pushed through her bra, poking at her shirt as Levi's hands fondled her breast. She stood in front of him sitting on the sofa as she pulled the t-shirt over her head. The shorts she was wearing found themselves thrown to the floor somehow and she straddled him. The lovely, waxed sight of Allison's plump pussy stared down at Levi's erect dick, dripping wet with anticipation. She eased down onto him as her walls began to grip and pull him inside of her, the feeling they both felt sent electricity threw their bodies. Her juices flowed as he held onto her hips while she slowly slid up and down on his shaft, sending his mind into a sense of euphoria. The sex was in a word amazing, and Allison was on cloud 99 as Levi's manhood pushed its way to the very end of her canal, filling her up with his hardened muscle. She tried to hold on, but the first tingle of an orgasm began electrifying her body as Levi's thumb rubbed her clit. He could feel her walls constrict, squeezing every inch of him the more his thumb rotated around her swollen clitoris. The flood gates opened and Allison wrapped her arms around Levi's neck as her body gyrated on his dick but all the jitters brought on an explosive orgasm for him also. They both didn't last as long as they wanted to as the fast strokes slowed down to deep grinds as they held each other. The young couple couldn't believe what they just finished doing as they looked in each other's eyes, but the ecstatic feeling immediately dropped when Levi's phone began ringing. He looked at the screen and it was Mr. Chou calling, Levi got nervous thinking the Asian father could see him with his daughter. He answered the phone, but Papa Sha was on the other end,

"I know you with her, yea. Tell dat slant eyed she devil she be next. I run this city. Me! Mutha fucker!"

YEAR 2020

The year started off terrible for Allison with her uncle, her father and Justin all meeting the Grim Reaper on the night Levi brought her home. They were at one of the shops trying to find the three guys and the girl that robbed Allison's store when Papa Sha showed up. The Haitian drug lord didn't come to the store to talk this time and his entourage surrounded the store with automatic weapons. Mr. Chou and his brother attempted to shoot their way out through the front door while Justin tried escaping out the back door with his own gun drawn for battle. The fire power was too much for the brothers as they both were taken out in a blaze of gunfire in front of the store. Unaware to his surroundings as he ran out Justin was shot in the back of the head as soon as he exited, the entire scene was a slaughter. Police tried to find any evidence to who actually committed the crime, but Papa Sha made sure to confiscate all the security footage. Allison closed all three of the stores for almost a month trying to wrap her head around the idea that she would never see the men that meant so much to her again. Levi was there for her physically and emotionally, but he knew she had to get back on the hustle because her primary suppliers weren't trying to wait around for her to get her shit together. The late Mr. Chou's main source of product came from the Cartel. They understood the power struggle that was going on in New Orleans between the Vietnamese BTK and Haitian Hitman Clique, but they wanted their money. Allison fought with the idea of starting back up but fear of coming across any of the men that killed her father scared her the most. Levi knew he had to step up and get a grip of the situation because he didn't want any added problems coming from across the border.

Olivia was heading out to go shopping with Darlene and little Diamond at the mall when she came across an unexpecting site panhandling for change at the red light. At first, she didn't recognize the person standing at the corner until Darlene pointed her out,

"Mama that look just like Jazzy that use to stay with us."

"Nah, dat ain't her."

"Look mama, dats her."

Olivia couldn't believe her eyes but the high and mighty wanna be boss queen had fell off her throne. Thoughts of jumping out of the car and giving Jazzy the beat down of the century ran through Olivia's mind but she held her composure. The sight of the person that betrayed her family standing at the corner, in dingy tattered clothes, bruised skin and begging for change was what she needed to see. Jazzy had completed her usefulness for what Papa Sha needed from her and like so many others he threw her to the wolves. She found herself less than what she had ever been after the Haitian boss man had men after men run through her, leaving nothing left. The life of a street walker had taken its toll on her and the visual evidence was proof that Jazzy lost the battle as she stretched out aged hands for scraps. Olivia wanted to feel sorry for her but couldn't knowing what she had done to her family and made sure to make eye contact with her as she drove pass her standing at the corner. At the time Darlene was too young to understand all the things that were going on with her mother and the women that stayed with them. She thought they were her aunties because that's what her parents told her but as she got older truths began to come out to Darlene. She never really said anything to Olivia about her thoughts on the subject, but Darlene had her own judgments on her mother's former lifestyle. Looking back at the caliber of people her parents had dealings with when she was younger played a part in how Darlene conducted herself with her own child. Strict and stern with no slack on discipline was the direction she took with Diamond. As the loving grandmother, Olivia played her part in spoiling the terrible two-year-old, but Darlene seen it as hindering her disciplinarian type tactics and that brought on conflicts. The three of them were in the mall when the little toddler cried for a stuffed animal she seen in one of the stores and Darlene with her lips tightened scolded Diamond for her actions. Olivia stepped in,

"C'mon nah, she been good all day. Let her have the plushy."

"I'm not rewarding her fa something she suppose to do."

"Maybe if I rewarded you, you wouldn't be so damn mean."

"Maybe if you was a little mean, ya son wouldn't a went to jail as a teen."

After saying it, Darlene realized she had gone too far but the damage was done as she watched her mother just walk away from her. She tried to keep up with her in the mall but trying to manage that with a 2-year-old was futile and she lost her in the crowd of people. Darlene continued looking for different clothes for herself and her daughter while calling her mother's cell, but all her calls found a voicemail message. She got a text from Levi asking if she or Diamond needed anything but like always the message was ignored. Even after two years had pass Darlene still didn't want to have any associations with her brother. She had finally caught up with her mother standing outside of the mall at the front entrance where her car was parked. Olivia's head was down concentrating on a text message she just received when she looked up at her daughter,

"You ready?"

"Damn mama, you just leave us in there and don't say a word? Shit, I thought you left us fa real."

"First off, watch how you talkin to me. We ain't equal. I bat da piss outcha. No matter how grown you think you are, I'm still ya mama."

"I'm sorry but mama you just left us."

"I had to walk away from yo ass before I cuss you out."

"Why cause I was speakin da truth?"

"What truth? That yo ass spoiled rotten, you and yo brother? That you truly don't understand da shit I've been through to provide for y'all. To make show I keep a roof ova ya head. See da thing you don't realize is yes you seen some wild shit growin up but that's because that's da shit I allowed you to see. You never seen both of ya parents walkin da streets to make sure y'all had. You neva seen yo daddy sitting outside a hotel nervous as shit hoping he don't have to hurt nobody cause his wife in a room turnin tricks. You don't know what it's like to have to patiently wait for your husband to come home safe because he out with some grimy ass niggas dat would kill him just cause. So don't tell me I ain't do enough or did too little when it came to my muthafuckin kids cause muthafucka I literally bent ova backwards with a dick in my ass to make sho you neva went without. So, excuse my French but FUCK YOU Darlene!"

After her vent Olivia held her little granddaughter's pudgy fat fingers and walked her to her car parked in the parking lot as Darlene stood there without a reply on her lips. The sacrifices of her mother were laid out in front of her like a pamphlet and the disregard she held at first faded away. Darlene just followed her mother to the car, remorseful for how she acted earlier and knew the sacrifices her mother had done she would do for her own daughter if she had to.

Papa Sha had gained more control over what was coming in and out of the city without the influence of the Vietnamese, so he set his eyes on a more legal venture with Dante's shop. A quick visit to the business without his goons still had the owner of the CBD Wellness Clinic on edge but the Haitian played it cool. He showed interest in the products Dante had to offer but at the same time offered his service also. Papa Sha wanted desperately to get his hands in the cookie jar, but the Jamaican wasn't budging on his decision not to mix company with him,

"No offense but there's no need for you. My shop stays legal and you tend to change that whereva you go."

"You may want to reconsider brove. Dat gyal can't keep you."

"She and Jah has kept me this far. Me not change me mind on the subject. Respect."

"Respect."

Dante watched as Papa Sha walked out of the store and knew it won't be the last time he visits. He heard rumors how the Haitians took out one of the top generals in the Vietnamese gang and feared his store was next. Thoughts of increasing security at the store became top priority but a call to Eve to discuss it put everything into to action as she used her influence with a few NOPD officers. Word got around fast that the CBD shop had sporadic visits by law enforcement watching over the store and Papa Sha knew he had to come up with a plan. Eve started putting pieces together of her own plan as she reached out to Levi to go over some strategies. Dante didn't know Levi but anyone that wasn't a friend of Papa Sha was a friend of his.

Levi and Allison were at her main store when he got the call from Eve about confronting Papa Sha before he made a move. The young Asian princess didn't want anything to do with the plan Levi was hashing out and he understood her reasons. Still a little shellshocked over how her family members met their end was evident as Levi would catch Allison just gazing off at the front door. It was as if she was looking for Justin to come in clowning and joking like he always did when he came through. Levi knew the pain of losing an older brother and hid it from everyone close to him, but Allison needed that connection so that she knew it would get better. He asked one of the cashiers to watch the store while he had a heart to heart with Allie. He closed them both off to the noise of the store in one of the storage closets in the back and sat Allison down on a pallet of soft drinks. The look of despair was written all over her face as Levi told her,

"Please believe me when I tell you I completely understand where you are right now. I was 7 years old when my brother was killed in a drive-by. I was just 9 when my father was killed in prison. I know the pain you feelin right now. All you wanna do is scream out. Thoughts that everything coulda ended different if you were there."

"It's my fault they're dead. If I had my shit together I wouldn't have got conned trusting a muthafucka in the beginning."

"Don't do dat. Don't blame yaself for what somebody else did."

"How can I not blame myself? They were trying to fix my shit. My fuck up and they all paid for it. Whateva you need to get rid of that Caribbean asshole please ask me. My money is yo money right now."

Levi could see the fury in her eyes when she told him that and that she meant every word of it. As they went to leave out of the storage room Allison embraced him tightly as a thank you for being there for her. She told him she had an appointment to make and that she wanted him to be there with her for it. Thinking it was just a normal meet up with a client Levi agreed thinking she just needed him as the muscle for the job. They left the store and Allison headed to the French Quarter area, Levi thought she was going home for something, but she went pass her apartments. She parked in front of an old-style Creole Townhouse on Decatur Street that had a neon sign in the large pane window that read tattoo. Levi never been to the place before but heard stories from Justin about where he got his first tattoo with his dad. The shop had a tattoo artist there that specialized in authentic Asian art and most of the Vietnamese community went to them when they wanted something special done. Allison walked in with her escort at her side and Levi was surprised to see a middle aged African American woman sitting in the shop. The two women greeted each other in a Vietnamese dialect and the tattoo artist smiled at Levi's stunned expression. Allison was looking over a sketch that was made just for her as the artist turned to Levi,

"You okay over there? You look like you never seen a black person speak another language before."

"Nah, it's not dat. I just neva heard a black person speak Vietnamese before."

"Baby when you live in a country as long as I did, you betta learn the language. Hi, I'm Dèsirèe."

"Levi."

Dèsirèe offered Levi some green tea as she prepped her equipment to start Allison's tatt. Levi sat quiet as he looked over all the décor of the room that was covered in all sorts of artifacts from around the world. He could tell just from pictures and decorations on the walls that the tattoo artist had traveled numerous countries, but one set of items caught his eyes. Dèsirèe had a photo of her sitting in the Sahara with two members of a lion pride, but the African mask around the picture was what fascinated him. While Allison was taking off her top and unhooking her bra, Levi was full of questions about Dèsirèe's voyage to the Motherland. He asked about the hand carved mask and Dèsirèe was more than glad to answer all of his questions,

"Baby these masks embrace our culture, our heritage, the essence of who we are as a people. You put a mask in your home, facing the entrance and it wards off any evil coming in. We need every bit of assurance in these times and days."

Levi was amazed at all the information he received from the artist, things he never learned in school and welcomed it all. He calmly watched as Dèsirèe started working on Allison's tattoo that was being done on her side going up her ribcage. As the buzz of the tattoo gun filled the room the artist jokingly asked if Levi wanted to get an art piece done also. He didn't come to get one but thoughts of it ran through his mind as he watched the image come to life on Allison's skin.

Eve was getting ready to head out to meet up with a client for a private show when Dante surprised her at her door with a bouquet of tropical flowers. He always did little things that just made her smile from time to time and this gesture was a sure smiling moment. Eve put her things down as she let Dante come in,

"I'm sorry. Were you heading out love?"

"I had an appointment to make but I got time. I love the flowers."

"They are mere ascents to your beauty."

"Stop it. You be doin too much. What brought you here?"

Dante laughed as Eve wanted to get straight to the point as she always did but he did come over with a purpose. He heard news that people overseas had been getting really sick with a contagious virus going around and reports been saying a few incidents were in the states. Eve heard the same thing but paid it no mind as she figured it would die down like everything else. They sat there in a tense conversation discussing the what ifs of what could happen and the idea kind of scared Dante as a businessman. He was telling Eve about entire cities that shutdown behind the pandemic they were experiencing and told her they may be next in line. Eve was confident that it wouldn't get that far because she felt United States was better equipped than Eastern countries. She tried her best to convince him that everything would be alright,

"C'mon nah, you talkin bout third world countries. Da government ain't gone let it get dat bad. Wha cha need to be stressin bout is Mardi Gras comin up. You know how busy we gone be?"

"Yea. We may need to hire help."

Dante instantly switched to business mode and they began talking strategies for the upcoming celebratory season. Eve was all game for the conversation but realized she was late for her appointment. She grabbed her things as she escorted Dante to the door to leave and the savvy Jamaican gentleman took her bags from her as he walked to her car. Eve adored the chivalry in him, always holding a door for her or reaching out his hand as she steps down from an elevated point. The debonair in him was always an instant attraction but Eve tried to keep business and pleasure separate. She jokingly stated to Dante as he watched her get in the car that he better stop spoiling her or she'll get too use to it. He smiled as his response was that he couldn't help but to spoil her because it was his pleasure. At that moment she wanted to cancel her previous engagement and give Dante all of her but instead drove away. Watching him through her rearview mirror watching her drive away was like a connection she never had with a man. Most men were business opportunities to her, a way to get paid and get as much out of them as possible. Mainly because of the lifestyle she lived, the majority of men she dealt with wanted one thing from her and Eve made sure she was paid extremely well for her service. Eve laughed at dancers settling for 200 dollars for private shows knowing they would end up on their backs with a wet ass. Her going rate just for her to show up at a client's door was nothing less than a grand and the price went up for everything extra. Eve was taught by the best in the field and she excepted nothing less from the men she dealt with. As she parked in the valet section of the Royal Sonesta, Eve mentally prepared herself for the freaky corporate American businessman upstairs waiting on her. He was a blue-eyed prince to a construction company his father owned in New Orleans, but the prince was infatuated about being pissed on. Eve had been drinking cranberry juice along with a lot of water all morning for this one session and she was ready to bust. After getting off the elevator, she walked down the hallway in her sexy sundress to his executive suite, pushed open his door and pushed him to the floor. He laid there with nothing but pure anticipation on his face as she stood over him, hiked her dress up over her hips and squatted right over his chest. The release was an ultimate satisfaction for her, and the blue-eyed prince climaxed in his pants as the warm liquids soaked his custom Dolce & Gabbana shirt. Eve looked down at him as he sat up to lick the drippings from her pussy,

"Yeah white boy, clean it up. You betta eat it right too."

After dropping her daughter and granddaughter off at home, Olivia met up with her business partner Sam for a nice late lunch. Sam wanted to talk to her about a shipment of Codeine she heard was coming in from overseas and was wondering if The Cajun could intercept it for them. Olivia was game to making the extra money but knew they had to be careful, any word getting back to Papa Sha that they were on the come up would have a bad ending for them. Sam couldn't stand the Haitian, so she knew the importance of it all. The buzz of the city preparing for Mardi Gras kept Sam's head on a swivel looking at all that was going on,

"I can't see how you live in the city, it's too much for me. Slidell is so quiet and chill, y'all do da most."

"I can't see myself anywhere else, this is home. You know you like it outchere, stop frontin. Don't have me drag you to the French Quarters off of Bourbon Street."

"Please don't, I'm not that kind of gay where I need to be seen all the time. Bright colors, rainbows everywhere. I just like to chill and do me or you whichever one comes first."

"Sam stop playin with me."

"You wouldn't want me to stop if I start."

"Stop it!"

The two friends laughed as they enjoyed the rest of their meal together and went over plans to get their hands on the shipment of syrup coming in. Olivia was the craftsman of the plan while Sam was the muscle and they put it all together on a napkin at the table. It was as if she was writing out football plays how Olivia sketched out routes and different points to meet up with each other. Sam was enjoying the laid-back atmosphere and ordered some tequila shots from the bar. Before they knew it, they were three shots in and the two were ordering more drinks to go along with the enjoyable time they were having with one another. Like any other New Orleans' bar & grill making friends was plentiful and this one was no different when a gentleman bought the ladies a round of drinks. Olivia thought it was cute and Sam wanted to have some fun with him. Sam wasn't the average tattooed mannish butch but actually a very attractive female that just so happen to look good in men clothing with a tapered short top haircut. She gestured for the guy to come over to join them and he was more than willing. Olivia giggled to herself as the guy instantly showed attraction to Sam's sky-blue eyes and her brightly colored sleeve tattoo on her arm. She questioned him,

"You here by yoself."

"Most of da time it starts like dat but I will make a friend anywhere, ya heard me."

"You from round here?"

"Yeah, I actually got a spot round da corner. My bad, my name Travis."

"I'm Olivia."

"I'm Sam, short for Samantha. You really live in da Quarters? Stop playin."

The young guy started spewing everything about himself, from growing up with a strict rich judge for a father, living in Greece for a year and moving back home to be an abstract artist. Olivia sat there listening to him talk about how he lives in a loft that his father owns and was amazed how other people lived. How a person could be so privileged without a care in the world and walk away from it to follow a dream. It wasn't that she was jealous at all but just baffled at his logic. Travis bought another round of drinks for them all and Sam had to tell him to slow down,

"Keep feeding me these drinks and you gone start looking real attractive to me."

"Shid, say less. I'm trying to be yo Will and you my Jada."

"Lil boy, you not ready."

"Ain't nothin little on me but my pinky toe."

The trio laughed and enjoyed themselves as the drinks flowed through the night. Olivia was ready to call it when Travis invited them both back to his house. Sam's belly was full of mixed drinks and was feeling good, so she accepted the invite, but Olivia didn't want her to go alone.

Levi watched as Allison stood in the mirror and admired the amazing artistry Dèsirèe created on her. The tattoo was of an Asian style dragon that started at her hip, went up her side to her ribcage and ended going up the middle of her chest between her breasts. The color variations were astonishing with bright greens, reds, yellows and glossy blacks. Levi could tell Allison was absolutely pleased with the final finish of the tattoo as Dèsirèe rubbed ointment on it and the birthdates of the men she loss shined in the tattoo she just received. Seeing the dates on her saddened him too when Dèsirèe asked Levi a question,

"So, you next? What can I create for you?"

"Oh I neva had a tattoo done and dat shit look like it hurt like a muthafucka."

"I ain't gone lie to you. Yeah, it's gone hurt but you will love the pain afterwards."

"C'mon Levi, get one, it's my treat. You sat here and watched me get my first tatt ever. I wanna be there for yours."

Levi thought about it and the one thing he knew he wanted on him forever was the one thing he couldn't be close to. He wrote out his daughter's name on a sheet of paper and handed it to Dèsirèe as he sat down in the tattoo chair. The artist asked him where he would like for the tatt to be and the nervous Levi took off his shirt and gestured for it to go across his abdomen, right above his navel. While Dèsirèe sketched out her next creation on a sheet of paper, Levi thought about his daughter. All the things going on in his life he barely had time to attempt to spend time with her, but he always made sure to send money through Kareem.

Ronnisha was the same age as his niece Diamond and he knew if she was anything like her cousin the bubbly Ronnisha was a handful. After having her second child, Shalay strayed away from the "bad boy" persona and that axed Levi from the category of men she was interested in. She wanted better for herself as much as for her kids and Shalay knew in her heart that Levi wouldn't change. He wanted to but pressures were too great to step away from the game just yet and Levi accepted the distance from his own child. Not that he didn't care but that he truly did, and he also wanted more for her than he could offer. Dèsirèe had finished her sketch and pressed the paper onto Levi's skin, leaving an imprint of Ronnisha's name on him. She also added baby footsteps at the end of her name, Levi fell in love with it and was ready for her to start on his first tattoo. The buzz of the machine startled him but what tensed up every muscle in his body was that first initial stick of the needle breaking skin. Levi's eyes widened as he looked over at a smiling Allison who reached out her hand for support and he gracefully accepted it. Dèsirèe went across his skin with the poking needles, drawing blood and bringing on a pain Levi wasn't ready for, but he welcomed the pain knowing what the outcome would be. Allison took his mind off of the tattoo gun poking at his skin when she placed his hand under her shirt and palmed her breast with his warm hand. He could feel her nipple harden in his hand and she stated,

"You can rub the other one after you finish with yo tatt. Deal?"

Levi laughed through the pain at her and reassured her that he will remind her of her promise when the tattoo is done. The artist was almost done and was finishing up the final touches as Levi had become numb to the needle scraping across him. She finished off the tattoo with some clear ointment and told Levi to go check out the artwork he had just received. The image literally brought tears to his eyes after seeing his daughter's name scripted so beautifully across his stomach. Before the sentimental father could enjoy the image more, he got a call from Eve wanting to discuss a plan to the previous conversation they had about Papa Sha. All the emotional characteristics left Levi for the moment and he was in strategy mode as he and Eve talked about eliminating a cancer that has plagued so many people in New Orleans. Levi walked away so that he could have his conversation in private and Dèsirèe could sense something wasn't right. She pulled Allison to the side,

"Baby girl, I'm a need you to be careful with that one."

"Ms. D, he's fine. He just have to take care of so many people in his family."

"Baby listen to me. That boy right there got a lot of demons in him and that baby is having the fight of his life, inside. He wants to be normal and fine, but he can't right now. He reminds me so much of your father, bless da dead, he really do. Just be careful, okay."

Allison paid for the tattoos and thanked Ms. Dèsirèe for everything while she thought about what the middle-aged tattoo artist told her as she walked up to Levi still submerged in his conversation. She wanted revenge on the Haitians, but the young woman was still uneasy because she was terrified that she would end up losing Levi the same way she loss her family.

Travis along with his two lovely companions walked up Iberville Street laughing and joking the whole way enjoying each other's company. He walked up to an old-style Creole townhouse with a bright red door, snow white arched frame and brownish brick exterior. The ladies were simply astounded at the fact that a young man lived there on his own in the heart of the French Quarters. He walked them in and gave them a tour of the place as he pointed out the artistic creations of ironwork in the middle of his living room. The house was something a person would only see on a home design TV show. Sam looked over at Travis and complimented him on his talent but then told him to get undressed. Olivia and Travis both had the same perplexed expression on their faces after hearing her statement, but Sam repeated herself again as she walked up to the male host. Travis stuttered his words,

"Whoa whoa whoa. Wha cha mean?"

"You said da only thing small on you is ya pinky toe. I'm tryin to see somethin."

Sam reached down at Travis' crotch and attempted to grab a handful of meat but to her surprise found out the young man wasn't lying. Her eyes told it all as she turned to look at Olivia, who was so confused at this point because she thought Sam was strictly into women. She watched as her friend reached into the stunned man's jeans and pulled out a flesh toned python that rested on the top of his belt buckle. Sam pulled his jeans down to the floor and his dick bumped her in the face as she looked up at him. Still on her knees, Sam began to unbutton her shirt exposing her full D-cup sized breast nestled firmly in a black silk bra. The massive meat swelled in excitement as Travis watched Sam lay on the floor to undo the tight jeans she had on. He got down on the floor and helped her finish removing them and kissed her thick vanilla cream-colored thighs on his way up to her black silk panties. The woman laying on the floor with Travis was not the hardened tattooed female Olivia had gotten to know but instead a sensual sexy being that at the moment was turning her on. Olivia stood there watching in awe as the young artist explored Sam's body with his lips and tongue, licking every inch of her. She didn't know if she was turned on by how sexy Sam looked unclothed or how attractive the couple looked engaged with each other on the floor in front of her. The area between Olivia's thighs moistened when she seen Travis slide Sam's undies off and buried his face into her freshly shaven mound. Her moans of pleasure heightened Olivia's intrigue to what was going on in front of her and it encouraged Travis' oral performance more. He wrapped his lips around Sam's clit and his tongue twirled viciously, sending her into spasmic jerks. Sam was simply amazed at how well he knew the female anatomy and how to get it to an orgasmic climax so quickly. It was his turn to enjoy Sam's pleasure pocket as he turned her over onto her knees and caressed her soaked pussy with the head of his dick. Sam looked up at Olivia still standing at the door staring at the sexual encounter when she reached out for Olivia to join them. Hesitant at first, she slowly stepped forward as she watched Travis kiss Sam's back and his engorged manhood pressed up against her moistened lips. Travis watched as Sam undid Olivia's jeans and slid off her panties right along with them. The sight of Olivia's plump waxed pussy excited them both as Sam stated,

"Oh I'm definitely eating this muthafucka, c'mere."

"I'm next after you cause that shit looks delicious."

"I'm a need you to focus and slide dat big muthafucka in, I got this."

Olivia laid down in front of Sam like she was a full course meal, and the erotic stud did exactly that as she engulfed herself into Olivia's goodness. Olivia's moans and gasps aroused Travis so that he bit Sam on the ass in pleasure, but it was his time to feel pleasure too. He placed the head of his enlarged phallus at her entrance and Olivia could tell as soon as he entered because Sam gasped in all the air from the room. She could feel every swollen vein, muscle and inch of him as it slid deeper and deeper inside of her. It felt as if he was pressing against her stomach, and he still had dick left to put in. His strokes were immense, every pound brought on a new pleasurable feeling and Sam didn't want him to stop but she returned the favor with every lick on Olivia's clit. Olivia had had her share of females going down on her, but Sam took it to a whole new level and brought about the one thing only one man could ever get out of her. The more Sam worked her tongue on Olivia's clit the more pressure Travis applied to the juicy puss wrapped around his Johnson. Olivia couldn't hold back any longer and her orgasm exploded in Sam's mouth in a bursting squirt. She almost drowned from the blast but the 12 inches of exaggerated dick stretching out her pussy kept her on task. Travis pulled his meat from Sam and gestured for Olivia to come stand in her place, the two women happily switched positions. Sam laid down in front of Olivia and the oral escapade began as her tongue attacked her clit. Travis admired the sight for a moment but then pushed his way deep inside of Olivia, her reaction to the massive appendage had her reaching back in order to brace herself for the rest of the dick coming. Olivia wasn't as talented at eating pussy as Sam, but it was extremely pleasing to her. Her juices dripped to the floor as Travis thrusted deeper inside and Sam whispered,

"Dat muthafucka filling yo pussy up huh? Damn this shit feel good."

 Travis could feel himself get closer to busting and pulled out of Olivia, but he didn't stop the show as he began to eat her ass out. His tongue found its way deep into Olivia's ass and she couldn't do anything but hold on. She flopped to the floor and Travis turned her over on her back with her legs open wide so that he could finish the job. While he was occupied tossing salad with two fingers sliding in Olivia's wet box, Sam took the opportunity to give him some very desirable head. She attempted to go deep on the mass, but it gagged her as soon as it filled the back of her throat. Sam stroked the enlarge meat stick, sucking on his head as spit dripped down his shaft from her lips. The spit rolled down his shaft, onto his balls and rested in the crack of his ass. Still giving him head while he let Olivia cum in his mouth for her second orgasm, Sam played with Travis' ass. Olivia flipped around and the two were in a 69 position, so she could help Sam suck the large member. He was so enthralled into the juicy pussy in front of him, Travis didn't notice Sam pushing two of her fingers into his ass until the feeling was too intense. Olivia was balls deep in giving the best head he had ever felt and Sam was literally finger fucking his ass while spitting on her fingers for lubrication. The women had full control of him when Sam held his legs up so that she could get deep in while her fingers slid in and out. Olivia sucked and stroked his dick while he had his way with her throbbing juicy clit but then the young artist let out a deep moan of pleasure. Sam didn't stop fingering him, but Olivia pulled her mouth from around his manhood and like lava from a volcano his thick white cream erupted from his penis. Travis laid there exhausted as the two women stroked out the last ounces of his cum and they both took turns giving his head one last suck.

"I was not expecting this when I bought you two drinks."

"Me neither."

Eve was on her way home when she called Levi to tell him about the encounter Dante had with Papa Sha and went over what they should do to take apart the Haitians. She came up with a plan to get Sha alone with her at a hotel and Levi eliminate him there. Levi was completely on board with getting rid of the Haitian gang leader but didn't want to have his stepmother involved with the deadly arrangement. He knew if he steps to Papa Sha the implications need to be him and him only because the backlash from it would be epic. Levi didn't want anyone he had strong feelings for getting caught up in his vendetta. From the age of a young teenager, Levi been wanting to touch Papa Sha in a way that wasn't anywhere close to being pleasant and the time had come. He let Eve know he would take care of the situation and that he didn't want her anywhere close to him or his people,

"Mama, this shit gone get ugly real fast. I don't want you, my mama, Dee or Allison nowhere near them understood?"

"Allison? The Chinese girl from the corna-sto? I thought dat was Mook ole girl. Nigga y'all sharing females nah. You nasty."

"Mama, you gettin way off subject. And her and Mook been split."

"But c'mon now, that's yo homeboy ex. Ain't chu got a code or something? You shouldn't want to mess with ya homeboy's ex and she shouldn't want to mess with her ex's friend."

"It's not like that. We all good trust me."

Levi knew the code Eve was referring to and didn't want to cross it. The incident happened that day and they moved on from it. Even though he and Mook hadn't talk in a while, he even went to him personally about it, concerned his friend would look at him different. To his surprise, the now family man that Mook had become gave Levi his blessings in any future he had with Allison. The two never really made it official that they are a couple to anyone or even themselves, but they did everything a loving couple would do. The fact that Levi included her in the women he desired to protect proved that Allison was more than just a fuck buddy. As he stood outside of the tattoo studio, he ended the call with Eve when he noticed the concerned face of Allison waiting for him,

"Allie, what's wrong? You okay?"

"Nothing babe. You ready?"

"Hell yeah. You said I get to touch da other titty when I finish my tatt."

"Boy you stupid, c'mon."

"So you gone lemme touch da titty?"

Allison laughed at him joking around but in the back of her mind still wondered if Ms. Dèsirèe's words had any merit to them. She didn't want to jump to conclusions because of the type of man he is or was. Besides Allison knew she wasn't an angel herself. Taking over the Chou family business took more than book smarts on Allison's part and having a dark side was key to survival. She kept her thoughts to herself for the time being because she didn't want to hamper the joy of their relationship. They headed back to her place for the rest of the day and Levi was more than happy to do so because he kept joking about her promise to him,

"So, I'm a get to touch dem titties now."

Talks on the news got more and more intense about the virus Dante mentioned to Eve a week ago but it was all pushed to the back of everyone's mind as the Mardi Gras season had begun. The city of New Orleans was beaming with excitement with festivities brewing everywhere and Dante's CBD store was reveling in all the action. He's been in the city during the celebration but never as a businessman making sales and Eve's statement of how busy they would be was an understatement. Eve was in charge of inventory for the store and her constant orders for product to Jamaica had Dante worried he would have too much. To his surprise after just a few days of carnival goers stopping in his store for oils, gummies and pre-rolls, half of his inventory was sold. Eve just smiled at his comments when the store would fill up with people,

"Geezus, gyal! Where all deez people cum from? My lord."

"I told you we gone get busy. Now go grab a box of dem 100 count bag of gummies. These lil college kids over here wanna buy five of'em."

"Me just stocked up the shelf, Geezus."

Dante truly enjoyed how his business was taking off, but he didn't know it was going to skyrocket the way it did during carnival time. Patrons came back constantly to the store buying product, offering carnival beads to the employees and even young women flashing breasts to his Rastafarian brothers that stood guard in the store. It was truly nothing but a joyful moment for Dante and Eve but like a hurricane cloud from the distance darkness raised its ugly head. Dracko parked his dark blue Suburban in front and just sat there staring through the store's front window. Eve seen the vehicle out the corner of her eye and acknowledged

Dante's nudges to her shoulder with a nod when he seen the Haitian gang's lieutenant sitting outside. Aggravated that Dracko would run off customers with his bullish demeanor, Dante took it upon himself to step to the gang member. He took one of his big dreadlock guards as added protection as he walked out to the truck telling Dracko who was sitting in the passenger side that he had to move. The Haitian didn't even address the store owner as he continued to speak to him about moving from in front of his store. He instead turned up the radio to the suburban as he laughed at the driver whistling at women walking by. Dante got agitated at the disrespect and kicked the side of the vehicle but Dracko wasn't the one that responded to his actions. The tall slender driver stepped out of the SUV along with two passengers from the backseat and angrily stepped to Dante,

"Fuck wrong with you! Want my foot in yo ass!"

Before Dante could even reply to the slim giant, the Haitian member backhand slapped him with a thunderous blow that dropped him to one knee. Dante's guard instantly pulled a pistol from his waist and the gang members all drew down on the two Jamaicans standing in front of them while Dracko laughed at the site. The altercation had the crowd of parade goers along with customers of the shop scatter as they all ran for cover and Dante stood up from his assault. Tension was extremely high as the Caribbean counterparts had a standoff and the shop owner tried to defuse the situation. Still amused at how everything played out, Dracko stepped out of the Suburban and told the rest of his men to stand down. Dante's eyes showed an uneasiness as the Haitian gang's second in command leader stepped to him and Dracko just smiled,

"Pussy boi."

The sounds of police sirens could be heard in the distance, Dracko looked over Dante's shoulder as people still ran out of the store and he knew he had won the small battle. He got back in the SUV and they drove off as Dante watched the big vehicle disappear in the traffic. Angered at how the situation turned out, he turned to see the once packed shop completely empty and Dante walked in knocking over a display of his products. Eve wanted to comfort him because she seen he was upset but his level of outrage filled the room when he shouted for everyone to get out. As everyone was leaving, she could hear him furiously talking to himself in Jamaican patois, but Eve understood the tactics that were taken on the store. She knew Dracko did exactly what he came there to do and that is have the store lose out on money. She also knew if the Haitians were not stopped it would get worse for them even ending the same way the Chous did. Eve went sat in her car to gather herself trying to figure out a way to touch the Haitians the way they reached out and touched them. The statement was made and she wasn't going to let them have the last word.

Olivia was home anxious about the shipment of syrup coming in and her sidekick Sam with one of her female lovers was right there with her ready for some action. They were waiting for The Cajun to send the text letting them know the boat had docked so they could meet him at the port. Olivia was pacing with anticipation because she knew this would be a big lick for them if they pulled it off. Sam could see the anxiety of the job overwhelming her friend as she asked,

"Girl you need some weed? Or better yet how about some head to calm yo nerves. You dartin thru this house like you got ADHD."

"Shut up and no."

"You sure? A nice nut would relax you."

"Really Sam? Girl you stupid."

"Shid, I'm tryin' to help you out."

The joking around with Sam eased Olivia's mind a bit as she finally sat down. They changed the subject when Olivia whispered to Sam asking if she's been talking to their ménage à trois partner Travis. Sam found it amusing how secretive her friend was around the young female Sam had with her when she asked about the young stud. The manly female let Olivia know that all her partners knew that they aren't the only ones she has sexual encounters with and that sometimes she enjoys a man from time to time. In an earlier conversation, Sam told Olivia that she was bi-sexual but most of the time she dealt with women. Merely because she couldn't find a man that was comfortable enough with his manhood to deal with a woman with her aggressive mannish ways. The women giggled like two schoolgirls as they reminisced about their brush with the well-endowed Travis. Sam surprised Olivia when she told her that she went back for a second round and the youngster had her use a vibrator on him.

"I know you lyin'!"

"Nah, Mr. Big Dick like you to push shit up in his ass. He gets off on dat shit."

"You know you like dat shit too."

"Hell yeah! Plus he got a good stroke. Bring dat dick here boi."

"I can't, muthafucka felt like he was poking my stomach. Big dick ass."

"Shid, but he'll pull dat nut right outcha. Lemme stop talkin' bout him before I end up textin' him again. Muthafucka gone think I'm thirsty behind his ass."

They laughed as they all chilled at Olivia's house waiting on The Cajun to send the info they needed. Sam and her company were playing touchy feely while Olivia waited when there was a knock at the door. When Olivia opened it, there was Kareem with a medical mask on his face standing there looking for Levi because he had some urgent information about Olivia's granddaughter. The entire Daniels' household had come down with flu like symptoms except for him and Ronnisha. He wanted Levi to come get his daughter out the house before she ended up getting sick like everyone else. The concerned grandmother immediately started calling Levi's phone looking for him to answer but the cell just rang until the answering service picked up. Desperate to find her son Olivia called around to different people trying to get any idea where her son would be. She even tried asking Darlene but that was a dead end. Right when Kareem was about to leave, Olivia's phone began ringing,

"Ronald. Kareem over here and you need to go check on your daughter like now."

"I'm all da way Uptown, what's wrong."

"Boy, you askin too many damn questions. Get over there and take care of my grandchild."

Olivia hung up the phone with her son and told Kareem that Levi's on his way to the house. She asked Kareem how his mother was doing because she hadn't seen Delores Daniels for awhile and was concerned about the single mother. The description the teen gave her of his mother at the time was unsettling for Olivia, she heard news of people falling ill but no one close to her. Constant coughing, horrible headaches, full body aches, a fever and a whole host of other things. When he mentioned she couldn't smell or taste, Olivia knew it was the contagious virus that's been talked about all on the news. She asked Kareem if he had any of the symptoms his family members were having and he adamantly responded with an answer of no.

Levi fought through the Mardi Gras traffic trying to get to his daughter, not really knowing what was going on but knew he had to be there. He was at Allison's apartment when his mother called and immediately left after getting off the phone. Levi explained to Allie that he had a family emergency and she rushed him out the door before he could say anything else. Allison had some business to take care of at her stores and made her way there while Levi headed to see his daughter. Pushing through thick stop and go traffic was driving Levi nuts as he tried to figure out a way to get to Ronnisha faster. He tried texting and calling Shalay, but she didn't respond to any of it, so he called Kareem to find out what was wrong,

"What's good lil bro? What's going on at the crib?"

"Man look, everybody getting sick at da house, like everybody except for me and Nisha. She too little to be getting sick like they are and I was wondering if you can come get her."

"Man you know Shay not letting me take her out dat house. That's da last thing gone happen."

"She too weak to fight an argument."

"I'm a see. You still by my mama?"

"Yeah."

"Look have her meet me over there, I'm like ten minutes from there."

Levi rushed to get to his daughter but knew the only way Shalay would possibly let Ronnisha leave is if she's under his mother's care. All types of things were running through his mind as he drove up the street to the Daniels' home. He heard stories of people dying from the coronavirus and entire cities shutting down because of how fast it spreads. Levi was determined not to have his only child in those statistics, he knew it was time to change, if not for himself for her. His mother beat him to the house and the sight of his baby girl skipping around her grandmother's legs playing was all he needed to see. Olivia was standing on the porch talking to Shalay who looked like death had tugged at her soul. Shalay's eyes were swollen and bloodshot, her nose was fire red, her body looked weak, but she tried to hold a smile in front of her little one. Levi got out of his car and he could hear Shalay's hard raspy coughs as he made his way to the porch. When she looked up at him walking to the porch Shalay could see the worry on his face,

"Ronald, I'm fine. I just got a bad cold."

"Shay dat cough don't sound good one bit."

"I promise, I'm good."

To see that he actually cared about her well-being was a plus in her book but Shalay still didn't feel comfortable letting her only girl stay with her father. Levi pleaded with her to let Ronnisha stay at his mother's house and Olivia agreed that she will take care of the little one. Shalay reluctantly went along with the plan and Olivia happily helped her get clothes together for Ronnisha to stay a few days with her. Levi stood at the bottom of the steps just thinking about what he needed to do to be a better person for his beautiful daughter. The site of a joyous two-year-old just playing on the porch in her own little world while the rest of the world was in havoc was all Levi needed to see to know he had to change. Kareem came outside and Levi thanked him for getting in touch with them about Ronnisha. Just like what he was about to do he wanted the teen to do the same and step away from the lifestyle,

"Lil bro, you a real smart kid. Caught on to this shit quicker than I did but this shit got a short shelf life and I want more fa you. I can't let you work fa me no moe."

"Nigga what you talkin bout? We got this shit on lock round here, ya heard me. I can't walk away from deez bags I'm makin."

"Lil nigga this shit is chump change and yo life worth more than a couple of bags of loud. Just in case something happens to me, I need to know I have somebody I can trust to watch over my seed ova there. I wanna step away right now but I have a few things to finish. After dat, I'm done but I'm sorry to say it, you done right nah. Trust me when I say, I gotchu fam."

"Nigga, really? You gone just do it like dat?"

"Fareal, seeing Nisha and knowing she needs better put it all in perspective. I gotta do this, I got to."

It was like his current life was pulling at the life he wanted to have when a dark cloud covered the sun, the city turned grey and his cell began ringing with Allison on the other end. Levi could barely understand the words she was saying from all the crying she was doing but he understood that she needed him. Olivia walked out with two bags for Ronnisha when she seen her son getting off the phone,

"Mama I gotta run. I can't explain but I have to go."

"Ronald, this is your daughter. Come back to her."

Allison sat in the office of her store with the door locked, balling in tears, shaking in fear and her employees trying to get her to come out. Just moments earlier she was outside talking with one of her regular customers, an old lady from the neighborhood, who was just reminiscing about how good of a man Mr. Chou was to her. Even before her father's passing Allison loved to hear those feel-good stories about her father and the nice things he did for people. The elderly woman gave Allison a hug that simply felt like a grandmother's embrace before she went on her way but then anxiety hit when the young woman seen Dracko. The Haitian patron stepped out of the dark blue Suburban with three other gang members who were laughing speaking in their own tongue so that Allison couldn't understand what they were saying. Just from their gestures and acting out she knew exactly what they were saying as the tall slim driver pointed to the ground where her father took his last breath. Dracko stood outside lighting a thick blunt as his three colleagues walked in the store,

"Damn shame what happen heya. Old man had lot to live for. You da boss now, eh. You got lots to live for?"

"You need to leave."

"Cum cum now girl. Me just want to snack. Sha want to meal. Don't make us take it."

Dracko blew a big puff of smoke in Allison's face and before it cleared from her eyes, he was back in the SUV smiling. The store owner nervously stared through the windshield at the gangster and fear took over her entire body as her hands began to shake. She wanted to scream, shout at him, curse him and all of his family but Allison stood there frozen to the concrete. It was as if she couldn't move, stuck like a statue in fear but the sound of the store's door swinging open with the three Haitians walking pass her made her jump. Allison ran inside and went straight to her office as she could hear the Gangsters laughing behind her. She sat on the floor of her office with her back to the door, refusing to open it for anyone until she heard Levi's voice,

"C'mon Allie, open up. It's just me."

It was like her protective security blanket had just arrived and as she opened the door a relief fell over her for the moment when she first laid eyes on Levi's face. He walked her in the office and sat her down at the desk. Allison explained to Levi what she was trying to say over the phone and he could tell she was still shaken up from how her hands were trembling. No one was safe while Papa Sha and Dracko tried to make their mark on the city. Frustration bombarded Levi because he wanted to turn his back on what he felt she wanted him to do,

"Baby, you and me both know firsthand how dangerous dey could be. Why not step away from it?"

"Step away? Step away from what? This is my muthafuckin' birth right! My father, my brother and my uncle died for what they fought to build! I'm not givin' up shit to these banana tree climbing muthafuckas! If I gotta die in da exact same spot my family did, so be it."

"Say less. I'm a need some equipment and a throw away car."

Tears were rolling down her face when Allison gave him keys to one of her storage lockers. Levi left with one thing on his mind, getting back home to see his daughter's beautiful smile.

Olivia got back home with the energetic Ronnisha and called Darlene to come over with Diamond for a play date. Levi's sister had never seen the innocent little angel since she was born because she didn't want anything to do with anyone involved with her brother. Olivia talked her daughter into coming over, explaining to her that the child has nothing to do with what her and Levi had going on. Darlene agreed as she headed over to meet this bubbly child her mother can't stop talking about. While she waited for her daughter to arrive, Olivia talked matters over with Sam about the pickup that was supposed to happen that night over a text. Sam knew her partner had a family emergency to take care of and went without her to go meet The Cajun at the docks. She let Olivia know that everything was running smooth and that The Cajun had already grabbed what he could from the shipment. They all knew this was going to be a big score for them and would set them up right if everything goes to plan. Nerves got to Olivia cause in the back of her mind she always thought something bad would happen when she would take a step forward to being a boss. Sam kept removing all doubt from Olivia's mind that it was going to work out, but Olivia had her reasons until a text came through,

"Bitch da eagle has landed. I'm a see u tomorrow. We got some work to do cause this a lot of shit."

The smile Olivia released was like a weight falling from her shoulders. A knock at the door alerted Debo to stand guard but it was just Darlene ready to meet her niece. The two toddlers had never seen each other before but instantly became friends as Darlene and her mother sat watching them play together. Olivia sat there pleased that her daughter came over and just enjoyed the sounds of happiness in her home again, something she didn't realize she missed. Darlene started asking her mother if she heard the news about what the city was planning to do. She heard on the news before she left her house that the states were planning to put a stay-at-home order in place because too many people were contacting the Coronavirus in Louisiana. Olivia heard rumors but didn't believe it was true until Darlene turned on the news and the reporter confirmed,

"The President is getting more information from the CDC, but the Stay-At-Home Order looks eminent. The Governor and the Mayor has already confirmed that they will be putting things in place to start the order. Only first responders and essential staff are allowed out after curfew."

"Dafuck."

Olivia couldn't believe what she was hearing, it wasn't that she was worried about the virus and its dangers but that she wouldn't be able to handle her business with Sam. She shook her head and giggled to herself as she figured her earlier fears came back to haunt her.

The streets of New Orleans were vacant after the stay-at-home order was enforced but in Big Easy fashion residents broke the rules on large gatherings. Neighborhood block parties, impromptu second line events and even curfew breakers kept NOPD busy with citations the mayor wanted for every violator. The city was virtually a ghost town and for some residents the calm along with the silence was nerve wrecking but for Levi, it gave him time to calculate. After the encounter Allison had in front of her store with Dracko and the incident that happened at Dante's shop, Levi knew he had to touch them before they got any cockier. When he went to the storage locker Allison told him about. It was like a scene from the Matrix movie with the amount of guns on the walls. Levi grabbed an arsenal of supplies. He went back to his talents of his teenage years and boosted a car from a garage downtown to use while he hunts for Papa Sha. Levi knew the thug wasn't going to let government officials tell him what to do so he knew the Haitians would be out and about through the city. He didn't want to get Eve involved in his plan but when she filled him in on the Haitians whereabouts, she became his eyes. The gentlemen's club she was working at was having their last hoorah before the city shut them down for good and the place was packed with people. Eve kept an eye on Papa Sha, Dracko and their entourage as they flaunted their riches throughout the club. The Haitians were in full turn up mode as they bought up bottles, lap dances and Papa Sha wanted to take half of the girls back to his place. Eve could see the group looking around to leave as Dracko gathered his crew up and Papa Sha smiling with two armfuls of dancers following him to the stretched Hummer waiting out front. The club started to empty out when Levi got a text from Eve,

"They comin out."

"There go my bitch."

Levi was waiting across the street watching the Haitians get in their vehicles and his main target was Sha, but when he seen a carload of dancers jump in the Hum-V with him it changed everything for Levi. He wanted to slaughter the leader where he stood but he didn't want to have innocent people in the crossfire. He then focused all his energy on Dracko and his crew that were getting in the dark blue Suburban parked behind Sha's Hum-V. Levi was stalking his prey like a Great White and he could smell the blood in the water. The vehicles pulled away from in front of the strip club, making their way down Canal Street and then turned on Claiborne Ave as they headed towards the 7th ward. Dracko's SUV stayed behind Papa Sha's limo as they drove up the street, Levi followed them but kept his distance because he didn't want Dracko to notice him. He started swerving his car from side to side like he was drunk as he sped pass the Haitians and then got in front of them, separating them from the stretched Hummer. Dracko and his three-man crew laughed as they watched the "drunk driver" go from lane to lane in front of them. Levi knew he had their attention when they began flashing their high beams at him, speeding up to his bumper. The traffic light ahead of them gave the hunter the perfect opportunity when it changed yellow and then red. Levi slammed on brakes sliding to a halt in front the Suburban, making them stop suddenly also, as he watched the limo drive off. With an all-black .44 magnum resting on his lap, he stood by as he looked through the rearview mirror. Levi pulled a black ski mask over his face and waited for his chance to bring a fear to the Haitians they never experienced before. His heart raced as time seemed to stop, he laid his head back on the headrest pretending to be sleep and could hear the thumps from his heart. The light changed green, but Levi kept his foot on the brake and after a few seconds the big auto behind him began blaring its horn, he stayed still. The big SUV blew its horn one more time but the car in front of them didn't move and then the driver got out. Levi could see in his side mirror a tall slim shadow walking towards him, he gripped the handle of the semi-automatic he had and prepared to start his own personal war. The driver side window was already down when the tall Haitian slammed his hand on the top of the car trying to startle its driver awake. As soon as the tall Haitian stood in front of Levi two bright flashes lit up the interior of the vehicle and the first victim of the onslaught was claimed. Before the tall driver could even hit the ground, Levi grabbed the AR15 that was sitting on the passenger side and got out to finish the job he was there for. With tactical precision, he stared down the sights of the rifle and the only thing Dracko seen was the green dot focused on his chest. The automatic rifle began releasing its wrath from the hundred round drum that was feeding it and the hollow points ripped through the windshield hitting its targets. Levi started walking toward the vehicle in SWAT team fashion as he picked out points to attack as his bullets tore through the interior of the SUV. He watched as the lead projectiles disappeared into the bodies seated in the vehicle and every window shattered from the firearm's power. Levi fired until he expended every round and then turned to walk back to his car pleased with his work but then he heard movement. He turned to find Dracko struggling to get out of the bullet riddled Suburban, blood pouring from the Haitian falling to the ground. Levi pulled the midnight colored .44 from his waist, walked up to the bullet battered gangster who was fighting to stand. He could see the lieutenant of the Haitian gang was defeated but he didn't want to take any chances. Levi pressed the muzzle of his gun to Dracko's temple and opened his skull to the moon light as he pulled the trigger.

YEAR 2021-2022

A year had passed since New Orleans fell silent for almost a year straight because of the Coronavirus outbreak. The contagious virus that affected the Daniels' household and so many others had taken over the city for a while. Grocery store shelves had the bare minimum, most businesses were shut down or closed and a lot of people were afraid of getting sick. Right along with the virus outbreak, the nation started to finally open its eyes to an ongoing problem that has plagued people of color for so long. Systematic racism started showing its face in social media videos along with on the news and people were fed up to the point of riots, protest and even boycotts. The sun had begun to shine back on the city with virus cases dropping and residents of the city returning back to a somewhat normal life. Levi went into hiding after his assault on Papa Sha's right hand man. He left his car at the Greyhound bus station to make it look as if he had left town but actually, he was staying at his mother's house. Levi chose to stay with Olivia in order to keep a watchful eye over his family. He hadn't heard anything from the Haitians and their presence in the city had seemed to calm down, but it was still there. Levi just figured he would keep his head on a swivel until the opportunity arose where he and Sha would finally meet up. For Olivia, it was a sense of comfort that her son was back home because she didn't have to worry if he was safe or not. Even though the city had been on a lockdown, it didn't stop the criminal element because it never took a break. News reports of shootings, robberies and even carjackings ran daily but for Olivia knowing her son wasn't involved was a blessing. Olivia's only son had found content with not having to constantly hustle and began to finally think of ways to live a normal life. With all the time he had on his hands, he began to look at other options and searching through the classifieds for legal employment. Levi was making a change in his life but that didn't mean he completely cut off the people he grew to care deeply for. He stayed in contact with Allison, making sure she didn't need his help, he stayed on Kareem trying to make sure he keeps his nose clean and occasionally texted his sister but never received a response. For the first time in a long time Levi didn't have a plan but he was completely comfortable with that.

Olivia was taking her claim in the street market as she had a few of Sam's girls running syrup and pills throughout the city. Money wasn't rolling in heavily, but it was steady cash to keep them all pushing forward. Their clients were usually street hustlers that needed a quick reup on products they usually couldn't find elsewhere, plus dealing with a sexy woman was a bonus. Except for The Cajun and Travis, the crew was pretty much an all-female clique that ran like a machine. Sam pulled Travis in when she had to stash some product at his crib, he didn't mind it at all because Sam would occasionally bring around a female treat also. Olivia kept her day job merely for show because it wasn't like she had to have it, but it looked good on paper. She had thoughts of making it a family business but seeing how her son had changed Olivia felt it was best to keep him out of it for now. Being a mother, she always wanted better for her kids and seeing that Levi stepped away from the street life was a step in the right direction in her eyes. Olivia reached out to The Cajun to see if he had any work for Levi on the docks or knew of any jobs at the ports. The Cajun was happy to help out a friend and had her send Levi to meet someone at the Port of New Orleans. After she got all the information from her Creole partner, Olivia made sure to give her son all the details. Before heading back in the clinic from her lunchbreak, Olivia received a video call from her buddy Sam. Thinking it was just Sam checking in like she usually does, Olivia answered the call,

"What up chick?"

The screen was dark, but she could hear movement and thought Sam mistakenly butt dialed her. Right when Olivia was about to end the video call, her friend appeared in the screen with the biggest smile on her face,

"Somebody wants to say Hi and that they miss you."

"Ok."

Olivia was a little confused at the statement but then right next to Sam's face on the video call was an exceptionally large dick that looked very familiar to her. Sam started licking the massive muscle until she got to the helmet and inserted it into her mouth. She handed the phone to the owner of the enlarged snake and the only sounds Olivia could hear were deep moans of pleasure but then Travis' face popped up. Trying to hold a conversation with Olivia while Sam gave him some great head was a task in itself but he managed. She couldn't believe what she was watching but couldn't turn away as Travis turned the screen to Sam stroking his dick and attempting to deep throat him. Olivia forgot she was at work as she stood outside watching the personal porno and whispered to Travis,

"Play with her pussy."

His fingers began caressing Sam's clit, her moans let him know he was in the right spot and he couldn't help but to show Olivia. The screen was a close-up view of Sam's succulent juice box with Travis' fingers rubbing her swelling clitoris and Olivia moistened watching the act. Travis set the phone up so that the voyeur could see them both as he asked if she wanted to see him go inside her, all Olivia could do was nod yes. He sat on the sofa with his engorged manhood standing at attention, Sam straddled over him and eased down on Travis' fleshed pipe. Her plump lips parted as his helmet pushed its way inside, her soaked box allowed him to slide right in and her lips wrapped around his hardened phallus. As he pushed in deeper Olivia could see Sam's juices dripping down his shaft and they both simultaneously let out,

"Oh my goodness."

Right then Olivia knew she had to go because if she stayed on the call any longer, she would end up leaving work. Sounds of Sam moaning and whimpering to Travis' deep strokes began to get loud right along with the sounds of skin slapping together. Olivia was saved from her erotic torture when one of her co-workers came outside and Olivia quickly ended the call, but the sex sounds were already heard. The embarrassed nurse just smiled as she shook her head and went back into work but images of what she just witnessed kept flashing in her head.

Levi took the info his mother gave him and went to go meet up with the person The Cajun mentioned. He got to the Port of New Orleans on Tchoupitoulas and asked the guard where he could find a Leslie Wilson. Levi didn't know who she was and figured it was some old lady that worked as a secretary at the docks. He was completely off target when he seen Leslie walk up to him from the loading dock after the guard called for her over the intercom. Two simple words could describe the woman walking up to Levi, "Chocolate Goddess". Even though she was draped in Dickie pants, Dickie shirt, bandana around her head and steel toe boots, a blind man could see she was fine. Leslie was thicker than a cold bowl of grits but don't get it twisted by the hazel eyes and full lips, she was meaner than a rattlesnake. She worked in a field that was mainly run by men, most women didn't stay long working on the docks like Leslie did but she was more comfortable around men than women. Most newcomers would underestimate her stature because she wasn't that tall or big, but Leslie could work the strongest under the table. She went from a laborer to a forklift operator and assistant manager strictly on her work ethics but what she desired was running her own company one day. Leslie was a determined female that played no games with nobody. Levi got a firsthand experience when she noticed he was paying more attention to her breast than the words coming out of her mouth,

"Say bruh, I can waste my time doing something else than talkin' to you if all you gone do is look down my fuckin shirt."

"I'm listening."

"Fareal, I'm doin' my boy a favor and I'm a need yo full attention. Dis job gets dangerous sometimes. A 3-ton container fall off its hook and yo ass could get crushed if you ain't payin' attention. I ain't trying to be mean or nothin' but I'm a need you to focus."

"My bad, I gotcha."

Leslie continued giving Levi a tour of the facility as she pointed out what he would be doing. He knew the job would be manual labor but when Levi seen guys walking out of a large cargo container, he knew he was in for a test. Leslie brought him to the office to fill out some paperwork and told him to be ready for work the next day at 5 in the morning. As she left, he couldn't help but to get another glance at the big round ass she was carrying behind her. Levi finished the long application in front of him and then left to go see Allison because it was a minute since he seen her face.

It was the following morning, business started picking back up for Dante's CBD shop and Eve was surprised that the city lockdown last year didn't put too much of a dent in their overall profits. The businessman made sure to push his products as hard as he could with promos, free samples and even webinars to get information out to future customers. He and Eve were going over inventory like she always liked to do once a week to make sure they didn't need anything. Dante wasn't really concerned about the product at the time when he had such a beautiful woman sitting in front of him. He had done everything in his power to get Eve to fall for him like he had for her, but his business partner wasn't budging. They were counting the last of their inventory when Dante was called up front to talk to a customer. When he walked out from the back his eyes fell upon Papa Sha standing there with five other guys holding baseball bats. The ominous grin Sha always carried greeted Dante as he asked,

"Can I help you? And no, I'm not interested in doing business with you."

"C'mon now. Why you turnin' me down? Me cum heya as a friend of de islands to help anotha brotha and you continue to say no."

"I don't need your help. Now can you please leave me?"

"Bumbaclot. I no want to do this but you force me to."

Papa Sha looked at the five guys standing behind him and nodded his head. The sounds of glass shattering and furniture moving alarmed Eve who was still sitting in the back-storage room. She didn't know what was going on, but she knew it couldn't be anything good from the shouting and destructive sounds she heard. Eve rushed up front to find Papa Sha standing like a smiling statue as two guys were beating Dante and his security with bats. The other three goons were destroying the shop, shelf by shelf and didn't leave not one countertop or display untouched. The entire store looked like a tornado came through it, but it was all the workings of their own personal hurricane named Papa Sha. Eve shouted for them to stop as she pulled out a shotgun that was hidden behind the cash register and pointed it directly at Papa Sha,

"I have zero fucks to give right nah! If you don't get yo Fluxy ass up otha heya, I'm a light all y'all up!"

Sha and his five goons walked out the store as they kicked broken shelves out of their way and Eve ran to help Dante up off the floor. Eve's business partner was battered and bruised but not one broken bone that she could see. His security guard wasn't so lucky as he held his arm that had a bone protruding from the skin and blood pouring between his fingers. Eve's first aid training back in high school kicked in as she rushed to wrap the open wound and get both of the men to the emergency room. Dante was in extreme pain as Eve sat him in the front seat of her car, but his concern wasn't for himself but his Rastafarian brother that laid in the backseat. Eve rushed to lock the store up and bring the two beaten victims to the Emergency Room as quickly as possible. Her rage was at a 10, thinking about what just happened but she knew nothing would happen because they had no security footage of the crime just wounded souls. Dante could see the anger in her eyes and he was upset himself but he tried to make funny of the situation,

"Gal where you learn fluxy from? You tink you Jamaican nah."

"Boy shut up and keep still before you hurt something."

"Just funny to me to hear you speak patois."

Eve pulled up in front of the Emergency Room of University Hospital and ran inside to get a nurse to help her with the guys. Two nurses ran outside with two wheelchairs for the men as Eve gave as much information as she could to the head nurse on duty.

Sam was back home in Slidell after a weekend in New Orleans and like she always did when she first gets home was take her dogs for a walk. She took pride in her pure breed pitbulls, they were like her children and everyone in the neighborhood knew the lady with the trained guard dogs. Sam been in love with dogs ever since she was young, her father introduced her to pits when she was 8 or 9 and she has loved the breed ever since. Olivia had called to check on her friend just to make sure she got home,

"Damn bitch, you can't call or nothing?"

"My bad. Got home and my babies were waiting on me, so I had to take them on their morning run."

"Girl, you and them dogs. Debo get walked once a week maybe twice."

Sam shook her head at Olivia's last comment and began preaching to her about proper care for pitbulls. Sam's business partner started laughing at how serious she was about the matter, going over the benefits like it was an infomercial. Olivia quickly changed the subject because she didn't want to get scolded anymore and asked Sam how much weight she had left. The dog lover told her most of the inventory she had left was stored at Travis' house for safe keeping. Olivia was worried that Sam was trusting the young bull to much because of their sexual relationship and addressed the issue to her. Sam reassured her that Travis was very trustworthy, even helped sell most of their product and gave her a key to his place along with showing her his hiding spot that was under the fireplace. Olivia listened as Sam told her that Travis' fireplace had a false bottom to it where he use to hide his weed when his father would come over. The house Travis lived in had true history to it, the false bottom in the fireplace was created for runaway slaves that needed a place to hide for a day. She laughed when her friend said Travis had a deflated plastic sex doll in the secret storage when he first opened it for her,

"Sam stop lying."

"Girl, I can't make this shit up. He said it was from a Mardi Gras party and he forgot it was in there. But girl, the secret compartment has a lever that look like a lantern on the wall and when you pull it down, the floor slides open. Like you can literally lay down in that bitch, fareal. Some secret agent type shit."

Sam was laughing at Olivia tease her about her "fuck buddy" being a nympho and how he must be whipped behind her because he is giving up all the family secrets. The ladies were enjoying their conversation while Sam was finishing up her run with her dogs and Olivia was making her way to work. Sam seen a bright blue car in her neighborhood that was unfamiliar to her, but she paid it no mind thinking it was nothing. The car drove pass and she could see three men in there with black mask on their faces.

Because of the recent pandemic that plagued the state Sam just assumed it was three men that were still being precautious, she dismissed it and kept talking to her friend. Sam was a block away from her home when the sound of tires screeching alarmed her and her dogs, but it was too late by the time she turned around. The only thing she seen was two of the masked men with assault rifles, hanging out the passenger side windows, aiming directly at her, all Sam could do was close her eyes and prepare for the worse. The sounds Olivia heard over the phone brought her right back to when her son Brock was killed but this time it was a close friend. She shouted Sam's name in desperation to just hear her say she was okay but the only response she got was an onslaught of gunfire and Sam screaming. The gun shots ceased, car tires screeched away and Olivia listened to gurgling sounds as her friend lay dying on the other end. Her eyes blurred as the tears rolled down her face and car horns blew at her as they sped pass because Olivia was frozen at the traffic light that had turned green.

Levi's first day on the docks was literally the hardest he has ever worked in his life, but he wasn't going to let it beat him. He kept his head down and tried to look busy, but he didn't have to pretend too much because containers were coming one after another, off ships rolling down the Mississippi. The crew had a small break between ship arrivals when Leslie brought Levi a bottled water,

"Heya go rookie, you lookin' a lil thirsty. Gotta say, you surprised me cause you keepin' up."

"Preciate ya, I wasn't thinkin' this shit was this hard. How long you been here?"

"Bout four years, straight outta high school."

"High school? Girl how old are you?"

"I'm 22, why you lookin' all surprised?"

"Just how you carry yaself, I thought you was older."

Levi didn't know too many people around his age that had their shit together how Leslie did. She gave him hope that he could stay on the straight and narrow. She was far from dumb and realized college really wasn't for her, so she jumped in the workforce. Leslie seen Levi was different than the guys she was use to dealing with on the job, he didn't complain about any of the work and he pretty much stayed to himself. Being the only female on the docks, other than the ones that worked in the office, Leslie became accustomed to guys trying to flirt or take her out on a date. Levi didn't give off any of those vibes and he was actually nice to talk to. He really didn't mind kicking it with Leslie either because her milk chocolate melanin was definitely pleasant on the eyes, but Levi kept his cool around her. Not trying to get in her pants like the other men she worked with was truly appreciated by Leslie. Their next big job had finally arrived as the crane operators began taking containers off the ship and Levi prepared himself for another rough one, but Leslie had something else in mind. She pulled him over to where she worked at and told him she was going to train him on working with the forklifts. Leslie started showing Levi how the equipment worked and what he needed to do but then they were interrupted. The lead foreman came with an emergency call for Levi stating it was his mother. When he got to the phone, he found a frantic Eve on the other end asking if he had a chance to talk to his mother at all. Concerned that something went wrong,

"I seen her when I left for work but I haven't talk to her since, what's going on?"

"Dante got jumped at da shop this mornin', doctor said he got two broken ribs and some bruising but he gone make it.

His security guard all fuck'd up though, dey broke this boy arm and his jaw."

"You know who did it?"

"Dat muthafucka Sha and dem bitches dat follow him. Levi they fuck'd da shop up. I was trying to get in touch with ya mama, just to see if she could help me."

Like clockwork, what he was trying to run from kept tugging at his coat tail and Levi offered to step in to secure the store for Eve. He told his supervisor that he had a family emergency and went straight to the CBD store to meet up with Eve and try to contact his mother. The docks weren't too far from where Dante's shop was so Levi got there before Eve and waited for her to arrive. He peeked through the large display window of the store and seen nothing but destruction, not one thing wasn't smashed or kicked over. Levi reached out to his mother to see if she heard about what happened at the store but all he got was her answer service. Thinking maybe she was busy at work and couldn't get to her phone, Levi just waited for Eve to arrive. His wait wasn't long as he seen Eve's car pull up in front the store and the stress on her face was evident. Not saying a word, she just walked up to Levi, gave him a hug and opened up the front door to the store. They walked in and the sounds of glass cracking under their feet echoed through the silent building. Levi looked around not knowing where to start heard a phone ringing from behind the register, the only spot that wasn't destroyed. Eve ran to answer it just to hear a customer inquire about some items they were trying to buy,

"Baby da shop closed today and prolly tomorrow, doing some remodeling. I'm sorry. Ok, bye bye."

Levi went to the back to look for something to get all the trash off the floor with and Eve tried to salvage any of the products that wasn't damaged. While he was sweeping up glass Levi asked her if she heard from his mother and Eve just shook her head no. They both buried their heads in the task ahead of them and tried to clean up as much as they could. Time had got away from them and before they knew it 4 o'clock was approaching and Eve was ready to call it quits. She apologized to Levi for missing out on work and handed him a thick brown envelope,

"Heya, this for you."

"C'mon nah, I woulda came over here to help clean up anyway. I don't need this."

"I know you would but this for helpin' with dat Dracko problem. You didn't have dat to do."

Levi thanked her as he went to leave to go home and Eve locked the store up for the day. When he sat in his car, he looked in the envelope Eve gave him to find 10 grand wrapped in a rubber band and a thank you note, stating "wish it was more."

Feeling devastated beyond repair, Olivia drove back to New Orleans from Slidell after talking with detectives because they see she was on the phone when Sam was killed. The officers questioned her about Sam's associates, friends and family, anyone Olivia would think would want to kill her. The former partner stood strong because it wasn't the first time she ever been in a police interview or interrogation room. She knew not to say too much or too little when it came to them asking her questions, but Olivia truly didn't know who did it,

"Officer I really have no clue who would have done this. When we were on the phone, she was taking her dogs for a walk and she mentioned seeing a blue car in the neighborhood she never seen before but that was it. She didn't say anything other than that. I loss my son the same way and to hear those shots over the phone was terrifying. She never did anybody anything."

Olivia was just so hurt that someone would do her friend like that and truly wanted to help the officers find them. The police couldn't find a next of kin close to Sam, so they had her identify the body from a photo the coroner took of her face. Olivia looked at the picture and sadly confirmed that it was her friend, but she could see one of the bullets hit Sam in the face, right where her dimple use to be. Because they had no one else to give the property to the investigating officer handed her Sam's belongings and thanked her for coming. As she made her way back home, Olivia saw that she missed calls from a few people, like Eve and Levi, but one that stood out was several calls from Travis. He never really called her like talking about it and for him to call her four times back-to-back was odd, Olivia tried calling him, but his phone just rung. On her way home, she took a detour through the French Quarters to stop by Travis to see if he was home. Olivia parked in front of his place and sat in her car dreading having to break the news to Travis about Sam. Tears began to well in her eyes, but she fixed herself as she got out of the car and walked up to his door. After a few knocks, Olivia figured Travis wasn't there and called his cell one more time to see if she could reach him. When the phone started ringing on her end, she could hear the sound of Travis' cell ring from behind the door. Olivia began knocking on the door harder trying her best to get the young man to open up, but the house was silent other than the ringing phone. She went back to her car hoping the keys that the officer gave her in Sam's property had Travis' house key on it. Olivia went through the entire set on the key but finally the last key unlocked the door. She walked in,

"Travis? Are you home? It's Liv."

Olivia walked through the living room only to find it was empty but as she made her way towards the dining room, which was connected to the kitchen, she found Travis. He was completely naked, hanging upside down, nailed to the doorframe by his feet, with deep cuts all over his body like he was tortured. Olivia fell to the floor, sick to her stomach as her eyes couldn't look away from him. Sounds of blood dripping from his body onto the floor was like out of a horror movie. The slashes to his flesh were the workings of a demented individual, someone who didn't value life at all. The biggest slash was to his throat, that left his head barely holding onto the rest of him. The thick smell of blood in the air was suffocating and Travis' body hung there in suspended animation as if it wasn't real. She silently cried for the young man still bleeding on the floor from his wounds but then Olivia noticed his manhood was severed off and shoved in his mouth. She knew someone was trying to send a seriously deadly message and then everything started to fall into place with two people close to her dying on the same day. Olivia rushed to call Levi.

After stopping over by the Daniels household to leave half of the money Eve gave him with Kareem, Levi made his way home. He was pulling up to his house when he seen Papa Sha standing outside of his Jeep with two other goons. Levi knew the Haitian gang leader didn't know he was the one that killed his second in command or he wouldn't be smiling at him like he was, but he prepared anyways. Levi got out of his car with a large chrome .45 by his side, visible for all the Haitians to see,

"Man, wha cha want?"

"Why you look so angry towards me?"

"What da fuck you want?"

The sounds of Debo barking and growling from the window could be heard clear as day as the pit watched Levi stand outside. Papa Sha smiled as he looked up and down the street as if he was looking for someone to come, then asked Levi if he seen his mother. Suspicious to everything the islander had going on, Levi told him he hadn't seen her since breakfast. One of Papa Sha associates looked agitated at Levi's reply and began speaking Haitian Creole aggressively towards him. Levi tightened his grip on the firearm in his hand as he prepped to defend himself because the other gang member looked as if he wanted to fight. Papa Sha seen the tension rising and with two words deescalated the situation but not before handing out his own threat,

"I need you to tell your mommy to call me. Not tomorrow or the next day but today. I won't come back looking for her."

"Nigga she don't fuck with you no moe, ya heard me. What you want with my mama?"

"Maybe I go visit yo sister and that baby girl."

"Dawg you touch my fuckin sister and y'all gone need all of fuckin Haiti to get me off you, fareal."

Papa Sha's smile went away as he stared in Levi's fiery eyes and the two men didn't budge one bit. One of Sha's men tapped him on the shoulder and his smile came back as he went to get in his Jeep. Levi focused on the gang leader with nothing but animosity as the vehicle began to pull away. He walked up the steps to the porch and his cell began to ring, it was his mother calling. Levi answered the phone and instant concerned himself of his mother's whereabouts,

"Mama, where you at? That clown Sha was here looking for you."

"Baby, I'm ok. I'm on my way home."

"No. Lemme come and get you cause if he see yo car, he gone know you here."

Olivia agreed with her son and told him to meet her at her job because she's going to leave her car there for the time being, Levi immediately left. Knowing Darlene won't answer the phone for him, he called Eve so that she could get the young mother to listen to reason. Levi was in full attack mode after the words he heard come from Papa Sha's lips, but he had to make sure his family was safe from it all. He called Allison to make sure she was okay and the young businesswoman had more on her mind than worrying about the Haitians. She received a call from one of her dangerous suppliers out of Mexico that was adamant about her paying him on time. Allison had been falling short on payments to the Cartel member and his temper was running very thin with her. She ran the underground business she inherited like clockwork but with Levi no longer there, other customers and runners left to go elsewhere. Allison didn't want to beg him to come back because she knew why he stepped away in the first place, but she needed him. Levi wanted nothing more than to be there for her, but his family came first before anything. He told her that as soon as he takes care of a problem that just came up they would work something out. Levi pulled in front of the clinic where his mother worked and she came out with anxiety written all over her face. Levi immediately began ranting,

"Mama I know you be wantin' to take care of yo own shit, but this dude is threatenin' to hurt Dee if you don't meet with him. I'm not letting dat happen, Dee and Diamond ain't got nothin' to do with this. He done tore Eve shop up and put da Jamaican dude in the hospital."

"Ronald, they killed Sam."

"What!"

"Gunned her down in broad daylight while she was walkin her dogs, dey killed her like she was nothing. Dem muthafuckas shot her and her dogs, they shot her in her face. Then they went to a guy Sam had dealings with and tortured him right before slitting his throat."

"He gotta go. You gone stay at Dee house and I'm a let you know when it's safe to go home."

"No Ronald, I don't want you getting' involved."

"Mama, I was involved as soon as he called out my baby sister's name."

Olivia tried to talk her son out of going after Papa Sha, but his mind was already made up. The rage she seen on her son's face was years of built-up hatred he had towards the gangster and the determination in his eyes reminded her of his father. She knew right then there was no stopping what was about to happen.

Dante was released from the hospital, but his security guard had to stay for another surgery on his jaw. Eve pulled up to the front entrance of the hospital and the nurse pushed Dante out in a wheelchair as Eve rushed to the passenger side of the car to help Dante in. The cringe that came across his face hurt her more than it was hurting him as she watched him slowly sit down in the car. Eve got back in and told her passenger he will be staying with her until he's well enough to take care of himself. Dante didn't want to be a bother but the thought of being home trying to fend for himself was a scary thought,

"Tink you me love. I promise to not be any trouble."

"Boy shut up. You been tryin' to sleep at my house."

The two laughed as Eve made her way to her place but Dante was concerned about the condition of his store. He wanted to get his Rastafarian brothers in the shop to clean it up but was pleasantly surprised when Eve told him she had that done already. As they slowly walked into Eve's place, Dante sat down in the living room to rest while the host went to get him something to drink. Eve was in the kitchen when her cell rang with Levi on the other end,

"Hey. You find ya mama yet?"

"Yeah. I need a favor. Call Dee and tell her to stay inside. Dat muthafucka Sha riding around lookin' fa trouble."

"Wait, what's goin on?"

"Eve look, I just need you to convince her to stay her ass inside. Sha lookin' fa my mama and he came at me sayin' if she don't show up, he gone go at Dee and Diamond. Just please do dat for me."

"I gotchu. Please be careful."

Eve immediately got off the phone with Levi and dialed Darlene's number, but the young mother didn't answer. Worry began to set in as Eve kept dialing and redialing Darlene's number. Dante could see the torment on her face and suggested that she go to Darlene's house to check on her after hearing why Eve was trying to get in touch with the young woman. He even offered sending someone over to her house just to stand watch, but Eve didn't want to make the situation anymore uncomfortable than it was about to be. She wanted to call in another favor from her police friends but knew it would lead to questions being asked that she didn't want to have to answer. Eve sat there stressing and trying to reach Levi's baby sister but then Darlene called her back,

"Hey, what's up? You called me like four times. Everything ok?"

"Look baby girl, I just need you to listen to me. Ya brother is bringing ya mama over by you to stay for awhile. It's not safe for her to be at the house. I just really need you to cooperate."

"Da fuck goin' on Eve? What Ronald get into this time?"

"He didn't get into shit, he just tryin' his best to keep y'all safe."

"Keep us safe? I ain't involved in nothing they do. Eve it's something you ain't tellin' me and I'm a need you to speak up like now."

"Look, the store I work at, you know the CBD store? Well, it was vandalized this morning and two people got sent to the hospital. One of ya mama's good friends was killed in front their house around the same time. When Levi got home from work, this gang member was looking for ya mama and leaving threats. Dee, I need you and that beautiful little girl to stay inside. I'm a send somebody to sit outside ya house til this is over. Baby, please do this for me."

Scared for her daughter, Darlene agreed to cooperate and stay inside until told otherwise. Dante got on the phone with his people and sent over two cars to watch over the house.

A week had gone by since Olivia loss a good friend and it still had an awful sting to it when she thought about

Sam. She started to blame herself for how things went down, and depression had started to set in deep. Darlene tried her best to be there for her mother because she knew what she was going through in losing someone, but it all was a little too much. Olivia would just stay in the bedroom, barely eating. Darlene had her daughter to think about and that was enough to fill anyone's plate of responsibility. Levi had come over to drop off some clothes and food when Darlene met him at the door,

"Is this shit ever gonna end? Mama need help, help that I can't give her."

"I just need a little more time Dee. I promise this gone be over real soon."

"Really Ronald?! Really?! Cause you running all around like shit sweet and we stuck in this damn house like fuckin prisoners."

"I know, I know. How is lil bit doin'? I know she gettin' big."

"Ronald please don't ask bout my daughter like you care. Do you even understand that yo daughter will have at least a memory of her father if you was to die right now? My child will never know who her father is or was and that's all because of you. You Ronald! Get off my porch."

The pain of his sister still holding hatred for him went through his soul as Levi stepped off the porch and watched the door slam shut. He held onto that pain as he got in his car and drove off in search of Papa Sha. Levi been working double shifts, one at the docks in the morning and another at one of Allison's stores pushing product out. He had just finished his shift at the port right before dropping the packages off at Darlene's house and had a few hours to spare before showing up to work at the store with Allison. Levi knew the Haitian drug lord went into hiding after his deadly rampage a week ago which made finding him a game of cat and mouse, but Levi wasn't any ordinary cat. He knew if he could get to one of Sha's men it would force the Haitian out of hiding and the perfect subject showed its face standing outside the liquor store. Smoke was one of Papa Sha's "crash dummy" members that did all the dirty jobs none of the other gang members wanted to do, plus he was Sha's younger cousin. No matter what anybody says, everyone has a sin or vice that controls them and Smoke's vice was hard liquor. He couldn't stay away from it and would indulge in massive amounts of it in one sitting. Levi knew if he could get to Smoke in a way that was so dramatic, Papa Sha had no other choice but to come out of hiding. He followed the Haitian as he stumbled up the street like he always did every afternoon from a liquor store or a bar. The neighborhood knew the island accent speaking alcoholic, but no one messed with him because of who his cousin was, but Levi paid that danger no mind. Levi followed Smoke to his wooden framed shotgun house on North Dorgenois Street and seen the drunken Haitian couldn't make it pass the porch as he slouched on the steps. Smoke sat on the porch steps, holding onto the neck of an open bottle that was wrapped in a paper bag and glanced at the cars that drove by. Levi noticed, even though he was tipsy, Smoke still was somewhat alert to his surroundings, so a typical ambush wouldn't work on him. Standing across the street looking at him was about to bring some unwanted attention. He made his way to the corner store where he seen a neighborhood crackhead named Cindy who was standing in front the store panhandling. Levi walked pass her as he went in the store and his mind started rumbling with ideas as he grabbed a bag of Chee Weez along with a pineapple Big Shot. After paying for his stuff, he approached Cindy with a business opportunity that would make a lot more than what she was begging for. He offered her 60 dollars to do a job for him and the fiend was more than willing. All she seen was the money and the addicted went with the plan as Levi pointed her in the direction of Smoke's house, after giving her instructions,

"Nah Cindy, you run off with my money and I'm a knock yo head clean off. Don't play with me. Don't think I won't find yo ass."

"I know, I know."

"Go ova dere, do what you need to do and leave. Aight."

Levi walked a block behind his potential prey's home until he was standing at the fence of Smoke's backyard. Trying to keep from being seen Levi quickly jumped the fence and crouched down at the backdoor of the house as he put on some latex gloves. He peeked through the windows to make sure no one was in the home and seen the place was empty with Smoke still sitting on the porch. For a minute Levi thought Cindy stiffed him because he didn't hear her approach Smoke yet but then her raspy voice could be heard asking the homeowner if he wanted some company. His plan was working when Smoke agreed to some fun with the female and Levi pried open the back door as he snuck in. He did a quick search of the house to find a hiding spot while Smoke and Cindy were outside chatting. Levi ducked off in the closet in the bedroom and waited for his time to spring his attack. The closet door had shutters in it that allowed him to see the entire bedroom. Levi waited in the closet for Smoke to take care of his business with Cindy. He watched through the cracks as the two uncoordinated addicts attempted to satisfy one another, only to fall on the bed. The stench of musty body odor filled the room as the drunken Smoke peeled the dingy shorts off of the crackhead. Levi couldn't believe somebody would actually want to have sex with the degraded female but to see what Smoke was doing had him sick to his stomach. He closed his eyes tight like it was a horror story in front of him when he seen Smoke start kissing Cindy's belly and work his way down. Levi knew what was coming next and couldn't watch it because of the awful smell that was abusing his nasal passage. He knew the smell couldn't come from nowhere else but from between Cindy's thighs and for someone to put their face down there was horrendous. After Smoke got his taste of his sex partner, he laid on the bed so she could return the favor. As soon as Cindy started sucking him off, Smoke closed his eyes and Levi saw the perfect opportunity to strike.

Levi burst through the closet with his chrome .45 tight in his grip and Smoke didn't have a chance to raise his head off the pillow. Cindy screamed in fright when she looked up to see Levi pressing the barrel of the firearm to Smoke's forehead. She stumbled to the floor, cowering in the corner of the room and Levi shouted for her to get out of the house. Cindy grabbed her clothes and put them on as she ran to the front door. Once Levi seen that she was gone he focused on Smoke laying completely still under his pistol,

"Time for some fun buddy."

"Do you know who I be boy? You best leave now and I won't kill you and yo family."

"Friend by da time I'm finish with you. You gone wanna kill my ancestors."

Levi took the side of his gun and struck Smoke so hard in the face that he broke his nose. The Haitian's hands held his face in pain as Levi grabbed a handful of his hair and dragged him out of the bed onto the floor. The tough guy act failed to scare the intruder and Smoke began begging for Levi to not hurt him. The conspiring Levi released an ominous grin as he walked his victim to the kitchen and sat him at the table. He ripped Smoke's t-shirt off of him, after striking him in the face again busting the mark's lip and used the shirt as rope to tie the Haitian's hands behind him to the chair. Once he was secure, Levi started looking around the kitchen and Smoke started begging for his life because he could see this wasn't going to end well. The trespasser was tired of hearing his victim grovel for his life and shoved a wet dish rag in his mouth to shut him up while he planned out his next move. Levi pushed everything that was on the kitchen table to the floor and started laying different items on it in front of Smoke. The terrified islander looked down at the kitchen table as Levi placed a screwdriver, a butcher knife, duct tape, a hammer, nails and salt on it. The clicking sound of the gas stove right before the flame ignited on it startled Smoke as Levi just sat down in front of him and smiled. He wiped the dripping blood from Smoke's nose as he engaged in a one-sided conversation with him,

"See I really don't want you. Who I want is yo cuzin but dat muthafucka hidin' from me. He fucked up and threatened my family and he know how I am bout people close to me. So I figured, why not touch somebody close to him. Truss me, it's not you. It's ya cuzin."

Smoke's eyes got big when he seen Levi pick up the screwdriver but then the torturer went to the stove and sat the metal rod in the burning flames. When he walked back towards his captive, the first thing he grabbed was the butcher knife and sliced Smoke across the face. The gash was so deep that Levi could see the inside of the Haitian's mouth through his cheek. Smoke tried to scream but the duct tape Levi quickly wrapped around his mouth ceased any loud shouts or noise. The weapon of choice was then slowly pushed through Smoke's shoulder until Levi hit bone and then he twisted the blade in the human flesh. The excruciating pain Papa Sha's cousin was going through was only the beginning of his kidnapper's plan. Levi watched as the blood just poured from his victim's shoulder and thoughts of the threatening words Sha said about his sister enraged him more. He picked up the heavy hammer and with all the force he could muster up swung the hammer at Smoke's shin, crushing it under the pressure. The muffled cries rattled down to a whimper as Levi poured salt in his hand and then rubbed it deep into the wound on Smoke's shoulder, adding more pain to the injury,

"Like I said, this has nothing to do with you. It's ya cuzin I'm lookin' for."

Unknowing to Levi, Smoke had been tugging at the knotted cloth around his wrist and finally got himself free when he pushed Levi to the floor. The Haitian stood up to get away, but his shattered shin halted that plan when he fell to the floor. Levi jumped up, seeing his victim was trying to escape and stomped on the broken leg, sending a shockwave of pain through Smoke's body. Seeing that his hostage wasn't going anywhere Levi joked,

"Damn dawg. You knocked me clean on my ass, I wasn't expecting that one, fareal. Gotta make show if I tie somebody up next time I do it right. But I'm a make sure you don't move this time. Remember, it's not you, it's ya cuzin did this, ya heard me."

He went to the table to get the hammer along with the nails and slowly walked back to a crawling Smoke, who was still trying to get away. Levi turned him over making Smoke face the ceiling, put his knee in his chest and stretched out his victim's arms. With the hammer in one hand and a long nail in the other, Levi drove the nail through the victim's hand until it went through the wooden floors. He did the same to the other hand and Sha's cousin had no more scream in him as Levi stood over him. Remembering he had the screwdriver sitting in the flame on the stove, Levi walked over to Smoke with the hot tool in his hand and the brut was the last face he would ever see. He slowly pushed the hot steel into the Haitian's eyeballs, burning them both as they exploded from the white-hot heat. He then stood over his victim watching the agony he had caused and only wished it was Papa Sha laying on the floor instead. Levi searched Smoke's pockets to find his cell phone, called Papa Sha, turned the speaker on and place his pistol to the victim's forehead. When Sha answered his cousin's call, Levi ripped the tape from Smoke's mouth and the only sound that could be heard was screams for help. Papa Sha desperately called out his cousin's name repeatedly pleading for him to answer but the only thing that replied back was the loud bang of Levi's chrome cannon. His job was done and as Levi went to walk out the backdoor of the house, he found pleasure in hearing Papa Sha cry out for his cousin over the phone. So, he figured he would leave him a present to see when the Haitians gang leader arrived at the house to rescue his cousin.

YEAR 2023

For the first time in a long time the city went quiet when it came to homicides. Levi was comfortable enough that he allowed Darlene and Olivia to leave the house without an armed escort. Olivia was still struggling with the idea that her friend was murdered while she was on the phone with her. She had finally put the thoughts of her son's death behind her and the sounds of death over the phone brought it all back. Darlene still kept a tight lip and distance from her brother but finally having her mother out of her house was a plus for her. She enjoyed having her freedom from her family again and focusing primarily on her daughter. The threats from Papa Sha had seem to disappear along with his presence in the city, mainly because he flew back to Haiti to bury his cousin Smoke. Stories of the gruesome death spread through the city like wildfire as a lacked investigation went into the murder. Residents in the neighborhood heard how the alcoholic Haitian was stabbed, beaten and nailed to the floor but that wasn't the horrifying stories. Rumors that the victim was disemboweled, and his intestines were stretched across the room while still connected to him was a display of something truly dramatic. Some people started saying it had to be a psycho that did what they did to Smoke, and others were saying it was someone making a statement, but no one had any idea who actually did it.

Levi was at work at the docks when he seen Leslie arguing with a guy in one of the nearby warehouses. He usually kept his head down and stayed out of everybody's business but when he seen the guy grab hold of Leslie's shirt like he wanted to hit her, Levi got involved. He rushed over to rescue her from the angered man but before he could get close to them, Leslie struck the guy with a right cross. The guy fell back into Levi's arms and tried to charge back towards Leslie, but Levi snatched him by the back of his collar,

"Nah bruh, can't let you do dat."

"Muthafucka, let me go!"

"I put it to ya like dis, you swing at her and dey gone have to pull me off you. Get da fuck up outta heya."

The enraged man kicked over a trashcan as he stormed out the warehouse and Leslie nodded her head as a "thank you" to Levi as she walked off in the other direction. Shaking his head at the fact that Leslie just walked off without saying one word, had Levi wondering if he should have stayed out of it and he just went back to work. The day dragged on with container after container coming off the ships and Levi was ready to call it a day hours ago. He was waiting for the crane to drop off the last container in front of his crew when Leslie called him over to her. Thinking she had extra work for him to do, Levi walked over to her without a purpose. Leslie released a smile as he made his way to her and Levi looked a little baffled because she barely smiled at anyone. He looked behind him to see if anyone else was around and Leslie gestured for him to hurry up as she laughed at her co-worker. Levi stood next to her while she sorted through invoices of the day's workload and Leslie thanked him for earlier. She leaned up against him while putting the paperwork in order,

"I really appreciate you stepping up like dat. Anybody else woulda turned they head."

"Nah, I can't watch no dude manhandle a female. Especially not a country redneck handling a sister. Sorry if I overstepped."

"Nah, you good. Muthafuckas getting' greedy when them extra ends slow down."

"Extra ends do sound good. When you come across some lemme know."

Levi knew Leslie had a hustle on the side, but he never said anything. Just like he had his secret lifestyle with Allison and her business, he figured Leslie wanted to keep hers under wraps. Levi headed back to his station to finish up on their last load and Leslie told him to meet her at her truck after he clocks out.

Olivia was helping a patient check in at the clinic when she seen an older white man standing in the lobby, staring at her. She didn't recognize him but something about him looked really familiar to her. After helping a few patients, one of Olivia's co-workers informed her that she had a visitor in the lobby. When she walked up front the older man stood there,

"Hi, can I help you?"

"You may not know me, but I believe you knew my son, Travis Babineaux. I'm his father, Trevor Babineaux."

"Yes, I did. I'm so sorry for your loss. I heard about what happened on the news."

"Thank you. I was wondering if you had a little time. I had a few questions for you."

Olivia stood there anticipating a barrage of questions she wasn't ready to answer knowing Travis' father was a former criminal court judge. She told him she would be free to talk with him when she gets off and Trevor gave her an address along with his cell. Olivia started thinking Trevor was digging for information on who killed his son but then she remembered that she was at his house and maybe someone seen her. Nervousness began to set in as the day went on and it got closer to her getting off work. Olivia called Eve to see if she heard anything from her NOPD connects about the former judge and his deceased son. Any indications that put her around Travis during the time of death would be drastic and Olivia needed to get her story straight. She hadn't been questioned by the police about Travis' death, but she wanted to be ready for anything. Eve didn't hear a word but told her she would make sure the homicide detective she knew on the force would keep her in the loop. Olivia went to clock out for the day and braced herself for a treacherous game of chess when she met up with Trevor. The ride to the address he gave her turned out to be a hotel on Bienville Street, that sat atop a bar and as soon as she called his cell Trevor came out to meet her. Olivia could see the anguish on his face behind his son's demise and thoughts of Sam came into play with her own feelings. Trevor greeted her with a firm handshake,

"Thank you for coming. I know this may seem off or unorthodox, cause you never met me before."

"It's fine. I only knew Travis for a minute, and he was really a nice guy."

"I'm a get straight to it because I don't wanna hold you up. I'm just glad you came so I could get this out my mind."

Trevor started talking about Travis' case like he was reading it directly from the reports and asked Olivia if she talked to him on the day the forensic officer presumed, he was killed. Knowing they could access anyone's cell records she knew he knew Travis called her repeatedly that morning, but they never actually spoke to each other. Olivia told him what he needed to hear but also let him know she was in Slidell that morning talking with the police about her friend Sam. When she said Sam's name, she could see in Trevor's eyes that he knew something she didn't and right then the chess game began. Trevor asked her questions about her and Travis' relationship, how did they meet and have she's ever been to his house. Olivia had a feeling he already knew the answer and just confirmed it to him that she had been to his son's place a couple of times. Trevor had ordered some drinks from the bar and began talking casually to her about Travis' lifestyle, how he felt he wasn't hard enough on him and pretty much spilling out all his feelings. Olivia started to see where Travis got it from, just telling all his business and just listened to the father but she also stayed on guard with her replies. Her assumptions came face to face with her when Trevor casually mentioned the secret door in front of Travis' fireplace. She knew exactly where it was and the morning she went to his house, where she discovered his body, Olivia purposely left the secret door alone. Olivia held a perplexed look on her face,

"Secret hatch? Nah, Travis never said anything to me about that."

"I only mentioned it because very few people knew about it and after the police had left the house, I went back to look in it. You know, just trying to find anything and the stuff I found in there was disturbing."

"Like I said, Travis never told me about any secret door. I only been over there a couple of times."

"You don't know of anybody that he was dealing with or had beef with?"

"Travis was a sweetheart and everybody he encountered just fell in love with him."

They talked a little longer and Trevor thanked Olivia for coming. He walked her to her car and the heartbroken father confessed to Olivia his true motives for their meet. He had a private investigator look into Travis' private life after finding a lot of narcotics in the secret hatch and when he seen that his son called her on the day he died, he had to question her. Trevor literally cried to Olivia as he apologized for thinking she had something to do with his son's death. He also told her that he and the police believe the same people that killed her friend Sam are the ones that killed Travis. Olivia knew that already, but she didn't reveal that to Trevor because then it would implicate her in the murders also. She pulled Trevor to her as she held him in a tight embrace, and he buried his head into her shoulder and wept.

Since he was all healed up from the injuries he received during the attack in his store, Dante moved back to his place but that didn't stop him from coming over for dinner at Eve's apartment. It had become a frequent thing with them and Eve found herself looking forward to their alone time together. She studied a Jamaican recipe she found online and wanted to surprise Dante with her culinary skills in the kitchen. Eve was just getting the plates ready to dish up the night's meal when she heard Dante knocking at the door. She opened it to the Jamaican prince smiling at her as always,

"You right on time. I hope you hungry."

"Geezus gal, it smell good good in heya. Wha cha cooking?"

"Oxtail stew over jasmine rice."

"You must want me to marry you gal. Me haven't had oxtail stew in forever."

"Boy shut up and go sit down."

Eve got the plates together and dished their food as Dante patiently waited on his meal while telling her about the day he had at the store. The CBD shop been picking up in sales and Dante was truly thinking about expanding his business with another store. Eve was game for the challenge and proud of the work they both put in to make the shop a success. She brought him his plate and Dante couldn't believe she pulled it off recreating a homecooked delicacy like she did. They sat down to enjoy their meal while engaging in "shop talk" about how they wanted the next store to look. Eve listened to her business partner talk shop but was simply thrilled at how much he was enjoying her cooking. After she put away the dishes, they went to relax in the living room and Dante went on about how well they're doing with the store. Eve sat there for a minute to listen to him then blurted out,

"Could you please stop talkin' bout the store and fuck me already."

"Huh?"

"What da problem is? I need yo penis beatin' up my guts."

"Come nah gal, stop teasing me."

"See you think I'm playing."

Eve knelt down in front of Dante and began unbuckling his belt as he sat there watching in awe of her forcefulness. At first, he thought she was playing like she always did, teasing him and then turning away giggling but he got the shock of his life. She reached in to pull his manhood from his jeans and began stroking it while looking him in his eyes. Dante tried to hold his composure, but goosebumps covered his body as Eve pressed her soft lips against the head of his dick. She stood up and the sundress she was wearing simply fell to the floor as if it was released from her body revealing a completely naked Eve standing in front of him. The sunlight that was piercing through the sheer curtains in the living room seemed to dance across her caramel skin as she caressed her breast. Dante's dick stood at attention as he looked at Eve's immaculate frame while she pleasured her clit with her index finger. He couldn't take anymore just looking at her when she licked the juices off of her finger and he picked her up as he walked to the bedroom. Their tongues attacked one another, twirling around and exploring the other's oral cavity. Dante laid her on the bed and his dessert looked better than any five-star cuisine he's ever had. His warm tongue sent shivers through Eve's body as his lips latched around her clit and circular strokes whirled around. Her juices flowed as Dante slid his oral appendage deep inside her and Eve arched her back in order to press down on his tongue. As he licked the inside of her walls, his thumb massaged her throbbing clitoris and Eve was on cloud nine when he went back to sucking on it. The feeling was so immense that she thought it couldn't get any better but then Dante went a step further and slid two fingers in her. His oral performance brought on her first orgasm of the day, as she screamed in pleasure and the rudeboy wasn't done. Dante flipped her over on her stomach and Eve thought she was about to receive some harden steak between her thighs, but she got a thick tongue in her ass instead. His warm tongue found its way deep up in her taint, Eve couldn't do anything but lay there and take it. He rubbed her swollen clit while tossing her salad and Eve buried her face in the pillow in front of her. Dante pulled her up on her knees and started rubbing his stiffened staff between her moistened lips, Eve braced herself for his entrance. His head pushed between her soft succulent lips, splashing in her juices as she could feel every inch of the meaty vein entering her. He slid in and out as he gripped hold of her plump ass, but Dante wasn't ready for the grip Eve engaged around his dick with her walls. The sounds of sex filled the room as the two beings became one and sweat poured from both of their bodies. Dante looked at her ass bouncing and took the opportunity to slowly push his thumb in her hole. Eve looked back with a devilish grin,

"You can pull ya thumb out and slide dat dick up in there."

He looked at her to make sure she was serious and when she reached back with her hands to spread her ass cheeks, he knew she was. Dante pulled his hardened appendage from her soft supple pleasure pocket and eased it in her tight place. Eve cringed in the pleasurable pain of him entering her taboo hole and pleaded for him to keep going. She could feel his staff punish her tightness to the point where it felt wide open. Dante grasped hold of her hips as he looked down at how his dick just disappeared in her ass and her cheeks jiggled with every thrust. The more he pushed in, the more she wanted until Dante couldn't take it anymore and exploded, releasing all of his cream inside her. The two fell to the bed with his manhood still inside shrinking down in size as her ass squeezed out the last drops of his dick lotion.

Levi was making his way to his car when he seen Leslie getting in her truck, she gestured for him to come over when she seen him. He didn't know why but he found the chocolate tomboy extremely attractive. When he seen her take the oversized long sleeve Dickie shirt off, he knew one reason why. Leslie stood there with a white tank top on as she tied the sleeves of her Dickie shirt around her waist and she caught Levi staring at her full breast again. She shook her head as she laughed,

"You a true titty man. Yo ass cannot not look at some titties."

"My bad but you got dem sittin all nice n shit on display."

"Boy you stupid fareal. Well, I need you to focus cause I wanna ask you something."

"Yes, I wanna touch'em."

"Nigga!"

"My bad, focused."

After laughing at how silly Levi was, Leslie got serious and started telling him about her side hustle. Before the Cajun moved out to Destrehan to work at the ports out that way, he was Leslie's supervisor and taught her everything she knows. The two collaborate with each other on shipments that come through and sell whatever they could boost off the containers that land on their docks. The operation was bigger than just them two and Levi found out that the guy that he fought off Leslie was the first mate of a ship they do business with. The redneck had a few crates of military grade firepower that he was trying to get rid of and Leslie didn't have any buyers, so she told him no. Levi immediately knew who to call and with the shake of the hands became part of Leslie's little operation. Leslie stressed that she was trusting him with the information she was giving him and that it wouldn't be wise to cross them. Levi laughed,

"Girl we good, truss. You just be ready with da crates when I call you."

"Bet. Now I gotta go kiss this muthafucka's ass and get him to load it all in my truck."

"Dat's yo fault, you shoulda came to me first."

"Fuck you."

"Shid, I thought that's what we was bout to talk bout when you called me over heya. Thought you was bout to shoot yo shot."

"Negro, everybody dat smile at you ain't tryin' to fuck. Getcho ass on. Call me later when you ready."

Levi laughed as he walked off but in the back of his mind found Leslie's aggressive demeanor so sexy along with her frame and face. He called Allison when he got in his car to tell her he had some equipment that could bring in some much-needed money. Allison was eager to make some extra money because her Latino counterparts were getting frustrated with her lack of ends coming in. Levi heard stories of how dangerous the Cartel was but never had any dealings with them. He cared for Allison and wanted to do anything to keep her in their good graces. The closest he ever been to a confrontation with a Latin gang was the gang that gunned down his brother Brock and that left somewhat of a scar that still haven't healed. After a quick conversation with his Asian princess, Levi ran home for a quick shower and something to eat before meeting up with Allison at the shop.

Olivia was home trying to do anything than what she was doing at the moment and that was thinking about her deceased friend. She's had good friends before, mostly females that she worked the streets with, but Sam was different. Sam helped Olivia better herself when she was at her lowest and using multiple crutches to just survive. She showed the mother of two that life was more than hustling and constantly staying on the grind. It wasn't that Sam did anything spectacular or marvelous at being her friend, but her presence was a much-needed purpose. Besides being a great partner in crime, the spontaneous calls or text just to check in with heartfelt concerns of Olivia's mental health and everything in between was something that was going to be truly missed. Olivia tried not to but the more she thought about her friend the more she sunk in that dark place again and meeting Travis' father didn't help the situation any. She found some pills that were stashed away and a glass of Crown made it all look right to her. The slow creep of the medication's effects started to work its way through Olivia's body and her eye lids began getting heavy. She rode the wave into hallucinations of colored walls and swirling patterns until she began to doze off at the kitchen table. Olivia's pain of losing Sam to such a violent act brought back the horror of losing Brock the same way. She always wondered if she could have done something different, her son would still be with her. The blurred illusions of shadows whirled around in her mind as flashes of Brock, Roger, Sam and Travis haunted her. Olivia attempted to block them out with another pill, but it only got worse as her body fought with her psyche. The spirits wouldn't leave her alone as she scratched at her skin like ants were crawling all over her. Olivia was truly tormented over all the losses she encountered in her life and started to believe it was all her fault. A handful of pills found its way into her palm and she was about to take them all but a knock at the door stopped her. Debo's bark startled her as she tried to make her way to the door only to find her granddaughter Diamond standing in the doorway while Darlene stood on the sidewalk. Olivia tried to compose herself in front of the little one, but Darlene seen that look before. She knew her mother was either high, drunk or both and wanted no parts of what was going on. Darlene called for her toddler to come down off the porch to her as she looked at a shell of her mother,

"Diamond, c'mere baby."

"Bye, mawmaw."

Olivia watched as her daughter walked away without saying a word and her granddaughter waved bye. The pain continued for her like a dreadful cloud of demonic hands pulling her back in the house as Olivia drowned in sorrows.

Allison grabbed a small U-Haul van to move the shipment they were getting from Leslie and Levi texted his new connect that they were waiting on her. The 21st Century "Bonnie and Clyde" waited in the parking lot of a grocery store on Tchoupitoulas for Leslie to show. When

Mr. Chou was alive, he taught Allison to never be in the same place when a big transaction was going down, but she had to meet this female Levi hooked up with at his job. She never showed Levi a jealous side before when it came down to their relationship, but he could tell she was a little insecure when it came to him and Leslie. Levi paid the questions about his co-worker no mind, but he could tell Allison was just fishing for any kind of info. Leslie had finally arrived as she parked her truck directly behind the moving van Levi was in with Allison. She jumped out to greet the buyers as Levi opened up the back of the van and Allison seen competition instead of a potential partner. Levi introduced Leslie to his girl while he pulled the crates from the truck and loaded them in the van. Allison carried a fake smile as she shook Leslie's hand. The streetwise hustler could see straight through the Asian princess' smile and was feeling some type of way. Leslie was there to make money and looked pass the body language,

"I can always get more if you need it. Guy, I work with is always lookin' to dump off a crate or two."

"Shid, dats what's up."

"Levi nobody was talkin' to you."

"We could always use some extra. Just let Levi know and I gotcha."

"I'm a make sure to keep an eye out. I'll remind this dude to tell you cause he will forget. Forget his head if it wasn't attached."

Levi laughed it off as he closed the van doors and Allison went to the passenger side to grab a backpack with 60 grand in it. They made the hand off and Allison got back in the van as Levi walked Leslie to her truck. The co-workers parted ways after Leslie thanked Levi for their business and he headed back to the van as Allison watched him through the side mirror. He got back in the vehicle to make his way to the storage unit Allison had set up to hide the crates. Levi could tell the wheels in his girl's head was spinning out of control because mentally she wasn't with him. He asked her what was wrong, but Allison gave a nonchalant reply that it was nothing. Levi could tell nothing was going to get resolved and stayed on course to the storage unit with a quiet passenger in the van with him. Right when he pulled up to the storage facility, he got a text from Leslie,

"Say bruh, no offense but next time leave ya girl at home. Dat female really don't like me but I'm a make this money."

YEAR 2024

Dante walked in the shop excited to tell Eve about a new spot close to the French Market he wanted to turn into his second CBD store. During a delivery, he came across an older gentleman that was willing to part ways with his building if Dante would take over the mortgage payments. The place was cheaper than where they were and it was in a perfect spot for tourist, Dante was ready to sign the paperwork. Eve could see the pure joy in her man's face as he talked about what he wanted to do with the place and how he wanted to promote it. The joys of talking about their upcoming adventure was interrupted when eight undesirable characters walked in the store with Papa Sha. The Haitian drug boss had been in hiding for over a year and it was the first time Eve or Dante had seen him in the city. His presence had become an annoyance to Dante and the Jamaican was fed up with the bully type tactics to give up the store. Eve reached out for his arm as he lunged forward toward Papa Sha, but he pulled away from her grasp. Before the shop owner could get close to the darkly clothed Haitian one of his henchmen stepped in front of Dante,

"You don't want to do dat my friend."

"Fuck is you!"

"Me? Me name's Kirby. And from now on you talk to me and me only. Okay?"

"If you not buying, I need you out my store."

"I'm a let you have dis moment. It's your store today, it's my store tomorrow. We gone talk."

"Fuck outta here! I ain't givin' y'all shit!"

Kirby turned around and made his way to the exit with the rest of the goons that walked in there with him, leaving Papa Sha standing there alone. The Haitian gang leader stood there without the normal flare and fashion he use to always have about himself. He stood there in an all-black suit, black trench coat, black leather shoes and dark shades. Sha hadn't shaved in months or even comb the shaggy beard he had grown over time and the devilish grin he would have was nonexistent. He reached in the inside pocket of his suit and pulled the ugliest rag doll out that was covered in tattered clothes but resembled Dante's appearance. Papa Sha held the doll to his lips as he whispered to it and then placed it on the countertop, walking away leaving the doll in the store. The greenish dirt brown colored doll ominously sat on the countertop and its sunken white eyes seemed to stare at Dante. Living in New Orleans, a person will hear random stories about voodoo dolls, spells and potions but Eve had never seen one up close. She reached out to pick it up, but Dante quickly pulled her away,

"No! You don't play with stuff like dat."

"C'mon nah, it's just a fake ass doll. Sha just tryin' to fuck with yo head."

"Girl, dis is no game. Dis right here is a threat."

Dante slapped the rag doll to the floor and stomped the head, smashing it to pieces and Eve stood there, loss for words.

Levi went to go check on his daughter but was caught completely off guard when he seen the mother of his child holding a newborn in her arms. He figured it was Shalay's twin sister Alonna's baby but when he was told otherwise Levi questioned the new mother. Kareem along with Cedric both ran out to the front porch because they could hear their sister Shalay angrily shouting at someone. When they arrived, they found Levi standing on the sidewalk trying his best to get a word out but Shalay had full control of the conversation. She handed her newborn to her baby brother as she stepped on the sidewalk where Levi was standing,

"Nigga we agreed to co-parent. Co-muthafuckin-parent. Dat don't mean I sit here waitin' on you to figure out what da fuck you gone do. Nigga we ain't a couple and yo ass ain't no fuckin saint."

"Shay, I never said I was. All I'm saying is…"

"What?! Dat you don't want anotha nigga around yo daughter? Maybe if you come around more than just twice a muthafuckin year, you wouldn't have dat to worry about."

Levi walked away because he didn't want to argue with Shalay anymore and knew it was the best option for both of them. He knew there was some truth to what Ronnisha's mother was saying but he felt he was doing his best. As he was getting in his car, Kareem and Cedric came up to the car to give him some more disturbing news. Levi hadn't seen him, but Kareem and Cedric have as they told Levi that Papa Sha was back in town. After slaughtering his cousin, Levi thought he had run the Haitian off for good. He had to see for himself so he drove around Papa Sha's old stomping grounds to see if he could get a glimpse of the Haitian out and about. Levi traveled through the 7th ward, Gentilly and even went as far as to driving Uptown looking for any of the Haitians. Stressing over what Shalay had to say and finding out Papa Sha was back in the city Levi called it a day as he went to go check on his mother. He pulled up to her house and the sight of an unkept house screamed at him as he walked up to the steps. Trash along with random papers blew in the wind with an overflowing trash bin right next to the raised porch. Before Levi could even attempt to knock on the door, he began gathering the garbage together and throwing it all away. The front windows were dusty and dirty like they haven't been touched in days, he hadn't seen the house this bad since his mother's addiction days. All the signs pointed right to the idea that his mother had fell off and returned back to her old ways when he was young. Levi went to knock on the door and with the slightest tap the door slowly opened up as if it wasn't locked at all. Afraid something had happened to his mother; he quickly pulled his .45 from his side and walked through the house looking for her,

"Mama! Mama, you here? It's Ronald. Mama."

The house had a stench of stagnant water and mildew with a horrible body odor smell to it, he covered his nose with his hand. Levi thought the worse as he kicked beer cans, plastic food containers and dirty clothes out of his way while looking for his mother. Images of her laying somewhere dead frightened him but he was somewhat relieved when he came across a strung-out Olivia sitting on the kitchen floor. Small aluminum sheets, a burnt spoon, a belt and a few syringes all pointed to the one thing Levi was also afraid of. He picked his mother up off the floor and sat her at the kitchen table, red needle sized holes blanketed her arms. Levi thought she had her addiction under control but what he was looking at saddened him to no end and he had no words.

Leaving for the day, getting in her large bathtub with a glass of wine was the only thing running through Eve's mind as she got the last deposit ready from the store's day. Business was booming today with in-person customers and online customers all ordering everything the CBD store had to offer. Dante was ready to go too but thoughts of Papa Sha's visit with that hideous doll haunted him. He didn't let Eve know how dangerous the gesture was that Sha left that doll in their store, but he was definitely on guard. They both gathered their things as they made their way to the back-exit door and Dante made sure to turn off all the lights. Eve walked out to her car parked behind the building while Dante locked the back door, but his lady shouting his name in fear alerted him that something was wrong. When he turned around, there stood Kirby with Papa Sha and two other guys. Dante feared for his life but being Eve's protection was more important to him as he charged the men. Right when the angered Jamaican was in arm's reach of them, Kirby brandished a chrome .44 Magnum from his waist and pointed it directly at Dante's forehead. Like the smile Papa Sha use to always carry, Kirby released an evil grin at him,

"Now I remember I said don't address Sha anymore. You talk strictly to me now."

"We don't want no trouble. I just wanna take my lady home."

"Before I pulled dis out, you look like you wanted all de trouble. All de smoke, like da kids say. I tink you just da muscle of dis store and she de brains. So is she de brains or you? Who de brains?"

"She don't have notting to do with dis. Notting."

"I tink you lying. She smart, she definitely de brains cause you have none."

Kirby squeezed the trigger to the firearm and the loudest bang Eve has ever heard went off right in front of her. Dante's limp body simply fell to the ground with the top half of his skull splattered all over the exit door. His body twitched as it seemed to unleash the last remnants of life in him while the blood poured from the top of his head. Eve's screams were quickly muffled by Kirby who put his hand over her mouth, pushed her against her car and stared in her eyes. Being that he just murdered a man right in front of her, Kirby was extremely calm and told Eve if she mentioned anything to anyone, she would find herself right next to Dante. The terrified female was shivering as Kirby went over their plans for the CBD shop and how she would be working with them. She watched as the two bodyguard like goons picked her man up from the ground and threw him in a nearby dumpster as if he was trash. Papa Sha still silent just walked up to where Dante's body was laying before and dipped his fingers in the pool of blood that stained the concrete. He walked over to Eve and with a bloody hand smeared the deceased Jamaican's blood on her cheek. Tears rolled down Eve's face as she silently cried and watched the Haitians disappear into the night, leaving her there alone.

After a long night of trying to sober his mother up, Levi tired as all out dragged himself to Allison's apartment. He found himself standing at her door with the key in his hand and too exhausted to even turn the lock. Levi opened the door to Allison sitting on the sofa waiting for him with the meanest look on her face,

"Baby not today. I had a long day and you look like you ready to argue."

"Nigga I was just wondering where you been and you couldn't call."

"Da phone work both ways, you do know dat right?"

"You know where I'm at all da damn time. You da one bouncing all ova da city."

"Can I just go take a fuckin shower and relax before you start."

Levi walked off leaving Allison where she was and went in the bathroom. He could hear his cell ringing as he stood in the shower and let the hot water beat at his skin. The dirt and sweat from the day's chores rolled off of him as the water eased the stress he was going through. Allison walked in the bathroom barking about him not calling her all day and accusing him of being with Leslie. Levi knew right then it was time for him to get some space between him and Allison before the relationship became toxic. After cleaning up, he got out of the shower, dried himself off and began getting his clothes together. The upset feminine lover seen that he wasn't saying a word as she blared out at him her disappointment in him. When Levi pulled out a duffle bag from the closet Allison knew she had taken it too far but wasn't going to claim fault in her actions,

"So you just gone pack yo shit up? Get da fuck out den. Probably running to go answer whoeva keep blowin' ya cell up. Always got some shit goin' on with you."

"I'm leaving cause it's da best thing for both of us dat I give you all da space you need. I don't know what's wrong but you need some fuckin time to yaself to find out."

"Fuck you Levi!"

Levi looked over at her standing there furious one last time before walking out the door and knew their romantic relationship was pretty much over. He cared for Allison a lot but couldn't just stand there and take her verbal abuse anymore, especially after the day he was having. Levi got in his car and his phone began ringing again, thinking it was Allison calling to scream more hateful words he didn't even look at the screen. He was at the red light when he finally picked up his phone to look at all the missed calls and realized it was Eve calling all that time. When he called her back, Levi could hear Eve's voice shivering when she spoke and the unbridled fear in her words as she talked about this Haitian named Kirby. As much as Levi wanted to just leave behind all the unnecessary killing, he knew there was only one way to deal with someone so vicious.

Kirby wasn't like the Haitians that Levi was use to that lived in New Orleans, he was ruthless and commanded submission from any that crossed his path. He traveled back with Papa Sha from Haiti after burying their cousin Smoke. Kirby was Papa Sha's baby brother and unchallenged leader of a very dangerous gang in Haiti called the Goonies. They were known for dismembering their rivals and putting them out for display as a scare tactic for everyone to see. The Goonies also had the police force in their pockets, so no one really messed with them or even tried. Kirby was just as arrogant as his big brother Sha and they both believed in voodoo heavily. After Smoke's burial Papa Sha sought out help from a voodoo doctor who gave him a guide to follow,

"The island prince has to be eliminated for you to succeed."

Papa Sha took it to heart and felt he had to get rid of Dante as soon as he touchdown in New Orleans. He buried himself into the craft, brought with him artifacts that he thought would help him conquer his enemies and dragged his brother with him to terrorize everyone else. Kirby took pleasure in being an intimidation to what he considered the weak. He wanted nothing more than to find the man that tortured and killed his cousin. Papa Sha didn't know who the killer was, but he knew it had to be someone that was trying to make a point and Kirby was hungry for vengeance. Kirby attacked any organized group or gang that wasn't clicked up with the Haitians and Allison's operation was in his sights. The newly appointed lieutenant to Papa Sha's gang made a visit to one of the Asian princess stores when she wasn't there and left her a message. The message he left wasn't in words but a physical threat that left the store clerk with several stitches across his forehead and a ransacked store. The presence that the Haitians were back in the city was felt across all underground operations and Kirby was leading the pack.

Levi sat quietly in Eve's living room as he listened to her cry out over the loss of the one man she had fell for and the senseless murderers that threatened her life. He thought he had gotten rid of Papa Sha for good when he took out Smoke, but it was only a pause to what really needed to be done. Levi's brain started calculating scenarios to how he could cancel the threats for good, but he needed to find out who this Kirby character was first before he made any plans. He asked Eve if the new Haitian told her anything else besides the fact that they were going to take over the operations of her store. Everything was a blur to Eve, but she did remember that Kirby said he will come talk to her in a few days about shipments she will receive. Levi started texting Leslie about any cargo she knew of, that was coming in from the islands. Then he hit up Kareem telling him he had a job for him. The tactic he was going to use was straight out of the Haitians' handbook and Levi had to have everyone on board for it. He didn't want to involve the teen Kareem because he wanted the young man to focus on school, but he needed someone that was no longer in the game. Leslie texted back,

"Nigga what you got goin' on?"

"I'm tryin' to see something. You know of any?"

"My homeboy say a special crate comin in tomorrow. You want in?"

"I want da whole thing. How much?"

"Shid, lemme find out."

Levi had a few bands stashed away for emergencies but knew he would need more and dreaded calling Allison because he knew she had it. Eve wanted nothing more than to get rid of the nuisance that was sitting in her lap and reached out to a very well-off client. She knew he would want some favors in return for the money she was asking for, but it was better than the torture she was going through at the moment. The sexual appointment with Eve's rich client was set up and Levi was just waiting on a response from Leslie so he could put his plan in motion.

YEAR 2025

The shipments that came through the ports from Jamaica and Haiti were bundles of premium cannabis that was camouflaged in rolled up area rugs. The weed was such high quality that it couldn't be found anywhere in the states and Levi had all of it all to himself to do with it as he please. He gave half to Allison and sold the rest to a few young corner boys that was trying to make a name for themselves. Levi knew once word got around that someone was selling premium smoke for cheap, the Haitians were not gonna be happy. Even with giving away half of the product, Levi made all the money back that he paid for it and more, but he wasn't finish taunting the Haitians. He saved the rugs that were rolled up in the crates and made sure to leave one every morning for Kirby or Papa Sha to see laid out in front of their house. Levi wanted to drive them nuts trying to figure out who was harassing them, and Kirby set his eyes on the street hustlers. Papa Sha let his brother have full range of the gang as he spread them thin throughout the city trying to find the bandit.

Even though they didn't make it as a couple Levi and Allison were great as business partners. It was more than just making money with Allison when it came to Levi. It was a loyalty thing, respect to the man that took him in and showed him how the game was played. Levi still cared for Allison but her sly remarks when it came to any other female shunned him away from rekindling anything they had. It never failed if he got a call or text,

"Ya girlfriend callin'? You need to go?"

"Really bruh?"

"What? I was just askin'."

"You a mess fareal."

The promise Levi made to both Mr. Chou and Justin's grave that he would always make sure she's protected kept him by her side though. Allison knew he would never leave her out in the cold, but her insecurities held her guarded against a romantic relationship, so she tried to stay business like. Her shop was well protected after the one incident with Kirby assaulting one of her cashiers. Allison called on her father's connections with the BTK gang and they happily sent members to every one of her stores as protection on a daily basis. The mere presence of the tatted gangsters walking around and standing guard over the shops repelled any further incidents from the Haitians. Levi was confident and comfortable when leaving her by herself so that he could focus on the task at hand. Getting rid of Papa Sha and his entire crew was going to take a lot of work but Levi had it all under control. Allison helped out with monetary means along with equipment from her storage units because she wanted the Haitians gone as much as anyone else. Revenge was a much-desired meal she most definitely wanted a piece of when it came to Papa Sha.

Levi was burning his candles at both ends on a daily with working the docks with Leslie, inventory with Allison, making sure Eve stays sane and dealing with his mother's growing addiction. Somedays he would literally pass out from exhaustion when he would get home to his one-bedroom loft. After he and Allison broke up, he found a nice spot Uptown away from everybody, but it didn't stop Kareem. The youngest of the Daniels' boys would always find himself at Levi's place after his classes were over at Loyola University. So much that Levi gave him his own key to the place if he wasn't home. He had never had a little brother and the bond they had was stronger than neighborhood friends. Levi made sure Kareem stayed in his books and not in them streets, but he needed his help one last time,

"Say round, I'm only asking you to do this cause I can't rely on anybody else to do it right."

"Nigga, I gotchu."

"I know but I don't need nobody getting' hurt on this one. Go in, fuck some shit up and get outta there. Don't hang around there. Get ghost cause I know dem niggas gone be comin'."

"Fam, I got you. This ain't my first rodeo. Truss me."

Levi handed Kareem a stuffed envelope of money as he went over a plan with him that would draw the Haitians directly in his sights to take them all out. He already had Eve on board, who was tired of the visits from Kirby and Allison gave him the keys to all the equipment he needed. The convo halted when Leslie showed up at the door to talk about a shipment she heard about. She wanted to see if Levi wanted to get in on the product but then noticed Kareem and realized she knew him. Leslie went to high school with Kareem's siblings and the conversation went from business to cordial as she asked about his family. Kareem talked to her about his brother and sisters but couldn't get pass how fine the female was standing in front of him. Levi chuckled to himself, looking at how the young man's eyes just followed Leslie's body frame. The conversation stayed casual but then Leslie had to leave to go take care of some business. She told Kareem to tell his siblings hello for her and told Levi she would text him later as she walked out the door. Kareem couldn't wait until she left,

"Nigga, was that hazel contacts?"

"Nah nigga, that's really her eyes. Crazy huh?"

"Dat thick chocolate muthafucka fine as hell, shit."

"I know right."

"Tell me you hittin' dat."

"Nah my nigga, I wish I was tho."

"If you know like I know, you betta shoot yo shot."

"It's not like dat tho, she cool people and Ion wanna fuck dat up between us."

Eve was getting ready to have a soft grand opening for the new CBD store in the French Quarters she started. Not having Dante there was trying, because this was his dream and it was a battle every day for her as everything in the shop reminded her of him. Dante's death was still under investigation with NOPD and they didn't have any leads to who killed him. Eve wasn't really any help to them because she couldn't give the police any kind of information because she was in fear of her own life. With Dante no longer there, his Rastafarian brothers' presence seemed to vanish from the stores right along with their protection. Eve buried herself in her work. The sting of Dante being killed in front of her haunted her every time she got a visit from the boisterous Haitians. Along with moving her own product, they had her moving product for them also and she wanted nothing to do with it. Her first store went from supplying respectable customers that dabbled in the benefits of cannabis to fiends that were looking for pills or a heroin fix. Kirby and Papa Sha had ruined the image of the wholesome CBD wellness shop Eve imagined for the store. The store owner was outside hanging a sign to attract new customers to the shop when four young men walked up to the front entrance looking in. She welcomed the new customers,

"C'mon in, look around. Everything not completely set up but I got some things out y'all might like."

The young men smiled as they entered the shop to look around and that's when Eve recognized Kareem with them. She knew about Levi's plan but just didn't know when it was going to happen. Eve figured it was to keep her honest when questioned about any incident that occurs. She turned around to grab some gummies off the back wall one of the guys asked her about and when she turned back a black revolver was staring her in the face. The robber shouted for her to empty out her register while the other three began shattering and destroying everything in their path. She didn't open it fast enough for the criminal and he pushed her down to the floor snatching the register open at the same time. Kareem rushed over when he seen Eve fall and helped her up off of the floor but was surprised when he heard her shout,

"Nigga stop it! Stay in character!"

The young man slapped her in the face, walked off and kicked over a display as all four of them ran out the store. Eve picked herself up off the floor and looked around at all the damage that was created in such a short period of time. Blood began to fill her mouth from the lick she took and Eve spat on the floor as she called Kirby to tell him what just happened.

Levi knew it wouldn't be long before Papa Sha or Kirby would show their faces at the shop after hearing the store was robbed. He made sure that Kareem and his crew was far gone while Eve cleaned up the mess the young thugs made in the store. After the cops left, the store owner began sweeping up the mess left behind from the incident. The neighboring store owners had saddened faces of concern for their new fellow owner as they watched her clean out broken glass from the shop. Eve was talking to an older lady about what happened when a large Cadillac SUV pulled up in front of the CBD store followed by two pick-up trucks. The men that got out of the vehicles didn't look nowhere near as friendly as Eve and the elderly woman made her quiet exit as they walked up. Kirby got out of the SUV and immediately began directing traffic as he told the other guys what to do. Papa Sha walked up to Eve,

"No worries che. We will make this all new again."

She couldn't stand the sight of him but was grateful to have someone else cleaning up the mess the vandals left behind. Eve got pissed when Kirby started questioning her but at the same time sounding as if he was accusing her of the condition of the store. She got nervous but held her ground when the angered Haitian stepped to her because he felt she had something to do with the robbery. Kirby noticed broken glass was all over the shop and holes in the walls, but all Eve had was a busted lip. He figured if the robber would go this far to destroy a shop, they would do more damage to the person holding the money. Papa Sha ignored his little brother's accusations to foul play but didn't put it pass someone trying to make a statement,

"Relax fool, we got this."

"Fuck dat! She knows bruv, I can feel it."

Sha felt confident that whoever did this would find themselves under his blade and that everyone will know not to touch anything owned by him. The thing they didn't know about the whole situation was that Levi was across the street staring at them through the lens of a scope perched atop a very high-powered rifle. He had found the perfect spot in a vacant apartment that was over a small souvenir shop across from the CBD store. Levi sat in the shadows of the apartment, completely out of sight of anyone that looked up there, but he could see anyone that walked by. After Kirby had words with Eve, Papa Sha walked his brother out the store and Levi set himself up to take the shot that he knew would change everybody's life for the better. Kirby stood out front dictating orders to the four guys they were leaving at the shop to clean up while Papa Sha waited by the large Cadillac lighting a blunt. Levi had his crosshairs square in the middle of Sha's forehead, the thought of seeing his skull open up pumped his adrenaline as his trigger finger twitched,

"There go my bitch."

Levi's inexperience showed with the powerful firearm when he took his eye off his target when Kirby stood next to his brother. Levi pulled the trigger but instead of striking Papa Sha in the forehead, the projectile zipped pass him and ripped through Kirby's cheek, tearing through one side of his face. The blood splatter slapped Papa Sha in the face as everything went in slow motion and he watched his brother fall to the ground. Kirby laid there on the concrete, blood pouring from the large hole in his face and Papa Sha reaching out to him,

"No bruv, no. Get up! Get up!"

Another shot rang out as sparks from a ricochet struck the sidewalk next to Sha's feet and his bodyguard covered him. Screams filled the streets as rapid fire exited out of a darkened window across from the CBD store, several bullets hitting three of the five men standing outside. Papa Sha scrambled on the ground avoiding the onslaught of firepower aimed at him and his crew. Glass from car windows shattering followed him as the endless gunfire continued to rip through the vehicles he was hiding behind. The last bodyguard seen where the bullets were coming from and stood up to return fire but as soon as he was in sight of the gunman his head exploded. Levi's heart was racing, sweat dripping from his face and he patiently waited for the opportunity to take a shot at Papa Sha hiding behind the last vehicle parked at the corner of the street. The sounds of police sirens got closer and closer to where they were, but Levi stood his ground waiting for the perfect shot. His breathing calmed but the police were getting closer and he couldn't get caught,

"Fuck!"

Levi snatched up everything and darted out the back, leaving nothing but empty shell casings on the floor of the apartment.

News of a shoot-out in the French Quarters could be heard from every news station in New Orleans as the police chief gave his statement to the city begging for any leads. Levi sat in his apartment angered at himself for missing the chance to eliminate the cancer that plagued the underground. He stressed over how he could recapture the moment but knew Papa Sha would go deep into hiding after today. Levi grabbed his backpack to head out and meet with Leslie about a delivery she wanted him to make but he needed to go check on his mother first. As he made his way through the city, NOPD presence was heavy everywhere he went, squad cars patrolling every corner of the rough neighborhoods. He turned on his mother's street and the sight of an ambulance parked in front of her house brought all sorts of fear to his soul. A gurney covered in a large white sheet exited Olivia's home as Darlene stood there with her daughter and Levi barely put his car in park before running out to see what happened. Darlene looked at her estranged brother,

"Don't run up here like you care now."

"What da fuck happened?"

"What da fuck it look like Ronald?"

"Dee, I ain't got time fa this. What da fuck happened to mama?"

"She fuckin OD'd. I came ova to check on her and found her on da floor with a fuckin needle in her arm. Dats what da fuck happened. Da last person dat tied us together is gone so I don't have anymore damn ties to yo ass. Fuck you Ronald! Fuck you!"

Levi stood there as he watched the only family member he had left in the world walk away from him. A cloud of darkness weighed heavy on him and everything loss meaning to him, including his own life. Next to the bleakness he was feeling, Levi began to fill with rage when he seen a familiar vehicle in the distance parked up the street from his mother's home. He recognized Papa Sha sitting in the front seat of the Cadillac that was in front of Eve's shop and they locked eyes with each other. Oblivious to everyone around him, Levi drew a chrome .45 from his waist and briskly walked up to the driver side of the vehicle. With complete disregard of his safety, little to no remorse to anyone in fear of him with the firearm, Levi approached the SUV with fire in his eyes. The driver jumped out of the vehicle but couldn't draw his weapon in time as Levi rushed up and struck him across the face with the side of the large pistol in his hand. Levi jumped in the large truck and pointed the gun directly to Papa Sha's temple,

"Bitch you killed my mama? My fuckin mama?"

"Blood fa blood, eh."

"Oh you think this a game bitch!"

"No games, I'm too old fa games blood."

Levi swung his gun one time at Sha's face, busting his nose as he started the engine to the Cadillac. He sped off up the street while Papa Sha held his face in pain and Levi began ranting about how the Haitian ruined his life. Levi talked about how it was the Haitian's fault that his father went to prison, that his mother became strung out on drugs and how he couldn't get away from him. The Cadillac flew through red traffic lights, hitting street curbs at every turn and speeding pass shouting pedestrians who just missed being hit by the vehicle. Every chance Levi got, he hit the drug kingpin in the face with his gun until Sha's face was bloody. The Haitian started laughing to himself as his beliefs gave him confidence that no matter what Levi did, he would live through it all. Papa Sha knew, from the psychic readings he received, he took out the "Island Prince" that was Dante and no one else could stand in his way. Levi looked over at the Haitian in disgust when he told him what his father told him a long time ago,

"I see why my pops didn't except his heritage. Why he didn't tell nobody who his real daddy was. You muthafuckas sick as shit. I still don't know why dat old man had you as his lieutenant back in da day. Fuckin Haitians."

The words cut through Papa Sha like a knife as he began to realize that the "Island Prince" the voodoo doctor was referring to was, the seed of the one person he despised. Papa Sha didn't feel Roger was a true Haitian because he wasn't full-blooded like they were, but he carried the blood of his former leader and so did Levi. Fear began to set in but by then it was too late as Levi sped up Paris Ave towards another red light as he blurted out,

"If I gotta kill myself to kill you, I will."

The SUV blared through the traffic light as another car was crossing, clipping the back bumper and the large vehicle spun out of control as it went up the street. It looked as if it would never stop spinning but then the Cadillac suddenly halted when the front of it struck one of the columns of an overpass and the front windshield shattered. Papa Sha's body went airborne from the impact and flew up the street until it contacted the asphalt. His body flipped, spun and cartwheeled up the avenue in a bloody mess as it slowed down, resting on the sidewalk in a contorted shape.

YEAR 2026

6 months went by like a slug on a hot New Orleans' summer as Levi sat in Orleans Parish Prison on a Vehicular Manslaughter charge for the death of Papa Sha. He was content with how things played out, knowing that his sacrifice of freedom freed everyone else from the Haitian drug lord's tyrannist rule. The only downfall of the whole situation was that Levi found out Kirby wasn't killed during the shoot-out. The round that struck him ripped through one side of his face, shattering his jawbone but Papa Sha's little brother lived through it. Levi didn't give him a second thought, figuring if there was going to be any kind of retaliation on Sha's death it would come straight at him and not anyone else. Kirby didn't want any smoke from Eve because the robbery of her store and the shoot-out in front of it brought on protection from NOPD. Allison was off limits also because of her affiliation with the BTK gang and the occasional visits from the Mexican cartel. Kareem made sure Levi's daughter was taken care of and always kept an eye out for the safety of Darlene, but she avoided anyone associated with her disowned brother. Levi himself just had to sit and wait out the 5 year long bid in prison he received.

For the first couple of months, the days felt long to Levi because he was stuck in a two-man cell with a bunky who did nothing but bitch and moan about the quality of the prison. He couldn't understand how someone could be so hardcore in the streets but bitch up when locked behind some bars. Levi was at his breaking point with the cellmate as arguments became more and more frequent over what he felt was menial stuff. A lifer and tier rep could see the young bull was about to do something that could easily end up getting him more time in the prison pulled Levi to the side,

"Say blood, ask for a transfer before you do something stupid. Everybody ain't gone be on da same page as you."

"Man dis muthafucka complain all fuckin day. Complainin' bout dumb shit."

"I can see you just tryin' to do yo time and I know da shit workin' yo last nerve. Dats why I say ask to be transferred to anotha cell or even anotha tier. I'll send you to the right one to ask."

Levi thanked the OG of the unit for his help and went get his things together for a transfer off the tier. The deputy in charge of transferring inmates throughout the prison was actually the nephew to the OG and was also in charge of work orders in the prison. Levi got real cool with the officer and ended up getting on with the kitchen staff. The time started to fly by as 16-hour days in the kitchen cooking breakfast, lunch and dinner occupied most of Levi's day. He stayed busy even when he wasn't, passing out books from the library, dropping off laundry to the cleaning staff and even working with the janitorial crew on occasion. Levi wanted to fill his days up with doing something to make his time behind bars move quicker. His daughter was growing up and he didn't want Ronnisha to forget about him completely. Writing letters, sending gift cards and getting Kareem or Cedric to leave a present on the porch from him became a regular thing. Levi wanted his presence felt in some form or fashion when it came to his daughter. Along with his only child, he also stayed in touch with everyone else because he knew once he was released from prison he would get right back on the grind. Levi needed his connects to keep him in mind so when he did need them, they would be there. Allison stayed getting letters every other day, asking her how she's been, how's the business going and all. Since his mother was no longer with him and his sister was non-existent, Eve received all the family-oriented letters and she appreciated every one. Leslie even got a few letters, keeping their friendship strong during Levi's stint behind bars. Kareem was the only one that was honored enough to receive a call from him though.

Kirby had recovered from his wounds and his days were filled with getting revenge on the man that killed his big brother. The police charged it as joyriding that went terribly wrong, but Kirby knew it was a calculated hit on his family. He tried having someone get to Levi in the hospital, but the inmate was too well guarded when he was in there. When Kirby got word that Levi was being housed at Orleans Parish Prison for his sentence, he put out a hit on the prisoner worth 10 stacks to any Haitian in there,

"I want him head. I want him head on me nightstand."

Big Bank was the man behind the prison walls and a faithful follower of the Haitian gang Kirby had control of. He was given the name Big Bank because he was a mountain of a man, standing 6'8" and weighing in at 390lbs. No one really challenged the giant as he had the run of the tier he was in and when he was on the yard most if not all prisoners avoided him if they weren't in his clique. Along with a few others Big Bank had two followers, Frog and Lester who took pleasure in being the intimidating muscle of the crew. The Haitian crew ran the laundry department in the prison because they used incoming clothing as mules to bring in pills the gang was selling. The pill operation ran smooth because two of the deputies that worked at the prison made sure they didn't run into any issues. Big Bank kept extra money in their pockets and the guards kept prying eyes from snooping around the laundry area. When the order came down from Kirby that Levi was a marked man the extra-large Haitian wanted nothing more than to bleed the opp out. He sent his two pit bulls out to hunt for their new prey and they quickly came back with info on Levi's entire schedule. After hearing that Levi was working with the kitchen staff, Big Bank knew getting to him there was completely off limits. There was an order to things in the prison and the kitchen staff was a melting pot of every gang in the prison that literally united them all in a sense. As strong and powerful as Big Bank was, the kitchen employees were somewhat sacred to the entire prison system. The jailbird leader was frustrated trying to figure out a way to get to Levi,

"We hit him, it can't come back on us. We gotta be careful on this one but he a dead man. Dead."

Frog had found out that on occasions Levi helps with passing out library books when he's not in the kitchen. The three

Haitian gang members came up with a plan to get the opp then and make it look like a random assault.

       Levi was unaware to the hit that was on his head and went about his day like normal. His mornings were filled with prepping breakfast for every soul behind the prison walls, while his afternoons involved the mopping of football field length hallways. Levi didn't mind the hard work because it kept his thoughts away from the time he had to do in there. He went from one task to the other as the days blended into each other and the weeks turned quickly into passing months. One day Levi had some free time and grabbed a rolling cart from the library to bring around to a few on lockdown. He pushed the cart down the long catwalk as he stopped at every cell door asking if they wanted a new book to read. Levi was on the second floor of the tier, walking down the catwalk and was admiring the view of the city through iron grated windows. He could see cars going by on the nearby freeway and just imagined where they could be going as he continued to ask inmates who were locked behind bars if they needed any new literature. The second floor of the tier was pretty much bare as several cells were empty but maybe three cells. Levi was standing in front of the last cell of the tier and the stocky framed resident Lester was sitting on the bed, looking down at the floor when he was asked the question,

"Say round, you need a book?"

"Nah, I'm good."

"You sure? I got the Decisions series collection. Heard dat shit good."

"Aight. Gimme dat."

"You gone like dis. Dude who wrote it, from New Orleans."

Levi gathered the three books to hand over to Lester when he noticed a scrawny guy walking up the catwalk towards him. Thinking nothing of it because he figured it was just an inmate going back to his cell, the makeshift librarian took his eyes off of him. As he reached in between the bars to hand Lester the books he had for him, Levi's wrists were immediately snatched in. His arms were pulled through the bars as his face pressed hard against the cold steel and the skinny resident on the catwalk sprinted towards him with a short blade in his hand. Levi tried to scream when the first jab tore through the side of his flesh, but the lanky Frog wrapped his hand over his victim's mouth. The second jab pierced right between his lower ribcage and Levi knew if he didn't get free his last days on earth was going to come fast. He raised up his knee and pushed against the bars as Lester's sweaty hands loss its grip. Frog pushed the rusty blade into Levi's back one last time as the angered victim broke free of Lester's grasp,

"Bitch!"

The two men fell onto the railing of the catwalk which kept them from plummeting to the floor below and Levi was finally able to get his bearings. Still with the shank jammed in his back, Levi charged Frog wrapping his hands around his neck. Frog tried to fight Levi off of him, but the predator had become the prey as the stabbing victim overpowered the stabber. Lester pushed his way out of the unlocked cell he was in to help his partner but as soon as he got close, found his face connecting with a backhand swing from Levi. Frog shoved his fingers in the wound on Levi's side and the excruciating pain caused the victim to push the skeleton of a man over the banister to the hard concrete floor below. When Lester seen his friend go headfirst over the side, he attempted to do the same to Levi but again caught a fist to the face, stumbling him back two steps. The assailant seen he missed the opportunity and darted off because he could hear the rumble of prison guard boots coming up the stairs behind

Levi. The victim tried to chase behind the heavy-set assaulter, but his body had other plans as it collapsed under the trauma it just took.

The news of the attack on Levi brought back some horrible memories for Eve when she got a visit from one of her NOPD buddies that heard it from his brother. Seeing Dante lose his life right in front of her came rushing back to her. The loud bang from the gun echoed in her head, the sound of her lover's body hitting the ground was so clear and the smell of death filled her nose. It was as if she was there all over again and the feeling wasn't good at all. Thoughts of someone she truly loved being hurt again haunted her and she asked the officer if it was anything she could do to help him. The policeman had no information for her at the time but encouraged her to have faith in the medical staff at the prison. Eve had very little faith in people because of everything she's been through but at the moment she had to put all her convictions in some people she didn't know. After her police friend left Kareem came over just to check on her like he always did ever since the incident with the robbery. He felt bad for striking her that day, but Eve always made him feel better about the situation,

"Say youngin, we all had our job to do and you did yo part. Truss me when I say there's no hard feelings. We had to make dat shit look convincing."

Kareem appreciated her making him feel better about everything but with Levi being gone for so long he occupied his time at Eve's place a lot. She took him under her wing and taught him what it took to run a business. Kareem had street sense and book smarts but keeping a business afloat took a special skill in which Eve was more than happy to show him. He was like a sponge with everything she showed him and surprised his teacher every time with how good her student understood the business of being an owner. The companionship was something both of them needed at the time and their friendship got closer with every day.

Levi woke up in the infirmary and the all-white walls along with the all-white sheets laying over him was a shock to his system because he thought he had crossed over to the upper room. A nurse rushed over to him to calm him, but the disoriented inmate pushed the woman out of his way in an attempt to get out of the hospital bed. The infirmary's deputy walked over to assist in getting control of the situation as she asked,

"Mr. Sweed, I'm a need you to lay down now. It's ok, you in the clinic and you safe. You keep jumpin' up like dat and you gone bust dem stitches."

He finally realized he was in a safe place and the ordeal he survived was just a passing moment. The nurse was able to check Levi's vitals while he calmed himself but the man in him was mesmerized by the curvy frame of the deputy walking away. The pretty smile she carried while talking to passing doctors and nurses was a plus. The embroidered name Wilson had him wanting to know her better, but Levi understood his circumstances would deny any kind of advance with the thickly framed yellow bone. For now, he caught himself just appreciating the lovely view of the officer sitting at her post while doctors and nurses went about their day. Thoughts of who his attackers were began to invade his mind as another officer came over to get a report from him of the incident. His wounds began to sting of pain as Levi talked about what happened to him. He had no clue to who the assailant was that he threw over the railing until the officer asked him if he knew of a Haitian gang. Everything started to rush in, and Levi knew right then that he had a hit out on him but held his tongue with the questioning deputy,

"Chief I honestly couldn't tell you. Dat shit happened so fast, I was just tryin' to protect myself, ya heard me."

"You good man, it was all written in as self-defense on your part. I'm a need you to watch yo back though. You really can't remember anything about the other guy cause the cell you was talking bout was empty. Nobody was connected to that cell or the ones next to it."

"I don't know."

The officer finished his report with Levi and left him to recover in the infirmary as the inmate thought of revenge. Levi knew this wasn't going to be the last encounter or attempt on his life and he prepared himself for whatever was coming. The heavy-set man that ran away from him was etched in his mind and all he wanted was another chance at him with no interruptions. Determined to get out of the clinic was the only thing on his mind now.

A week in the prison hospital wasn't without its obstacles for Levi, with infection setting in one of his wounds and the occasional threats from the Haitians kept him on a constant alert. The one light to his days were oddly the sight of the clinic deputy Netta Wilson who always took care of him. The 5-foot 2 thick yellow bone was a welcoming sight of eye candy and her grayish colored pupils added to her sexiness. Levi would catch himself just staring at her succulent frame, a frame most women would pay for but hers was all natural with hourglass dimensions. Even though her uniform was her size, it was fitting tight in all the right places. Pants that hugged every inch of her and a top that looked as if the buttons would pop if she inhaled. Netta knew the majority of the inmates who came to the infirmary "eye fucked" her as soon as they seen her. Some would even go so far as to approach her. The hospital's deputy understood the type of business she was in, the element of characters that were in there and she knew men were simply going to be men. Levi admired the fact that the high levels of testosterone that filled the building didn't intimidate Netta one bit. He was even curious one day when he asked,

"Why you only work on the male side?"

"Too many females in one spot is a fight waiting to happen."

"Nah, you scared one of dem studs gone holla atcha."

"Nah, dats da least of my worries. I treat dem da same way I treat y'all, no love."

"Shid, you love me."

"Boy stop. Only things I love is my lil one and my paycheck."

Netta caught herself enjoying their small conversations mainly because it felt genuine and it wasn't some horny guy trying to talk her out of her panties. Levi's level of conversation stayed around family, friends or how each other's day was going. As much as he wanted to shoot his shot at her, the situation of him being an inmate and she being a sheriff deputy deterred him. Levi had his chances to pursue some more intense convos with Netta but held his will power intact when it came down to her. He had just finished talking with the infirmary's doctor, who was releasing him back to general population and the inmate took the opportunity to express his feelings. Levi told Netta he's going to miss their daily talks and that he appreciated her help. She joked with him saying she's always in the infirmary and if he wanted to he could always get shanked again to come visit. As he prepped himself to face the trials of gen pop and the obvious battle he's going to run into with the Haitians, Levi got some good news on his way to his cell. The deputy in charge of Levi's tier pulled him to the side,

"Boy, you made a good impression down there in da clinic. Got dem asking for you personally."

"Whatcha mean asking fa me?"

"There's only two inmates that work down there and one of'em transferring next week. Most guys here gotta be veterans to work in the clinic but one of da nurses along with da infirmary deputy asked for you personally. Don't mess dis up. Most guys don't get da freedom to roam da facility like dat."

Levi thought about it and knew this was his chance to make the best out of a bad situation. He just had to figure out how to get the Haitian crew off his back next. That was something that had to happen and soon before it was too late.

YEAR 2027-2028

Kareem started working for Eve at her CBD shop in the French Quarters and the young man had become a true protégé to handling the business. Eve was at the point where she was able to trust him with ordering new inventory, making the schedule for the other employees and even dropping off deposits to the bank. He proved to be a true asset to her, and she showed him everything it took to run the business. With no children of her own, Eve took to Kareem like her son only second to Levi who they both were so ready for him to get out of prison. Letters that he was doing good was like a gift to read when they received them, and Eve made it her mission to visit as much as she could. Her visitation time helped her more than it helped Levi, seeing him in good spirit and not seeing stress on his face was a plus. Eve would joke with him, stating that she's going to send him a cannabis filled care package every time she came to visit. One day Levi replied,

"Mama don't play. I may take you up on dat one day, ya heard me."

"Boy shut up. You mind yaself in there and stay outta trouble."

Knowing her son, Eve could tell he really meant it and knew he was plotting on something from the inside. She always would try to tell him there's a better way, but Levi wasn't trying to hear that. Stuck behind bars, he felt the system was set up for him to fail. Feeling his destiny was already written, he encouraged Eve to put her energy into keeping Kareem out of jail. With his mother gone, his sister non-existent in his life, Kareem and Eve was the only family he had left. Levi seen the potential in the young man and knew Eve's savvy in business would be the perfect fit for him. She would glow when she talk about how good Kareem is and how fast he catches on,

"That boy gone be something special. He's a true businessman with a heart of gold. Always lookin' out for people but keepin' it real with dem too."

"Yeah, his whole family like dat. Real cool people. I never told nobody but when I was small I envied dem."

"Why you say dat?"

"Don't get me wrong, not sayin' my childhood was bad or nothin' but they just had it all. My daddy was my superhero but dey daddy was like a real live superhero. Dude was built like a action figure and dey mama sweet as hell. Mrs. D always looked out fa us."

"Baby, yo parents did what dey needed to do to give you da best life dey could."

"I know but shit wasn't sweet and dats why I stay on Reem. I want him to be better than me. Dats my lil bro."

Levi prided himself on keeping Kareem on the straight and narrow because he truly wanted better for him. Eve adored the fact that the youngest of the Daniels' clan looked at Levi as a big brother and the love the two had for each other.

Levi was gathering some dirty linen from the infirmary to take to the laundry room when he seen Deputy Wilson sitting at her post. He could tell something was wrong with her because she wasn't carrying her usual joyous spirit, she carried every day at work. Levi didn't want to pry in her personal life, but he felt they had somewhat of a bond between them. When he walked up to her he could see the agitation in her eyes,

"Hey, you good?"

"Yeah, I'm good. Where you going?"

"I gotta take these sheets to laundry, so they could be clean for tomorrow. You wanna take me?"

"Yeah, I need to walk around."

The two walked the halls of the prison, passing several tiers and picking up extra linen that needed to be washed. Levi noticed he wasn't the only one that found Netta crazy attractive when they would make stops at the different control booths. Some of the male detention officers would break their necks trying to get Officer Wilson's attention. Promising her days of pampering if she would agree to a date with them or even a chance to just chill with her. Netta paid them no mind as she made her moves through the building while Levi kept himself busy with his chores. The whole time they made their way to the laundry room, Levi could tell his company had something taxing on her mind that was really bothering her. He attempted to get her mind on other things as he joked with her,

"Everybody shootin' dey shot at you. I ain't know I was walkin' with a celebrity."

"Stop it. Half dem negroes married. I ain't got time for none of dat, not tryin' to ruin nobody happy home."

"Maybe it's not a happy home you never know but you still got da single half to go through. Who you givin' the privilege of access to you?"

"Nah, none of dem interest me like dat. I can't do fuck boys. But now I got a question for you since you wanna get all in my business. You always talk to me every day, ask me about my lil girl and my mama all the time but you neva shot yo shot. Why is dat, you scared?"

"Neva dat. If my situation was different and I wasn't on the wrong side of these bars, I would have been shot it. But I can't take that chance in here."

"Maybe taking a chance could work out for you, ya never know."

Levi was stuck after hearing Netta's last comment because he didn't know how to take it. He didn't know if she was serious or just joking around like she usually does but the prison resident was very curious. Levi changed the subject and asked if everything was okay at home. Netta was hesitant at first but then she opened up and told her prison buddy about her ex. She started to go on about how he refuses to help with the child-care of their daughter. Levi thought about his own child and how he would give anything just to see her. He encouraged Netta that everything works out in the end and that her baby daddy would regret his actions in the long run. They made it to the laundry room and Netta waited at the huge steel double doors talking with one of her colleagues while Levi brought in the dirt garments. The two deputies had no clue as to the tension that filled the room when Levi entered but the inmate knew exactly what he was doing. Levi purposely went to the laundry room because he heard the Haitians ran that department and he needed to see the guy that helped attack him. Every eye in the steamy room was zoned in on the man who killed Papa Sha and threw one of their brothers over a balcony. Levi was there for one reason and one reason only as he scanned the room for the stocky guy that set him up. He almost gave up looking for him but then a mammoth of a man came walking from the back and following close behind was the target Levi was searching for,

"There go my bitch."

When Lester locked eyes with Levi, he lunged forward towards him, but Big Bank halted the advances because of the guards close by. Levi released an evil grin knowing they couldn't do anything about him and headed back by Netta who was waiting at the exit door. Knowing he was able to fuck with their minds real quick was all the pleasure he needed. Plans were coming together in his head as to what he wanted to do.

Leslie was doing her usual hustling outside of working on the docks when she pulled up to one of Allison's stores with a shipment she got hold to from an unmarked crate. When she looked inside the crate the surprised dock worker found several stuffed teddy bears, but they weren't stuffed with cotton. The stuffed animals were full of heroin, cocaine and pills ready for distribution, but Leslie needed to find a seller. Allison was willing to buy all the pills and coke off of her but left Leslie with all the heroin to deal with. As Leslie was on her way out the curious cat in Allison prompted her to ask,

"It's none of my business but I just needed to ask. You and Levi still kickin' it? How he doing?"

"Kickin' it? Da fuck you mean?"

"You and Levi a couple, right?"

"Girl stop it! Dats my dawg. We just cool and dats it. He was yo nigga. Well, until he wasn't. Dats on y'all."

Allison didn't know what to say after hearing Leslie's reply and watched her drive away heading over to meet up with a buyer of her remaining product. The hustler laughed to herself as she thought about what Allison asked her. Leslie went to meet up with Kareem because he said he had someone in mind that could buy the rest of the Chiba from her. She really didn't want to drive around the city holding down two kilos of heroin in her car and hoped Levi's homeboy had a trusted connect. Leslie was cool with working with Kareem for two reasons, one because of Levi and second because she was really good friends with his brother Cedric. She went to high school with him and knew the family was some loyal folk when it came to their friends. Kareem was at the shop with Eve going over some upcoming orders when Leslie pulled up. Leslie knew Eve was a down female when it came to under the table actions. She just didn't know how cool she would be with them conducting a street deal at her shop. She called Kareem outside to meet up with her so they could discuss their next move when Eve came out. The store owner could see she had a teaching moment on her hands when she seen the two talking,

"I'm a tell y'all this. Don't ever do shit on a public street where anybody could walk by and hear yo convo, Reem you know betta. Do dat shit behind closed doors. Leslie bring yo lil ass inside."

"Yes ma'am."

The two immediately listened to the wise woman as they took their conversation in the back office away from ear hustlers and Kareem talked to Leslie about moving her product. He told her that Levi been looking for a way to get ahold of some work to move behind bars. Kareem said he would hold the packs for Leslie at the shop until Levi get back with him. The hustler usually didn't accept promises of payments from people, but she knew Kareem and Levi was good for it. Besides she was happy to get the packs off her hands and knew she would definitely get paid later.

Morning came around fast for Levi as he sat up in his bunk looking around at the four walls of his 8 by 8 cell. His body had gotten accustomed to being up early because of his new medical room gig but today was Sunday and the infirmary was closed. Levi usually worked in the kitchen on them days, but he wanted to stay in. His cellmate was roaring like a Mack truck hauling a heavy load as he snored in his sleep. The low chatter of nearby inmates could be heard as they woke from their own slumber and Levi got himself dressed because he knew count would be coming soon. The day started like any other day, guards walking around like they didn't want to be there and residents plotting on what they could get away with. After a coded conversation on the phone with Kareem, Levi had become one of those residents and he was trying to see who he could use to reach the outside. He knew the two kilos of heroin Kareem had stashed would sell like crazy on the inside. Levi's brain was scrolling through names like a rolodex of different deputies he knew was down for making some extra ends. A lot of them worked for the Haitians, bringing in their product and the others freelanced favors for a few inmates. Levi needed to find someone he could trust and that was a task in itself because he didn't trust anybody behind those prison walls. He was in the cafeteria getting breakfast when he seen Netta standing with two of her co-workers, watching over the room. The sexy redbone released a smile when they made eye contact with each other and a light came on in Levi's head. He didn't want to use her, but he knew if he played his cards right, he could get her to take care of him in more ways than one. After finishing off some not so appealing oatmeal, toast and runny scrambled eggs, Levi walked over to throw away his tray. He walked pass Netta heading back toward his cell and grazed his hand against hers. The sheriff deputy made up an excuse to leave her associates in the mess hall and followed behind Levi. He could feel her behind him as the sound of her combat boots hitting the concrete floor echoed down the walkway. Netta called out his name,

"Mr. Sweed."

"Yes ma'am."

"Where you think you goin'?"

"Ummm, back to my apartment."

"I need you to do something, follow me."

Netta walked him down an empty hallway of vacant offices, Levi was skeptical of her intentions but went along with her anyways. She unlocked one of the office doors, walked in and the unsure inmate looked over his shoulder to make sure no one seen him walk in behind her. Netta shut the door and the only light in the room came from a small window in the far back of the office. With the lights still off, Levi knew she didn't bring him back there to talk and went for it all as he rushed in for a kiss. Netta pulled at his bright orange jumpsuit as the buttons popped loose and Levi tugged at her uniform unbuttoning her top. They undressed each other and both parties were pleased at the sight standing in front of them. Netta's purple laced bra held her 40 double D's up like they were on display for Levi to enjoy. The bulge growing in his shorts was a pleasant sight to see as she caressed it with her fingertips. Levi pulled her uniform pants down to a matching pair of purple lace panties that were already moistened from Netta's wet pussy. With her pants and undies down to her ankles, Levi picked her up and sat her on the desk in front of him. He put her legs on his shoulders, pressed his lips against her moist lower lips and slid his tongue deep inside her tasting her delectable juices. Netta squirmed as his tongue swirled around her clit and he gripped her ass burying his face into her fat pocketbook. She could tell Levi was talented at his oral skills as he nibbled on her throbbing clit, and she held onto the end of the desk. The head she was receiving became so intense that she had to cover her mouth before she screamed out her first orgasm with him. Levi felt her juices roll down his chin as he stood up between her legs and his manhood pressed against her. Wiping his face, he looked down at her waxed "Mound of Venus" and read the tattoo above it that said,

"Warning!"

Levi disregarded all cautions and knew he had to get in there to see if it was all true or just a distraction. The heat in the room raised another degree as he pushed his way inside her and her walls welcomed every inch of him. Slow strokes of his dick slid back and forth with ease as Netta's love liquid surrounded Levi's hardened appendage. The strokes increased as the feeling brought on more and more pleasure but Netta's moans had to be muffled by Levi's hand as she began to squirt out another "Big O". He attempted to hold out on his nut but after seeing her squirt all over his dick, Levi returned the favor. He pulled out, stroking his meat as he released his load all over her warning sign tattoo and she reached down as she helped squeeze out the last drip. Breathing hard following a very eventful encounter Netta smiled,

"Now that's how you shoot your shot."

A few weeks went by and the secret lovers' encounters in the vacant offices continued as Levi enjoyed being deep inside of Netta. During one of their conversations while getting dressed he mention a package he needed her to get for him. She had already got in too deep, bringing him in a burner phone and Netta seen nothing wrong with the request. He guaranteed a three-way split of the profits if she could get him the package from Kareem. Netta didn't know what she was getting into messing with Levi, but she was about to find out as she met up with Kareem to pick up the contraband for him. The young sheriff deputy was a little nervous about the meet up but wasn't naïve to the lifestyle because she came from a family that collaborated with the underbelly scenes of the city. Netta chose to go in a different direction unlike her older brothers and her daughter's father who all were still deep in the game. She seen with her cousin's death that the corner was not a life she wanted for herself or her child. It was something about Levi that pulled her in and had her dismiss the obvious consequences she could face if she got caught. Netta knew of the other deputies who had a double life, working for or with residents inside making sometimes twice as much as what they make legally. She figured it was her turn to grab the opportunity her new fling laid out for her. The two strangers met up at Lake Pontchartrain and Kareem seen exactly why Levi got Netta on his team as soon as she stepped out of her car. The thick yellowbone had on some grey tights, a New Orleans Saints cropped hoodie and the sexiness glowed around her like an aura. She looked like an IG model from a FashionNova page as she walked up to him with the cutest smile on her face. For a few seconds Kareem was stuck on stupid as his eyes scanned over the exquisite frame standing in front of him. Netta had come accustomed to the male species looking at her as a snack and usually she used it to her benefit but today she was all business,

"Hello!"

"My bad. You got out the car and I loss all train a thought."

"Really? I'm a need you to focus. Like for real for real."

"Bet."

Kareem realized the healthy thoroughbred standing in front of him was all business and no games, so he jumped in line too. He reached in the back seat of his ride and pulled out a black backpack that had 2 kilos of heroin in it. Kareem had already broken one kilo down to individual baggies and asked Netta if she needed help with the other one. She giggled as she informed her new partner this wasn't her first rodeo weighing or bagging product. Netta's nerves seemed to calm once she tossed the backpack in her car and her mind began calculating her moves when she gets back to work. Her street smarts took over and Kareem could see another side of her that resembled his mentor, Eve. Netta started to actually relax around Kareem and the lifestyle she ran away from felt comfortable in her lap. She didn't want their encounter to look like a meet and drop to any onlookers so the vixen entertained Kareem for a while. Her company was well welcomed as it gave Kareem more time to admire Netta's naturally exaggerated build and then it got even more entertaining when he noticed her tattoos. The paw prints that outlined her hips were real nice to look at but the lower back tattoo of a Chinese symbol surrounded by rose vines over her big round ass was a delight to see. It forced his hand as he inquired,

"How many tatts you got?"

"Including the ones you see, I got about 6 of'em."

"Six? Lemme see."

"Boy you a mess, I see why you and Levi friends. You can see most of dem dependin' on what I got on but one of dem the only way you seeing that is we fuckin. And I don't think we that cool."

"Shid, I'm cool if you cool."

"Boy stop it. You and Levi definitely brothers. I'm a need you to focus on what we need to do and not my tatts."

"Well, I'm a need you to cover dem all up then, cause my focus not on work."

"Well next time I'm a wear a moo moo dress and some fuzzy slippers. Would that be better for yo focus?"

Kareem and Netta started laughing at each other as they clowned around about how serious she was at first compared to now. Kareem chuckled when Netta teased him about how his mouth fell open when she walked up to him. The two really clicked once they got to know each other and the possibilities had potential but the elephant standing in the midst of them halted that thought. Kareem was loyal to his pretend big brother and that made Netta off limits even though Levi was locked behind bars. Netta on the other hand had no problem with it because she knew she was just there to serve a purpose for Levi and there was no real connection other than sex. She could see Kareem was different than the brothers she was use to dealing with and he was very appealing to her because of that. Netta caught herself flirting with him and Kareem desperately tried to fight the urge to return her actions. He could see she was a woman that went out to get what she wants, and any man would be a fool to turn her down. Kareem became that fool and stepped back but Netta left something on his mind before leaving him at the Lake. She leaned in, put his hands on her soft round ass and ever so gently pressed her full luscious lips against his. Kareem watched the sexy body of Netta walk away from him and wanted nothing but to follow her. She got in her car and before pulling off told him,

"Don't be no stranger, text me later."

Business was popping for Levi with the new product he introduced to the fiends behind the prison walls. He really wasn't trying to make a killing at selling the heroin he had but just to ruffle a few feathers in taking money away from the Haitians. Levi's plan was working, and Big Bank wasn't happy about it at all. He and Lester had devilish plans for the upcoming jail house drug lord. The two had another ambush set up for their enemy but what they didn't know was that Levi was expecting it. He was able to sneak away a razor-sharp scalpel from one of the unaware doctors in the infirmary. A doctor, who paid attention to none of his surroundings on a regular day basis. Levi knew the Haitians would try something and he needed an edge on them for backup because the only one who really had his back on the inside was Netta. The moment he was waiting for was close at hand when Levi returned back to his cell to find his bunky was gone for good. When Levi asked one of the guards where he went the deputy replied,

"He requested a move and we granted it. Looks like you got da spot all to yaself, all alone."

"Yeah, I see."

Levi was a little suspicious of the deputy's response because the guy he shared a cell with pretty much stayed to himself and was about to be released in a week. To ask to be moved all of a sudden was kind of strange to him. Once in his cell Levi could tell his things were searched through and whoever it was tried to make it look normal. He knew they were searching for his stash. It was as if the entire cell block knew something was going on because eyes stayed on him as he walked through the dayroom. Whispers went silent as he walked by and new faces were evident on the block when Levi scanned the room. He knew the Haitian gang was about to make a move today and he kept his head on a swivel, suspecting everyone. Levi didn't want to be cornered in his cell, but he also didn't want to be ambushed from behind either. He kept his back to a wall and watched every individual that came in his path. Tension was high and his stress level was through the roof as Levi attempted to look normal on the outside. He carried on with his day like any other but made sure he had his shank tucked in his sock ready for whatever happens. Levi gave up on an ambush when he went to the showers to clean off the day's dirt and that's when he was approached. Naked as the day he was born, covered in soap and vulnerable to everything. Levi seen Lester charging towards him with a sharpened toothbrush handle in his hand. As soon as the assaulter was in arm's reach of him, Levi connected a closed fist to Lester's face staggering the juggernaut back a few steps. When he seen that his attacker was stunned from the hit, Levi advanced striking him again in the face all the while avoiding swings from the sharpened plastic shiv. Lester was blindly swinging his hand in an attempt to keep Levi off of him because the two strikes to the face quickly closed both of his eyes. Levi seen that his opponent was frantically trying to keep him off and rushed in to tackle him to the floor. The big man dropped like a load of bricks on his back with Levi on top of him but a deep slice to Levi's shoulder made him retreat back. Lester gained his bearings as he got up off the slippery wet shower floor and made his way back towards Levi,

"Bitch I'm a gut you like a catfish."

Blood poured from Levi's arm like a faucet and the huge brut lunged towards him with nothing but bad intensions. Levi's back was close to the shower wall when Lester tackled him to the floor. In the process of them falling to the ground Lester's forehead hit the brick wall, pushing his head back. Levi heard a loud crack as if bones broke and Lester's limp body slumped on top of him while the water from the shower continued to spray on them both. The big man over judged his attack, wrapping Levi up to the ground and hit his head on the brick shower wall snapping his own neck. Levi crawled from under Lester as the giant laid there dead with the pointed toothbrush handle still clasped in his tight grip. He quickly grabbed his clothes to put them on and exited the shower room to surprised eyes looking at him walk to his cell. Levi knew it wasn't over and the next attack could happen at any given moment. Sleep was a luxury now and closed eyes could end up closed forever if he didn't stay alert.

The next morning Levi got up to rumbles from the deputies investigating the death of Lester in the showers. None of the other inmates were talking and the incident was ruled an accident, stating Lester slipped in the shower breaking his neck. Mostly everyone in the cellblock knew what really happened but no one was saying a word about it. Levi tried bandaging himself up that night in his cell, but the wound was still bleeding something serious. He went to his regular workstation at the infirmary and met up with Netta,

"Hey, I need a big favor."

"It is too early in da morning and I am not suckin yo dick. I ain't even have my coffee yet."

"Really Netta? I'm fareal, I need you to look at something."

When she heard him call her by her first name she knew it had to be serious and brought him over to any empty exam room. Levi eased his arm out of his jumper and shock was all over Netta's face when she seen the bloody makeshift bandage on the upper part of his shoulder. She peeled the blood-stained napkins off to a deep gash that still had a little red liquid trickling down his arm. Netta seen doctors close up wounds before but she didn't want to take a chance on messing up on someone she cared about. She told Levi to stay put while she went to get one of the doctors, she trusted to keep their mouth shut of the incident. The doctor came in, quickly stitched him up and gave Levi a few pills for the pain before leaving him with Netta. Levi sat there quiet because he could see the look on Netta's face went from concern to agitation after the doctor walked out. She stood at the closed door with her arms folded,

"What happened? And don't tell me nothing cause that damn gash wasn't nothing."

"I had a situation and I handled it."

"You handled it? Look more like dey handled you."

"You should see da other guy."

"Ronald, I ain't playin' with chu. Did this have to do with dat dude in da shower? We can't be havin' no heat comin on us. Did anybody see you?"

"Ain't nobody talkin' in there. Most of dem dudes knew what was goin' down."

"Bet. Dat mean I gotta getchu outta there. You gone have a new bunk by da end of da day. Just keep yo head down."

Levi appreciated Netta as he walked up to her to give her a kiss, but the deputy turned her head as the approaching lips connected to her cheek. The inmate smiled as he mentioned his play brother's name to her and Netta replied that Kareem is very nice to her. Her eyes lit up when she spoke his name and Levi knew right then that he had to step back from the deputy. He knew their relationship was based on crooked business actions and the occasional freak session. Netta was looking for more and it was something Levi couldn't give her at the moment. They would always have that connection, but it was his boy's turn to step in to give her what she needed. It was a double-edged sword Levi was working with because he knew if it seemed to her that he gave her his blessings, her happiness would work out for him in return. They stayed business partners as the plan continued to go in his favor to aggravate the Haitians.

Netta's words came true and she had Levi moved to a safer cellblock which was closer to the Infirmary. She had him moved just in time because Big Bank was on a rampage over his right-hand man finding death's grasp in the shower. The incident was ruled an accident to the prison system but everyone on that cellblock knew the truth. Levi's new cellblock was full of OG's that were there to serve their time and had very little tolerance for the nonsense from the younger generation in the prison. His cellmate was a mean old man that liked things a certain way and had no problem making that clear,

"Say lil man, I've been in this cell by myself for 5,496 nights. Neva had a issue, neva had a situation dat couldn't be fixed. Now I greed to let you stay here as a favor, but you bring yo problems to my doorstep and I'm a bleed you out in da dayroom and act like I ain't know you."

"We good Chief, we good. I'm just tryin' to stay outta trouble, do my time."

"Boy don't try and play me, don't do dat. Yo name hot as fish grease right now but my money on you though. Dem island boys needed some competition. Just make sure you keep yo shit quiet. Move in silence and don't let dem know yo next move, until it happen."

"Preciate dat my G. What's yo name? It seems you already know mine."

"Neville. Neville Wilson."

"You not related to Deputy…"

"Keep dat shit to yaself. Where you think she keeps yo backpack youngin'?"

Neville opened a secret compartment in the wall that had all sorts of contraband hidden in there along with the black backpack Netta brought in the prison, full of latex balloons packed with heroin. The old man was finishing off the last five years of his 20-year sentence for distribution. He was a big-time dope dealer in New Orleans when he got pulled over for a simple traffic stop and the police found 4 kilos of coke in his car. Neville could have snitched on his co-conspirators for a lesser sentence but that would have involved the rest of his family. One thing he was, was loyal to his bloodline and took everything the judge threw at him. Neville was also Netta's last living uncle on her mother's side of the family.

Levi went about his day like normal, confident that he had a safe place to sleep. Plus, his workplace was heavily secured with deputies he could trust. He gave up on working in the kitchen because the Haitian gang's presence was very evident in there. But things started looking different in the Infirmary too. Netta wasn't at her normal post when he walked in and the deputy there was one of the sketchiest of them all. Levi didn't ask or say anything but knew something was up. The sheriff deputy working in the Infirmary worked for extra ends along with looking the other way when paid to. He prepped himself for the worse because he knew it was coming in the form of vengeance. Levi went on with his day, gathering dirty laundry, emptying out trashcans and making sure the clinic was clean for the doctors. He was taking out the trash to the dumpster when he was approached by an overzealous young Haitian gang member who rushed him in the alleyway. The two rumbled with each other, throwing blows that would knock out the average man, but Levi stood his ground. As quick as the fight started it was over in seconds and the young thug took off running down the hall leaving Levi breathing heavily. Spitting out the blood that filled his mouth on the concrete, Levi walked back inside ready for battle but there was no one around and the hallway back to the Infirmary was vacant. He carefully made his way back to his station when he seen the deputy standing in the doorway,

"Excuse me Chief."

"Dats a nasty cut on yo lip there buddy."

"Yea, slipped on a bag outside and fell."

"You might wanna bob and weave next time. Neva know when dat next bag might pop up on ya."

"Right."

Levi didn't say anything and left the guard to his duties, he knew today was going to be a rough one. Lunch time came around and the clinic cleared out as the doctors left with the nurses to enjoy their meal. Levi backed himself in the corner eating on a wet ham sandwich and keeping his eyes on the front door. He could hear chatter in the hallway and figured it was time for another confrontation but then seen Netta rush in. The deputy that was standing guard tried everything to keep her from the clinic, but she knew something wasn't right. Netta walked up to Levi apologizing for leaving him at the prison hospital, stating her commanding officer had her take a resident to the Medical Center. He was so pleased to see a caring face, Levi thought nothing of it but knew his trials weren't over quite yet. Netta could only protect him in the clinic but that was going to be over in a few hours and he had the rest of the day to go. Levi knew the rival gang was going to try something and he mentally readied himself. The clinic was emptying out as the staff dwindled down to one nurse and an on-call doctor but Netta stood ground until her shift was over. Levi left out when she did and the concerned deputy walked him back to his cellblock as she preached to him to watch his back. It was something Netta didn't have to tell the inmate because everybody and everyone was an enemy at this point to Levi. He knew the gang leader Big Bank had a hit out for him and the target was big on his back. Levi chilled in his cell while all the old heads sat in the dayroom watching talk shows on the TV. He felt safe sitting in the company of the older prisoners because they were respected, and the cellblock was neutral to everyone. Levi was sitting on his bunk with his head down when he heard Neville shout,

"Say young blood!"

When he looked up, Big Bank was standing in the doorway of Levi's cell. The mountain looked as if he filled up the entire exit and Levi knew this was about to be one hell of a fight if the beast charged him. Big Bank began walking toward Levi insulting everything about him, knocking over stuff in the cell and disrespecting his place. Levi attempted to say something and Big Bank swung so fast that it flew his opponent back. Levi quickly got up from the floor because the giant brut was charging towards him with his fist clinched for war. The victim charged and a barrage of swinging hands struck Big Bank in the face, stumbling him back. He knew right then that this wasn't going to be an easy task for him because Levi was not going to back down. The monstrous man raised his leg and kicked Levi in the chest throwing him back. He then straddled on top of him dropping down club like blows from his closed fist. Levi caught glimpses of Big Bank's angered face in between strikes from his fist and returned a few of his own but it didn't phase the giant. After having his way with his prey, he picked him up from the floor, turned him around and wrapped his enormous arm around Levi's neck. The attempt to gasp for air was completely cut off as Big Bank's muscles squeezed tighter and tighter. Levi pulled, scratched and tugged at the huge arm around his neck but it didn't budge one bit. His body became weak, his arms felt heavy and his vision blurred as Levi started to fall unconscious. Big Bank could feel his victory nearing and whispered in his enemy's ear,

"I'm a make show when I get out, I do yo dick suckin sister da same way after I fuck da shit outta her."

Levi's eyes popped open with rage as his hand reached down in his sock to retrieve the scalpel tucked in there. He gripped the handle as tight as he could and swung back with all the force he had left. Anyone close by would think a woman was being assaulted from the high-pitched scream that came next as Big Bank's tight hold was released. Levi took in a deep breath as he got himself together and then looked down at the defeated giant laying on the floor bleeding from between his legs. The handle of the scalpel was sticking out from Big Bank's crotch that had a pool of blood pouring out. Levi was stuck thinking he was about to get another charge but then Neville shouted,

"Lil man, getcho ass outta here."

"Nah, this all me ole school."

"Boy if you don't take dis damn knife, flush it and get da fuck. I got this."

Levi listened to the old man but before he left Neville told him to punch him in the face real hard. The old gangster had a plan, but it had to look convincing to the coming guards that were in route to the cellblock. Levi had just flushed the broken scalpel down the toilet when the riot unit came running in the dayroom towards Neville's cell. Two of the riot guards pulled a limp Big Bank out of the cell with a trail of blood behind him and Neville calmly walked out with his hands behind his head. The old man looked at Levi and winked his eye with a smile as the guards escorted him out of the dayroom for questioning.

YEAR 2029

Release day came early for Levi after an extensive investigation into the stabbing of Big Bank. Neville took the charge claiming the big brut came in his cell threatening him with death and the old man was forced to defend himself. Big Bank had a reputation for being violent and using his size as intimidation to weaker inmates. Old man Neville made it sound very convincing and the bruises to his face conspired with his story. Levi was in debt to Neville, but the old man thought nothing of it because he was looking out for his young cellie. The elderly inmate was only charged with having contraband in his cell in the form of a shank which was a slap on the wrist for him. Big Bank on the other hand had to live the rest of his life taking testosterone pills because he lost both of his testicles in the stabbing. Before leaving Levi made sure that Neville's commissary was full and kept it full the rest of the time he was locked up. His favorite girl and Neville's niece wasn't there to see him off as one of the Sheriff Deputies escorted him through the Intake Department. Levi was ready to run out the building when he seen the sunlight shine through the glass double doors. The double doors brought back memories of when he was a teen causing a ruckus in the streets and problems for his mother. Levi was locked up when his mother was buried and all he could think of was her at the moment as he signed the paperwork to his freedom. He pushed open the doors as he inhaled the fresh air, happy to be a free man again. Waiting outside for him was Kareem and Allison who were both excited to see their boy back home. Allison ran up to Levi and jumped in his arms, he was confused towards the amount of affection she was giving out, he just stared at Kareem over her shoulder. Levi's homeboy couldn't do anything but laugh to himself as he asked,

"So what's the first thing you tryin' to do? Shrimp sandwich? Daiquiris? Or you tryin' to smoke something?"

"Boy you know I don't smoke. Tell da truth, I just wanna go see my mama."

"Bet."

They all got in the car and Kareem drove straight to Providence Memorial Park where Levi's mother Olivia was laid to rest. Providence was one way in, one way out, vast 4 plus acre cemetery which held many families' loved ones and the final resting place of the renowned gospel singer Mahalia Jackson. This was Levi's first time visiting his mother's grave and it was an extremely emotional moment for him when he seen her name etched in the granite tombstone. He stood there silent as his eyes blurred from the tears filling them up and the site of his mother's final resting place was literally set-in stone for him. Allison attempted to comfort him, but Kareem held her back because he knew what his brother was going through. Kareem's father was just yards away from where Olivia was buried and he couldn't bare looking in the direction of Cedric Sr's gravesite, feeling he was a disappointment to his father. All three of them have felt the loss of a parent to the hands of someone else but Levi felt it was his fault because he didn't do more to help his mother.

Kareem had kept up the payments on Levi's apartment while he was locked up along with stacking up the money from the packs he sold in prison. The newly ex-con was sitting on a nice payout after all the money was split up between everyone. With a place to stay and money in his pocket, Levi knew he couldn't jump right back into the game after just getting out of prison, but the adrenaline was itching at him to get back in. He suppressed the urges by going back to working on the docks with Leslie, but temptations were there too. His female partner in crime would always have extra jobs come up that needed Levi's assistance in some form or fashion. Allison also had work for him that involved moving weight from Texas to the Florida Keys on occasion. Levi made it his purpose in life to keep Kareem out of the game because he and Eve seen so much in him. Kareem didn't like it because he felt Levi was keeping him from making a big payout,

"Say fam, I'm tryin' to grind and bring home da bags too."

"Round, I know but I don't need you out in dem streets like dat. I need you to make it, ya heard me. Do it betta than me. Da legal way."

"Dat shit gone come in time but I need to make some stacks right nah."

"Fam, I got you. Just stay away from this shit. You got a good girl in Netta and business doing good at Eve shop. You good. You don't need these problems I got. I need you to be da one dat make it, ya heard me."

Kareem knew his big bro was speaking truth to him and agreed to stay away from the lifestyle and seek a much more desirable way of living. His biological big brother Cedric had already begun that journey with a career in the medical field and a wonderful marriage to his wife Denise. Kareem was 6 months away from his degree in Psychology but the aspirations of running his own business was what drove him.

Levi was getting ready to clock out of work when Leslie came to him about a package, she acquired from one of her regular customers. Leslie had already talked with Allison who was expecting the delivery, but Levi really didn't want to see the Asian Princess at the moment. He wasn't in the mood for dealing with the clinginess Allison had been throwing off lately. True enough Levi took in the perks of Allison wanting him around all the time because he spent a few years in prison. The soft touch of a woman was much needed and she supplied that on numerous occasions. Levi reluctantly took the box,

"You couldn't find nobody else?"

"C'mon nah, take one for da team. You know you like her cakes."

"Oh, now I'm on yo team? But I like yo cakes more. When you gone let me play coach?"

"Nigga stop playin' with me. Go drop off da package, hit me up later."

"You gone slip up and let me take you out one of these days."

"Bye Levi."

Netta stopped over at the CBD shop, to meet up with Kareem after she got off from work. The two newly found lovebirds couldn't get enough of each other. As soon as Netta seen her dreadlock Prince standing behind the counter she had to taste his lips, the kiss was welcomed with a warm embrace. Before they knew it the two left the other employees in the front of the store and made their way to the back-storage room. Kareem couldn't resist those soft grey eyes of Netta when they stared at him the way they were at the time. Besides, the way the top of her uniform was open revealing her lush plump breast demanded attention. Kareem sat her on the wooden countertop and began giving her all the kissing attention she needed as he unbuttoned her top. He reached in her pants as two fingers found her throbbing clit and began massaging it. She squirmed to the rotation of his fingertips around her clit and her juices started to surround them. The excitement was as intense as it could be when Kareem slowly slid his fingers in and out, the sounds of gooey goodness filled the room. Netta in return reached down to pull out what she really wanted playing inside her wet walls. She stroked him until he was rock hard in her hand, her fingers gliding across hardened veins that wrapped around a stiffened muscle mass. Kareem could feel she needed some deep penetration therapy as she pulled at his manhood still tucked in his shorts. He pulled her down from the countertop as he unzipped her pants and pulled them down along with her panties. Netta followed his commands as he forcefully turned her around and bent her over the tabletop they were standing at. She held onto the edges of it as her head laid on the cold wooden slab and Kareem prepared to enter her warm pocket. He leaned over, moved her hair from her face to lick her earlobe and right when she could feel him push his way inside of her, he bit down. Netta could feel every inch of him slide deep inside, every curve of his dick fill up in her until his balls pressed against her lips. Kareem stood up straight as he clasped his hands on her waist and watched her ass jiggled with every thrust he gave to it. The Yin Yang tattoo surrounded by rose vines on Netta's lower back was hypnotizing to him as his hardened appendage seemed to disappear in her plush goodness. Kareem's strokes banged in with force like he was mad at her and Netta enjoyed every impact as her juices flowed, dripping down her thigh. She knew her man and knew he was getting close to exploding as she mumbled,

"I want dat nut in my mouth. You bet not cum yet."

Netta's pussy grip squeezed down on him like she was milking his orgasm to the front and Kareem couldn't hold on any longer as he pulled his meat from her hot cumber patch. She immediately knelt down in front of him, pushed her mouth around his shaft and sucked out every ounce of his cream. Kareem's knees weakened as he watched Netta make his dick disappear between her full luscious lips swallowing his volcanic blast. Netta thought their session was over after her big gulp but Kareem had to finish her off and laid her down. He held her legs up while he locked his lips around her clit and his tongue twirled in her juices. Her clit jumped with every flick of his tongue against it, making her anticipate the next stroke and wanting more. She couldn't believe he had her going again as he slid two fingers deep in while he sucked on her. Kareem's oral talents led his tongue all around Netta's clit like a tornado would in a trailer park. The task was almost done when Netta started to feel tingles of energy roll up her spine in the form of an orgasm, she held on. Kareem latched on her clit like a leech and refused to release her until Netta shivered out a spastic orgasm that was followed with splashes of her own feminine squirts. Her body jerked as fluids shot from between her plump waxed lips like a water gun and Kareem enjoyed the sight of it all. They put their clothes back on as Netta laughed to herself about how Kareem had her and told him she didn't come over for all of that. That her visit was actually business related and Kareem replied,

"That was business, I just took care of it. Shid."

"Shut up. Levi left something for me with Eve. He said you would know where it is."

Kareem had been working at Eve's shops for a while, stayed away from the game like Levi asked and he finally saved up enough money to open up his own business. He was finishing the final drafts to submit to the bank for his business loan when Netta first came over. The thought of him opening his own business excited them both but Netta had plans of her own. She was still moving product for Levi in the prison and became really good at it. The young female sheriff deputy had been bit by that "fast cash" bug and she was all in. Kareem tried to convince her to slow down and step away while she had a chance before she gets too deep into the game but Netta wasn't listening. She had a daughter to take care of on her own along with a house and a sheriff's salary wasn't going to cut it for her. Netta came over to pick up the package Levi left there and a lover's quarrel ensued. Kareem offered to get her a job working at the shop with him, but he couldn't compare to the money she was bringing in with the packs she was selling. Netta felt she was smarter than the criminal family and lifestyle she ran away from at first,

"C'mon nah, I got a sweet set up. You and me both could be makin' paper here. How I'm a walk away from dat?"

"Baby I got some things in da works. We gone be good. Just gone take some time."

"I know you got yo shop you tryin' to open up but we could be sitting on some stacks in da meantime."

"This shit don't last long fa people like us, Netta. Why you think I stepped away from it?"

"You ain't step too far from it if I'm still pickin' up from you."

"You right, I ain't got nothing for ya today."

The confused look on Netta's face was priceless as Kareem walked off leaving her standing there. She followed him asking for her product and Kareem told her it was all gone, that he sold it to another buyer. His attempt to save her from herself seemed to backfire as the argument escalated. Netta's confusion turned to anger as she yelled at him for taking money out of her pockets, threatening to tell Levi about it all. Kareem didn't budge with his decision and ignored her bickering as he politely asked her to leave his store because she was causing a scene. Netta stormed out and Kareem knew he had created a problem that needed to be fixed soon as he sat in the office looking at the two kilos of coke in a duffle bag.

Levi showed up to one of Allison's corner stores to drop off the shipment she was waiting on from Leslie. The sexy store owner was a sight to see in all her seductiveness, but the delivery guy dismissed it as if she was covered in a burlap sack. Levi was all business as he brought the package to the back room and Allison keyed in on the mood he was throwing out. She kept everything professional, brought him his money for his service and informed him she had another drop off for him that needed to be in Mississippi. Levi looked in the satchel to see 4 kilos of cocaine, a large Ziploc of mollie and around 4 pounds of premium chronic,

"Dem Sip Boys lookin' like they tryin' to stock up. I just left dem like a few days ago."

"You know dem country bumkins smoke more than they sell."

"True dat. So they need this by tomorrow morning? Cool."

"It's like a two-hour drive there. I could come with ya, if you like. We could chill in Biloxi after the drop."

"I don't think so Allie."

"Fa real? I'm talkin' two friends goin' on a road trip. Would you tell Reem no?"

"Be yo ass ready at 5 and I don't mean 5PM either."

"5? Duh fuck."

"Yes, 5. I ain't tryin' to sit with dem two teeth in da mouth ass rednecks after dey done hyped up on moonshine. If you can't make it, I can go by myself."

"Ok, 5 it is."

Levi was about to leave when he got a text from Netta telling him about what happened with Kareem. Allison could see the agitation on his face as he was texting and asked what was wrong. When he broke down what was going on the gangster side of the store owner came out. Levi listened as Allison told him that the sheriff deputy could become a problem if she wasn't satisfied. He understood the pros and cons of under the table dealing with law enforcement, although this was a little different than payouts Levi felt this wasn't going to end well. If Netta started to talk too much to the wrong person, it could endanger the whole operation, and everyone could get caught up. It was something Levi knew couldn't happen and from the text she was sending him, she was on the verge of spilling everything. Allison offered to have her taken care of for good, but Levi didn't want Netta's daughter to grow up without a mother. A lesson was going to have to be taught and Levi knew the right people to teach such a lesson when he had Allison get in touch with her suppliers. A group of men that didn't tolerate no back talk, no disloyal acts and intimidation was their main form of communication. Lords de Tampico was the Mexican Cartel that supplied Allison with 70% of her product, an agreement her father made before she was born and a deal she still has to honor til this day. Alejandro Millena was always fond of Allison and most of the time her feminine charm could get favors done without a problem. She knew if she called in this favor it would lead to her having to return the gesture, but the problem Levi could have in Netta had to be resolved. Allison told her partner she would make a few calls and get back with him later.

Netta had just left the grocery store with her daughter after picking up a few things for tonight's dinner. The little princess skipped alongside the grocery basket her mother was pushing as they both sung the old "Baby Shark" nursery rhyme. Netta walked up to the trunk of her car as she let her daughter Nevaeh get in the back seat. A large dually truck with a longhorn hood ornament on the front was parked right next to them and the doors swung open. Netta loaded her groceries in her trunk as two Spanish men walked pass and one of them smiled stating his daughter sings the same exact song. Netta laughed,

"They can't seem to get dat song out of their little heads."

The well-dressed clean-cut gentleman then asked her if she could give him directions to get to Crowder Boulevard. Netta knew where the street was but her focus was on the other guy that was with him, she couldn't stop staring at his face that was adorned with tattoos. The two men were like night and day, one silky hair pulled into a curly ponytail dressed like a GQ model while the other looked like a stereotype of a Latino prisoner covered in tatts. Netta started telling the guy directions to Crowder when he mentioned a cross street that really caught her attention, it was the street she lived on. The debonair charm he had at first seemed to disappear as his eyes locked with hers,

"I have a friend that lives around there, cute three-bedroom house she's buying. Nice neighborhood and all but she needs to get in touch with my buddy Marco in Cellblock D."

"I don't know who you are but you need to leave."

"Oh my apologies, I'm Alejandro. You work for me now. You don't contact Levi anymore. You don't contact Allison anymore."

"Do you know who I am? I can cause you and yo buddy Marco a lot of problems, try me."

"You don't contact Kareem anymore. And yes, I do know who you are Netta Wilson, sheriff deputy of Orleans Parish. Like I say, you work for me now. Oh, and tell

Nevaeh uncle Alejandro loves watching her in dance class, she is freaking adorable."

The two men walked off, leaving Netta standing at the back of her car shaking in fear, terrified that her daughter's life was in danger. The dangers she thought she was smart enough to avoided walked right up to her like it was nothing and threatened her entire existence with a smile.

YEAR 2030

The year couldn't start off any better for Kareem because it was the grand opening of his barbershop "Hard Headz" and his entire family was there to celebrate with him. With help from his mentor Eve and funding from Levi, the young entrepreneur was able to become a legal contributor to the community. Levi couldn't have been any more excited for the man he considered his little brother on that day, but it was all shadowed by who he saw walk up to help cut the ceremonial ribbon. Kareem had all of his nieces and nephews help him open the store and standing there with the biggest smile on her face was Levi's daughter Ronnisha. The 12-year-old hadn't seen her father since she was 2 and wouldn't have recognized him in a line up but Levi knew that beautiful face from anywhere. He stood back as he just watched her prance around in the shop with her siblings and cousins. The building was packed with people, from certified barbers, stylist and plenty of future customers along with the Daniels family. Eve came over to give Kareem a gift, the very first dollar he had made at her shop, incased in a wooden frame. Levi watched the joy in the building as if it was a living being blanketing everyone there and wanted nothing more for his daughter than that. Shalay walked up to him with a chubby bundle of joy on her hip,

"Stop staring at her and go talk to her."

"I can't."

"Why not Ronald?"

"Cause she's gonna have some questions for me I can't answer right now."

"She's way smarter than you think, her and her brother Khori are my little nerds. How's ya sister doing? You still hangin' with Desmond and Mook?"

"I couldn't tell ya where Darlene at, she don't talk to me. Dez been dead over a decade now and me and Mook haven't spoken in a while. He a family man doin' his own thing."

"I'm so sorry to hear about your mother, she was a beautiful woman."

Levi leaned over to the little girl on Shalay's hip, smiled at her and tickled her little chubby cheeks making her giggle. He walked off to allow the Daniels family to enjoy the accomplishment of their sibling. Before leaving, Kareem's mother Delores stopped Levi at the door and thanked him for taking care of her son when he was out in the streets heavy. Delores wasn't blind to what Kareem was doing but the single mother had three other children she had to take care of. Her words cut through Levi like a knife but not in a harmful way. The fact that someone thought he did some good in the world was an emotional rollercoaster he wasn't ready for. Levi kissed Delores on the cheek and thanked her for the kind words as he left.

The favor Allison called for that took care of the Netta problem came to collect as Alejandro showed up with a new business offer that the store owner couldn't say no to. The suave Latino told Allison that she would be in charge of a new escort service that would supply the Big Easy. He already had a line of girls ready to work the scene and a growing clientele that favored the discrete functions of the business. Alejandro never liked his hands in any of the dirty work of what he had going on, he was more like a Conductor to an underworld orchestra and Allison just became the new instrument. She reluctantly agreed to operating the escort service and the Cartel leader told her where she had to be. So much went through her head of women being forced into a sex trafficking ring, with promises of being let go once their profits give them freedom or they die trying. Allison seen news reports of women being held in dingy warehouses, trap houses and even big rig trailers only to be let out to perform sexual favors. She was torn with the idea because she was a woman herself and couldn't see making another woman do such a thing, but she knew she had to. Allison knew if she turned down the job the dangers of dealing with the Cartel was going to have her in a situation she didn't want to be in. After Alejandro left, she got in touch with Levi because she felt he was the only person capable enough to deal with the condition that was placed in her lap.

Levi met up with Allison at the address she texted him but the house he pulled up in front of was nowhere near a dingy warehouse or a rundown trap house. They were in the middle of the Garden District of the city and everything about the area screamed "old money" or rich bastards. It was an area of the city Levi stayed away from because it always had a strong police presence, and he would stick out like a sore thumb. The old 1960's two story home with tall columns looked as if it stared down anyone that walked up to it, with its wrought iron gated front. The long driveway that went up to a carport on the side stopped right alongside the house. Levi couldn't imagine some pimp shit was going on in such a historical looking building but when the door opened, he knew this wasn't a wholesome family household. Cartel like gangsters roamed the bottom floors while half naked young girls walked around showing off their assets. The whole set up reminded him of how his mother and father had things when he was younger but on a much larger scale. Allison held onto Levi's hand like a safety blanket when this short Latino thug walked up to them,

"You gotta be Allison, I'm Jose. Alejandro told me you was comin."

Jose was like a Mexican gangster movie typecast with his leather pants, bulky silver belt buckle and pointed alligator boots. He walked them through the huge house showing them the operation he was so proud of like it was his baby. The large house was just that, a large house because downstairs was where the Cartel kept crates of automatic weapons, kilos of narcotics and bundles of cash. Upstairs was mainly where all the girls stayed, packed in the four bedrooms up there. Jose gave them the rundown of how the escort service operated and what they were asked to do. It was merely a drop off and pick-up process but if any problems were to arise, they would be in charge of taking care of it. The Cartel member warned them that the last guy that was in charge of the operation found himself on the wrong end of Alejandro's machete,

"These girls here are professionals, they know how to pull at ya heartstring. Hector call himself falling in love with one of them and tried to run away with her. Joker found him and fell in love with what Hector's insides looked like."

"Joker? Who is dat?"

"Do ya job, bring in da bag as you say and you may never have to meet Joker. He's not da friendly type."

Levi seen these guys were not to be played with and was skeptical about getting involved with them, but Allison needed him. He wasn't disappointed in what he seen walking around upstairs though, the women were gorgeous and every one of them looked exotic. Allison on the other hand looked at them as helpless women that needed a way out, but she soon found out otherwise. While Jose was going over how the operation went with Levi, the newly appointed madame talked with her employees. Allison pulled a few of the girls to the side and found out they were there voluntarily. Some were paying off a debt for being in the states, some paying off a family debt to the Cartel and others volunteered because it was the only way they knew how to make money. All of them were young with the oldest only reaching 21 and the youngest just clearing 18 by a month but all of them seasoned street women. One of the ladies by the name of Satin was a 19-year-old seasoned vet,

"Mami, this is what I do. I make them happy and they pay me. If I have a problem, I call Jose and he fix it. They still pay me."

"But what if…"

"They Pay Me. And I like it. I bring home da bags baby. Aye."

The brothel had become a safe haven for them and the Cartel members were protection in their eyes. Allison listened to all of them and started to see it wasn't the captive dungeon like images she had in her head. She was drawn in like they were and started looking at them as money bags. Satin even offered to give Levi a free "taste test" of her talents but he passed on the proposal. The women were definitely how Jose described them, professional and it had become evident that they knew how to handle any man in front of them. Levi found himself as a premium cut of beef in front of a pack of wolves when a gorgeous specimen by the name of Cashmere approached him,

"Papi, you are so fine."

"Nah, I'm good."

"You sure? I could make you better."

"Allie, I think it's time to go."

Allison laughed at how desperate Levi looked to her for help from the young vixen that was grooming him, the two left after getting all the information they needed from Jose.

After leaving the Brothel and a long conversation on how they could make this all work out for them, Levi dropped Allison off at her apartment. He knew how the business was run, he had firsthand experience from a young age watching his father and mother operate an escort service. Levi understood then that sex sells just as much if not more than drugs and he was right in the mix now. His mother didn't think he was paying any attention to her, but the youngster then was just soaking it all in for this moment. Levi also had Eve on his side who even though was retired from the business still had connections. It was funny to him how he would end up doing the one thing that his parents did when they were his age. Levi found himself heading back to where it all started for him. He was driving through his old neighborhood, just reminiscing over old memories when he noticed a car that had been following him at every turn. It became a game of cat and mouse as Levi took his followers on a scenic route of the 7th ward. He made sure his chrome .45 was close by when he pulled over and the dark tinted car stopped right behind him. Levi got out of his car to address the stalkers behind him with his shining tool in his hand but then a big SUV came screeching to a halt in front of his car. The late Papa Sha's baby brother Kirby jumped out of the SUV with a Desert Eagle in his hand,

"You BITCH!"

Levi ran for cover as the Haitian gang leader started to let off several rounds in his direction. He darted down a slim alleyway between two shotgun houses as two gang members chased behind him. Levi dipped under one of the raised houses for cover and watched as the two Haitians searched the backyard for him. Trying to keep as quiet as possible, he laid motionless under the house in all the mud and trash. He laid there, with his pistol focused on the guys walking pass him. One of the gang members chose to look under the house for Levi but a bright flash of light was the only thing he found. The loud blast from Levi's gun and the opened skull of his partner scared the other Haitian into retreat. The hidden target quickly shimmied from under the raised house as gang members scattered around the front of the house looking for him. Police sirens in the distance had the Haitians run back to their vehicles as Kirby shouted,

"I'm comin for you bitch! I'm comin for you!"

Levi escaped the ambush with a few scrapes and a raised heart rate, but he survived it as he quickly made his way back to his car. He knew he had to go on the attack before Kirby could jump out on him again. Levi sent a message to his new comrade Jose as he zipped through the neighborhood away from outcoming police cars.

Jose met up with a paranoid Levi who was still covered in the soot that was under the house he hid under. The calm and cool Cartel member convinced his unnerved partner that his enemies are now their enemies. The two went back to the Brothel where Levi could calm down and get his head around Kirby's attacks while Jose set up a plan of attack of their own. Levi was chilling in one of the rooms upstairs after a hot shower when Cashmere walked in to be some distracting company for him. The sultry almond toned Cashmere could read body language better than anyone and seen that he was not in the mood for sexual pleasures. Instead, she just snuggled in the bed with him, with her soft, thick thighs sprawled across his and her head resting on his shoulder while she softly caressed his chest,

"Papi, you ok?"

"Yeah, I'm Gucci."

"Good."

"Why you here? Jose sent you in here?"

"No, I come cause I want to. You don't want me here? I leave."

"Nah, you good."

Levi didn't think he would be laid up with such a beautiful woman and not have sexing her on his mind, but he was.

His mind was racing with the dilemma he was in because he knew Kirby was not going to stop until one of them were dead. Levi was realizing just because he was out of prison the price tag on his head was over. Kirby was still hell bent on revenge for his brother's death. Cashmere tried to get his mind off what was pestering him as she had him lay face down on the bed and she massaged the tension in his shoulders. The young seductress rubbed his tense muscle into complete relaxation and Levi almost fell asleep until he felt her skin press against his. Cashmere had taken all of her clothes off while giving a much needed rub down and laid on his back, pressing her sensual warm body against his. The smell of sweet strawberries filled his nose as Cashmere kissed on Levi's earlobe and neck. His arms were stretched out on the bed and her hands glid across his muscles until her arms matched his. Her breast pressed against his back and Cashmere's body seemed to turn into an anxiety blanket that felt so safe to Levi that he didn't want the feeling to end. He turned his body around under her until they were face to face and Levi stared into her deep brown eyes,

"What are you doing little one?"

"Making you feel good Papi. Don't you want me to make you feel good?"

"Nah, I can't be doing dis with you."

"You sure? Cause he telling me different."

The Latin Princess was talking about the hardened shaft of Levi that was pressing against her inner thigh. Her gentle kisses on his lips only made his manhood stiffen more as she began whispering sensual Spanish phrases to him, phrases Levi had no clue what they meant. Cashmere reached down to grab a handful of Levi's rock-hard muscle and slowly eased herself onto him. They both relished in the moment as his manhood slid deep inside her and her juicy walls wrapped around him like he belonged there. His girth filled her up as her moist muscles massaged his staff while she went up and down on him. Levi gripped her hips as he gazed at the beautiful creature riding him with nothing but pleasure on her face. Her full breast bounced along with a slight jiggle every time she slid back and forth on him, every stroke feeling better than the last. Levi started pushing back as each stroked pleased Cashmere more and more but then the door to the room swung open with Jose standing there,

"Aye yo, hurry up. We gotta go."

Levi sat up to leave but Cashmere wanted to finish what she started as her hips continued to rotate around on his still hardened appendage. The feeling was too good to walk away from, but Levi knew he had something way more important to take care of as he pulled himself from inside her. He hurried to put his clothes on before he changed his mind looking at the sexy Spanish fly staring back at him.

Jose did his research on the Haitian gangster's crew and sent out some spotters to find Kirby's whereabouts. He received a call from one of his boys that Kirby was at an apartment complex across from a University in the Gentilly area. The Haitian had his whole crew at the apartments and Jose was ready for a battle. Levi, a little thrown back at the amount of support that was coming with them asked,

"Dawg, all these dudes coming?"

"Hey, Alejandro always said. You mess with one of us. You mess with all of us. So yes, we all coming my friend."

"Dem Haitians crazy as a muthafucka and Kirby the craziest."

"He don't know crazy, I give no fucks. Fuckin pendejo!"

They headed to the apartments in two cargo vans and a big pickup truck, every member holding their weapon of choice. Most of the men that came along had automatic rifles or pistols, but the true dangerous ones were the ones that spoke very little to no English. They were the ones that carried nothing but razor-sharp custom-made machetes that look like they could cut through bone. The Lords de Tampico Cartel was known for beheading their rivals in vicious attacks and the Haitians were their new rivals. The ride to where Kirby was, was filled with blunts being passed around and chatter of laughter between the passengers. Levi's mind was focused on finishing what Kirby had started, getting rid of a menacing foe that threatened everything around him. Jose asked him how the beef between them started and after hearing the entire story of the Haitians' terror, Jose wanted them all dead. The Cartel's vehicles pulled up in front of the complex and all the doors swung open as if a SWAT team was exiting out. They all darted in the apartments and anyone that showed the slightest aggression towards them were faced with absolute domination. The machete wielding warriors attacked with precision swings leaving victims gutted, missing limbs or gashed open skulls. With a ski mask over his face, Levi sprinted through the courtyard looking for his target with marksmen covering over his path, eliminating any adversary that got close. Some residents of the apartment complex screamed as they ran for cover themselves during the chaos. The Haitian gang was confused and didn't know which direction to look because the Cartel was coming from all angles. It was a complete massacre of the gang as a few got off shots killing maybe one or two Cartel members, but it didn't compare to how many were loss by the Haitians. A small group of three gunmen stood over as protection for Kirby but a barrage of bullets from the windows took them out quick. Kirby was there all alone; three dead bodies laying at his feet and screams of the last of his crew being slaughtered outside. It was right out of an action movie, the way Levi kicked the front door open with nothing but his chrome .45 in his hand. The loud commotion of the Cartel members getting rid of Kirby's gang could be heard as Levi ripped the mask from his face and walked up to the chanting thug. The Haitian sat on his knees shouting,

"Olorum Papa, strike him down! Strike him down to my feet! Him take me brotha! Now him take me life. I curse you half-breed. You will die by the blade."

"I already did and came back, duck ass nigga. Let's see if you come back from dis bullet bitch."

Levi placed the barrel to Kirby's forehead and the blast from the firearm was like a release of stress for him. It was like a weight fell off his shoulders and disappeared with the life that use to be in the Haitian's body. Jose rushed in shouting for Levi to leave because he knew the police would be there soon. They both ran out pass a horde of dead bodies laying throughout the complex. Levi let out a sigh of relief because the gang that tormented him since birth was dismantled.

Breaking news reports were all over every TV channel in New Orleans about the deadly gang war that took place in a quiet apartment complex in Gentilly. The metro area was in complete shock because of how horrific the attack was. Reports of a shootout was pretty much a norm when it came to gang activity in the city but descriptions of dismemberment of the victims was a little too much for everyone to handle. People only heard of that from other countries and not in the states, it was a lot to take in. Levi sat on the edge of the bed in front of the TV with Cashmere laying by his side looking at reporters describe what they were able to see. He wasn't looking at the news with any admiration to what happened that night but to make sure there wasn't any suspects identified. The news went on and on about the massacre that took place but then a small report of a terrible car accident caught his attention. The flash of an overturned Suburban in a canal with the description of a man that sounds exactly like Kareem's brother Cedric changed the mood quickly. Levi immediately called his adopted little brother to make sure,

"Hey lil bro, is Ced ok? I just seen da news."

"Dawg, I have no idea. Da doctors are still back there workin' on him and nobody came told us shit yet."

"Fam, you need anything please let me know. How is Mrs. Dee and ya sisters holding up?"

"Man, they doin' as good as they can. I just hope…Shit! I gotta go!"

Kareem hung up the phone and all Levi could hear was women bickering in the background before the call ended. He wanted to be there for the Daniels family like they have always been there for him, but Levi had bigger things on his plate. Alejandro walked in, a visual reminder to Levi that what took place earlier was another favor that would eventually have to be paid. Levi had Cashmere step out because he figured the Aztec descendant was coming in with a favor request. At this point he didn't care what he was asked to do because he was that grateful that his rivals were gone. The Cartel boss man knew his new employee was skittish against organized gangs but was loyal to anyone that was loyal to him. Levi showed that he was fearless when it came to completing a task and Alejandro needed a man like that on his team. The gang leader spoke to him as if he was making a business proposition,

"I can see we have an understanding. You do for me and I do for you, no questions asked. Do you believe we can continue like that?"

"I think we good. Long as I ain't asked to be a damn escort."

"Haha, no Ese. But I may call on you to take care of some particulars from time to time. You will be compensated though."

"Say less."

The two were in deep conversation as they ended up leaving the Brothel and walking the Garden District neighborhood. It was mainly an all-white neighborhood and the two men casually walking its streets stuck out like a sore thumb. At first Levi continuously looked over his shoulder expecting to see a police car pull up on them, but he noticed how Alejandro carried himself. He paid attention how the confident Latino walked the streets like he owned the block, like he belonged there and no one dare ask him otherwise. They made their way to a "mom and pop" corner store that sold po-boy sandwiches. Alejandro couldn't stop talking about how he fell in love with the New Orleans style sandwiches when he first moved to the city. Levi found out the Cartel had been taking stake in the city since the rebuilding started after Hurricane Katrina. Cartel members took hold of construction sites and they started using them as shell companies for their more lucrative operations. Alejandro was the son of a ruthless Cartel boss that met his end at the hand of a rival, he and Levi had a connection that way. After hearing what Jose had to tell him about how everything went down with Levi and the infamous Caribbean gang, Alejandro felt he had a true ally now. They sat at a park bench, discussing the direction Alejandro wanted for his inherited business, all the while enjoying a couple of shrimp po-boys and pineapple Big Shots. The time was going good until some clueless young thugs seen what they thought were two easy marks. A scrawny hoodie wearing kid, that looked no older than 15 showed the handle of a gun tucked in his waist and asked,

"Hey, you got some change for me?"

Levi started to reach for his tool, but his companion smiled as he shook his head no to him. Alejandro reached in his jeans, pulled out a handful of coins and laid them on the picnic table in front of the young criminals. The skinny leader got frustrated with the Mexican sitting in front of him, thinking he was being disrespected and slapped the coins off the table, as he pulled the firearm from his waistband. Levi could see fear in the young hoodlum's eyes and knew a scared criminal was a dangerous one because they're unpredictable. He was about to solve the juvenile delinquent problem, but Alejandro stopped him again as the young leader started threatening to shoot them both. The Cartel boss smiled even more,

"My friend, you don't know me…"

"Muthafucka, we ain't friends, ya heard me. You playin' round and gone get y'all popped."

"Like I say, you really have no idea who I am. I could be a blessing or a curse for all of you. Just like that little red dot on your shirt could be your blessing or curse."

The young thug looked down at his chest to witness a small red light shining on his shirt. When the other juveniles seen the illumination, they all sprinted out of the park area in fear of being shot. The solo culprit was frozen in fear as Levi snatched the firearm out of his trembling hands and Alejandro walked up to the youngster, handing him a business card. The youngster looked over the shoulder of the Spanish man in front of him and seen the red light disappear from a black box Mercedes parked at the end of the park. He helplessly watched Levi empty out the gun he took from him and put the bullets in his pocket. Alejandro handed the youngster back his gun and the smile his was carrying went away,

"Go to that address on the card and tell them I sent you. Cross me again and I won't be your blessing, understood."

"Yes sir."

"Get yo lil ass outta here."

YEAR 2031-2032

Levi found himself becoming comfortable working as a chaperone for Allison's escort service. The women also found themselves feeling safer when "El Semental Negro", which meant the Black Stallion, was with them on a job. The professional marriage was a perfect setting and business was picking up fast with a new girl arriving at the Brothel almost one every other week. Allison had a time trying to keep up with all the names, the new faces and the continuous demand for escorts. She started to look at men in a whole new light as if all of them were just horny devils looking for their next nut. Allison became attached to some of the girls, looking to get them out of the life they were in. She caught herself finding jobs for them outside of the escort service, which didn't go well with Alejandro or Jose. The two men discussed it with Levi before stepping in,

"Hey, I know she's your girl and y'all have a long history. Fix this because this can't happen anymore."

"I gotchu, I'm a talk to her."

"I like her. Her and her father, God bless the dead, brought me a lot of money. I'm not like the police, I don't do warning shots."

"Gimme some time, I'm a talk to her."

Levi knew Alejandro meant what he said and had no problem eliminating whatever problem he had, even if it meant getting rid of Allison permanently. Allison had already coasted Satin and Legacy from the group, finding them both jobs along with housing. She was taking money out of the big boss pockets and Levi knew it was going to be a real issue. Cashmere was even in on the takeover as she worked from the inside with Allison. Levi let the Asian Princess know through a text they really needed to talk after he gets back from Texas. He was making a delivery for Jose and picking up a package from some of the Cartel members in the state. Levi had made runs for Jose before, but he never had to bring anything back with him. He never asked any questions and did what was asked of him every time. It kept a smile on the Mexican mob boss' face and in his good graces.

The 9 and half hour ride felt crazy long for Levi, mainly because of the amount of product he was transporting in the cargo van with him, the New Orleans native was ready to get rid of it all. He knew it was just his nerves messing with him but every vehicle that passed looked like law enforcement. Levi made it to the address Jose gave him and the warehouse looked abandoned when he pulled up in front of it. Before he could put the van in park to make sure that he had the right address, bright spotlights shined on the van and two men approached him. They directed him towards the large double doors that opened up to Alejandro's little brother Gabriel standing there waiting. A suave Latino like his older brother, Gabriel was a well-dressed man, thick black wavy hair that hung to his shoulders and adorned in gold chains. He had a scar in his face that went clean across, from the right side of his forehead to the left side of his cheek, like someone sliced him. His thick Spanish accent was the first thing you would hear as he shouted for his workers to hurry up. Gabriel ran the business in Texas and was nothing like the calm collective older brother, if anything he was a complete asshole. He was ruthless just like his late father and his arrogance was through the roof. Levi got out of the van to an automatic rifle toting thug patting him down for weapons. The Mexican gang leader stood there watching over the process,

"So you're the cabrón negro doing all my brother's biddings."

"I'm a let dat negro part slide cause I know dat means black in Spanish."

"Look at you learning a new language. Damn white people said y'all was ignorant, good boy."

"Watch it pendejo."

Gabriel chuckled at the fact that he didn't intimidate Levi one bit and admired the way the newcomer stood his ground. He had one of his goons drive the van in the warehouse while he escorted Levi to his office. Once inside, the warehouse was just like the house in New Orleans but on a much greater scale. Wooden crates stacked on one wall was like a gun candy store carrying almost any and everything for any kind of gun fanatic. Further to the back was a complete process center for all the narcotics the Lords de Tampico distributed throughout the states. Then there were makeshift rooms that housed all the half-naked women walking around in the warehouse. Levi was amazed at how they had the place set up but was dumbfounded that the police wasn't kicking the doors in arresting everyone. Gabriel had complete control of the situation plus he had the chief of police and the mayor in his back pocket for added insurance. It was what fueled his arrogance because he felt untouchable in the city of

Brownsville, Texas. After the van was parked in the warehouse and the doors were closed Gabriel walked Levi up to his office. Once they were upstairs, Levi could see that the makeshift rooms were created with partition walls that were absent any type of ceiling. The view from Gabriel's office window looked over the entire warehouse and everything could be seen from there. It was three rows of five rooms with one girl in each room. The area was made like a single efficiency with a twin bed and a nightstand in them. The girls there were nothing like the ones in New Orleans because these girls looked strung out, dirty and neglected. Levi was looking out the office windows at the set-up Gabriel's crew had put together and couldn't believe how they were operating. Gabriel wanted to have a drink with Levi while the warehouse crew got the cargo ready for the van. Levi sat on the sofa in the office next to a half-dressed female who was in there with them. Before he could even get himself comfortable, the disoriented feminine company leaned over and began pulling at Levi's belt buckle. Confused as to what was going on, he pushed her off of him,

"Fuck wrong with dis bitch."

"Oh she just a head hunter. Anybody around her is subject to get sucked like a straw."

"Man y'all wildin'."

"Nah, we just make sure these putas trained well before they get to y'all."

The operation wasn't completely explained to him, but Levi was starting to realize that the women that worked for the escort service wasn't exactly volunteers. He could see that some of them just looked trapped in a dangerous situation and Gabriel was the epitome of dangerous. The mean little brother handed Levi a bottle of premium Tequila and snatched the high female off the couch by the back of her hair, pushing her out of the office. Gabriel was aggressive towards all the residents of the warehouse, especially the ones that failed to please him. He was known around town as "Pitbull" because he was so aggressive, Levi found it funny when he heard the nickname. Thinking back to when he was younger and how he use to be, Gabriel's antics were comical to him. Levi could read a person from the first meet and seen that Gabriel was putting on a show, to show that he was tough to the outsider. He sipped on the top shelf Tequila while waiting for the workers to get his van ready with whatever the cargo was, he was bringing back to New Orleans. Levi knew it was a long ride back and was just ready to go but the sound of men arguing caught both of their attention. Gabriel stepped outside of his office to see his men dragging and beating two people through the warehouse. The man and woman were bloody from head to toe with cuts and bruises all over their bodies. One of Gabriel's men ran up to him to explain that the two tried to steal a duffel bag full of cocaine and the guards caught them sneaking out the back. The warehouse foreman walked down the stairs to the thieves as they looked up at him in total fear begging for their lives. Levi stood at the top of the steps watching the whole thing as the two accused looters cried out in a Spanish language. Gabriel already had an idea what he wanted to do but looked up at the outsider to see what he thought about the situation,

"So amigo, what you think I should do?"

"Say man, a muthafucka steal from ya once they steal from ya again."

"Exactly."

Levi knew the business they were in and a thief was the most hated in the field but didn't know the caliber of judgement Gabriel had in mind. He watched as the warehouse kingpin instructed his men to stuff the two accused in steel drum containers. The two thieves begged and pleaded for mercy as the lid of the containers was sealed over them. Gabriel then shoved a water hose in the only airhole left in the containers and began filling them up with water. Frantic screams from the containers were replaced with gurgling as the water spewed from the top and then there was no sound except for water hitting the floor. Gabriel calmly walked over to Levi and told him to go get a hotel room while they clean up and that his van would be ready in the morning.

One of Gabriel's men dropped Levi off at a hotel close to Downtown Brownsville for the night. The New Orleans native didn't realize how tired he actually was until he seen the bed in the room. Levi laid across it and instantly started falling asleep but that was interrupted with a knock at the door. With one hand wrapped around the handle of his favorite pistol and the other holding onto the doorknob Levi answered the door,

"Who is it?"

"Ariana, Gabriel said you needed some company."

"I'm good. You can go back."

"I can't."

When Levi heard the female's response, he opened the door to a beautiful young Hispanic woman standing there with a six pack of sodas and a bag of tamales. She walked in the room and placed the food on the table, Ariana was beyond beautiful and Levi couldn't take his eyes off of her. Ariana told him that Gabriel sent her to be his company for the night and that they could do whatever he liked. She started to slip the thin strap of the satin slip dress off her shoulders and Levi stopped her. As much as he wanted to see what was under there because Ariana was so damn fine, Levi just wasn't in the mood and could tell something wasn't right about the whole situation. He sat her on the side of the bed while he sat at the table in front of the six pack and asked her why she couldn't go back. Ariana looked a little confused at Levi's question because most of the men she met in hotel rooms didn't want to talk at all. This guy sitting in front of her was different, he carried himself differently and his feelings showed through his eyes. She didn't expect to be treated like a human being and this man sitting in front of her brought out an emotion she wasn't ready to express in front of him. Ariana's big brown eyes began to well as she got up from the bed and went to the bathroom. Right then Levi knew something just wasn't right as he mumbled to himself,

"What da fuck is going on? I am not a damn counselor."

He slowly walked over to the bathroom and tapped on the door, asking Ariana if she was okay. The door swung open to her gorgeous smile and bright face as she replied that she was fine. They went back to the table where the food was, and Ariana started to tell Levi all about the authentic tamales she brought him. She asked him where he's from, about his family and where he wanted to be in 10 years. Levi never really gave thinking 10 years in advance a chance because he lived day to day for so long. The exquisite temptress in front of him got him thinking about his future and then he returned the same question back. Ariana gave him an answer as if her life was over at that very moment as if she had nothing worthwhile to live for. It baffled Levi to hear someone had nothing to live for and it gave him more questions to ask her. Ariana told him how her father was a member of the Cartel and that he owed them massive amounts of money that was lost in a drug bust in Houston 8 years ago. The Cartel gave Ariana's father an ultimatum, give up his daughter or the entire family perish, she was only 15 at the time. Levi couldn't imagine making such a decision that would endanger his only child in such a way and finally understood why Ariana said she couldn't leave. Her mother moved to Dallas and she was all alone in Brownsville with no one but the Cartel to rely on to survive, so she did what she was told. They stayed there and talked most of the night until they both fell asleep in each other's arms until the morning, a feeling Ariana had never felt before. The banging on the door awoke both of them as one of Gabriel's workers came to pick Levi up. Before he left, he asked in a whisper if Ariana wanted to get away and Levi could see that the young prostitute was scared to answer him. He knew he was taking a dangerous risk, but he told her anyways,

"If you wanna go be in the back parking lot of this hotel and I'll take you with me."

Levi got back to the warehouse where Gabriel was waiting for him with the most annoying smirk on his face, the van was loaded and parked out front ready to go. He handed Levi the keys to the vehicle and told him not to have too much fun with the cargo. Levi hadn't looked inside yet and figured it was just a normal shipment like any other but when Gabriel told him all the girls went to the bathroom already, he was a little puzzled. The van had six girls in it from the warehouse that Levi was bringing back to New Orleans with him to work as escorts. He didn't know he was about to be a part of the human trafficking the Lords de Tampico had going on in their organization. After talking all night with Ariana about how the Cartel operate and acquire their girls, Levi was conflicted with the situation. Most of the girls there were paying off a family debt to the Cartel or was a victim to a kidnapping and forced into prostitution. Levi knew he had done some diabolical shit in the short time he had been on this earth, but he couldn't see doing this continuously. Gabriel mentioned that the steel containers from last night was dumped in the Rio Grande,

"After I shot a few holes in them, the motherfuckers sunk like a rock my friend. Looks like the river got some new residents."

It was as if he was sending Levi a message not to mess with him or else. Then like a light switch changed the subject and asked about the company he sent over last night. Levi played as if it was nothing and told him that he left her in the hotel room. Gabriel chuckled as he told him all of his stock know their way back home. The arrogance of Alejandro's little brother was sickening to Levi as he got in the van to leave. He was a thug by nature and had no problem taking a man's life if it called for it but the degrading of a woman as property was too much for him. Levi knew his mother and father had a prostitution reign that they operated for years but all the occupants were voluntary. He watched as a young kid, women come in and out of his house but none looking as frightened as the women sitting in the back of his van. Levi drove back to the hotel and parked in the back parking lot like he promised Ariana. He waited a few minutes looking for her to come out the back exit, but everything was quiet with no one in sight. Levi had given up on rescuing the young female from the trap she was in and began driving away but was abruptly stopped when Ariana ran in front of the van. They locked eyes and Ariana's beautiful smile showed she was ready to go with him as she got in the front seat. Levi made his way to the freeway,

"I thought you changed yo mind."

"No. I seen when you pulled up, I just had to make sure it was just you."

"We got company though."

Ariana looked in the back of the van to see some of the girls from the warehouse and tears began to flow because she knew where they were going. She knew not to ask if they could receive the same saving treatment as her because that would be too dangerous, but the thoughts ran through her mind. The van buzzed down the freeway on its way back to the city and Arianna's eyes were as wide as silver dollars. She had never been outside of Brownsville Texas because Gabriel had her and all the other girls terrified to take one step pass the city limits. The warehouse pimp's tyranny along with his ruthlessness was still evident when he called Levi's phone and the women in the van heard his voice over the speaker. Their curious stares as to what new encounters they would face in a new city was replaced. Their eyes full of complete fear when Gabriel asked if the driver seen Ariana. Levi knew the beautiful defector would soon be missed and a search for her would commence. Arianna was petrified as she slumped down in her seat believing the New Orleans' hood would give her up but that wasn't the case. Levi gave the most convincing reply and Gabriel seemed to believe every word. The call was ended as the escort crew made their way down the interstate to New Orleans, but Levi's mind was rolling with ideas of what he had to do with Ariana.

After a group text with Eve and Allison, Levi had an idea for his Ariana situation, and he needed the women for help. The sign stating "Welcome to the city of New Orleans" put a time limit on everything for him and he knew the clock was running fast. Always ready to help her adopted son out, Eve met Levi by the old Tipitina's building on Napoleon Ave because it was off the grid to their Latin counterparts. Levi parked on the side of Eve's car and rushed to get the Mexican princess to safety as he opened the door for her. She turned to the women in the back of the van telling them she would come back for them and to be quiet about what happened,

"No me viste. Understand?"

Levi's small bit of understanding of the language knew Ariana told her friends that they didn't see her in the van, and they all agreed. Their secret was kept, and he watched with a confident heart that he did the right thing as Eve quickly pulled off. Levi didn't want to know where Ariana was headed because he knew she would be safer that way.

He knew Eve would make sure she was taken care of. He headed to the Brothel with the rest of the women in the van with nothing but conflict going on inside of him. Levi wanted nothing to do with the transport of the women but knew if he didn't deliver, everyone he loved would be in danger. He was already taking a risk with getting Ariana out of there and doing anymore could be detrimental. It became a known fact when he pulled up in the car port of the brothel and Alejandro was waiting for him,

"Hey my brother. Didn't know if you was gonna show or not. Gabriel still looking for one of his girls after you left. You ain't see her?"

"Why you think I wasn't gone show? But nah, last time I seen dat female was when she came over to my room. Dats bout it. She prolly out makin' sum money, she be back."

"Nah, they know to check in. We make sure they know to check in. Rules. All my people know to follow them."

All the girls got escorted upstairs to their rooms while Alejandro went over what he had planned. The boss man was a true entrepreneur when it came to expanding his business and he had his sights on getting goods imported. Alejandro was looking for a shell company to use as a docking station for a lot of his products because he began to notice unwanted eyes staring at his brothel. To get in his good graces again, in an attempt to pull his mind away from Ariana's whereabouts, Levi mentioned Eve's CBD shop and how she always had product imported to her store. Alejandro thought about it and told him to set up a meet with Eve just so he could get a feel of the store. Levi didn't want to get his stepmother involved but the damage was done and the boss was expecting results.

Levi was heading to go talk with Allison about the escort service after getting yelled at by Eve for setting her up with a dangerous crime boss. He knew she would be completely against it, but he assured her that Alejandro just wanted to see how she ran her company,

"Mama, I promise. He just wanna see how you do shit. No strings attached. No business propositions. No bullshit."

"Ronald I'm telling you, shit start soundin' funny and it's gone be me and you."

Levi pulled up to one of Allison's stores and she was outside talking with two NOPD officers who stopped by like they always did. Just watching her, reminded him of her father and how he always made sure to keep an added security blanket close by. Mr. Chou knew he couldn't make his money without having a few officers on his side to make sure his business ran smooth and Allison was doing the same thing. Levi walked by as if he was going in the store to buy something but went straight to Allison's office to wait for her. He didn't get the chance a lot, but Levi sat there in silence trying to clear his mind of the women from the warehouse. It was bothering him that those women didn't have a say in what or how they lived and all the money they made they would never see. Levi was in deep thought and didn't see Allison walk in when she bumped him to get his attention. She could tell the wheels were rolling in his head and knew that look he was giving off meant he was about to do something that might end up being dangerous. Allison sat down behind her little desk,

"I set your friend up with some cash and she's on her way up north. I can see something on ya mind. What you got going on up there?"

"This shit not cool. If a female wanna sell a little ass to make some money, I'm good with dat. But this shit right here is not what's up."

"Sex trafficking never is. Why you think I take the risk? If I can save one of dem, I'm good."

"Allie, you should have seen deez females man. It was like dey were herding fuckin' cattle."

"I can only imagine but what you gone do about it?"

YEAR 2033

Levi had a war going on inside and the possible end results scared him. He knew if Alejandro found out what he was doing the fallout would reach pass just killing him. Levi was torn between what he was use to and what he felt was right. The thought of his own daughter came into play because most of the women who started working for the Cartel was Ronnisha's age or younger. With help from Allison's connections and Cashmere who was doing it because she would do anything for Levi, his mission was a go. He knew he couldn't just snatch up a bunch of girls and take them away, for several reasons besides the Cartel retaliating on him. Some of the women in there were so far gone that they were brainwashed to believe this was the only way and others were so loyal that they would snitch. The selection had to be random and the girl picked had to want to get away from the situation she was in, that part was Cashmere's expertise. Levi wondered why the young vixen never attempted to run away,

"Cash, I really appreciate yo help but I can set you up with a place to get outta here."

"For what? Who gonna help you then Papi?"

"I'm just sayin'. You out here risking yo shit watchin' deez girls get outta here but you still up in here."

"Papi, you cute. You know da last guy I had sex with? You. They don't use me in they escort stuff. I work da strip clubs and recruit da guys who pay for it. So to watch some of dem get outta here is a plus for me Papi."

It was always business for Cashmere and she didn't see it how Levi did. She figured there would always be a man out there that would rather pay for sex and she was just there to make her profits. Cashmere didn't fear Alejandro's Cartel how most of his members did, mainly because she was pretty much untouchable, being that she was Joker's little sister. Joker and Cashmere had been working for the Lords de Tampico since they were kids. Joker quickly moved up the ranks as their enforcer and Cashmere respectfully moved right up with him. There wasn't much a female could do in a male dominated gang but when Cashmere introduced the possibilities of an escort service, the boss was hooked. They originally had her as the madame of the operation, but she was more comfortable recruiting clients in. Cashmere didn't like the fact of how they were getting girls in forcefully and not by choice. When she found out that Levi wanted to free the ones that were trapped in, she was all game for it. Cashmere knew if she got caught, her saving grace would be her big brother. Just like most of the crew was afraid of Alejandro more feared the "El Coco" or the boogeyman that was in the form of Joker. Levi never met the 6 foot 3 Mexican and never wanted to but what attracted Cashmere to the New Orleanian was the fact that Levi was just like her brother in so many ways. Joker had the reputation of being the most dangerous man connected to the Cartel but with Cashmere he was a gentle giant and protected her as such. She never flaunted her undisclosed power around, but it was very much known that she was not to be played with. Levi didn't know how important her alliance with him would be when he first met her and appreciated everything she was doing. He had her filter through the numerous amounts of girls in the brothel, to find one that desperately wanted out, Cashmere was good at reading people. After the right girl was found, Allison would set up a fake appointment with a fake client and Levi would always drive her to a hotel where she would never be seen again. The operation was almost flawless, but Levi knew it wouldn't be like that forever, Alejandro was not a dumb man and would figure it out sooner or later.

Alejandro met up with Eve months ago to see how she ran her stores and also how she was able to get special products imported. He offered to become a silent partner in her business in return she allowed some of his products delivered to her stores. Eve respectfully declined the proposal because it reminded her of a certain Haitian she despised, and she never wanted to deal with that situation ever again. Unlike the two deceased Haitian gang leaders, Alejandro respected Eve's wishes and only asked that she help him with starting up his own CBD shop,

"I'm only asking for this favor because you are a citizen of this wonderful country and they won't ask you too many questions, love."

"So you just need me to get the paperwork started and get the right certificates signed? I'm not running your company for you honey."

"No, no, no you won't be running anything. I just need you to start it up and I will take it from there, I promise."

Alejandro's charm was definitely a factor in Eve's decision to go along with the plan and Eve's undeniable beauty along with her womanly strengths was an attraction for him. The deal was made with a handshake and Eve got on the ball with getting Alejandro's small company started.

She didn't like the fact that Levi got her involved in with the Mexican gang, but she understood she was the distraction for Levi. It was easy for her to get another store ready for its grand opening with her credentials and Alejandro's bank roll, no one suspected a thing. Signing over the shop to another company was even easier and the Cartel businessman had a legal business he could operate without discretion. The Lords de Tampico boss man wanted to celebrate with her on his new establishment with dinner and she reluctantly agreed. He tried to shower her with extravagant gifts, but Eve's previous employment prepped her to the point where the gifts weren't so exciting to see. The nonchalant thank you was like an aphrodisiac to Alejandro because he never dealt with a woman like Eve before. Most of the time all he had to do was smile and say something sexy in Spanish and most American women would fall to his feet. Eve was different, a true challenge and the Cartel leader accepted the test. Eve could tell he wasn't use to the type of woman she was, strong, dominant and knew what she wanted. She seen that she could have a little fun, so she did just that. Eve had dealings with several powerful men on different levels and Alejandro was no different than them. The celebratory dinner date was at a rented out Gautreau's Restaurant in the Freret area and catered by the head chef who went all out for the high paid customer. Eve was impressed at how the Latin gangster went all out for her, but she refused to give him the pleasure,

"So this what you do for all your business associates?"

"Associates? I can't even get a partnership?"

"Nah buddy, you ain't ready for my partnership."

"Mami, I'm ready to part anything with you."

"Are you?"

Eve's subtle flirts were all accepted by Alejandro and she in return shot down every one of his advances like a sniper. It was a true game of "cat-n-mouse" where Alejandro really thought he was the cat but, in this case, Eve was the one doing the hunting.

Allison had set up another fake appointment for a girl they were about to free from the demanding escort service the Cartel had going on. She made the reservations at the hotel room and gave Levi all the info he needed. Allison had reached out to a group that was experienced in working with sex trafficking victims and they found them housing out of state. The people would meet with the girl in the hotel room and convince her to leave everything behind in order to start a new life somewhere else. They had a 90% success rate with most of the victims and were confident that the one Levi was dropping off would go right along with them like all the others. Levi pulled up in front of the JW Marriot of New Orleans hotel with a young woman by the name Courtney who looked nervous as hell. Courtney had been working with the escort service for a week or so and Cashmere was sure she was ready to get away from the Cartel. Nights of convulsion type crying after every date with a different man was a tall tale sign that she was not built for this lifestyle. Courtney was scooped up by one of Gabriel's men who met her online. She thought he was a nice Latin guy who just so happen to like all the same things she did. The only thing was during the first face to face meet she was drugged, kidnapped and repeatedly sexually assaulted until she complied to their wishes. The gang members had her mind so fucked up that she truly believed that she had to have sex with different men to keep them happy with her. Levi told Courtney the room number to go to,

"Hey, go up there, do what ya gotta do. I'll be down here if ya need me."

"I'm a see you when I get back right?"

"Of course."

"I just wanna see ya face."

"Girl, get outta here."

Courtney got out of the car, went inside and Levi backed into a parking spot where he could be facing the front entrance. The operation called for Levi to stay at the hotel just in case something goes wrong and after 30 minutes went by it went as wrong as it could. Levi seen five of Jose men dart in the hotel with nothing but delivering pain on their faces. Right when he was about to get out of his car Jose tapped on his passenger side window. The Cartel lieutenant got in the car and Levi thought he was about to meet his end, but Jose just told him to drive off. The car was silent as Levi drove down Canal Street and then Jose's cell started to ring, it was Alejandro on the other end telling Jose where to meet him. The angered Mexican told Levi where to go as he ended the call with his boss only to start telling Levi how disappointed he was with him. Thoughts of just stopping the car and fighting it out with Jose crossed his mind but Levi knew he wouldn't win against the large pistol resting on Jose's lap. He stayed silent as he drove down to the end of Canal Street which ended at Greenwood

Cemetery. Greenwood cemetery is one of the oldest cemeteries in the city, only falling second to the 3 Saint Louis Cemeteries. The gloom of the cemetery could be felt to the bone in the city's night sky as Jose made Levi get out and walk up the alleyways. The shine of flashlights blinded him for a quick second as Jose pushed him forward towards the bright lights. When Levi's eyes focused, he could see Alejandro sitting next to an old tomb with a few of his men close by, Cashmere and a very large Mexican he assumed was Joker. Alejandro lit a Habana cigar while one of his men patted him down searching for any weapons. Levi didn't know what to expect because Cashmere was standing there with fright written all over her face. She mouthed off silently that she was sorry, and Levi shook his head as to comfort her that the situation wasn't her fault. After he was searched, Jose walked him face to face with Alejandro and the boss had a lot to get off his mind,

"I truly thought you were ready to make some real money and not that change you been bringing home working with Allison. I actually believed you would work out, despite some of my people saying otherwise. I guess your connection with the Asian Princess distorted your mind to the bigger picture. I'm really disappointed in you Ronald but I believe this can be fixed."

"Alejandro, I apologize, but I don't have anything you want or need."

"You don't my friend, but you do know someone that does."

"I'm lost. What you talkin' bout?"

"Go head and facetime that beauty Eve for me."

Right then Levi's stomach turned in knots because Alejandro was bringing in the only family he had left. The screen glowed in the dark as the facetime icon blinked waiting on Eve's response but once she answered Alejandro snatched the phone from him. Cashmere screamed in fear as one of Alejandro's henchmen kicked Levi in the back of his legs, putting a sharpened machete to his neck and making him kneel in front of him. Eve was confused because she seen the Latin gangster smiling at her on Levi's phone, but she carried on a casual conversation with him anyways. Alejandro then informed Eve, in the calmest voice, that she would be giving away both of her stores to him in return for Levi's life. He told her that her stores would be the only payment he would agree to that won't involve him having Levi's head as a parting gift. Alejandro then turned the camera to Levi kneeling down in front of him with a machete digging into his skin.

Frightened for her son's life Eve quickly agreed to Alejandro's demands and told him she would be bringing him the keys to both shops. The Cartel leader smiled one last time at a terrified and crying Eve as he ended the call before throwing the phone at Levi. Alejandro had his men stand Levi up while he continued to puff on his cigar,

"Levi, I like you and that's partially the reason I don't have you buried in one of these damn old ass tombs. It's time for you to retire from this line of work. Most men don't get a chance like this one so I think you should take it because next time I won't be so kind. Now as for your lil friend Allison, that's a different story. I gave her too many chances. But hey, she finally gets to meet Joker."

"Alejandro don't do this. It was my idea, don't take it out on her. She was just trying to help."

"Help? Like she did when she had us chop Desmond and his lil buddies up? Please tell me you knew cause she sure did. She was pissed that Desmond left her innocent lil cousin at that motel. Luckily it was one of our first hangout spots. We had a little fun with her, she had a tight ass, but we brought her back. When Allison found out what happened she was the one that put out the hit on his head. She said she really didn't like Desmond anyway. We had to honor it. It was business, nothing personal, but business with that lil Vietnamese puta done ran its course."

Levi couldn't believe what he was hearing but knew it had to be true because Alejandro had no reason to lie to him at this point. He thought Allison was being truthful about how the incident played out with his close friend and her uncle being upset about his daughter. The Cartel leader started laughing when he seen that Levi had just realized he had been lied to all this time. Before sending him on his way, Alejandro schooled Levi on one main rule he had to follow in the game and that was to only trust blood. The Mexican gangster told him that he has several loyal members in his group but the only one he trusts is the word from his brother and even then, sometimes he doubts that. He went on talking in depth about trust and how it affects any kind of relationship as he glanced over towards Cashmere. For the first time in years Joker was afraid but it wasn't for himself, it was all for his little sister standing in front of him. The young vixen stood there strong with a face of stone ready to accept whatever punishment Alejandro was about to hand out but inside her heart raced expecting the worse. Levi could see that Alejandro was leaning toward a life-threatening discipline for Cashmere and spoke up for her like he did earlier. He begged for the boss man to look the other way in her case and Alejandro really considered the request, but some sort of law had to be laid down. Joker's eyes locked on the words coming out of his leader's mouth as he banned Cashmere from the entire Cartel, and everything associated with them. She was ordered out of the house she lived in, she couldn't stay at none of the other houses they owned or motels they operated. She couldn't work at none of the high-end clubs they worked and any money she had at the time was no longer hers but the Cartel's. Cashmere was completely cut off from the Lords de Tampico and it wasn't anything Joker could do or say. Alejandro told the two former employees to get out of his face before he recanted everything he just said and they both began to walk away. Levi had finally come across a man that was truly more dangerous than he was but was grateful for his leniency. He was following behind Cashmere out of the cemetery happy he still had his life intact but then Joker grabbed him by the arm. The oversized Mexican stared Levi face to face,

"Just know if it wasn't for Cash, I'd be ripping yo skull from yo fuckin' shoulders right now. But know I'm a have fun with ya China girl."

After talking with Alejandro about her son's safety and giving up both of her CBD stores for that safety, Eve immediately went looking for Levi. She found him uptown sitting in front of his house sulking in his sorrows with a bottle of half empty Crown in his hand. Levi was never one to smoke or drink and Eve knew right there this was one of the hardest days for him. She had never seen him without a fire lit in his eyes, that desire to go out and grab whatever he wanted, he looked completely defeated. Eve thought it was because of being caught by the Cartel after smuggling away some of their girls but for him it was the thought of Eve, Darlene, Ronnisha or Diamond being hurt because of him. Tears fell from Levi's eyes thinking about how his actions had already struck pain to his life with the loss of his brother Brock, his mother's death and how his own sister tore him from her life. Just the idea of the torture Alejandro was capable of terrified him,

"Mama I thought he was gonna hurt you. I was really scared they was gone go look for Nisha or Darlene."

"Ronald everybody is fine. He made me that promise that he won't touch any of us. We don't have to deal with him anymore, he got what he wanted."

"Mama I'm sorry bout pullin' you in this shit. You lost everything cause of me."

"As long as you safe and sound that's all that matters to me. That building can be replaced, you can't."

"But that was yo bank roll."

"Don't you fret yaself bout that, you know I know how to bring in that bag. It's time you figure out yo options now."

Levi knew Eve was speaking the truth and having a criminal record didn't give him too many options. He didn't want to but working at the docks with Leslie full time was the only possible solution he had. Levi started to look at the whole situation as a blessing and not a curse because he was finally able to step away from the life that took so much away from him. The thought of actually being there for his daughter physically and not just financially could truly be a thing for him.

YEAR 2034

The rehabilitation rescue Levi, Allison and Cashmere had going was all taken down by the innocent face of the last girl Levi dropped off, Courtney. The young street walker was so caught up in the brainwashing Jose put in her head that as soon as she discovered what was going on, she ran to tell it all. Once Alejandro found out about it the anger that raged through the gangster had everyone in that hotel room on his hit list and everyone involved on the butcher block. It wasn't until it was too late that Courtney realized that she had signed her own death warrant because the orders was to eliminate every soul in the room. The five mercenaries Levi seen run in the hotel that night tied all three of the people up in the room including Courtney and executed them all. The only news report that came out was of a Caucasian female that was found dead in a hotel bathtub of an apparent suicide. Another report of three out of towners, each shot one time in the head was found in their van by the river. When Allison saw the news of the three in the van, she knew the Cartel knew about them. She tried calling Levi, but all her calls went straight to his voicemail, and she assumed the worst had happened. It wasn't until she woke up in the middle of the night and seen a large shadow standing at the foot of her bed that she knew the truth. The large shadow choked Allison out until she fell unconscious and when she woke, she was strapped to a dingy bed in an abandoned house in the lower 9th ward with Joker. Joker took pleasure in torturing people, and he took his time with torturing Allison. Mr. Chou's daughter died three days after her kidnapping because Alejandro wanted her hell to be stretched out as far as her body could take it. She had finally given up after bleeding out from the severed limbs Joker had cut off during his time with her.

Eve didn't let the Cartel situation set her back for long and was back on the grind as usual. Because she was a veteran in the exotic dance industry, she got right back in the mix but not as a stage performer. Eve knew the ins and outs of the industry, what it took to be an exotic dancer and used her experience to her benefit as she became the "house mom" in several strip clubs. She would move from club to club with her suitcases full of things dancers needed for their day to day and became "Mama Evelyn" to a lot of girls. After the Cartel incident she noticed Levi got a little distant with fewer calls and text, but it never stopped her from reaching out to him from time to time,

"Boy wha cha doin'? You do know the phone work both ways, right? Why I gotta always be da one to call and check on you?"

"My bad mama. Just been working almost every day at da docks except on Sundays and even then, I'm running deliveries for Lez. Just been keepin' busy, that's all."

"With all dat keepin' busy you keepin' outta trouble too?"

"Yes ma'am."

"Don't play with me boy."

"Serious, I been chillin'. I go to work, and I go home. I'm a straight homebody now."

Eve was proud of the man he was becoming and happy that he made it out, unlike a lot of people they knew. Her memory was blanketed with gravestones and "R.I.P." shirts from people she looked at as family. The only family she had left was Levi and Darlene and that was a task in itself because Darlene still didn't want anything to do with her own brother. Eve tried her best to reconnect the siblings, but Darlene was as stubborn as her father was and it was no budging her. The single mother strived to raise her child away from anything that resembled the life she had, and the teenage Diamond only recently found out she had an uncle by the name Ronald. The inquisitive teen would always ask questions about him, but Darlene would deny it all. The disgust she held for Levi ran so deep that she literally erased him from her life completely.

Levi kept his head down, under the radar but that didn't mean he didn't dabble in the occasional drop off here and there. He still had his connections with a few guys from the underbelly of the city that weren't associated with Alejandro's crew, who had the city on lock when it came to moving product. He had Leslie's shipments to keep up with though and her deliveries were booming so much that she was considering opening her own store. Levi and Leslie became like a package deal when it came to making under the table orders from the docks. She had learned so much from The Cajun that she ended up taking over his area in Destrehan after he retired. Levi reconnected with his neighborhood friend Mook and got him a job working on the docks with him. Being a family man now, Mook didn't get into the extracurricular activities like Levi because he wanted to be a role model for his teenage son Jason. The image was something Levi strived for because he always kept his own child in his mind. Seeing how some of the teens in the city were wilding out with violent crimes Levi definitely wanted to be there for his daughter. It got so bad that looking at the news at night was just a notification to let everyone know who was killed on that day in the city. A breaking news flash always frightened him when a young teen was involved because it was a nightmare Levi never wanted to experience. He continued to keep tabs on her through Kareem and to hear she was in the top of her class in school plus an accomplished published painter had Levi the proudest father in Louisiana. Clippings from newspaper articles and magazines stayed sealed in a photo album at home of all Ronnisha's works. Everyone knew how honored Levi felt when talking about his only child and "Babygirl" as he so affectionately called her. He looked forward to calls and text from Kareem about her but a text he got from Kareem today had him concerned. As soon as Levi got off work, he called his adopted brother,

"What's good lil bro? Yo text said it was an emergency. Da fam good?"

"Levi where you at? We gotta talk."

"I just got off work. What da fuck wrong? Where Nisha?"

"Levi I don't wanna talk to you bout this over da phone. Can you come to the…"

"Where da fuck is my daughter Reem?!"

The words that came across the speaker of Levi's phone was like gunfire striking him directly in the heart. Everything began to sound muffled and his vision went blurry as Kareem told of an incident that occurred at a church festival. Ronnisha and her brother Khori were shot at by some goons who came to the festival looking for trouble but when they left, they left Ronnisha dead in her brother's arms. Levi had never felt faint before but after Kareem's words ripped his heart out his chest his legs and arms went weak. He fell to his knees on the side of his car in the parking lot and it was as if his soul poured out of him in his tears. The pain he felt was greater than any he had ever felt before in his life, but it began to be replaced with nothing but anger. Kareem knew Ronnisha's father was changing his life around for his child, going from the criminal known as Levi to the well-respected citizen named Ronald. The thing is he needed the ruthless "Levi" back because Kareem had nothing but revenge in his heart behind his niece, Levi was filled with that same rage by the end of the call. When he stood up next to his car the city looked different to him, dark in the daylight, dead at nighttime and everyone was a suspect until proven innocent. Levi was determined to find who murdered his only child or leave the city of New Orleans a scorched section of earth.

When news of Ronnisha's murder got to Leslie, she did everything she could to console her friend. She knew the young teen meant the world to Levi and the agony he was going through was unimaginable. Leslie caught herself spending days and nights with him just to be a shoulder to lean on because he was completely out of tears. The pain he was going through sent Levi across every emotion possible and back again. He blamed himself for not protecting her, he cursed whoever was responsible, he cried out because he knew he would never see her face again and he feared the police would never solve the case. Levi pleaded with the only person he felt could help and that was Leslie at the moment,

"Right now I know if I ask around, I'm a accuse everybody."

"I gotchu."

The emotional cycle had passed, the tears dried up and Levi didn't want to talk anymore. The man he buried a year ago came back and he wanted nothing but blood. Leslie knew

Levi had a dark side, but he always carried himself in a lighthearted manner around her. The man that she was talking to now was calculating, determined and unsympathetic to everything around him but she knew the reason why. Leslie canvased the city trying to find anyone that knew about what happened at the church festival. People talked but as for who the shooters were, they stayed silent because everyone was scared of being called a snitch. One night after making one of her deliveries at a bar, Leslie came across a very talkative bartender who overheard a conversation he shouldn't have. A rival between two dealers ended in one of them getting cornered and trapped under a barrage of gunfire. The bartender pointed out the guys who were talking about the shootout to Leslie and she immediately brought the news back to Levi. She didn't know she almost signed one of those boy's death warrant because what took place next was unmerciful. Levi casually went to the bar the next night and found his mark there. He bought several drinks for a few people, befriended the young man and they had one good ole time. When the prey finally fell victim to all the amounts of alcohol in his system, Levi was more than willing to drive him home. The thing was the drunk awoke naked on the docks tied to a chair in an empty storage container with nothing but Levi staring him down. The young man feared he was about to be sexually assaulted by some sick sadistic male rapist, but he was so wrong. Levi beat and tortured the pawn until he told him everything he needed to know about that day. He had the informant so petrified that his life was in constant danger that he left the city for good after being let go.

Kareem and his family were completely devastated over the senseless loss of Ronnisha, but a bright light came to him in a text from Levi that he had information on the killer. He met Levi at his shop to talk privately about what he learned and Kareem wasn't ready. The informant told Levi that two rival dealers, Garu and Kush had been having altercations on the regular, nothing too dramatic. Garu was with his crew at the church festival and they just so happen to catch Kush slipping while he was hanging out with his family. Kareem was a little confused because he still didn't know why or how his niece and nephew got stuck in the middle of some street beef. Levi told Kareem to sit down,

"Dawg, Kush goes to Texas A&M and so does Garu."

"Deez niggas go to school with my nephews?! Khori gotta know one of dem."

"Nigga, Kush is Khori. He been selling hydro at school since he been there. Garu is his rival and dem niggas been beefing for da longest."

"Nigga I know you fuckin lyin'. Tell me you playin'."

"Wish I was but dats why dey was shootin' at Khori. Dem niggas was really tryin' to get'em. My Babygirl was da one who lost her life though."

"Why da fuck he ain't tell me? Why da fuck he ain't tell da police?!"

"C'mon now Reem, you know if he would have told dem it was over some drug dealer shit and he was one of da dealers, Khori would have went straight to jail and you know dis."

Kareem went to the safe in his office and pulled out an envelope with two stacks of 50-dollar bills in it. When he tried to give it to Levi, he shook his head no, but Kareem forced the money in his hand. It wasn't like it was payment for the info he just got or for the hit that was just mutually made but just a gesture of some sort. The heartbroken father walked away to go search for Garu and no one was going to stop him from finding him.

Eve seen on the news about the ongoing investigation into the murder of a young teen at an annual church festival and was floored when she seen Shalay Daniels talking to reporters about her daughter. She felt for the mother's loss but knew this was too much for Levi too handle on his own but every time she would reach out to him her calls went to voicemail. Eve would pass by his house to check on him, but he was never home, and his absence began to worry her. She started to think the worse and there were very few people around that could reach him that she knew. Eve didn't want to bother Kareem because of the situation the family was in, but she had no other choice in the matter. When talking to Kareem it was as if he was being extra secretive with her,

"Look Reem, I just wanna talk to him. He not answering none of my calls and I'm startin' to get worried."

"I'm a see if I can get to him, I promise and I'm a get back to you."

"I'm serious Reem. I got nothing but time today. I will sit in yo shop til Ronald show up."

"Okay okay, I'm a get him to call you."

Kareem knew Eve wasn't playing about her son and meant every word. She nervously waited by the phone for Levi's call with the worst thoughts going through her mind. Eve knew her son and knew he was out for revenge on anyone that had anything to do with Ronnisha's death. She could only imagine what he was going through but terrified that he would end up just like his late daughter. Eve sat on her sofa reminiscing about when she first met the crazy intelligent adolescent Levi. How smart he was in school and how protective he was about his family. She thought about how innocent he was back then, in a dysfunctional family and still seen the good in some people. Tears ran like a river down Eve's face because the little boy she loved so much was this endangered grown man now and she couldn't do anything to help him. He was all the family she had left after losing her love to a senseless violent act and losing her best friend to a drug overdose. Levi meant more to her than she knew, and it pained her not knowing where he is or if he is okay. Her suffering melted away when her phone lit up and it was Levi's name flashing across the screen,

"Ronald, where are you?!"

"Well hello to you too."

"Boy don't play with me. I been calling yo phone for da past three days now and you sent me straight to voicemail every damn time."

"Mama, my bad I just been busy. You know how it is."

"No, I don't know how it is. Had me stressin' ova here. Are you okay?"

"Mama, I'm fine. I promise. Just got some shit on my mind dats all."

"I know baby and I'm so sorry about Babygirl. I just don't want you to do anything stupid or dangerous that might get you in trouble."

"Too late for dat."

"Ronald!"

"Mama, I gotta go. I love you."

"Ronald!"

Levi found himself driving all over the city looking for any sight of the young drug dealer by the name of Garu. He didn't find the guy he was looking for, but he did get a lot of info on his associates and the Lords de Tampico was the main supplier for him. Levi never wanted to see anyone from the Cartel again after surviving a potential execution, but he knew he would have to in order to find the murderer. He went to the house in the Garden District, but the place was completely vacant without a soul in sight. Levi knew of the other spots Alejandro had control of and went to them only to find them empty too. He found Jose's number in his cell and called,

"Levi? Fuck you calling me for?"

"I really need to talk to Alejandro."

"Alejandro don't want nothing to do with you ese. Remember? You dead to us."

"Muthafucka look. You don't put Alejandro on this muthafuckin phone, when I find you, I'm fuckin yo skull with a muthafuckin 12-gauge, ya heard me."

Levi heard silence on the phone for a couple of seconds and then Alejandro picked it up laughing,

"That's the fire I missed right there ese. Come talk to me."

Levi listened as Alejandro told him where his new spot was and immediately headed out to the deep parts of New Orleans East. The drive felt long because his patience was running thin and Levi just wanted to look the man responsible for killing his daughter in the eyes. He knew going to the Mexicans was a dangerous move, but he also knew Alejandro had an idea where Garu was and he needed that information. It was going to be like walking in a lion's den, but it was a risk Levi was willing to take. He drove on the dark back roads from the Interstate 10 onto Michoud Blvd, turned in a secluded neighborhood off the boulevard and up to a large two-story house at the end of a cul-de-sac. Huge palm trees outlined the front of the house as the U-shaped driveway was lined with several top-of-the-line automobiles. Levi's presence was anticipated as two henchmen walked out to greet him and escorted the visitor inside. He stood at the front double doors of the house looking around and seen two familiar faces staring him down with hatefulness in their eyes. Jose and Joker didn't understand why Alejandro allowed Levi to come see him, let alone still be allowed to breathe but they didn't question him. The boss man came down the stairwell with a big smile on his face,

"There goes the luckiest cabrón in the city of New Orleans. My condolences, I heard about your daughter. Very sad."

"No offense but…"

"Funny thing when people say, no offense. More than likely they about to offend you."

"Alejandro, I just need to find Garu."

"My friend I don't know where he is. He went into hiding after word about someone looking for him got out. Plus, he's one of my guys, I can't just give him up. I'll be missing out on the money he brings in if I give him to you."

"It would be a lot easier to replace one muthafucka. Replacing a whole crew gone be hard. I'm not threatening you at all but if I can't find Garu, I'm a have to settle for everybody dat work for you."

"Hahaha, that's why I liked you Levi. You have the biggest balls."

"And I give zero fucks."

"You get pass Joker and I'll send you in the right direction to find your mark."

Levi turned around into a solid fist lunging from Joker, striking him square in the eye. The Latin brute continued his attack as he kicked his victim to the ground and jumped on top of him. Levi attempted to cover up as the blows rained down on him like a hailstorm. A collaboration of loud chatter and cheering could be heard from the crowd surrounding the assault as they encouraged Joker to continue. Levi caught a glimpse between punches that Joker wasn't concerned about protecting himself as he swung at his soon to be casualty laying on the floor. With one quick swing of desperation, Levi's knuckles found its target, hitting Joker in the throat and cutting off all his air. The big Mexican fell to the side trying to gasp for air and in seconds the table was turned with Levi on top. He stood to his feet and began walking away but the crowd didn't let him leave. Levi turned to Alejandro and the gang leader told him he had to finish his job first. He went over to Joker who still was fighting to breathe and committed to pounding him with vicious blows to the head. The Cartel hitman reached down in his boot and pulled out a black .38 Special with all intent to end the battle with one gun blast, but Levi grabbed hold of the pistol. With the barrel of the gun pushed up under Joker's chin and Levi's finger pressed against the trigger, he looked up at Alejandro,

"I just came here to find Garu."

"Only one way you gone find him, my friend."

The pull of the trigger let off a loud bang and Joker's body went limp as Levi stood up with blood all over his clothes.

The crowd slowly disbursed, Alejandro told Levi to go clean up in the guestroom and all the information he needed would be waiting for him.

Levi was given Joker's car after he got the information he needed from Alejandro and was headed to talk with an old friend. He pulled up to a well-known strip club on Chef Menteur and walked in the smoky club looking for the one person who could help him. They locked eyes and Levi gestured for Cashmere to come over,

"Hey."

"Hey Papi, I missed you."

She sat on his lap and never missed a beat as she began to rub on Levi's chest. He could see the exotic dancer was all business as always, but he was there for one thing and she was the one with the info. Levi was told that Garu was hiding out at a girl's house that maybe Cashmere knew and he needed to know everything the dancer could tell him. He slid a crisp 50-dollar bill in her cleavage as he asked about Garu's girlfriend. Cashmere remembered a girl that use to live next door to her in The Frenchman Warf Apartments that Garu would always visit from time to time. Levi knew exactly where the place was,

"You think she still lives there mami?"

"I just moved from there like a week ago, so she should still be there. Papi please tell me you not gone hurt her."

"Have you ever heard of me hurting a female? C'mon now, that's not even my style."

"I'm sorry, I know. Well it looks like you working Papi so I'm a let you go."

Cashmere kissed Levi on the cheek and started to walk away but Levi's conscious began tugging at him over the incident that took place earlier. He stopped the dancer and attempted to explain to her what happened. She smiled as she was the comforter to him because she knew already and told Levi she was sort of happy to see him,

"My brother called me earlier and told me you were on your way to Alejandro's crib. He also said you wasn't leaving that house alive because he was going to kill you. When I seen you walk through those doors, I was relieved."

"I'm sorry."

"It's ok, he went out da way he wanted, in battle. Did he suffer much?"

"No."

"Good. Now go find that puta."

Levi left for the apartment complex Cashmere told him about, he's been there before, so he knew the landscape and the hiding spots. He sat in his car in plain sight as he watched the front of the apartment where Garu's girlfriend lived. Shadow images flashed across the window curtains and Levi could only imagine it was the one person that destroyed all his dreams. He had to have a positive confirmation before he just stormed the apartment like he wanted to because he didn't want to be wrong. One wrong move and the flight risk could disappear forever. His patience finally paid off as Garu walked out on the balcony of the apartment smoking a cigarette. Levi smiled,

"There go my bitch."

OUTRO

Levi was an Angel surrounded by Demons. Or was he the Demon? It really depends on how you viewed him. Did he do everything for survival or was he just doing it all because that's what he wanted to do? Some feel that your life is already planned out for you at birth and others feel that your life is what you make it. Levi made the best out of what was laid out in front of him, and he used it all to benefit him the best way possible. Some friends became family, and some family became enemies but Levi pushed through it all, never wavering from who he was. So, who was he?

Biography

Ralph Edgerson Jr. was the youngest of three, born and raised in New Orleans Louisiana. He always had a wild imagination but didn't start writing stories and poems until high school. Impressed with his visual writings in class an English teacher introduced him to Journalism where he honed his skills even more. After high school Ralph thought of majoring in Journalism in college but life had other plans for him. He joined the work force and writing fell to the backburner of his mind. After meeting his soulmate in September of 1995 Ralph focused on family and his first born arrived in November of 2003. 2005 came and life again had other plans for Ralph but this time on a much greater level. Stripped from everything he knows; Ralph moved his family to Houston Texas for a new beginning but that didn't come without trials. Thoughts of the unknown and uncertain brought Ralph back to an old friend that allowed him to vent in a way of literary release, in 2006. It was just a way to occupy his mind for the time being, but the creation of the "Decisions" saga began without him even knowing it. Ten years had passed, and writing fell off again for Ralph as he focused more on family, but he still occasionally wrote poems. He met a poet on social media that really enjoyed his poems and she suggested he have them published. Ralph let her read over the short story "Decisions" he wrote ten years ago, and she immediately wanted to have the story published. In July of 2018 Ralph Edgerson became a published author and his five-star rated urban novel "Decisions" arrived. In June of the following year he had the second installment of his first book published and he hasn't stopped writing since. Ralph enjoys creating dramas that keep his readers enthralled in the storyline and hearing readers fascination with the story and the characters. What he loves the most is hearing the excitement from his children saying, "My father is an author."

Levi's Labyrinth